# BEYOND THE
# DARKENED FOREST

# BEYOND THE

# DARKENED

# FOREST

A Seventeenth Century Historical Novel

## Peter R. Hawkins

**To order additional copies of this book, contact:**
Xlibris Corporation
0-800-644-6988
www.xlibrispublishing.co.uk
Orders@xlibrispublishing.co.uk
00000

15.11.2012.

To James and Suzie,

From traffic lights to romps in
the Seventeenth Century, there
must be a link !!
However, I must admit the research
was fun !!
I hope all is well in your World,
and give my Kindest regards to
Peta. There are certain chapters
in this that I think Nick would
have enjoyed.

Take care, folks.

Peter S-B.

Adventure, passion, love, romance, and tragedy, together with humour and commerce, are at the heart of the book, which is centred on the Forest of Dean in the English county of Gloucestershire, with an added maritime flavour set against the backdrop of the Bristol Channel and the south-west coast of England.

The early part of the century was still verging on lawlessness, with an intriguing change in attitude towards commerce, money, sex, and power.

The emergence of wealthy merchants and industrial families and the power they wielded then started to bring about a lasting change to the British way of life.

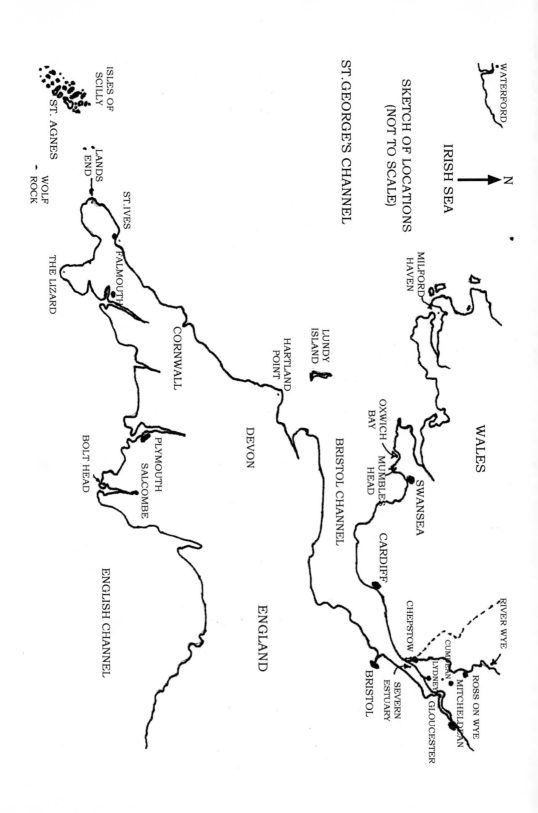

# CHAPTER 1

The tall, cloaked figure walked the streets of the Irish port of Waterford for many hours during the night and early morning of a day in the spring of 1586. Usually a man of instant decision, he was not used to being faced with a dilemma. Flecks of dawn light were beginning to show on the horizon as he stood beside one of the large cannon on the east-facing rampart of the city's defences.

'Do we stay or do we go?' he mused to himself out loud.

'Sir?' queried a garrison soldier who was walking past him as he had asked himself the question for the thousandth time. The cloaked figure turned to face his inquisitor.

'It's all right, Sergeant. I was talking to myself.'

'Yes, Major, I quite understand. Good morning to you, sir!' the sergeant said as he saluted and then returned to walking his rounds.

Major Sir Richard Crighton looked up at the sky, half smiling to himself as he returned the salute saying, 'So it is, Sergeant, so it is', a comment that the sergeant failed to hear as he was now remonstrating with a soldier he had found leaning against the rampart wall, apparently half asleep.

The encounter seemed to trigger a decision from the major as he turned and walked down the rampart steps and made his way to the harbour, where he boarded a Dutch-built flyboat that lay alongside the dock. Walking towards the high stern of the vessel, he was greeted by the captain.

'Good morning, sir. I trust you're well this morning?'

'Thank you, Captain, extremely well,' the major returned. 'I've decided that my wife and I will join you for your trip to Chepstow after all, so could you make ready a cabin for us?'

'Yes, of course, sir. We'll be catching the noon ebb tide. The wind seems to be set fair from the north-west, so hopefully we'll have a fast trip as long as we get the Bristol Channel tides right,' he said, smiling. Captain Larkswell was a veteran of those waters and of the tides that governed his journeying around the Irish Sea and south-western coast of England.

'Our cargoes are stowed and secured, so I shall await your arrival. I hope your wife will be up to the trip, Sir Richard. She's not long till she's due, is she?'

'No, not long. It's not the sea trip that is my worry, Captain. It's going overland to get her home to Gloucester which is my main concern. What cargo do you carry by the way?'

'Mostly woollen goods, with some French wines as well. And as a precaution, sir, we sail in company in an effort to deter attack by our privateer friends,' the captain replied to his owner's son, whom he had known since he was a child.

'Ah, the one thing I forgot to mention is that I suspect my wife's maid will be travelling with us, so if you could ensure there is also a cabin for her, I would be grateful. We'll see you well before noon,' the major said brusquely, turning away and going down the gangplank, across the dock, and into the town.

'Are you sure about this, Richard?' his wife asked, as they sat in a large sumptuous room of her parents' house that was next to one of the largest churches in the city.

'Yes, as long as you feel up to the journey, my love, that's what really concerns me.'

'Of course, I'm up to it!' she replied in her soft Irish brogue. 'I know you'd prefer our children were born in England, so as one of your father's ships is here, we might as well take advantage of it. Have you cleared your leave with the colonel yet?'

'Yes, when I was on my way back from the docks. He didn't seem to have a problem with it.'

'He wouldn't, when a peer of the realm's son asks for leave. I suspect he saluted *you*,' she laughingly responded.

Richard looked at his tall Irish wife, with her tumbling hair and wonderful soft smile, a smile that could melt the hardest of hearts. She was heavily pregnant with two babies, and he hoped his English pride would not be the cause of a problem for her. What had that Irish midwife told them?

'You've got two in that stomach. Either that or you've been with a Waterford giant!'

'Typical Irish humour,' he reflected.

'I'd better go and tell my parents what we have decided, although after our talk with them yesterday, I don't think that they'll be too surprised,' his wife continued.

Both her parents had thought it a good idea that they should go, although they both agreed the decision a little late. But the one thing they had insisted on was that if they did go, their daughter should take her maid, Martha, with them.

'She's English. She wants to go back to England, and she tells me Gloucester is not far from her home in the Forest of Dean,' her wealthy wool merchant father had said.

Much as he loved his daughter, Granuaile, the troubled times of the city made him feel that it would be safer if she had her offspring in Gloucestershire. Also, Richard's father had commented on a recent visit to the family in Waterford that there could be a problem with the inheritance if the children were born in Ireland. Although he liked Richard's father, he took that as a coded warning for the future of the unborn infants.

'It appears that it would be better for everyone if our grandchildren were born in England,' he'd said dismally, consoling his tearful wife after their daughter told them what had been decided.

It was a little before noon that saw the major and his wife waving a somewhat sad farewell from the high stern deck of the *Magdolin*, as she slipped her warps and manoeuvred into the centre of the river with only her top gallants set on her foremast for steerage, and with the assistance of three oar-powered pulling gigs belonging to the harbour.

Joining the two other vessels that were bound for the Bristol Channel, she started to catch the ebb tide and the north-westerly wind that would take them down the twisting River Suir, into the wide estuary, and then out into the Irish Sea.

After an uneventful sea crossing, with a fair wind and favourable tides, the *Magdolin* lay to her anchor in a small bay on the South Wales coast that was sheltered from the wind, and waited for the tide that would take her on up the Bristol Channel, the lower reaches of the River Severn, and then finally up a short section of the River Wye to Chepstow.

Oxwich Bay was a favourite waiting place for both inward and outward-bound vessels that plied the Bristol Channel, especially when the wind had any north in its direction.

Lady Granuaile Crighton lay on her bunk and asked her husband, 'How much longer do I have to suffer this ship's motion?'

'For about another fourteen hours from what the captain has just told me,' her husband responded. 'There was a time when we were about ten hours out of Waterford; I thought we were going to see the birth of our first two children a little earlier than expected!'

'You still might unless you get me off this rolling coffin pretty quickly,' she replied with a note of desperation in her voice. 'And where's Martha? I haven't seen her for the last couple of hours.'

'She's still leaning over the starboard rail counting starfish!'

'Why does this boat roll *so* much or isn't that a question for the military?' Granuaile grumbled.

'Because it has a relatively flat bottom so that it can navigate our shallower rivers and estuaries, and that means when we are at anchor, she rolls more.'

'I've noticed!' his wife replied. 'And it also makes pregnant ladies think their babies are imminent, which in turn makes them irritable.'

'I've noticed *that* too!' the military man answered, leaving the cabin to seek out the captain.

True to the mariner's word, fourteen hours later the *Magdolin* edged her way up the two miles of the River Wye leading to Chepstow Docks, letting the flood tide carry her with only her mainmast spritsail set to give her steerage. She also had two of her own gigs launched and attached to her bow, so that oar power would help her manoeuvre on some of the tighter turns.

'The last bend before we come to the docks is the worst for a boat of our size,' Captain Larkswell commented to Sir Richard, as he helmed his vessel up the river.

As they approached the bend that he had spoken of, the captain swung his charge out into the middle of the river to take a wide swing, and his boatswain in one of the gigs noisily urged his crews to pull as they had never pulled before, and *Magdolin* swept effortlessly around.

Half an hour later, they were safely moored alongside the dock, and the passengers disembarked.

'Have a safe journey home, Sir Richard, and my kindest regards to His Lordship,' Captain Larkswell said as the couple mounted the carriage that was to take them to the Gloucestershire estate of Richard's father.

'I hope that the carriage gives you a smoother ride than the old *Magdolin*, My Lady,' he addressed Granuaile while he helped Martha mount the steps of the carriage, 'and safe deliverance for your little ones.'

'Thank you for your good wishes, Captain,' Granuaile replied with a laugh, 'but I suspect the highways of Gloucestershire will be a lot rougher than the waves of the Irish Sea.'

Neither the carriage driver nor his passengers were aware of the three horsemen that fell in behind them as they left the docks and took the Roman Road towards Gloucester.

Four hours later, the highwaymen struck.

Granuaile and Martha were both asleep and Richard was dozing when he became aware of shouting in front of the carriage, which stopped with a sudden jolt.

Two pistols were fired, the shots killing both the driver and groom. A third pistol was pushed under one of the cloth curtains of the carriage into Richard's neck and discharged, killing him instantly, spraying the whole of the interior with his blood and the force of the shot wedging his body into a corner.

Now wide awake, both women let out piercing screams. The protective coverings were ripped off each of the windows by two of the horsemen; the third had dismounted and held the guide reigns of the carriage team. The two peered inside and then jumped from their mounts, becoming too preoccupied with the female passengers to bother recharging their pistols. Letting go of their horses, they wrenched one of the doors open, first dragging a hysterical Martha from the carriage, followed by a now quiet and icy calm Granuaile.

Martha lay on the ground still screaming while her mistress struggled up from where she lay and went over to her, kneeling down and putting her arms round her. She turned and looked at their attackers with a look of utter contempt on her face.

'So you attack defenceless women, do you?' she hissed at them. The two men she addressed smirked at her and then purposefully but slowly started to recharge their pistols.

'Especially when they're rich and good looking,' the taller of the two replied, still leering at her with a toothless grin. 'And I've never had a pregnant bitch before!'

'You won't have one now either. You'll have to kill me first!' she warned, releasing her maid, levering herself up, and walking towards him, whilst at the same time drawing out a long narrow-bladed knife with a beautifully decorated handle from beneath her cloak.

The move so panicked the man he had to look down to complete the priming of his pistol, which he finished at the exact moment Granuaile reached him. She swung the knife upwards with all her strength, as she had been taught, its blade entering him at an angle just below his ribcage, piercing his heart. Then with a sharp twist she pulled it out, dropping the knife and catching his pistol as he crumpled to the ground. She span round and with two hands brought the weapon to bear on the second attacker at the precise moment he levelled his own at her.

Without any hesitation she squeezed the trigger, the pistol ball hitting him in the forehead, killing him instantly. As his body dropped, Granuaile felt a hammer blow from the shot fired by the highwayman. It was accompanied by a searing intense pain below her left shoulder, the impact spinning her around before she fell to the ground with a loud scream.

The third of the thieves was still trying to hold on to the now rearing first pair of horses in the carriage team, who went high in the air with flailing front legs. As they crashed down, one of the horse's metal-shod hooves caught him across the face, splitting it open to the bone and dislodging his left eye from its socket. He shrieked in agony and grabbed his face, letting go of the guide reins as he did so. The four horses surged forward, knocking him over and trampling him underfoot, dragging the carriage over him. Terrified, they turned and bolted, taking the now unattended carriage with them.

The man's broken corpse lay on the ground, all life crushed and taken from him. The whole attack and its aftermath had taken less than three minutes. Granuaile managed to drag herself along the ground to where the still screaming Martha was lying.

'Martha! Martha!' she shouted. 'Stop it. Stop it for God's sake. They're all dead!' With that, she clasped the wound where the thief's pistol shot had penetrated her side and fainted.

Granuaile regained consciousness to the smell of dank wood smoke and the sound of low voices. She tried to turn her head but failed to because of the bindings around her shoulder, neck, and chest. She stared up, slightly puzzled at the sight of sods of earth above her, sods of earth that appeared to be supported on a rough, tree branch frame.

She then became aware of a woman kneeling beside where she lay, bathing her forehead and moistening her lips with clear tasting water.

Granuaile asked where she was in a barely audible whisper.

'You're in a charcoal burner's hut in the Forest of Dean,' the woman replied with a smile, 'and you appear to have been shot, by the look of your wound.'

'Highwaymen stopped the carriage, killed our driver, groom, and my husband. One then attacked me. But where's Martha?' she murmured, before losing consciousness again.

The woman continued bathing her forehead, until she heard a man's voice calling her softly from the door. She turned, smiled, and getting up as quietly as she could went out into the sunlight.

'How is she?' the man asked.

'Not very well. She's lost a lot of blood, and the ball from the gun that was fired at her is lodged between two bones below her shoulder. She has just passed out again, but before she did she asked about someone called Martha. Tell me again how you found her.'

'John and I were coming back along the Roman Road from Lydney after delivering that cart full of charcoal we loaded yesterday. We heard the sound of several gun shots from somewhere in front of us, followed by a lot of screaming. It all went quiet for a few moments, then a carriage and four came past us going like the wind back towards Lydney.

'There was no driver, but it looked like there was someone inside. It passed us so quickly that we didn't have a chance to stop it. We pulled up for a bit and waited till everything seemed to have gone quiet before carrying on around the next bend. It was a horrible sight!'

The man appeared genuinely upset and stopped talking for a few moments, going to stand beside the second woodsman to whom he had been talking outside the hut.

Continuing, he said, 'There were bodies scattered all over the place! When we jumped down from the cart, John counted five men and one woman. All the men were dead, but the woman was obviously alive as she was moaning and writhing around on the ground. There was blood everywhere. We didn't want to stay around in case of more trouble, so we lifted her into the back of the cart and then quickly checked the men's bodies.'

'For valuables!' the woman said quietly.

'Yes, all right, we checked for valuables! We also collected four pistols, two off the ground, two from the bodies, and a long bladed knife covered in blood that lay nearby.'

'I hope you didn't forget the ammunition and primers for the pistols!' the woman added sarcastically, looking accusingly at the two wood colliers.

'No, we didn't. But *there was* only one woman,' he continued in a whining voice.

He looked back at his wife, who was undoubtedly going to have a lot more to say about the fact that they'd searched the bodies, so he decided to carry on.

'There were three horses grazing nearby which we couldn't catch, so we left as quickly as we could in case anyone came along and saw us, then we came back here.'

'So there was no other woman?' she asked.

'No, I've just said that. The only one was the pregnant one who we've got in the hut.'

'I'm puzzled! There's nothing to tell us who she is. She is obviously wealthy as can be seen by her fine clothes, however blood-soaked. She speaks with an Irish accent that I can barely understand, she's very tall, and I'd say she was pregnant with two babies! But she wears no jewellery, although it looks like she did because you can see where it's been ripped off her clothes, and her fingers look as if rings have been pulled off them as well.'

'That was not us!' the man said defensively. 'We found no jewellery on any of the dead when we searched them.'

The woman gave her husband a meaningful look.

'Of course, you didn't want to stay around in case anyone came, but you had time to search the bodies!' she repeated with mounting sarcasm.

Just as the woman was warming to her task of remonstrating with her husband, there was a wail from the hut, so she immediately returned to her patient.

The woodsman's wife started bathing Granuaile's forehead again as she was sweating so profusely, also moistening her parched lips with some clear spring water.

'Thomas!' the woman called out to her husband who was idly talking to his friend.

'Yes, Mary Jane?' he said as he came in through the hut door.

'I'm going to need help. You and John get yourselves off to the village and bring Caenwen back with you. Tell her about the woman. Ask her to bring all the herbs that she uses to treat serious wounds, and tell her that I don't think it'll be long before our lady starts to give birth to possibly *two* babies. So could she bring anything that will be of help with that as well. If she wants money, then *you* give it to her!' She gave him a long withering look after she spoke and then added, 'And if you find a priest, bring one of them too!'

Thomas sensed the urgency in his wife's voice, so he and his fellow charcoal burner quickly put their horse into its cart harness and set out for the little village in the Forest.

Granuaile regained consciousness once more and looked pleadingly up at Mary Jane.

'It doesn't matter about me, but please try and save my babies. Will you promise me?'

'There *are* two then?'

'Yes, so the midwife told us' came the faint reply.

'What's your name?' Mary Jane gently asked.

'Granuaile.'

'Granuaile, I'll do everything I can for them, I promise you. But where are you from?'

There was no reply, as the prone figure had fainted once again.

Four long hours later, she died—died with the effort of giving birth to two babies, died from her wounds inflicted by a highwayman.

They showed Granuaile both of her children minutes before her death. She smiled and touched each of them with her uninjured hand.

'I pray your lives are good, my sons, and that you find true happiness and love. Call them *Gearoid* and *Glendon*, please,' she whispered in her soft Irish accent that neither Mary Jane nor Caenwen could really understand or barely hear.

With those final words on her lips, Granuaile slipped into the care of the Almighty.

The two women gently covered her and then immediately started tending to the newborn infants. Caenwen had brought two village women with her who had recently given birth so that the new arrivals could at least be fed with a mother's milk.

'Now what do we do?' Mary Jane questioned with a worried frown.

'Well, the two women that I've brought with me both lost their babies in childbirth, that's why they have so much milk to give. Let nature take its course with both of them, and we'll see what happens, shall we?' the lady of the Forest herbs replied with a conspiratorial smile.

'What names did she say?' Mary Jane suddenly asked, with slight panic in her voice.

'Was it Grundwell and Gumshu?' Caenwen answered, somewhat doubtfully.

'This one must be Grundwell because all he's done is grumble and drink well since I put him to my breast!' the first Forest mother said.

'And this one must be Gumshu because all he's done is chew my nipple with his gums!' laughed the second Forest mother.

'As I said, Mary Jane, let nature take its course,' Caenwen murmured softly.

'I have to thank you for all your help, Caenwen. I gave Granuaile my promise that I would look after her children, but I pray to God that I am able to keep that promise.'

'*We'll* keep it, *we'll* keep it!' Caenwen assured her. 'And looking at those two mothers, I think the problem is resolving itself. The legend and stories surrounding our Irish lady's name certainly described her well. I've never seen such courage and determination to stay alive during a birth. Other than her name and that she was obviously from Ireland, you have absolutely no idea who she was or what she was doing travelling along the Roman Road?'

'I've none whatsoever. She must have been of good family though with those fine clothes, and Thomas said the coach and team were of the best. He did say he thought that there was a crest on the carriage door, but it passed them at such a speed, he wasn't sure,' Mary Jane replied.

'She wore no jewellery or rings that might give us a notion?'

'None, Caenwen. Thomas says there wasn't, and I do believe him. The only thing that could have been hers is the knife, and we can't be sure about that. But it is a fine one with a long blade and beautifully carved and decorated handle,' Mary Jane answered, going into the hut and bringing it out so that the lady of the herbs could look at it.

'That'll pay for the funeral,' Caenwen commented, examining the knife. 'I can sell this in Mitcheldean if you would like me to? Fran and I are going there in two days' time, and I know several men who might be interested in buying it,' she continued.

'That's a very good idea. I hope your daughter is well, and growing up fast I suspect?'

'She's fine and will be taking over from me soon. She loves herbs and tending to the sick and injured. She's already practicing on animals!' Caenwen replied with a grin.

John also returned to the hut with another horse and cart. The two charcoal burners had realised when they got to the village to pick Caenwen up that it would take two carts to bring everyone back from the burn site.

The two men had been friends since childhood, sharing adventures, girlfriends, and trouble. But now they were older, married, and worked together, they tried to avoid trouble as much as possible. Neither of them had expected to find so much of it on a simple delivery of their charcoal to Lydney.

'John Tapper, how's that wife of yours?' Caenwen asked, as the carts made their way back to the village from the site of the hut and charcoal burn.

'Fine, thanks, Caenwen, but I suspect we shall need your assistance very shortly,' he responded with a wide grin.

'That's the trouble with you men. You forget ten minutes of passion and fun can give your wives nine months of problems, followed by several hours of acute pain!' she snorted.

John's cart was carrying the newborn infants, the two Forest mothers, and Caenwen, with Thomas's cart carrying Mary Jane with Granuaile's body. It also had an extra passenger that they had picked up on the way—an Anglican friar in a brown serge habit with a large copper cross hanging from his neck on a hand-woven leather thong. He was quietly saying prayers over Granuaile's body as the procession wended its way back to the village.

The two carts parted company as they came to the outskirts, Thomas's going to the church whilst John's took the two babies to their respective feeding mothers' cottages, where they alighted and with Caenwen's help were settled into their temporary homes. John then returned to his own cottage to see his wife, Josephine, who although heavily pregnant, still managed to gave him a welcome that made his toes curl.

He told her what Caenwen had said about him getting ten minutes of fun. She looked at him with a mischievous twinkle in her eyes and smiled, tossing her long, curly chestnut hair.

'Really, was it that long, John Tapper?'

Trying unsuccessfully to ignore the inference behind her remark, he told her about meeting the friar and how he had joined the group to look after Granuaile's body and escort it to the village church.

'Yes, I met him earlier. He was here in the village. I liked him straight away and all the children did as well. But I thought he was going to another village towards Chepstow tonight?' Josephine asked him, a little puzzled.

'He was, but turned round so that he could be with her,' her husband quietly answered.

'But he didn't know her!'

'"*God knew her, and I work for God,*" the friar had replied when Thomas had said the same thing to him,' John told his wife.

Josephine looked at her husband and smiled. 'Go down to the church and ask him to come here for something to eat, and also say we can offer him somewhere to sleep.'

'Are you sure? You must be very close to having our baby.'

'I am sure. If I give birth whilst he's here, then he can help Caenwen, can't he?' she replied with a giggle.

As the three had their meal together, Josephine suddenly sank down on to a stool, clasping herself and complaining of intense stomach pain. Father Benedict ran to fetch Caenwen, leaving a terrified John gripping his wife's hand and giving her repeated assurances that all would be well.

'No more ten minutes of fun for you, John Tapper!' she managed to say through clenched teeth, sweat pouring from her brow.

'Have you ever helped in delivering a child before, Father?' Caenwen asked as she positioned Josephine ready for the arrival of her firstborn.

'No, but I have delivered many calves on my father's farm in Somerset!' he said as he held tightly on to Josephine's hand, as John had just passed out and was lying prone on the floor of the cottage.

'If you're inferring I'm a cow about to drop a calf, Father, may my calf give you hell throughout her life!' Josephine managed to gasp in between instructions from Caenwen to push.

With one final effort and a huge scream, a baby girl thrust her head into the world, a baby girl that within a minute nestled in her mother's arms, with a recovered John bending over, kissing and caressing both his wife and his daughter, saying, 'How wonderful, how wonderful, my first child, and oh so beautiful!'

'Well, you only have to look at the mother', the friar said gently, 'to behold the beauty of her child.'

'That does not absolve you from the inference behind your remark about delivering calves, my friar!' Josephine returned with a tired smile. 'And I've decided on a name. She's going to be called Maisey.'

'Oh dear, I'm sorry, John! I think I might just have a lot to answer for. Josephine and I were talking before we had our meal, and I told her my favourite girl's name was Maisey, after a wonderful heifer on my father's farm,' the friar admitted guiltily.

'I'll forgive you, Father. We've had so many arguments about names over the last few months it's a relief she's picked one that we can both agree on,' John replied with a smile.

Father Benedict leant forward and made the sign of the cross on the foreheads of Josephine, John, and baby Maisey, asking the Lord for his blessing on the little family of happiness.

Caenwen and he walked out into the evening air, the friar to return to his vigil by Granuaile's body that lay in the church, and Caenwen to set off to the other end of the village to assist in yet another birth.

'Full moons always increase the number of births we get,' she told the rather bemused friar, 'and I can't give you a reason either. Let's hope this next one I'm about to deliver is a girl too, and then we've had two of each tonight! And you needn't suggest more farm animals' names to the parents either! They've decided that it's going to be Daniel if it's a boy and Ursula if it's a girl!' And with a smile and a wave, she disappeared into the dusk.

The following evening, Granuaile was laid to rest in the small churchyard on the outskirts of the Forest village, after a simple service given by the rector of Mitcheldean, assisted by Friar Benedict.

The mourners were few, but those who did attend were those who had been closest to her when she died, those who had given her the greatest hope for the lives of her two children.

They were also the ones who were sworn to absolute secrecy, lest their actions be discovered by others and be punished for breaking the laws of man, whilst upholding the will of God.

No one ever came looking for either Granuaile or her children.

But a family in Ireland stayed in mourning for their daughter for the rest of their lives, whilst a family in England mourned their son, and their heir, for generations to come.

# CHAPTER 2

The noise of the children's laughter was beginning to annoy the rector of Mitcheldean, who was paying one of his infrequent visits to the church in the little Forest village of Cumdean.

Standing at the lectern, he had been trying to read a part of the scriptures of which he was particularly fond, but it would seem that the children of the Forest were intent on disturbing him. He strode out of the already open door and glared around to find the culprits.

Six children were in a heap on the grass, grappling with a large figure in a brown serge habit, all of them screaming, shouting, and laughing.

'Enough!' yelled the ill-humoured cleric, striding over to the squirming heap of bodies, grabbing one child by her long chestnut hair, and pulling her clear of the others.

'I won't have any more of this!' he shouted as he raised his hand ready to give the restrained child a cuff to the head.

Two of the six-year-old boys in the heap saw what was about to happen and immediately scrambled up and ran at the rector, both of them cannoning into the side of his legs and knocking him off balance.

To try and save himself, the cleric let go of the girl's hair and put his hand out as he toppled over. The rector, although not very tall, was of a rotund build, and the weight of his body impacting upon one of his fat but unexercised arms resulted in him screaming in agony as it snapped like a twig.

Undeterred by his scream or the man's office, the young girl sat on his chest and with clenched fists started pummelling him.

'Don't you pull my hair. Don't you pull my hair because it hurts me!' she yelled at him, her small fists going thirteen to the dozen.

The two boys, meanwhile, sat on his legs to stop him kicking out, at the same time trying to bite through his hose to extract their own retribution for his actions.

Father Benedict struggled up from where he had been fighting with the children and walked over and prised Maisey off the rector, her arms still flailing the air as he did so. He put her on the ground with a sharp rebuke, and she stood where she was put, still glowering at her quarry. The two boys had succeeded in their efforts to inflict more pain on the reverend gentleman, who was clutching his arm whilst shouting and trying to kick them off his legs.

The friar then grabbed both Grundwell and Gumshu, putting one under each arm and depositing them down beside Maisey. With his back to the pain-ridden cleric, he gestured for them to disappear. The two boys obeyed instantly, but Maisey took a step forward as if to continue her attack. A huge arm shot out and caught her, and then the friar bent down and hissed in her ear, 'Go, Maisey Tapper, go!'

Maisey departed the scene, not at a run but with an indignant walk, swinging her hips as she did so.

'May my calf give you a lifetime of hell!' her mother had said to him when she was born. 'This is definitely a bad start, but I wonder if things *might* improve,' he muttered to himself, as he turned to deal with the ill-tempered clergyman who was still lying on the ground.

'Rector Clarence, that was an *awful* fall you took,' the friar said in his most sympathetic voice, 'and you dressed in your best frock coat and britches as well.'

'What do you mean *fall?* I was attacked by three of those horrible little village urchins!' he screamed back at Benedict.

'Excuse me, sir, they certainly did not attack you' came an indignant voice from one of the girls who was standing in the group who had been fighting with the friar. 'We were all playing with Friar Benedict when you walked past us and tripped over that fallen branch, which is over there,' she said, pointing down at the offending branch lying on the ground.

'That's quite right, Sophie,' Caenwen confirmed as she and her daughter Fran walked up to the group. 'I was standing by the corner of my cottage when it happened,' she added. 'Now let me have a look at that arm and see what damage you've done to yourself.'

There was another scream of pain from the cleric, as she had given him no warning that she was going to take hold of him to have a look at the injured arm, and he had tried to pull away from her.

'Come now, Rector. That didn't really hurt, did it? If you would accompany Fran and me to my cottage, we'll set it to a splint.' With that, she and the friar lifted the clergyman to his feet and led him away to attend to his arm, hobbling and complaining bitterly.

An hour later, the Reverend Clarence left the village, driving his trap himself as all the villagers were suddenly too busy to take him back to the rectory in Mitcheldean, especially as they would have had to walk three miles to return home.

As he left, attempting to drive the pony and trap with his one good arm, he shouted to the friar so that everyone could hear, 'I'll never come back to this village, never. I hope your church falls into wrack and ruin and that you find no one to take your services. Be warned, I shall be telling the bishop all about this day!'

The pony took fright at all the commotion and all but bolted as the cleric yelled and gesticulated, inadvertently flapping the reins that he held in his uninjured hand. Pony, trap, and the now panicking rector, were last seen by the villagers disappearing down the track to Mitcheldean at an extremely brisk pace.

'That looked a little dangerous!' the friar remarked to Caenwen, as he walked off to find the children who had been involved in the clerical fracas to ensure that all was calm again and no one had been hurt.

A month after the rector's warning, the bishop came to take matins at the Forest village church. At the beginning of his address, he leant on the edge of the pulpit and said in a quiet voice to the assembled congregation, 'Which three children were involved in the disturbance with Reverend Clarence?'

Gumshu, Grundwell, and Maisey stepped forward without any hesitation, Maisey looking defiant, the other two looking resigned.

'Tell me exactly what took place, please, and I want the truth,' he asked gently.

Maisey repeated the story to him, down to the last detail, still looking defiant but slightly tearful by the end of her explanation.

The bishop was silent for a few moments whilst he pondered his reply.

'I have been trying to rid myself of that man for three years, almost since the day of his arrival! You three managed to rid me of him in a matter of minutes, for which I thank you. You'll be delighted to know Reverend Clarence is leaving Mitcheldean within the next few days, but I would ask one thing. When his replacement comes, please, children, don't try to beat and eat him. We have few good clergy left!' he said, with all but a smile.

He waved the youngsters back to stand with their parents.

All through the service, the bishop kept glancing at the two tall six-year-old boys who had owned up so readily. They were taller than the other village children; they were going to be good looking, and they obviously didn't lack courage.

They reminded him of someone he knew, but he could not think who that person was, much as he would try.

A short time later, the bishop walked through the churchyard as he loved to do when he visited this part of his diocese. He had been the rector of Mitcheldean twenty years previously, and this little church had been part of that living.

He stopped in front of one grave with a headstone simply marked *Granuaile.*

Realisation suddenly dawned on him, realisation that he had found the answer to the question he had been asking himself all through the service, since first seeing the children.

The two boys bore a striking likeness to Sir Richard Crighton when he had been that age. The bishop had known him because his father's estate was within his Gloucester diocese, and he had preached at the estate church on special family occasions; he had officiated at the funeral of the young heir when he was laid to rest in the family crypt, some six years ago.

Bishop Robert Galbraith stared at the grave with its simple headstone. He turned slowly and walked over to sit down on the low churchyard wall under a young oak tree. Looking at the grave again, he began to think over everything that had just come to light.

'Hullo, Robert,' Caenwen's soft Welsh voice said from the other side of the wall behind him. 'I thought I might find you here!'

He felt her soft hand gently caressing his neck. He reached round and took hold of it, and turning his head slightly, he brought it to his lips, holding it there whilst he kissed it time and again. He got up and turned completely round to face her, still holding her hand to his lips.

'You are as beautiful as when we last met, and your voice still evokes every memory that I have of you!' he said with a trembling voice, tears welling up in his eyes.

It had been twelve years since they had last met, twelve years since he had last tried to persuade her to marry him, twelve years since yet another refusal. Every time he had visited the little Forest

25

village since then, she had ensured that they hadn't met, even though it had broken her heart.

'I am a healer, a country girl and that would turn your parishioners against you. You know that, Robert,' she had told him twenty years previously, when they had first fallen in love.

'I will give up the Church and come and live a simple life with you, but please give us a chance. You cannot deny a love like ours,' he had pleaded on bended knee on each of the occasions he had asked her to marry him, but her answer had always been the same.

'No, Robert. Your calling is *the Church*, and I have no right to ask you to give that up. Your God needs you because there are precious few men of the faith who will serve him as well as you will!' She had remained adamant in her reply.

'How is our daughter?' he continued in a low voice, still holding her hand and gazing into her eyes.

'Fran is healthy and wonderful, and *so* excited about meeting our bishop,' she replied.

Robert looked quizzically at her.

'I knew that you would work it all out once you had seen the two boys and then Granuaile's grave. But I don't want to talk outside in case we are overheard, so I've arranged for you to have some refreshment with me. When I asked your chaplain if you could, he didn't seem at all surprised by my request, my love?' she said, ending with a question.

'He arranges the money I give you,' Robert answered with a smile. 'He's the only one I can trust.'

They walked around the churchyard, he on the inside and she on the outside. The only time they let their hands part was to pass something in their way. They met at the gate, where raw emotion overcame both of them. They kissed and hugged each other, oblivious to all else, not caring who saw their passionate embraces, their tears, or their kisses.

They sauntered slowly back towards Caenwen's cottage, both still gazing into the other's eyes, arms tightly entwined. Then without a sound, Fran ran up from behind them and took the bishop's other arm and gave it a squeeze, beaming up at him as he turned to her, a daughter recognising her father and a father acknowledging his daughter.

Robert looked back at Caenwen with an obvious question in his eyes. It was the question she knew he would ask her as soon as they had met.

She had also known the answer she would give him, when she had stood behind a small pillar in the church and watched him talk to the children earlier in the day. The thought had made her both nervous and excited as to what the future could hold for them both.

Alone in the cottage, while Fran and Robert's chaplain went to visit the village families, the two talked about the two Crighton children.

Caenwen told him everything she knew about Granuaile, and then Robert told her about her origins, her husband, and his family.

He sat and thought for a long while, with his future wife sitting quietly on his knee, her arms encircling his neck.

Speaking quietly, he said, 'We have to think about the welfare of the two boys, Grundwell and Gumshu. Caenwen, I'm intrigued. Please tell me how on *earth* they came to be christened with those two *very* peculiar names?'

She told him exactly what had happened and how they came to be named. He turned to her with a broad smile on his face.

'A Welsh woman trying to understand an Irish woman, those two boys never stood a chance to get their right names, did they, my love?'

Caenwen giggled as she gave the bishop a bite on his neck for his cheek.

'Seriously', he continued, 'these are dangerous times for certain of the aristocracy, but I'm not a politician, so I can only go on what I've heard. Those two boys are obviously happy, well looked after, and are amongst people who love them. Nothing we can do will bring their natural mother or father back.

'Granuaile's parents know she is dead. It's just that they have no grave at which to grieve, unlike Sir Richard's parents. If they were told where she was buried, then the existence of the two boys would become known, and I think that would be dangerous for them *and* for all those who helped them, however well meaning.

'Whether or when that will ever change, I don't know. But I now agree with you, it is a secret that is best kept from all but those who need to know, and that includes the boys. How many people *do* know?'

'It's only you and I who know the full story. The others only know fragments,' she replied after some thought. 'And there are only eight of those now, all sworn to total secrecy.'

'I'm afraid we are going to have to trust a third person with *all* the facts, someone who the people of the Forest respect but who at the same time is capable of holding such a dangerous secret, someone who can tell the boys only when the time is right. It all needs to be recorded on a document so that there can never be any problem with the accuracy of the facts,' the bishop mused.

'What about someone like a friar?' Caenwen asked, suddenly sitting up straight.

'Friar Benedict!' he responded.

'He's visiting the Tapper family now, which he often does.'

'I know!' Robert replied. 'He told me he would be here when we met two weeks ago.'

'You know of him, and you've met him?' Caenwen asked with raised eyebrows.

'Yes, we meet quite regularly. We both work for the Almighty. Even if the friar sleeps under a hedge and I in a palace, we're all equal in the eyes of the Lord,' Robert continued with a smile. 'And I learn a lot from my friendship with people like Father Benedict. I already knew exactly what happened when the children took on Reverend Clarence, but I needed to hear it from them. I also have to hear regularly that the woman I love and my daughter are safe and well.'

'You're a crafty old fox,' Caenwen whispered, cuddling up to him again.

'I'll show you who's old,' the bishop said, moving his hands gently across her breasts.

'Not until we're married, Your Lordship!' she started to say, but then changed her mind and succumbed to the man that she had loved so much, for so long.

Two hours later, Father Benedict sat in the cottage, talking to Bishop Robert and Caenwen at length, and then writing a detailed account using materials that Robert's chaplain had provided.

'That could be dangerous information you hold, my good father. Guard it well!' Robert warned quietly. 'And should you feel that it needs to be passed on for some reason, then pass it on to someone who you trust as much as we trust you with the same instruction. Only tell the boys when you think the time is right!'

'I will, my lord. That I promise you,' Father Benedict said, kneeling in front of Robert, taking his hand and kissing his ring. As he rose, the friar wished them both all the happiness in the world before quietly closing the cottage door behind him as he went out.

'That's the bit that will take me some time to get used to,' Caenwen said thoughtfully.

'That's done for the office, not the man, my love.' Robert smiled. 'And as I said earlier, all men are equal in the sight of the Lord.'

'But *I* wonder if the Lord knows how good a man *you* are, Bishop Robert Galbraith?' his lady countered.

'Well, if you could put in a good word for me, it probably wouldn't come amiss,' a contented Robert replied with a mischievous grin, with obvious reference to their lovemaking earlier in the afternoon.

'Robert! And *you* a bishop too!' Caenwen laughed, exaggerating her Welsh accent.

The two six-year-old boys crawled through the undergrowth towards the charcoal burners' hut. They froze when one of the two wood colliers came from watching the charcoal kiln burn to relieve himself. Gumshu began to giggle when the man passed air as well as fluid, and Grundwell had to dig his friend hard in the ribs to stop him. When the woodsman had finished and gone back to watch his burn, the two friends turned to each other.

'It's a good job the girls aren't with us. Maisey would have been *bound* to have said something then,' Grundwell whispered.

'And Sophie would have screamed and run off!' added Gumshu.

The boys had given the two girls the slip earlier in the morning. They had told them that girls didn't climb trees, so when the girls responded as they knew they would by climbing the nearest tree they had made good their escape.

'They're *not* going to be happy!' Gumshu called to Grundwell as they had raced off, splashing across the stream just outside the village.

The boys suddenly realised that they missed having the girls with them, so they crawled back through the undergrowth and went to find them.

'When we next get the chance, we'll bring the girls back. The man might do it again, so we can see what they do.' Grundwell grinned as they ran back across the stream.

The four youngsters played together as often as they could, but even at the age of six, they, like most of the children of the village, had their parts to play in helping their family to survive. The girls helped their mothers in the feeding of the family, grinding corn to make flour for the family bread, collecting wild berries and herbs, and making the pies that were filled with the gathered fruit.

Maisey said to Sophie when they were out collecting berries from one particularly thorn-ridden thicket early one morning, 'I'm going to have servants to do this for me when I'm grown up.'

'I'm going to have *lots* of servants so that they can make the bread as well,' Sophie observed, looking down at her hands which she had burnt on the oven stones that morning, when she was helping bake the village bread.

For their part, Grundwell and Gumshu had already learnt the art of snaring rabbits and bigger birds from their fathers. Gumshu's father was also an expert at catching fish with his hands, the fish that lurked in some of the pools of the larger streams in the Forest. Samuel and Nathan also instructed their sons well in the art of keeping alert to the approach of the royal bailiffs who patrolled the woodlands, guarding the royal game.

Lying on his mattress one evening, Gumshu heard the arrival of a gamekeeper at the door of the cottage. He heard his father, Nathan, vehemently denying that he had ever touched a royal deer, never mind shot one.

'You can search this cottage all you like!' he said to the man and his assistant. 'We will, Master Whorston, we will,' replied the royal official and promptly took him at his word.

When they came near to where Gumshu was lying, they moved quietly round him as he pretended to be asleep. Their search of the cottage eventually yielded nothing, neither deer meat nor musket. After they had left, Gumshu got up, and he and his father removed the raw venison steaks from beneath his mattress, putting them back in the cool part of the cottage where his mother kept her meat and fish and his father hid his gun.

'You will get flogged and deported one day!' his mother said to her husband.

'They've got to catch me first,' Nathan replied to his wife with a wide grin.

'They've been here twice in the last month, so they must know something,' she retorted. 'Please stop teaching Gumshu about poaching. We only have one child, and I don't want him deported with you,' she continued in a worried tone.

The next day, the family moved to the hut by the charcoal kiln that Nathan had built in the Forest. Once the kiln had been lit and the burn started, the aroma of cooking meat floated across the clearing, but with a strong wind blowing, the smell soon disappeared.

Venison had not been mentioned again by either Nathan or Sarah, nor had there been any further visits from the royal gamekeeper. After some persuasion, Nathan also returned his borrowed firearm to a fellow poacher who lived in St Briavels, close to the castle and church.

Grundwell, too, was the only child in *his* family.

'I wish I could have some brothers and sisters,' he said to his mother one evening. Elisabeth looked at Samuel with a troubled face.

Samuel Fordes smiled at his son, saying, 'I only need one son to light my charcoal burns, and one child is quite enough, thank you.' He then quietly changed the subject and started talking about the following morning's fishing expedition with Gumshu and his father.

Grundwell thought about what his father had said and decided he was quite right about only needing one son. His biggest thrill was when he was allowed to climb on top of the charcoal kiln after his father had lit the centre and put the plug in the chimney hole around which the kiln had been built. He would then slide down into his father's waiting arms. It never impressed his mother though, because he usually ended up ripping some part of his clothing or getting a face full of smoke if he didn't put the plug in quickly enough.

'If I had any brothers or sisters, they'd want to do that too, so I couldn't do it every time,' he thought.

The subject was never talked about again, either by parents or child.

A week later, the boys returned to the hut, and this time they had Sophie and Maisey with them. The four had done their usual trick of meeting outside the churchyard gate, going there separately so that they did not arouse the curiosity of the other children from the village. It wasn't that they didn't like them; they all had other friends as well, but the four of them always found they got bored with games of hide and seek, tag, kicking a pig's bladder around, or building dens. They wanted more exciting things to amuse themselves.

The girls had also been stopped from playing with their dolls outside their cottages after Sophie's mother had caught the two of them hanging their rag dolls on a tree, and then letting the two boys throw stones at them.

'What were you thinking of?' Josephine angrily asked Maisey when she had been told about what had happened.

'We were pretending they were witches,' Maisey replied with an innocent look on her face, the reply causing her father to near choke over the drink he had been quietly enjoying.

There was silence around the wood colliers' hut, so the four children kept crawling closer.

'I thought you said we'd see someone having a wee?' Maisey enquired accusingly, looking back at the two boys.

'We didn't know they'd have gone,' Gumshu whined.

'Don't grovel!' she snapped back. 'You know I hate it when you do that.'

She looked over at Sophie and grinned as she said it because it was something that she'd heard her mother say to her father. She had then asked Father Benedict what it meant.

'You shouldn't have been listening,' the friar had said, when she told him where she had heard it.

'You said the best way to learn words was to listen to other people speak them,' she retorted with one of her indignant looks.

The friar coughed and then explained what it meant. He thought it better not to mention the conversation to her mother and father.

On Maisey's instigation, they jumped up, ran to the hut door, and peered inside.

'It smells of smoke and other horrible things, and I'm not going in there,' Sophie said emphatically.

'I'm not either,' Maisey agreed. 'Sophie's right. It's horrible!'

'You're both scared,' Grundwell challenged. 'Well, we're going to go in, so you both wait here.'

Where upon the two boys ventured into the gloom of the hut to explore the inside.

There was nothing to be seen but some rubbish lying on the floor, several old blankets, some old straw mattresses, and two discarded stone flints. Gumshu bent over and picked them up. He struck the two stones together, not just once but several times, watching the sparks fly off and land on the floor.

'Don't!' Grundwell cried out.

His warning came too late; the sparks ignited one of the dry straw mattresses and flames immediately flared up, spreading at an alarming rate. The hut also started to fill with thick white smoke. The girls, who were standing at the door, both screamed and ran back into the clearing. They stopped and turned round to look at the hut which now had smoke billowing out through the door.

'The boys!' Maisey yelled and started to run forward again towards the hut, followed closely by Sophie. Just as they did so, Grundwell appeared at the door, dragging a choking Gumshu with him. The three of them pulled their friend over to the opposite side of the clearing, where they all collapsed on the ground. Gumshu was still coughing but not as badly; he sat up with smoke-induced tears running from his eyes. They all looked at the hut, which was now enveloped in smoke and flames, sending a plume of smoke high into the sky.

'I think we'd better go!' Sophie exclaimed.

'Well, there's one thing. If those charcoal burners are lost and can't find their way back to their hut, they'll be able to find it now!' Grundwell said by way of reply, rolling over and looking up into the sky.

The four children leapt up and headed back into the Forest as quickly as they could run, heading back towards their village, only pausing to let the boys wash themselves in a stream so that they didn't smell of smoke quite as much.

'What were the children up to yesterday?' Josephine asked Sarah and Elisabeth the following day when they met at the spring behind her cottage.

'I don't know. They were definitely up to something, but they seem to have taken a vow of silence,' Elisabeth replied with an indulgent smile.

The charcoal burners hut had burnt itself out; no one noticed the smoke coming up from the Forest, so no questions were ever asked, not even by the men whose hut it was.

Year on year, the four friends found pleasure in each other's company, the boys growing taller and the girls more striking. The games and adventures of childhood started to give way to the beginnings of complex relationships between a girl and a boy, as the four friends matured into the beginnings of adulthood.

The annual maypole dancing that started as a children's frolic began taking on a more serious meaning. The four's parents now watched their teenage children dancing with ribbons and flowers around the maypole that was drawn around the village, mounted on a decorated cart pulled by one of the villager's oxen.

'It's the only day of the year that Maisey gets up early without being yelled at,' her father remarked as they watched the youngsters go by, dancing to the music of the pipe and the drum.

'And she was up and away into the woods well before dawn this morning,' her mother said with a knowing smile.

'That's funny, so was Gumshu!' *his* mother added with the same smile.

Two fifteen-year-old friends stood by a tree on the outskirts of the village, the boy carving into the tree's bark, the girl watching him with a smile playing on her face.

'Now everyone will know that we love each other,' Maisey said softly.

'You don't think they already know?' Gumshu asked, smiling back and taking her hand.

The two carried on with their evening walk, down towards the babbling Forest stream that flowed past the grass bank that was their favourite place to sit, the place where they used to sit and dream.

# CHAPTER 3

'But they're only seventeen!' John exclaimed when Josephine gently broached the subject of their eldest daughter wanting to marry Gumshu.

'They've loved each other ever since I can remember, John. Who knows what the future will bring?' she replied softly. 'And he has done his best to help us since your accident in the mine.'

John sat and reflected on that remark from his wife. She was quite right, as she usually was. Gumshu had been more of a son to him since he crushed his leg on that fateful day, which saw his greatest friend killed and he left with a useless limb. He quietly cursed himself for failing to carry on working the charcoal with Thomas all those years ago. But the pay that the mine owner had offered him to extract coal was a lot more than he could ever have earned with Thomas.

He smiled to himself. He had taught Gumshu all he knew about charcoal burning. He had sat in the Forest clearings with him, watching him build the kilns from the wood of the small trees and saplings that he had cut down. He had told him the best way to get the *burn* alight and then how to regulate it to get the best charcoal. In the end, charcoal and Gumshu had been his saviours because no one would employ a man with a shattered leg.

'Well, at least it will stop all those flowers being scattered outside our front door every time they celebrate the maypole dance. I've never seen as many as we had this year. The boy must have a secret supply in those woods.'

'I think he had a little help from our daughter with that,' Josephine replied with a laugh.

Her husband looked at her with a knowing look, adding, 'Not the only thing he got, judging from the grin that he had on his face for about a week after.'

'John! That's my daughter you're talking about.'

'She's *our* daughter, Wife, and we both know how enthusiastic we are about such things, don't we?' he said, sliding his hand up her skirt and then between her thighs as she tried in vain to pass where he was sitting.

She stood still for a moment about to protest, and then drew breath and sighed as John found and caressed the soft lips of her cavern of desire.

'That's not fair, John,' she said in a husky voice, dropping the wooden bowl that she was carrying and turning towards him.

He slid his other hand up her skirt as well and pulled her to him as she lifted her garment and straddled him. With one arm round his neck, her free hand searched for and found his erect manhood, releasing it from his britches, guiding it to the entrance of her now moist and willing passion. She then lowered herself down on to him and slowly but purposefully began to gyrate her lower body, with John holding her buttocks to keep her close to him.

'Can they?' she whispered, caressing and kissing him. 'Can they get married?'

'Right now, you can have anything you want!' he replied with mounting breathlessness, as his manhood penetrated deep into his lady's organ of joy.

Sometime later, Josephine went in search of her daughter to tell her that her father had agreed she could marry her childhood sweetheart. As she was about to go out of the door, John looked at her.

'You planned that didn't you, Josephine Tapper? You are a crafty wench!' He grinned.

'How could you possibly have such thoughts, John Tapper? You are such a wonderful lover. How could I ever resist you?' she said as she flashed him a departing smile.

The two families met and talked of the forthcoming marriage of their son and daughter, both knowing some of the history that surrounded Gumshu.

'Neither family has any wealth, so I think we should just give them our blessing,' John said to Gumshu's parents, whereupon the four began to celebrate the imminent union of their children with copious amounts of ale and mead.

'I thought *we* were supposed to celebrate our forthcoming wedding too?' Maisey said as she came into the cottage later in the evening, to find all four parents in a state of total inebriation, unable to stand or talk, the only method of communication being by giggling fits.

'I think they must have agreed on satisfactory terms!' Gumshu grinned, putting his arms around her waist and kissing the top of her head as he stood behind her at the cottage door.

The wedding was a true Forest village affair, with the Reverend Gyles Stollard and Father Benedict leading the bridal procession from John and Josephine's cottage to the village church. After the simple ceremony of placing the ring on Maisey's finger and the joining of their hands, which were then covered by Gyles's vestment, the couple paraded round the village on a flower-bedecked cart drawn by a grey plough horse, followed by the crowd of wedding guests, which consisted of the whole village and the two holy men.

Mary Jane, now alone after Thomas's death during the previous winter, walked back with Father Benedict from where the procession had ended to go to the little churchyard. They stood in front of Granuaile's grave, the friar saying a quiet prayer, Mary Jane with her head bowed, deep in her own thoughts and memories.

As they turned away to join the wedding feast, she quietly asked, 'Do you think she would have approved of her new daughter-in-law?'

'I have no doubts whatsoever, and she would have had enough time to think about it! Those two have been inseparable since they could barely walk. Maisey even used to help him when I taught them about reading, writing, and figures. I often wondered what he'd ever do without her, but that question doesn't arise now,' the father replied with a smile. 'I have to teach someone else now,' he continued with a look of childlike enthusiasm on his face, rubbing his huge hands together in anticipation.

'Surely you're not going to give the village children a lesson today?'

'Children? Good Lord no, certainly not. Today, I'm going to teach that rector of Mitcheldean how to drink and appreciate real village-brewed ale and mead. He needs to know before he retires!' the friar replied.

'Aren't you going to eat first?' Mary Jane enquired, as she knew the tables were groaning with an array of temping foods; there was also a pig roasting on a spit, a favourite of the wandering emissary of the Lord.

'The pig and I will become acquainted in due course, but first I must instruct my pupil!' came his reply, floating back on the wind as he bounded across the meadow with his habit flying, rushing towards where the tables for the wedding feast were laid out with food, ale, and copious amounts of mead.

Two months later, Grundwell and Sophie also married, in the same fashion as their friends. And the rector had remarked a day prior to the ceremony when he was talking to one of his churchwardens, 'I'm really looking forward to the day. Two more young people getting married, and myself getting another lesson from the friar on the consumption of local produce.'

Grundwell and Gumshu settled into wedded bliss with enthusiasm along with vigour, and into their chosen profession as charcoal burners with resignation and indifference.

'I told both of them when they were fifteen that they would never make anything of themselves as far as charcoal was concerned,' Grundwell's father grumbled crossly. 'And things haven't improved a lot!'

'They have to do it though. They have wives to support now, and judging by the dedication to lovemaking of my daughter and son-in-law, it won't be long before I could become a grandfather,' Maisey's father had replied with a knowing grin.

Neither couple had a cottage of their own, the main reason being that they could not afford the rent, but there was also a shortage of available cottages in Cumdean. This meant that living with their respective wives' parents was the only option open to them.

'Privacy and the opportunity of lovemaking are a constant problem when we are home in the village!' Gumshu confided to Grundwell on a day when they had been discussing the benefits of their developing semi-nomadic life as charcoal burners.

The only opportunity they could have to be alone with their wives was when they were working, as both men now had their own registered Forest sections for producing charcoal. That meant they built their own huts so that they could live on the site where they cut the timber, assembled the kiln, and then attended the burn for the two days that it was alight.

When Maisey came to stay at the first hut that Gumshu had built since they were married, she put her hand on his shoulder, looked at it, and then up at him, laughing.

'You won't set this one on fire whilst we are still in it, will you my love?' It was a question for which she received a sharp slap on the bottom and was then carried into the hut. With Gumshu's attention being held elsewhere, it was fortunate that the kiln burn was successfully underway at the time, so there hadn't been a need for any immediate work to be done on it.

Grundwell's Forest section was some two miles distant from Gumshu's. He, too, had built a hut so that he could have Sophie with him as he worked. Her only complaint was the constant smoke that drifted through the hut once the burn had started, but she had to admit that it was a small price to pay for their privacy.

'I can be as noisy as I like when we make love out there in the Forest,' she told an amused Maisey with relish, when they were back in the village after one particular burn. 'I just worry in case we get visited by any village children during the day!'

Nine months later, the plague struck the Forest village. How it arrived no one knew, but it decimated the community, striking at family after family, taking some and sparing others, young and old alike, leaving widows, widowers, orphans, and broken hearts in its wake.

Gumshu, Grundwell, and their wives were delivering two loads of charcoal to one of their customers in Lydney when they heard news of its arrival in the village. They were told by another charcoal burner and his family who were making a delivery to the same forge.

'What do we do? Stay here or go back?' Gumshu asked the others as they stood round the man's cart with frightened and worried looks on their faces, agonising over the decision. There was a dreadful silence as each became immersed in thoughts about the safety and well-being of their own families.

'I think you may have a problem getting back into the village anyway. Rumour has it that there will be a ring of soldiers around the whole area by tonight to stop people leaving,' the wood collier told them. 'Luckily *we* haven't been in the village for weeks,' he added.

'Yes, but I doubt they'll stop people going back in,' Grundwell replied thoughtfully.

Gumshu walked across the Roman Road to look out towards the River Severn. Grundwell came and stood beside him. 'What do you think we should do?' Gumshu repeated.

'Sophie is pregnant, so as far as I'm concerned she stays away. Whether she agrees or not is another matter,' Grundwell said quietly.

'In that case, I think you should *both* definitely stay away. Does Maisey know?' Gumshu asked in a low voice.

'Sophie is telling her now,' Grundwell replied as they walked back across the road.

When they joined their wives, the two women were clutching each other, both crying. Without a word, each of the wives took hold of their respective husbands and held them very tight. The two men looked at each other, not knowing quite how to react.

'With getting the charcoal ready that we have just sold, *none* of us have been in the village for over a month,' Gumshu declared in a decisive voice. 'Therefore, I suspect we won't be infected. Our parents would tell us to stay away, we all know that. You two have a baby coming, therefore, that is your decision taken for you.' He paused, trying to bring his many emotions under control. 'We can do nothing even if we go back, except bury the dead,' he continued. 'If we try and nurse the sick, the chances are that we'll get sick too. Therefore I think we *all* stay clear and live with our consciences, and at least we'll carry on our family lines,' he finished, adding the last bit of his answer more to ease his own guilt than using it as an argument. He would one day realise the enormity of his words, should he remember them and ever be told of his true blood line.

Grundwell readily agreed, and reluctantly the two women also saw the sense behind the decision.

No Lydney tavern or inn would give them accommodation when landlords realised they were from Cumdean, but luckily they found an abandoned fisherman's shack on the foreshore of the Severn Estuary, about a mile from the outskirts of the town.

With the money they had been paid by the forge's owner, they bought food, blankets, and clothing from the shops and then made the best they could of their temporary home. They built a fire from the plentiful supply of driftwood they found on the tideline. Gumshu produced two flint stones and struck them together to get a spark to light the tinder.

'I'm getting quite good at doing this now,' he remarked, a comment his wife and two friends did not find the slightest bit amusing under their present circumstances.

They took the two horses out from their carts' harnesses and tethered them close behind the shack, the animals grazing contentedly on the open salt marsh grassland.

Looking at them, Grundwell commented, 'There's our emergency food supply should our money run out.'

'Yes, that's fine, but if we do have to kill and eat them, we'll put you two in the shafts of the carts to take us home,' replied a serious and tearful Sophie, as she and an equally tearful Maisey sat outside the door of the shack on an old oak form.

With the other charcoal burner and his family from Cumdean living in a nearby shack, the group were left in peace as no one from Lydney was going to risk infection by going anywhere near them.

They passed the time by collecting driftwood, trapping rabbits, and gathering other food sources from the marshes and shoreline, cooking them with the wild herbs and berries they found in abundance on the surrounding grassland and bushes. They talked much about the future, but thoughts of their families were never far from their minds.

They returned to the Forest village nine weeks later once they heard that the military ring had been withdrawn, taking that as an indication that the danger of infection had passed.

The Reverend Gyles Stollard stood and looked around the village, openly weeping.

Silence echoed around the Forest—no children's laughter, no women's chatter, no men's shouting; there was even silence from the village dogs.

He knelt down as if in prayer. But it wasn't prayer that made him kneel; it was anger, it was frustration, it was a sense of betrayal by his God, and he could not come to terms with any of it.

'Why? Why? What have these good people ever done to deserve this?' he cried out in frustrated anguish.

Fran heard, Father Benedict heard, Sophie's parent's heard, and all ran from where they were to try and give some solace to this kind and elderly cleric who felt so humiliated and betrayed.

Father Benedict lifted him to a standing position and tried to stop him ripping off his neck cloth and dark top coat of office.

'No! Gyles, no! That is not the answer. These people will need you now, more than ever!' he said, giving his friend a firm shake. 'Think please, I implore you. I will also need your help, help that only your experience in years can give.'

The rector bent his head for a few moments, then raised it and looked the friar in the eyes.

'Forgive me, I indulged in self-pity for a time then, but your words are spoken with wisdom. But why, Benedict, why? Where is our God?' he cried out again.

Father Benedict looked at his distraught friend with deep compassion.

'Gyles, I have no answer for you. You must find that in the faith that you have in the Lord,' he responded in a gentle voice.

The others had all gathered round to see if they could help.

Fran spoke quietly, 'Rector, if you'd allow me, I have a herbal drink that calms as well as fortifies. May I offer you some?'

Recovering some of his composure, Gyles looked at her and with a smile on his face asked, 'Is it anything like the ale that the friar has taught me to drink? My wife says he has led me astray and I shouldn't succumb to temptation again, not unless she's with me!'

'Do you know, Fran, last time I went to the rectory to have supper Anne drank more than I did, and she still managed to talk sense!' the friar interrupted indignantly. 'And she brews her own superb mead,' he added with a heartfelt sigh.

'She's a brewer's daughter, but I never dared tell anybody,' Gyles admitted.

'All those wasted years, and I never knew!' the friar murmured, shaking his head.

The rector looked at those around him as he drank the draught that Fran brought him, and he marvelled at the courage that they had all shown by remaining in the village whilst the plague had raged.

He had heard how Fran had dispensed her herbal remedies, with no thought of her own safety.

He had heard how Benedict's tireless pastoral care had saved many from self-harm, and had helped hold the village community together.

He had heard how the survivors had buried their dead and cleaned infected cottages, whilst still managing to feed themselves, keep their sanity, and retain some humour.

And he marvelled; he marvelled at the human spirit in the face of adversity and death.

'The presence of the soldiers did *slightly* put one off flight!' Sophie's father readily admitted to him when Gyles mentioned his admiration of all those who had stayed. 'Anyway, thank God the youngsters had the sense to stay clear!' William added.

'Which youngsters do you mean?' Gyles asked.

'Sophie, Maisey, Gumshu, and Grundwell,' the worried man replied.

'Do any of them know that their parents are all dead apart from you and Lisa, and that Maisey's two sisters are dead as well?'

'No, they haven't come back yet, but now the soldiers are gone, I suspect that they will be very shortly. Unless, of course . . .' his voice trailed off with a very concerned sigh.

'Benedict was right, I am needed here!' Gyles suddenly said, refastening his neck cloth and straightening his coat.

'You are both needed, sir,' William responded.

Father Benedict held a sobbing Maisey as she stood in front of her family's grave in the churchyard. She shook as she stared at the plain wooden cross that simply said '*The Tapper Family*'.

He had buried them in one grave so that they could be together in death, as they had been in life.

Other families had been laid to rest in a similar manner, out of compassion as well as necessity. He had knelt for many hours in the little church before taking that decision. And as he had quietly said to the Lord, 'I not only need guidance on pastoral questions, but with a practical one as well. Lack of grave space is becoming a problem!'

Maisey went silently back to the cottage and started to clean. She cleaned without stopping for nearly a day and a night—not hearing, not seeing, and not speaking.

Gumshu watched her, watched her deal with her grief as well as her guilt.

He *too* was grieving for *his* parents; he *too* was trying to deal with his guilt at not being with them to share their suffering and he had no doubt, their death as well.

On the second evening, he walked down to the Forest stream and sat on the grass bank, buried his face in his hands, and wept, wept like he had never wept before.

Maisey came from the village and sat beside him, gently putting her arm around his shoulders and pulling him close to her.

She tenderly kissed the side of his head and said in a soft voice, 'I love you, as I always have done.' And there was no need of any further words between them.

They sat in the same position until dusk crept over the Forest, then still without speaking, they got to their feet and returned, hand in hand, to the cottage with the Forest spring behind it, the cottage that was now their home and not shared with anyone else.

Grundwell and Sophie sat in front of the fire in the cottage that was now *their* home, the cottage that used to be home to Grundwell's parents. He too had grieved, but no tears had flowed. He stared into the fire, thinking his own thoughts. He wasn't sure how he felt, but a terrible sadness ran through him. He and Sophie were also sharing a silence generated by grief, and there were no words that could be said in sympathy. He reached over and took her hand, gently pulling his wife to him. He then slowly felt her stomach, feeling for the life within. He wanted to feel the life of the future.

'1604 will be a year I shall never ever want to look back on,' he reflected bitterly.

The village of Cumdean started to show signs of rebuilding its shattered community, with the addition of new faces to add to those who had survived. Many sought a new life—a new life with new hopes and new dreams. Women with babes in arms emerged to stand at their cottage doors; children of all ages shed their mantles of isolation, and once again the sounds of play and laughter rang around the woodlands and glades of the Forest.

The early morning sounds of the miners, quarrymen and foresters going to work yet again echoed around the wooded hillsides and valleys. The church congregations started to gather once more, increasing in their numbers as the embattled parishioners began to rebuild their faith as well as their lives.

But however much the communities were recovering; the memory of those who had died would never be forgotten by those who had lived.

The two friends returned to labour in their Forest habitat with some reluctance and little enthusiasm.

'Why are we doing this?' Grundwell asked Gumshu one day as they left the village at dawn, bound for their designated workplaces.

'Because there is nothing else we can do' came the short reply from his friend.

'There must be something else. We're young, fit, and healthy,' Grundwell muttered.

'And married!' Gumshu shot at him.

'Ah, I knew there was something else,' Grundwell grinned, as he had just had to deal with a sickly Sophie.

The conversation was temporarily forgotten over the forthcoming years, both families increasing in number, with Maisey and Sophie seemingly trying to outdo each other in the production of little ones.

When Maisey had twins, Grundwell joked to Gumshu, 'That was cheating! One at a time please!'

'I couldn't agree more!' Maisey declared, when Gumshu told her about their friend's remark.

Much to the delight of the villagers, Gyles Stollard and his wife Anne retired and came to live in the village.

'I shall have my own resident master brewer!' laughed an ecstatic Friar Benedict when they told him of their plans.

When Grundwell and Sophie had the first of their family christened, he and Gyles raised their mugs of mead to Baby Alice at the celebrations that followed, with a toast to her happiness followed by the question *'Who's next?'*

To which a blushing Maisey had replied, 'I think that'll be me!'

So the two men of God had taken that as an extremely good reason to celebrate the forthcoming event, as well as the present one.

Grundwell looked at Gumshu as he still remembered their conversations about the future when they had been bemoaning their dislike of working the charcoal.

'It looks as if we won't be finding out what is beyond the Forest for some time yet then!' he observed with a wry smile.

# CHAPTER 4

Both families paused and then turned to look back at the Forest behind them; even the dogs seemed to hesitate.

It was as if the leaves on the trees were waving them off on their adventure of life, whilst at the same time the darkness of the seemingly intertwined trunks of the woodland was closing the door on their pasts.

Each of the adults was lost in their own world of successes, of failures, of pains, and of pleasures. It was as if all the tears and laughter over the past few years had accumulated to give them a send-off, with the gusting breeze stirring the leaves to emulate the sounds of laughter, and within the silences, the imagination could hear the tears flowing like the Forest streams.

The children gambolled down the gently sloping expanse of rough grass, blissfully unaware of their parents' innermost thoughts.

Ahead of them, some two miles distant, lay Mitcheldean. The smoke from the hearths of the houses lay around the roofs and tall brick chimneys like a soft, wispy blanket. There seemed to be no breeze at all within the valley that cradled the town, in spite of the hour of the afternoon.

'Best be getting on,' Gumshu said, nearly tripping over one of the dogs that was chasing a hapless rabbit. 'We've a way to go yet, especially with the little ones.'

The remark broke the mood for all of them, so turning back so that the town was the object of their gaze, they gathered children and dogs and increased their pace. They put their reflective thoughts and the Forest to the back of their minds, for the time being at least.

When they got into the town, and after some discussion, they split up, having decided that it would be easier for two smaller family groups to find somewhere to sleep.

'This doesn't feel right!' Gumshu stated after a few minutes.

He scowled at a lady of ill-repute who had appeared out of the shadows, giving him a meaningful look. Seeing the look, she retreated back into the safety of the darkness to await further potential clients.

Gumshu enjoyed admiring pretty women, but definitely not when his wife and family were close behind him.

'What did she want?' Maisey questioned. Gumshu shot her a glance, and silence lapsed between them.

'Anyway, what doesn't feel right?' she asked.

'Splitting up from the others,' he replied, narrowly avoiding putting his foot into what looked like a very foul-looking water course running at the side of the street. The stench confirmed he was right to be cautious, and he made a mental note to be more careful in future.

'At least in the Forest', he thought, 'they dig holes for such things and mark them with a briar.'

They continued their way further into the town, every turn revealing something new for the children to look at. They had never seen so many people before, except for the yearly visit to one of the local town fairs. Gumshu kept asking people who were passing by if they knew of anywhere they could stay. Those who bothered to stop kept telling him to go to one of the inns. What they didn't know was that Gumshu and his family were in the town to try and earn money, not spend it on expensive places to sleep.

'I think, Maisey, we *had* better find an inn. It's starting to get dark!' he finally said in a reluctant voice.

They were, at that moment, passing down a narrow street which had rather run-down looking houses on either side, most of which were in desperate need of paint and repair.

After some hesitation, Gumshu knocked on a door behind which he could hear raised voices. A stocky woman opened it. Her look softened when she saw the tall handsome woodsman in front of her.

'Yes?' she enquired, looking at him with obvious signs of arousal.

'We're trying to find somewhere to sleep, and I wondered if you might know of anywhere,' Gumshu answered, endeavouring to avoid her gaze.

'How many are you?' the woman asked, noting Maisey's presence with some disappointment.

'My wife and me, plus four little ones and two dogs,' he replied.

'You're lucky,' the woman answered. 'We do have a room spare. Come in, all of you, and I'll show you. You'll all have to sleep together, mind.'

There was a calculating look in her eye, Maisey noticed, with not a little apprehension. Gumshu was a good looking man, and she knew by experience that most women found him attractive, with the result that many had tried to ensnare him.

She smiled to herself. Gumshu had been hers from when they could barely walk and nothing or any one had ever changed the way they felt about each other.

Grundwell and Sophie fared much better. They and their three children had only gone a few hundred yards when a smartly dressed woman came up to them.

'Are you looking for somewhere to stay?' she asked in a very pleasant and well-educated voice.

'Well, yes, we are, but we don't know where to look, and we definitely can't afford to go to one of the inns,' Sophie replied, slightly taken aback by the woman's direct approach.

'Follow me then!' the lady instructed.

She led the way down a wide street with affluent-looking houses on either side. The light was fading, but Sophie and Grundwell could see the house that she stopped at was large, smartly presented, and had three storeys. Shafts of candlelight shone out of the glazed peephole in the front door and some of the uncovered windows on the ground floor, dancing like moonbeams on the faces of the people passing by in the unlit and darkening street.

The door opened into a huge room, with a large fire hearth set into a substantial recess on one of its long walls. The fire embers glowed red with heat, giving power to two iron cooking pots that were supported above it. There was a strange accompanying smell, not unpleasant, but enough for the three little ones to notice and pull their mother's skirt.

'What's that smell?' Alice whispered.

'Spiced rabbit simmering in one of the pots over the fire' came the reply from a darkened corner of the room.

The children jumped. None of them had noticed the figure bending over a bench when they came through the front door. The man straightened up and came into the flickering candlelight, his hands covered in blood, the sleeves of his tunic still bearing pieces of fir from when he had skinned the rabbit. He glanced at the smartly dressed woman.

'And who might they be?' he questioned.

'They're going to be staying for a couple of days,' she replied.

'Do they have any money for rent?' he said, looking slightly puzzled.

The woman looked at Sophie for a reply.

'Yes, we do,' she said, trying to ignore the man's gaze which had fallen on to her obvious full figure. 'I'm not very happy with this', she thought, noting the man's somewhat dark and rugged appearance as well as his interest. She felt a strange feeling of foreboding in the pit of her stomach.

Alice persisted with her question, looking up at her mother's face.

'But what's the smell?'

'That's cinnamon. We add it to the cooking pot to make the rabbit taste good,' the man replied, a reply that left the Forest family looking slightly quizzical.

'I'm a wool trader, and we sometimes trade our wool for spices from the Far East, cinnamon being one of them,' he said by way of explanation.

At that point, the man realised that those simple woods folk had no idea what he was talking about, so he returned to his bench and to the skinning of another rabbit, quietly cursing the absence of his house servant. 'Falling off that wool sack was not the brightest of actions,' he reflected, 'even for John.'

The woman showed the family up to their room, and the children's eyes lit up, as they'd never seen real beds before, let alone had the chance to sleep in one.

The two families settled into their respective lodgings. Rents were agreed upon in both households, which would include the cost of food and drink. As water in towns was never drunk because it was so filthy, ale, mead, or wine was drunk by the adults and milk by the children. Listening to the conversation about the drinking arrangements with keen interest, the children of both families decided that towns were definitely the place to be, even at their ages. In the Forest, the closest they had ever got to alcohol was the dregs from their fathers' mugs after a celebration, and that was only if they were quick enough to beat the dogs.

The woodland streams had always been a good source of drinking water, as long as the drinker would be upstream of any animal carcass. That meant that ale, wine, and mead were reserved specifically for fun, pleasure, and inebriation, not as a replacement for water.

Although some members of the two families had gone to their beds and fallen asleep, others commenced a night of lust and adventure, namely Gumshu and Maisey.

Gumshu's night had started when he had come up the stairs on the way to the room they had been given on the third floor. Stocky woman's man, husband, or whatever, Gumshu didn't really know, had handed him a flagon of somewhat dubious-looking nature.

"Ere,' he said, 'this is bit of a present for you and your wife. I won't charge you anything.' Then he scuttled off into the darkness, his disappearing candle casting a ghostly and flickering light down the somewhat unevenly floored corridor.

Gumshu held his own candle in a position to light up the flagon top; he then deftly removed the ill-fitting stopper, sniffed the now exposed liquid, raised the container to his lips, and took a tentative sip.

The taste was that of a mixture of honey, hops, and something that he could not identify. All the same, he took a deeper draught the next time as the taste was not all that unpleasant. The second draught settled the matter; he'd drink it, but as to sharing it with Maisey, that was questionable. He always had a cunning plan when he shared anything with her. He'd eat or drink a good quarter of what was supposed to be shared before he'd offer any to her.

Maisey had been well up to this little trick of Gumshu's. Knowing him as she did, she would inadvertently expose part of her ample breasts or shapely thigh, and when his gaze was averted to the part of her body that had been exposed, she would then deftly remove or drink a bigger portion of the proffered item than she was entitled to. The only problem was that Gumshu would sometimes take her action as intention of desire, and would act accordingly.

On that particular night, once he had executed the first part of his supposedly cunning plan, he went up the remaining stairs to the room that they had been given, quietly raised the latch, and crept in. It was a large room, peculiarly shaped, because part of it actually overhung the street. All the children and the dogs were in the same room, so Maisey had hung up a rough woollen blanket that she had found in a chest, attaching the ends to the exposed beams that formed part of the roof so that she and her husband could have some privacy.

Gumshu's candlelight showed that the four children, as well as the two dogs, were lying asleep in a tangled heap on a series of straw and horsehair-filled sacks in one corner of the room, covered by another rough blanket that Maisey had found.

In the candlelight it was difficult to establish whose leg was whose and whether they were canine or human. On the other side of the room was the area for him and Maisey. She had lit her own candle and was propped up on a similar sack as the children, but underneath her was a thin horsehair-filled mattress. Two woollen blankets had been roughly thrown on top of the mattress. Gumshu dropped the blanket dividing the room, flopped down beside her, and offered her the flagon, minus the stopper that he had lost coming up the stairs.

Maisey took the first of many long draughts from the flagon, dutifully passing it back to her husband for his turn. She, too, noticed the taste that she couldn't place, but such was the effect on her taste buds that she chose to ignore it. Gumshu carefully placed his candle beside the makeshift bed so that the effect of the two candles was to bring the man and woman together in a fusion of flickering, softly moving light.

It was not long before the couple were exploring each other with hands and tongues. Gumshu slid his hand into the loose top that Maisey was wearing, gently pulling it off one shoulder, then the other. The material cascaded down, exposing her two full breasts crowned with brown erect nipples, showing her mood and anticipation. Gumshu then moved his head down so that his tongue found and then gently encircled first one nipple and then the other. His right hand caressed the underside of each of her breasts before he moved it over her soft belly, searching out the abundance of her forest and the beginnings of her moist cavern of ultimate pleasure.

Once found, he slid his fingers back and forth over the most sensitive areas, his fingers lubricated by her juices of passion. With his other hand, he gently pulled the rest of her dress off, and as he did so, he caressed first her back and then the soft areas of her shapely buttocks, seeking out all her most erogenous zones. Eventually Maisey lay back on the scattered blankets, resting her head on the sack, softly moaning and writhing with pure ecstasy as Gumshu's mouth and tongue followed the course of his hands and fingers.

She then brought her hands down from behind her head, pulling up Gumshu's tunic as she did so. Bending from the waist so as to not disturb the pleasures that he was bestowing on her, her hands found and caressed his erect and responsive organ.

She rubbed her soft cheeks and breasts over his back, and as she did, she released his shaft, taking hold of his shoulders and giving them a sharp twist so that he then lay beside her. She bent over him and started attending to his manhood again, using her hands, probing tongue and mouth with soft and full lips. Gumshu moaned with appreciation, pushing his body up, seeking more attention from the woman offering forth so much pleasure.

Maisey's long chestnut hair cascaded down over her neck, shoulders, and breasts as she sat up to move her position to straddle her lover. As she did so, she reached forward and grasped his two hands and guided them back to caress her soft-skinned and ample breasts. Kneeling over him, she then matched her cavern to his enlarged instrument of carnal desire so that as he entered her soft and moist passion, he did so with a smooth and sensuous movement. At the same time as she lowered herself on to him, Maisey leant back slightly so that as his organ penetrated deep inside her it gave her the most ultimate of sensations.

She then commenced a slow but erotic movement of the lower part of her body, at the same time rising and then purposefully pushing down on to his pulsating manhood with all her power, giving them total consumption of each other. Slowly, she pulled his hands from her breasts and placed them on either side of her gyrating hips, returning hers to caress her own breasts and hardened nipples. His powerful hands then held her where she had placed them, moving her to exaggerate the already sensuous actions of her ample and beautiful body.

Both the man and the woman then became totally immersed within their own minds and fantasies, lost to everything that was around them but joined together within their own world of lustful eroticism and love. After what seemed an eternity within their own universe, a combined ultimate fulfilment was achieved, a fulfilment announced by a mind-blowing climax of movement and breathlessness, accompanied by a deafening crescendo of sound.

After a few moments of recovery, Maisey gently drew herself off her man's depleted manhood with a loud sigh of total satisfaction and pleasure. She then lay alongside her woodsman lover, with both of them silent, gently kissing and caressing each other but eventually drifting off into the oblivion of a drug-induced sleep.

Gumshu awoke the next morning, just as the greyness of the dawn was penetrating into their room, giving it a strange and ghostly appearance. His back and arms ached somewhat, and his head seemed to pulsate in a way that it had never done before. He rolled over and gently caressed his lady, but she was still oblivious to the movements, sounds, and light that were trying to recall her from her erotic dream land.

As he gazed around the room, his attention was drawn to the boarded dividing wall, the other side of which was obviously another room of similar nature to that which he and his family shared. The timber boards contained an abundance of knots and fissures, with two of the bigger knots appearing not to have any centres.

Gumshu was slightly puzzled, but it went out of his head as the children woke up and descended on him to play, to have their usual rough and tumble. The chaos was added to by the presence of the two young dogs, both of which joined in the fun, their excited barking increasing the already loud cacophony of sound being created by father and children. Maisey groaned and accepted the inevitable; it was time to wake up and arise, something that she was not particularly good at even under normal circumstances.

Grundwell and Sophie's night had been far less adventurous; with no love potions available, they had slept solidly once the novelty of a heavily curtained four poster bed had worn off. The whole family was in one room but with no dogs, as theirs had been left in the Forest with Sophie's cousin, who had taken over their license to continue charcoal burning.

They had eaten well the previous evening, as their newly acquired landlady and her husband, Mary and Edward Kingscote, turned out to be kind and generous. After the meal, they had all sat around the fire in the candlelight, listening to Edward's tales of voyages to far-off lands, of exotic foods and spices, and of people of strange origins. Even the children were fascinated to start with, before they had dropped off to sleep in their parents' arms.

Alice snuggled up to Mary as if she had known her all her life, and Edward noticed a look of sheer contentment on his wife's face, one that he had never seen before.

Grundwell was fascinated by the stories. Having been a woodsman all his life, he never knew such places and peoples existed. He asked question after question of his host, and seemingly, both had warmed to each other by the end of the evening.

'I wonder if he wants someone else to work for him,' Grundwell asked Sophie when they eventually got their children to bed and had settled down themselves.

Unlike Gumshu and Maisey's, their bed was comfortable, not just a hard horsehair mattress on the floor. The room was large and well furnished with four small chests and three other smaller beds that held the children. To have been actually allowed to sleep in such treasured items as those beds was indeed an honour. 'An honour not usually bestowed upon passing strangers,' Sophie had reflected thoughtfully. There was even a wooden pail and bowl in their room so that they could fetch and use water for washing, a novelty which the three children were not so enthusiastic about. There was also some family discussion as to what purpose the earthenware pot under each of the beds served, but Mary's polite explanation had solved that particular mystery for them. She also showed them the newly erected building in the back toft of the house, explaining the toiletry function of that as well.

'Well, you heard what he said. As they have no children, he sees no point in making the business any bigger than it is now, so I really can't answer you,' Sophie replied to her husband's question. 'But I'm slightly puzzled though. This room could have only been furnished with a family in mind, but they don't have one. I find that a bit strange,' she continued, gazing around the candlelit room before she closed the bed's heavy curtains. Sophie turned to look at her husband as he hadn't replied; he was now asleep and beginning to snore quietly. She gave him a dig in the ribs, in case the quiet snoring should develop into anything any louder, looked over to check the children, and then extinguished the candles. Sleep was soon upon her, but in her case, it was neither drug nor lust induced.

The family were up around dawn, as they heard movement and noise coming from down the stairs. Daily life had already begun in the big room. John, the manservant, had managed to drag himself away from his sickbed and had come in from the small hut where he lived at the back of the house. He had always been well content with his living space, however small, as it was close to the animals and fowls he tended and importantly, it was next to the house's brewing shed. In the town of Mitcheldean, John's brewing skills were nearly as famous as his record for the consumption of alcohol.

John's need of his bed had been abruptly curtailed by a bedside visit the previous evening, when his employer had made his feelings on malingering servants abundantly clear.

The family seated themselves around a large oak table with Mary and Edward. John and the maidservant, Estor, placed bowls of hot porridge with rye bread in front of them. Edward began to wonder if they'd ever eaten before, such was the enthusiasm of consumption shown by the family from the Forest.

After eating their meal, Grundwell asked Edward if he knew of anyone who needed someone to work for them, as he was somewhat desperate to find work.

'I don't know,' Edward replied, looking thoughtful for a minute. 'What can you do other than make charcoal?' There was no malice in the question; it was just a fair observation.

'I have a strong back, good hands, and a willing brain,' Grundwell answered.

'How long did you work the charcoal?'

'From when my father used to let me climb the charcoal kilns he had built so that I could plug the chimney holes after the fires had been lit, and that was when I was about five or six. But I've had my own registered section of woodland for the last nine years, until we decided to come and see what the town had to offer,' Grundwell replied, looking at Sophie.

'Well, I'm looking for someone to move the wool bales around. It seems John here has an aversion to such things,' Edward said.

John muttered something rude by way of defence that none of them heard, and then fled out into the toft at the back of the house; whether to tend the animals, go to his hut, or visit the brewing shed it was unclear.

'You can try it and see if we suit each other. We can talk about pay later,' Edward offered.

Grundwell and Sophie looked at each other again, and she nodded her agreement.

'I'll do it,' Grundwell replied. 'When can I start?'

'Well,' Edward said, 'tomorrow would be as good a time as any. I have several loads of wool coming in, and you could help with the unloading. We could go up to my warehouse now, and I can show you what happens to the wool once it has arrived.'

Grundwell felt that opportunity might well be the chance he had been looking for. He had never been work shy, and the prospect of a new venture filled him with some excitement. He had always disliked sheep, but he thought that he could actually learn to like them, especially if it meant he could earn more money *and* it got him away from charcoal. Any concerns or thoughts about his friends then evaporated with his enthusiasm for the new job.

Gumshu and Maisey managed to calm the children and the dogs before going down the stairs to the main room of the house. There they too sat around a large square table on old oak forms. Maisey helped the lady of the house prepare a simple breakfast of oats, ale, and milk, not up to the standard that Grundwell and Sophie had found but still very welcome.

They had established that the husband and wife who were their landlords were called Daniel and Agnes Richmond. They worked as servants for a man who owned a small iron works on the road to St Briavels. He also owned a large house on the corner of Craven Street, but was presently living with his family in Cardiff whilst developing a new iron works there. With no plans to return, his two domestic employees had no work and more importantly for them, no wages.

Taking in lodgers to earn some money had been the subject of heated discussion when Gumshu had fortuitously knocked upon their door the previous evening.

Maisey noticed that she was getting some very admiring looks from not only the husband but also his wife, which rather concerned her. She was used to lustful looks from the menfolk of the area, but to have similar looks from a woman, she found rather disturbing.

Gumshu had the same odd feeling that Agnes was blatantly staring at both of them a little bit too much and with a look that wasn't simply out of interest. Her husband, too, seemed to have a permanent leer on his face, and again, that bothered the young woodsman.

After breakfast, he walked up to their room, leaving the family downstairs. Once on the small landing, he opened the door that obviously led to the adjoining bedroom. He slipped inside, closing the door quietly behind him. The hessian sack over the window made it too dark for him to see, so he cautiously walked over and pulled it back to let the light in. His heart sank and went cold at what he saw when he turned round.

There, close to the dividing wall, were two stools. Each stool was positioned below a knot hole in the boards of the dividing wall. Looking through first one hole, then the other, cold realisation dawned on Gumshu, realisation that his lovemaking to Maisey had been witnessed by the two people who had given them a bed for the night. He also realised that the drink that they had been given had obviously contained some form of, well, he didn't know what. His head was still throbbing gently from the memory, and he could still taste the combination of honey, hops, and the unknown additive.

Rage enveloped him. He flew down the stairs, his feet barely touching the treads. He burst through the door of the room where they had eaten their meal, not even bothering to press the latch down. His first sight was that of the husband. In one gigantic stride, he was across the room, caught hold of Daniel's throat, and threw him against the rough stone wall, snapping the man's head back as he did so. The powerful woodsman then pinioned him against the stones, pushing his face within an inch of the other man's.

'What was in the drink? What was in the drink?' he yelled.

The man's eyes bulged with terror; he could hardly breathe and croaked something that Gumshu had no chance of understanding. At that moment the man's wife came up behind him, raising a large iron cooking pan ready to strike him.

Maisey then joined in the fray. She didn't know what it was all about, but she saw her husband in a total rage and about to be attacked by a female that she didn't like or trust, so she hurled herself across the room, her momentum and side impact knocking the woman off her feet and sending the pan crashing to the floor. Maisey bent down and picked it up and swung around ready to attack again. At that moment, the two dogs suddenly realised that their master and mistress needed assistance.

They bounded across the room, attacking the man's legs, inadvertently biting Gumshu's buttocks and ripping his tunic as they did so.

The woman struggled to her feet, only to be downed again by a pan-wielding Maisey. To add to the totally chaotic scene, the four children were screaming in terror at all that was going on.

Once again, the woman managed to get up from the floor. This time she was close enough to the wall to be able to snatch a knife that was hanging from a hook.

Maisey took aim with the iron cooking pot again, swung it round, and managed to hit her husband's impending assailant on the head. This time her blow was accurate, and the woman swooned to the floor, unconscious, the knife skittering across the stone-flagged floor.

The pan-wielding Maisey then tried to pull the dogs away from the two men. Unfortunately, the animals had now warmed to their task, blood was everywhere, and most of it seemed to be flowing from Gumshu's bottom. In the end, Maisey had to take a swing at them with the cooking pot to stop the canine attack, connecting with both of the dogs' hind quarters as she did so. With howls of pain, they shot under the table, joining the hysterical children who had retreated to the same location.

The noise in the room was deafening.

Gumshu was still yelling at his prisoner at the top of his voice, totally oblivious to the chaos that was going on around him. Daniel's face went a rather odd shade of blue, his bulging eyes rolled, and he became deadweight in Gumshu's arms. At that point, Gumshu let his quarry loose, and the man slid slowly down the wall, emitting a rather strange wheezing sound as he did so.

Maisey set about retrieving the children from their refuge and trying to calm them down. The task was made more difficult by the dogs that had taken a definite dislike to their mistress on the grounds of mistreatment by a cooking pot, and so kept growling at her.

In the meantime, Gumshu tried to revive the man of the house by pouring a handy jug of ale over him. Daniel groaned, showing there was still a form of life within. That turned out to be a big mistake because Gumshu then resumed his grip on his landlord's throat and promptly dragged him up the wall, reversing the journey that the man had just made in the downward direction.

Again he yelled, 'What was in the drink?'

This time the man was in a better position to answer, because Gumshu had moved and slackened his grip on his throat in order to allow some form of speech.

'We mixed a love potion in it from the Far East,' he managed to squeak, his eyes full of fear and apprehension. 'A friend who works for a local wool merchant got it for me!'

Gumshu resisted the urge to give the man's head a twist for revenge. He simply let him go and turned away, then thinking better of it, he turned back and gave his quarry two powerful blows in the solar plexus. The man groaned and fell to the floor, clasping his stomach with both hands. Walking over to Maisey, Gumshu took two of the children from her.

'Go and get our things from the room. We're leaving now,' he said in a quietly controlled voice, as the anger he had shown earlier had abated.

He looked straight into her large brown eyes, bent forward, and tenderly kissed her forehead. 'I'll explain later,' he whispered and then squeezed her hand.

'Leave the children with me,' he said, taking hold of the other two of their offspring whom Maisey had been holding.

She quietly obeyed him without question, as she knew by experience when not to argue with him. Letting go of the children, he went to sit down, then realising his mistake when he put his full weight on the stool seat, he got up at a far faster rate than when he had sat down. He transferred his gaze of dislike to his two dogs, who realising the impending danger, exited through the door that Maisey had left open and disappeared to lurk at a safe distance.

Before leaving the house, Maisey bathed the bites on Gumshu's bottom with a lotion she found in the cupboard in the large living area. Next to the lotion, there was a big red bottle with a peculiar type of stopper in it, a type that she'd never seen before.

As she examined it more closely, she realised that she recognised the smell coming from some spillage on the shelf. It was the same smell as the liquid she had been drinking the previous night. She removed the large coloured bottle and placed it in the old sack bag that contained some of her belongings. 'I will investigate the bottle contents later,' she decided.

The family left the house, leaving a scene of total devastation behind them. Agnes had partially regained consciousness just before they left, but feigned a relapse on grounds of common sense when she looked into Gumshu's eyes. Although it crossed her mind that her lodgers had not paid her, she thought that asking for any payment was a step too far, so she held her peace.

'I told you we shouldn't have separated from the others,' Gumshu said with a slightly concerned tone in his voice. 'I hope that they've fared better than we have!'

They then set off to try and find their Forest friends, with the two young dogs following behind at a discreet distance.

# CHAPTER 5

Grundwell's conducted tour of Edward's wool facility proved a lot more interesting than he had anticipated. The substantial wooden building was on the outskirts of the town by a large fast flowing stream, a ten minutes walk from the house on Craven Street. Within the building was a gigantic storage area for the wool, with several large work rooms leading off. Those were for the preparation of the wool before it was woven into cloth in the final area.

The biggest room was used for *scouring*, or cleaning, the greasy wool after its arrival, using warm water either on its own or mixed with potash, pig dung, and stale animals' urine. Edward told him this was to extract all the impurities, as well as the lanolin, from the raw wool, and the addition of animal waste and potash made the process far more efficient than using only warm water. Once the wool was removed for drying, *washers* then hand-skimmed the residue that was left to collect the lanolin, which he then sold to the local apothecaries.

Grundwell's stomach heaved as the wool was placed in large trays with the washing mixture to be worked by the *washers* using bare feet to tread the wool into the wet mixture. Edward smiled on seeing his face, explaining that they were now starting to use a new process where the wool was put into large vats, and hand-operated wooden paddles then agitated the wool and fluid before it was removed and washed in ordinary water. When Grundwell asked about the water supply for the process, Edward indicated the stream with a wry smile, as there was a certain amount of controversy about its use.

The following room was also as large, but divided into two. The first part was a drying area where the washed wool was dried; the second was a *carding area*. Edward explained that it was a process not unlike using two large combs to comb and *tease* the raw wool, thus taking out any knots and aligning all the strands so that the *carders* could shape the wool into small rolls. That enabled the *spinners* to put the rolls into their hands and then feed it into their spinning wheels in a continuous process, each roll creating a long thread.

The next room contained the spinning wheels, where the newly washed and carded wool was spun into a yarn, the yarn being made up of several threads, the number of which governed the thickness. Edward told him that they stored the spun yarn on small wooden frames, which made it easier for handling by both the *spinners* and the *loom operators*.

Hand operated wooden looms abounded in the next room, all except in one part which had ten large and incredibly noisy, complicated machines that were each being operated by two weavers, giving a far finer weave than the smaller looms, with much larger quantities of cloth being produced.

The noise was so loud that it began to hurt Grundwell's ears.

Edward shouted as they walked. 'Those big looms are to my design, helped by a loom maker from Gloucester. Until a few years ago, weaving was something done mainly in the home using very small looms. What I'm trying to do is make it a commercial proposition, along with many others, it has to be said. Once I've got the design right, then I'll apply for a patent, but there's bit of a way to go yet! The weavers who operate them unfortunately also have to spend a lot of time repairing them, but they do produce a large amount of fine cloth, when they work!

'Although we employ a lot of people here, as you've seen, we also have others spinning and weaving in their own homes. These we call *outworkers*. We provide their spinning wheels and hand looms and then supply them with the carded wool. We collect the woven cloth from them and bring it back here to be stored with the cloth we have produced ourselves. When there is enough to make up a full cartload, we take it to the fulling mills that can be found on some of the rivers and streams of Herefordshire. The only problem is that I get involved in transport costs with it all. The slowness of our transport doesn't help either because I'm able to sell all the cloth that I can weave, so there is a need for speed.'

'What's a fulling mill?' Grundwell tentatively asked as they reached a quieter part of the building, keeping to himself the fact that he also didn't know what the word *patent* meant.

'It's usually a water mill, where two fuller socks are connected to the water wheel by way of big wooden beams. These *fuller socks* are large, heavy wooden hammers that beat the loosely woven cloth, once it has been soaked in a water and clay mix. This beating aligns and tightens the woven yarn. Once that is done, it is washed again to get the clay out and returned to me. We then dry it on large frames called *tenter* frames, which you will see in the next room we come to. Once it has reached that stage, I can then sell it to any English or Welsh cloth merchant who may want it, or we can transport it to Chepstow, where it goes off by ship to say Ireland or to ports such as Bristol or Plymouth, from where it can be exported to one of my overseas customers. I also have a lucrative trade in exporting raw wool, either as I buy it in or scoured and treated in the process I've already explained,' the business owner answered.

Grundwell was also slightly bemused as to why Edward was in the cloth trade at all. Most local businesses were timber, coal, or ore based, with the woollen industry being centred further to the east of Gloucestershire.

Edward explained that he was originally from north Herefordshire but had met Mary, who was a Forest girl, so he had moved to Mitcheldean, bringing the only business he knew with him. At the time, it had not made a lot of difference in which area he operated, as the woollen trade was well established countywide. But with increasing competition from northern England, that trade was now in decline.

Luckily, he had always concentrated his efforts on establishing a lucrative export market, aligning it with expansion of his home business. Dealing in raw wool as well as yarn and woven products had not only protected *his* business from the downturn Gloucester suffered, but had also allowed him to expand by taking up clients abandoned by failing wool merchants in southern England.

'Diversified markets and finer cloth are the secrets to my success,' he declared in conclusion to an eager and impressed retired charcoal burner.

The following day, Grundwell started his life in the woollen industry.

Having left Sophie and the children in Mary's safe and enthusiastic hands, the two men departed for the warehouse well before dawn; as the first of four loads of wool was due to arrive about an hour after first light.

By the time the last of the four wagons had been unloaded by mid-afternoon, a sweating Grundwell was not quite as keen on sheep as he had been initially. It wasn't the weight of the vast bales of raw wool that was the problem; it was the size and the fact that he wasn't used to handling such ungainly loads. The other problem he had was with Edward's two usual unloading staff, as they and the cart driver simply sat and drank ale, offering him no help at all, other than to make sarcastic remarks about his unloading technique. The driver he could forgive, as being a Hereford drover he was more used to moving sheep and geese around the country than unloading vast sacks of raw, greasy wool.

However, as for the two others, Grundwell saw no reason for them not to help.

The wool trader and his new employee walked back to Craven Street as dusk fell.

Edward asked, 'How was the day's work unloading?' He was aware that there had been four oxen carts of wool to unload as he had purchased them from an estate up beyond Hereford on a buying trip some ten days previously.

'I found the sacks difficult to handle because of their size, not just their weight,' Grundwell told his employer truthfully.

'Were you not given the handling hooks?' Edward asked with a frown.

'Handling hooks? What are handling hooks?'

Edward smiled in sudden realisation. 'I think you had better have a word with your two fellow loaders in the morning!'

Grundwell then became aware that his working day had been made considerably more difficult than it should have been with no tools as well as no help. Not vengeful by nature, the following day would be a definite exception for him, he decided.

Looking at Edward slightly awkwardly, he said, 'You and Mary took us in off the street two days ago, for which we are grateful, but we really need to find a permanent place to live now I have hopefully got full-time work.'

Edward thought for a minute. 'I have a very small cottage on the far side of the town, in which we lived when we were first married. It was rented out, but the tenants have moved to Leominster to find work in the hat or cap trade. We'll work the rent back and knock it off your wage if you would like. You'll have another few minutes of walking to and from work, but I suspect that that will not bother you particularly after all the walking you did in the Forest.'

Grundwell reflected that it was no wonder that John left his sickbed to return to work after a visitation from his employer the previous night. One did not refuse or argue with Edward, and certain things were not even up for discussion, like not accepting the cottage.

He made his mind up to emulate that man in as many ways as possible in the future. There was also something else. Having seen his workplace and slept in the treasured beds at Craven Street, he was convinced that Edward was not the poor man he made out he was. Most men bragged and showed off their wealth. He suspected that that man had no need of such practices. When he said that his was the largest woollen business in the south-west, Grundwell had no doubt that it was.

The duo arrived back at Craven Street some minutes later to be greeted by smells of exotic cooking, an enthusiastic but enquiring Sophie, a contented Mary, and three children desperate to tell their father of the day's happenings with chickens, piglets, and lambs.

'Yes, it's been a good day,' he said in response to Sophie's questioning look. 'We need to talk later of a place to live, and I think Edward might have the answer for us.'

Sophie's look betrayed her relief. She had that same feeling in the pit of her stomach about Edward when he had walked through the door earlier, the same feeling that she had had two nights previously when she first saw him skinning the rabbit.

It quietly disturbed her, but she couldn't explain why.

Mary and Edward persuaded them both that it would be better if they stayed with them at least until the following Friday. As it was then Tuesday, they would then have the chance to go and look at the cottage they were being offered and get it ready to live in, although Edward said it was.

'What does he know?' Mary said. 'We'll go down in the morning and check, won't we, Sophie?' Sophie readily agreed.

'And', Mary stated, 'anything this young family are short of, we'll make sure we get it for them, won't we, dear?' Mary shot a long, pointed look at Edward before the man could even think of a response.

'Yes, dear,' he said with practiced ease. After nearly twenty-five years of being married to Mary, he knew when it wasn't even worth putting up an argument. He did privately wonder, however, how that the young couple had come to be their lodgers without warning and why Mary had taken such a shine to Sophie. She also seemed totally besotted by the children. 'Ah well', he reflected to himself, 'perhaps this is the family she never had.'

The following morning the two men set out to the wool warehouse again, leaving Mary and Sophie to dress the children before going to look at the cottage. There were mutterings from the youngsters about the need for their presence on such an outing, preferring to remain and play with the animals and chickens in the back toft. However, resistance crumbled after a few sharp words from Sophie and some treat bribery from Mary.

The cottage was some ten minutes walk from Craven Street in the opposite direction from the warehouse. Passing through the town, Sophie made a mental note of the location of the shops that were in some profusion in the centre of Mitcheldean. She smiled to herself as she noticed that they were passing one of Grundwell's favourite inns, The George. He was not a heavy drinker or regular customer of such establishments, but occasionally, when he could afford it, he felt the urge to have company other than his nearest and dearest. It was invariably followed by a morning of suffering and tiredness, with promises of no repetition.

Sophie's regret was that in most cases her shopping trips would have to be limited to just looking at the items for sale, with little chance of buying anything. There was not often spare money for luxuries other than the occasional family outing to one of the local fairs. It used to frustrate and upset Grundwell.

The problem was that not only did he dislike making charcoal, he also felt it had no future and would never earn him enough to give his family the luxury that he craved to give them. Mary was well aware of Sophie's mood as they walked on to reach the part of the town taken up by cottages and houses.

'Things will change, you know,' she commented without looking at the younger woman at her side.

'Maybe, but maybe not,' Sophie replied, trying to regain control of the children, after a passing street trader had shown them some small toys on a tray that was hanging round his neck.

'Well, if it is any help, Edward seems to think your husband has a future with him and the wool, and that's only after two days!' Mary said quietly in an effort to cheer her up.

Edward and Mary had discussed Grundwell when they had gone to bed the night before.

'He's got a good head on his shoulders and a willing pair of hands,' Edward had commented. 'And he also has a tremendous amount of drive and ambition.'

He did not mention to Mary his slight concern about him being overambitious as he could be accused by his wife of making judgements too early, but he did have a gift of assessing people very quickly and being proved right over time. His father had once told him that the first impressions of people were usually the correct ones, and that was something that he had never forgotten.

The little party turned off the busy main street and walked along a quiet lane, with several cottages scattered on either side.

To the relief of the children, the small party stopped outside a small single storey building, built of stone, with a roughly hewn slated roof. It was of similar pattern to the other cottages except the last one on the street, which was constructed of a timber frame, with lime-washed wattle and daub walls and a thatched roof. Beyond that cottage was the track that led to the outskirts of the Forest.

'This is our old cottage,' Mary said with a nostalgic look on her face. 'As Edward told Grundwell, this was our home when we were first married. In fact, we were married at the Church of Saint Michael, which is on the rise just above the main street.'

Sophie turned to look in the direction in which Mary was pointing and noted the imposing-looking church, whose spire rose above the rest of the houses like a demanding finger beckoning the parishioners of Mitcheldean to worship.

After unlocking the somewhat large lock on the door, with a key that matched its size, Mary led the way in. As well as not being very clean, the cottage smelt of damp and old cooking. Mary sniffed and in an effort to let some fresh air in opened the door that led to the large toft area at the back of the building.

Frowning slightly, she said with a resigned air after looking outside, 'I don't think the previous tenants were very good at cleaning or keeping the toft tidy and cultivated.'

'That is a bit of an understatement!' Sophie thought as she investigated the cottage.

It had a large room with a deeply recessed fire hearth at one end. At the other end were two rooms, with a wide boarded dividing wall, which was obviously the sleeping area, judging by the horsehair mattresses on the stone floor. The rest of the furniture in the main room was rough but functional, with two oak settles, a high-backed chair, four stools, and a substantial large rectangular table. Cooking pots adorned the wall by the fire hearth.

Sophie smiled to herself. That really was a palace compared with the charcoal burner's huts that she had endured over the years, and although it was damp, she preferred that to the incessant smell of smoke. It was, in fact, similar to the cottage that they had had in Cumdean, but that had had a thatched roof, although without a toft at the back, just an open grassed area that led into the glades of the surrounding woods.

Mary looked at her and then said with a smile, 'Well, Sophie, what do you think?'

Sophie beamed her reply without speaking. The children had done a quick tour, decided which mattresses they were going to sleep on, and then had disappeared into the toft. Alice reappeared with whoops of delight as there was an outside shack that housed a privy, but with a wooden seat over the hole. The huts and cottages she was used to just had a hole dug in the ground behind them into which, being the fidgeting type, she had slipped on more than one occasion and had had to be rescued by one of her parents. That was why, according to Grundwell, she had such a loud voice, well practiced by bawling for help.

So the ladies set to on a cleaning frenzy after Mary had been to one of the shops in the centre of the town to purchase some cleaning implements. She and Sophie worked silently for a time, but Sophie was aware that Mary kept stopping and watching her, smiling each time Sophie caught her eye. The children played happily in the toft and then along the lane, where they encountered some boys of a similar age to Alice. After some slight differences between them, the children settled down, and any passing stranger would have thought that they had been friends for most of their lives.

In the wool building, friendship was the furthest thing from Grundwell's mind. When he and Edward had arrived that morning and unlocked the building, the first of Edward's men to arrive just happened to be the two men who had supposedly worked with Grundwell the day before. Edward made a tactical withdrawal, leaving the three together. Grundwell went to the box where Edward had told him the handling hooks were kept, took one out, and turned to face the two men, over whom he had three advantages.

His first advantage was being just over six foot in height. The second was that with broad shoulders and extremely thick biceps, well highlighted by his sleeveless tunic, his profile was not unlike that of a fully grown Hereford bull. And the third and final advantage was that he was totally calm.

He walked towards his quarry with exaggerated slowness. The two backed away from his advance, looking first to the left and then to the right for a means of escape. But Grundwell had chosen his ground well. The only means of escape for them was through the door behind Grundwell.

'We need to have a little talk,' said Grundwell in a low voice. 'And we're going to have it now!' he continued in the same tone. He advanced a little further.

The two objects of his gaze were now sweating with fear, their backs pressed against the timber side of the wool shed. One fell on to his knees with an ashen face.

'For God's sake, it was only to see if you could do it. We meant you no harm,' he snivelled. 'Please, please don't hurt me!'

The fact that the plea was made in the singular, and not the plural, was not lost on Grundwell. He shifted his gaze to his second target, a little shrew of a man with a turned-down mouth and eyes that were too close together. He suddenly darted forward to try and make his escape under Grundwell's guard.

Grundwell's foot shot out and tripped him up, sending him flying forward like a bird launching itself off a wall. In this case, the bird had no wings, and the man hit the floor with an almighty slap, smacking his face on the rough stone with a resultant red film spraying around him. He lay totally inert.

The first man, seeing all that had happened, placed himself in an even more incumbent praying position, and Grundwell was not sure whether he was praying to God or to him. At that point, he leant forward, picked up the now screaming man, and hung him by his tunic on a peg that was sticking out from the wall of the warehouse.

Turning back to deal with the second man, Grundwell was surprised to note that he had regained consciousness, turned himself over, and was now trying to emulate a spider, using arms and legs, sliding along on his bottom and heading towards the door. Unfortunately for him, he got the angle of exit wrong and collided with the door frame. As he had gained considerable momentum during this exercise, he hit the timber with the back of his head at some speed, with the result that not only did he knock himself out again but he also cut his head open, depositing even more blood on the floor.

'Ouch!' Grundwell said. 'That must have hurt!' Without more ado, he picked the spider man's body up and hung him up in the same manner that he had dealt with man number one. He then drew up a box and seated himself facing the two loaders.

Man number two regained consciousness after a short time, but sad to say, neither he nor his praying accomplice retained their composure. They both started shrieking and wriggling around, feet and hands flaying about. The pegs were not very strong, with the inevitable result that they broke. The two men tumbled to the ground, first lying in a heap, and then, making use of the legs that God gave them, exited through the open door as fast as their wounds and pride would let them.

'But we haven't had our little talk,' Grundwell called after them in a hurt voice.

Edward came back after all the commotion had died down and was not surprised to see who the victor was.

'We now have some serious work to do, young man.' And he indicated for Grundwell to follow him.

The warehouse was now frantically busy, one reason being that with the delivery of wool the day before, to which Grundwell's still aching limbs could bear witness, Edward was demanding even more production from his staff.

The washing room was at full capacity with both the trays and the new vats in use; the waste animal products were being used in some profusion. Grundwell's stomach turned over, as it had done previously. He did, however, try and ignore his feelings of nausea as Edward's workforce was of a mixed gender, and he didn't want to show anyone, especially the women, that he was so sensitive to certain smells.

Watching the operators at work, he was impressed at how thorough they were with the wool washing, although as Edward had told him, some of their customers preferred the wool unwashed, as they thought it easier to spin, and made better yarn with the lanolin present. Some of the spinners also thought it easier on their hands, as it made them softer. The whole warehouse was alive with chatter, laughter, and light-hearted banter between the men and women, all without affecting production, Grundwell noticed.

Edward took him aside so that he could hear him speak above the noise of the looms which were all in action again, making any form of speech useless.

'There is something that I haven't mentioned,' he shouted. 'There are only certain times that the farmers can shear their sheep, and the fleeces we use are very slow growing. I buy and stockpile as much wool as possible during those times so that I can regulate our production to suit the market's demand. Sometimes though, I have to lay workers off through lack of wool, which can lead to some unpleasantness amongst the people who work for me. I do explain it all to them before they start here, so they have a choice. Employing some 115 people, including outworkers, I have to be very careful with my costs, and idle workers don't make me profit,' he continued with a wry smile.

The two then moved on into a quieter part of the building, where Edward was obviously continuing to watch the performance of his workers, as his eyes were never still.

'Why don't you use other fleeces as well, say from Wales, so that production can be increased and be more regular?' Grundwell asked. 'It would also enable you to build up more stock to protect yourself from any unforeseen problems with supply,' he added.

Edward shook his head. 'No, the Ryeland fleeces we use are famous for their quality all over the country as well as abroad. I don't want to spoil that reputation or reduce the prices. I can sell all the wool I can get, either as raw wool, yarn, or cloth, so why change?'

At that, he turned away to talk to another member of his workforce. Grundwell assumed that the matter was now closed.

After supervising the work in the warehouse for some hours, Edward took Grundwell to meet some of the outworkers. Word had spread about the wood collier's disagreement with the two loaders, and he had to smile at some of the comments. Most of the admiring glances he got were from the women of the workforce, something that pleased him.

Walking back to Craven Street, Edward appeared completely relaxed and in absolutely no hurry to reach home. They chatted over a wide variety of subjects, from charcoal to wool, to life in general. Grundwell was totally unaware that Edward was not only testing his ability to talk but also his knowledge and experience. Just before they reached Craven Street, Edward offered him the job of warehouse foreman. The old supervisor had moved to Oxford to be closer to his wife's family, and a replacement was urgently needed.

Grundwell was staggered by the question but eagerly seized the opportunity that was being offered.

'I want you to do two weeks trial first. If we suit each other, then we'll look at your wages,' Edward stated. 'And what you don't know about wool and commerce, I'll teach you.'

The work of cleaning the cottage was progressing well, Sophie reported to Grundwell after supper. She couldn't stop smiling. The news of her husband's new job had also made her extremely happy, and she suddenly felt optimistic about their future.

Sensing their mother's mood, the children were taking full advantage of the situation, especially when their father seemed to have been affected by the same good humour. However, Alice just had to push it that little bit too far when Mary found her smuggling a piglet up to the family's bedroom.

'I don't think your mother or father would be too pleased with that,' she quietly chided. 'But when you go to your new house, you can take two of the piglets with you!'

Sophie caught the last bit of the conversation and shook her head slowly. 'Thank you, Mary, most kind!' she said with a grimace, followed by a broad grin.

'I could spare a chicken or two and a lamb,' Mary quipped, warming to her task, with a grin to match Sophie's.

Alice listened to the conversation, not realising the humour behind it all.

'I'll look after them and clean them and everything,' she piped.

'Where have I heard that before?' Grundwell interjected, remembering all the animals that Alice had brought back to their Cumdean home in the past with the same promise.

Grundwell and Sophie visited the cottage the next morning. To the delight of the children, they were allowed to stay with Mary at Craven Street and continue with their plaguing of the animals in the toft. Edward disappeared to the warehouse again, glad to escape Mary before she regaled him with a list of items to be purchased for the cottage. He did, in fact, go through the back of the house to escape detection, but as he swung round the corner at the front, she was standing at the door with a wry grin on her face.

'You've forgotten two things, my love,' she called with a twinkle in her eye.

Edward feigned total innocence and muttered something inaudible, but he still went up to his wife to hear the inevitable rebuke.

'One is you haven't kissed me goodbye.' That Edward always did as a matter of principle as well as pleasure.

'And the second is?' Edward questioned, as he corrected the first omission.

'You forgot the list of things I want for the cottage!'

Edward already had his hand out so his dearly beloved could place the list in it. He smiled a smile of the guilty and turned to go. He thought to himself that she always was two thoughts ahead of him, which was quite disconcerting for a man like Edward.

The young couple explored their new home like a pair of excited children. Sophie and Mary had done a thorough job, and the cottage was immaculate, although there was still a lingering smell of damp.

'That'll soon go when the fire has been lit, and it has been going for a few days,' Grundwell commented, looking at the hearth and then up the chimney to make sure it was clear of any obstructions.

Sophie smiled at him. 'I will never rid myself of that smell of smoke, will I?'

# CHAPTER 6

Maisey, Gumshu, and the children searched for their Forest friends for about three hours, stopping people in the street and asking if they had seen such a family.

Eventually, they sat down to rest on the top of a grass bank that was outside an imposing-looking church. The two dogs had also caught them up, having investigated every street smell possible on their meanderings behind the family.

The party looked around them and took stock.

'This is silly,' commented Maisey. 'They could be anywhere.'

She was tired, her head throbbed, and she was still in a state of shock after her husband explained to her why he got so angry with the Richmonds about what had happened the previous night.

'Yes, you're right,' Gumshu replied, easing off one of the shoes of their youngest son, whose shoe bindings were causing blisters on his feet. 'What are we going to do?' His question seemed to be aimed at the sky rather than at Maisey. 'What are we going to do?'

They both gazed out towards the Forest and neither spoke. The children started to play somewhat noisily, rolling down the grass bank. The little one seemed to have forgotten that one of his feet hurt. At that moment, a young cleric from the church came through the lych gate and down the bank. He immediately started remonstrating with the startled children.

Gumshu was in no humour for such behaviour, so he got up with some care because of his dog bites and strode down the bank, gaining momentum as he went. By the time he reached the bottom, he was out of control. He cannoned into the hapless curate, knocking him over. Gumshu also lost his footing such was his downward momentum and finished up on top of the cleric, who was by then yelling for divine intervention.

Rolling off him, Gumshu was about to offer his apologies, when the curate upped and fled back up the bank and through the lych gate, shouting words that even made the worldly Maisey blush. There was a loud bang as the main church doors shut very firmly. Gumshu thought he heard bolts being drawn, but he couldn't swear to it.

'That's it!' he said in a loud voice. 'We're back to the Forest and Cumdean.'

Maisey lay back on the grass and looked up at the scudding clouds. She, too, had had enough of Mitcheldean, so she was not about to argue with him. The hut and woodland section were still there for them if they wanted it, and they had told their landlord they still wanted their cottage. That was unlike Sophie and Grundwell, who had passed their registered area of woodland on to Sophie's cousin and had stopped paying rent on their Cumdean home.

That decision Gumshu had thought a little unwise at the time, but Grundwell was adamant about it. Maisey started to wonder what had happened to their friends, as there was no sign of them at all. It wasn't unusual that they had lost contact; it had happened quite frequently over the years when one or other of the families had decided to make their own way for a time.

They gathered up their belongings and took the first lane they came to that led off towards the Forest track, retracing the previous day's footsteps. They passed stone—and slate-roofed cottages scattered on either side. As they came to the end of the lane, they passed the only timber-framed cottage, which had lime-washed walls and a thatched roof.

The way back was accompanied by silence from even the children. Gumshu was thinking that this was yet another failure in his life, while Maisey's mind was wandering back to their lovemaking the previous night. She shuddered involuntarily at the thought that those terrible people had witnessed such a private moment between herself and her husband, a time of all-consuming love, and they had degraded it totally. She felt abused and nauseated.

The Forest that had closed its doors behind them the previous day seemed to suddenly reach forward and enfold the family in comfort and sympathy, much as a mother surrounds her hurt child with arms of warmth and understanding. Maisey's eyes were filled with tears of relief to be home. They walked into the Forest through familiar wooded glades, over quietly babbling streams, along tracks where their happy memories danced with the sunlight that filtered through the leaves and where familiar smells stirred emotions of happier times.

They at last came to the clearing where their last charcoal burn had been, and there on the outskirts of the woods was the small hut that Gumshu had built. They collected the bedding that they had so recently discarded, and then continued on towards the Forest village.

Now in familiar territory, the children and dogs ran ahead, the air filling with the noise of children's laughter and barking dogs.

They emerged from the woods to be greeted by some of their neighbours, who were delighted that the family were back but intrigued to know why so soon. Without answering their questions, Gumshu and Maisey walked to where their cottage waited for its two wounded occupants. Gumshu quietly closed the door once they were both inside, leaving the children to play with the other youngsters of the village. He had noticed his wife's earlier tears but had left her alone, sensing her thoughts and mood.

He took her into his arms to offer her reassurance, but she slowly pushed him away.

Looking up into his face, she simply said, 'There is something I must do.'

He looked at her with warmth and understanding and quietly opened the door so she could go out again. He didn't attempt to follow her, but leaving the door open, he collected some kindling and started to light the fire in the large hearth at the far end of the room.

Maisey, meanwhile, had made her way to the churchyard on the outskirts of the village. As she walked, she collected a bunch of softly scented wild flowers. Going through the wicket gate, she walked hesitantly across the uncut grass to a tiny grave under an overhanging oak tree. It was close beside a low stone wall that divided the cemetery from the adjoining fields and woodlands.

She knelt down and placed the flowers against the rough wooden cross at the head of the grave, the cross that simply bore the word '*Katherine*' lovingly carved on it.

'We're back, my little one,' she said quietly, her voice charged with deep emotion, the emotion that can only be stirred when a mother looks upon the grave of her dead child. She buried her face into the mound of earth and soft grass, her arms flung out as if trying to encircle the tiny body within. Grief, once again, came forth like an unchecked river in flood.

Her own body became racked with her sobbing, and the sounds of her desperate crying echoed around the small churchyard, heard only by the now silent songbirds.

Some time later, Gumshu stood by the wicket gate watching the outpouring of sorrow from the woman he loved. His eyes filled with tears and his whole form began to shake. He turned and walked a short distance away, where he leant against a tree, dealing with his own grief. His two dogs, which had followed him when he had come looking for Maisey, sensed his mood of desolation and lay down beside him, their muzzles inches away from his boots, their eyes resting on his.

After about an hour, Maisey came back through the gate. Seeing her husband with his back to her, still leaning against the tree, she quietly went up beside him and gently took hold of his hand. Together, and without speaking, they started to walk back to the cottage. Both of their faces bore the scars of the tears that they had shed, tears that had been shed in profusion. The evening was drawing in, and the sight of their other children laughing and running towards them broke their mood. They gathered them into their arms and took them into the now warm cottage. Food had been left for them by other villagers, so there was soon the smell of an evening meal being cooked over an open fire. It was accompanied by the sounds of children's laughter and family chatter, simply, a family happy to be home.

The next morning, Gumshu was up as dawn broke. Village men folk and a few of the children were already on the way to their places of work. He stood by the cottage door and in the half light started talking to some of the men. Three or four who he knew well took the time to linger awhile.

'Off to a new burn?' asked one.

'Thought you were going to seek your fortune in the town,' joked another.

'Ah, Maisey made him come back. Too many women in them towns,' quipped a third.

Gumshu smiled and quietly replied to all the jesters, 'Decided towns aren't for us. Too many things we don't know.' His face reflected the seriousness of his mood and the feelings behind his reply. The men caught his drift, and the humour ceased abruptly. 'Trouble is, I don't want to go back to the charcoal. The family are tired of living in a hut for half the year because of me,' he continued. 'And I've had enough of it too.'

'So what now?' asked Ralph, his special friend. 'You've still got to pay the rent *and* buy the food.' It was a point that Gumshu had been considering most of the night as he quietly lay alongside Maisey, with sleep being the furthest thing from his mind.

'Don't think so loudly!' she had said sometime during the night. He had responded by moving his hand over her breasts in an effort to stimulate some interest.

'And you can cut that out! You never know who's watching,' Maisey murmured.

They both suddenly had a fit of the giggles and rolled round, hugging each other under the threadbare covers. He kissed her on the nose and then slapped her bottom. Suddenly, they both knew all would be well in spite of their experiences in Mitcheldean. They lay on their sides with their arms wrapped around each other, both deep in thought.

'Seriously, what now?' she had said, which was much the same question that Ralph was asking him now. The answer was that he really didn't know.

'Well,' Ralph said, taking the initiative, 'you know that I'm the foreman at Cottrells' mine, just a way towards the west of us.'

'Yes, I remember because you always come back home grey,' Gumshu replied with a broad grin. That was a joke between them as Gumshu always teased Ralph about the fact that even after a thorough wash after work his hair still stayed grey.

Ignoring the remarks, Ralph carried on, 'Well, we have too few mine workers at present, so why don't you come and join us? The rewards are fair as long as you work hard, and I don't doubt you will. After a year and a day, you would be entitled to start a mine or quarry of your own, as long as you get extraction licences from the landowner and the Crown, as well as conform to the requirements of the St Briavel's Hundreds!'

Gumshu looked at him, not understanding a word of what his friend had said.

'How about I just come and dig coal out for you?' he returned. 'Starting now!'

'Good, now you'd better go and tell Maisey what you're about,' Ralph replied, setting off with the others, leaving Gumshu to follow on after he'd told his wife about his new job.

Ralph smiled to himself. 'Now who's going to be going home grey!' he muttered. 'Gumshu, my boy, you're going to get the wettest seam I can find!'

Ralph had explained to Gumshu some time previously that the reason for the grey appearance of the Forest of Dean miners was due to a seam of grey clay that ran between the floor of the Forest and the seams of rocks and coal below. When it rained, water from the woodland floor filtered down through those seams, taking some of the grey texture from the clay with it. That mixture was then deposited on the miners who were working underneath.

Ralph and Gumshu entered the mine workings from a large gaping hole that had been driven into the side of a valley. All around the entrance was the residue of the excavated material that had been cleared by the miners before they could get at the coal seams. Gumshu remarked that it all appeared to be very close to the entrance.

'We are restricted in how far we can spread the surplus by the Government,' Ralph retorted, somewhat testily. 'Sorry, it's a bit of a contentious issue with us colliers. It's yet another way they have of regulating the size of our mines, and therefore how much coal we take from the ground!'

'*They* being?' Gumshu questioned.

'The Crown, who seem to think they can not only dictate output, coal price, transport costs through tolls but also take away some ancient rights that we hold as Forest of Dean miners. It doesn't seem enough that they already control our rents and levies. They want *everything* their own way, including trying to dictate the size of our mines.'

Gumshu understood Ralph's frustration as the charcoal burners had restrictions placed on their production as well. That was done by limiting the size of the trees they used as well as the quantity, hence the need to be licensed. The heavy reliance on the Forest timber stocks by other industries, ship building and mining being but two, was made more damaging to the resource by the refusal of the Government to insist on a programme of replanting.

'It seems', Gumshu said, 'that you are restricted when there is a shortage of resources above ground, and where there is no such shortage underground, they still restrict you.'

'Huh, it's all about money, power and politics!' Ralph coughed as he spoke and then went on coughing, much to Gumshu's dismay.

Eventually, he stopped after taking a long draught of cider from a flagon that had been put on the floor by a passing work colleague.

'Give it back to me later, Ralph,' the man called out, as he disappeared into the bowels of the earth. Having regained his voice after the coughing fit, Ralph took Gumshu down the sharply sloping floor, deeper into the mine. It was a hive of activity.

They passed carts being dragged up to the entrance, laden with the coal that had been hewn from the coal seams. Small agile ponies were harnessed to the carts, the majority being led by children. Gumshu recognised some of the young boys he had seen earlier that morning. There was little or no laughter from them now, only looks of misery and despair.

Water spilled from the roof of the first large chamber of the drift workings, seeping through the clay, shale, and rock above. Occasionally, there would be a small fall of mixed debris from the roof or walls of the chamber. But everywhere there was water, incessantly dripping and covering everything with a clinging grey film—the ponies, the carts, the children, and the men. It was a grey, dank, and dangerous world, created to achieve but one thing—the extraction of coal; coal that would be used for the powering of metal forges, of which there were a multitude within the Forest; coal that would be used to power the local lime kilns; coal that would be used for the fires in local cottages, houses, and mansions; coal that would be sent to the cities, towns, and villages in the county and well beyond.

Gumshu reflected on the use of charcoal and wondered if coal would ever take its place. Coal didn't have to be replaced, but the basic ingredient of charcoal did—trees, and that was expensive, adding to the problem that trees took years to grow. He was sad, not for himself, but for all the other families that he knew who depended on charcoal for their living. He could see the gradual decline of that Forest industry in time. Gumshu reflected on the conversation he had just had with Ralph, about it being about money, power and politics, and how coal seemed to be at the heart of it.

Ralph was speaking to him, and it snapped him back from his thoughts.

'I think that I'll put you with Joshua, who is a good man with a lot of experience. He will show you as much as he can about how to win the coal out of the seam and how to dig and hack out a tunnel. They call him the Mole!' The Cottrell mine foreman repeated, realizing that his friend's mind had been elsewhere.

He turned around and yelled up a small darkened tunnel that led off the chamber.

'Joshua, can you come out for a minute?' There was a muffled sound of a voice by way of reply.

Two minutes later, two feet appeared, followed by a body and then by a tousled grey head. Joshua had emerged. Covered in the usual grey film, he smiled in welcome at Gumshu.

Ralph explained to him that he wanted him to show the latest addition to the workforce how they dug tunnels and what was involved in extracting coal from the actual seams. Ralph then disappeared up the candlelit chamber.

Joshua sat down and first explained to Gumshu about the tools that he would need. At that precise moment, Ralph reappeared carrying two differently shaped shovels and four different types of pick.

'These were Richard Owen's,' he stated quietly. Joshua shot him a glance that was hard for Gumshu to miss. Ralph saw Joshua's reaction and the fact that Gumshu had noticed.

'Richard was killed by a roof fall yesterday,' he said by way of explanation. 'I'm sorry, but we do have to carry on, accident or not. We have to get the coal out, and we have to sell it. Whatever happens in the mine, we still have to pay all the running costs, and we still have to feed our families.' He faltered as he knew Joshua and Richard had been friends.

'There was no one to blame but Richard,' he continued. 'He was trying to cut down on the roof and wall supports so that he could excavate quicker. The support timbers were there, at the entrance to his tunnel, but he took a risk and he paid the price.'

Joshua was silent. Then he said, his voice barely a whisper, 'Ralph, the timbers were put there *after* the fall. You know it and so do I!' Looking at Gumshu, he said, 'This is a very dangerous business and many are killed working these deeper drift mines. But the owners and their partners don't care.' He looked accusingly at the foreman as he spoke.

Ralph turned on his heel. He wondered how many others knew about the timbers.

Joshua looked at Gumshu, nodded, and then carried on, 'I'll show you what I can, and then it's up to you.' He took hold of one of the spades. 'This one we use for digging out the clay and shale. This one, which is broader, we use for shovelling the coal or debris back towards the entrance of the tunnel and then loading the cart, which takes it up to the surface so that it can be stockpiled.'

Taking hold of one of the picks, which were of different lengths, Joshua demonstrated how they hacked at the rock to expose the coal deposits. With another, he showed him how they broke the coal out once they had exposed the seam. He also explained the easiest way to work in the confined conditions created by the low and narrow tunnels. He ended with a warning.

'Whatever you do, make sure you shore up the roof and if need be brace the sides from the *start* of your tunnel, depending on what type of ground it is. Because if you don't and there's a fall, usually it will kill you. If there are no shoring timbers, always wait until the gang who bring them to you have done so. Remember that they have to go into the Forest, cut the trees, trim and cut the shoring timbers to various lengths, and *then* bring them to you. It all takes time, so make sure you give them plenty of warning.

'Water is another danger, especially near old workings, and that can come at you from any direction. If you come across really wet patches, don't dig into them. Try and work round them and then tell Ralph. If you dig into such an area, and there's a lot of water behind it, you could release a deluge that could drown you, as well as the rest of us!' he cautioned.

With that, the grey mole was about to crawl back up his tunnel when he thought about something else and turned back to Gumshu.

'When you come in the morning, make sure you also help check the supports in the main chamber because if that chamber caves, then you're dead! And always make sure that you've got candles to light your tunnel and stick torches as backup. Not too many, mind. Remember, flames burn air. Little air, you can't work properly. No air and you're dead!' he said. 'And get Ralph to explain about gas too!'

Gumshu's last sight of him, for the present at least, was of his booted feet disappearing into the darkness. 'I wonder if it's being so cheerful that keeps him going,' he reflected, at the same time moving smartly out of the way of a bolting pony with a half loaded cart behind it and a yelling child running alongside, grimly hanging on to the driving reins. The new collier was about to call some advice to the child, but by the time he had gathered his thoughts, cart, coal, pony, and child had disappeared up the incline to the mine entrance at an impressive turn of speed.

By the time that incident had passed, a somewhat deflated Ralph came down the incline and silently indicated that Gumshu should follow him. He took him to the top level chamber of the mine and showed him the start of a fresh tunnel that was going to be driven to establish a new coal face. Timber shoring timbers lay nearby.

'We'll start this together, and I'll take you into the coal seam. Then I'll explain about the dangers of gas, how we get ventilation, and how we deal with water,' he said in answer to some of Gumshu's questions that he had asked as they had made their way up the labyrinth of tunnels. He listened to his friend's advice, watching him operate with shovel and pick and trying to learn as much as possible, including how to brace the roof and walls as well as continually *listen* to the ground noises around him, exactly as Joshua had warned him.

'Keeping alert could well save your life', Ralph stated with a wry smile, 'as well as being in a position to get up and run should the need arise!'

Gumshu thought about the advice that both of the miners had given him about always listening to what the ground was telling him. He concluded that miners had to have the hearing of a bat, the speed of a deer, the agility of a contortionist, and the strength of a giant. His deceased father-in-law had also once told him that miners needed the love of a good woman. 'The last two attributes I have, but the others I will have to acquire,' he reflected with a wry grin.

Most of the village children were at the top end of the village, being entertained by Friar Benedict who was making one of his frequent visits to the village. He was always there when he was needed and had a knack of turning up at the right moment. That was unlike some other clerics in the area, whose sole purpose in life seemed to entail getting the people of the Forest into their churches so that they could fill their collection boxes. Gumshu called it furthering their own ends. Other people called it something less charitable.

On this visit, Father Benedict was distributing some simple wooden toys that he had whittled during the long evenings when he wasn't walking. Those evenings were becoming more frequent the older he got, he freely admitted to his friends. He had called in to see Maisey and shared a mug of ale with her, listening to her recall the family's adventure of the time that they had spent in Mitcheldean.

He thought there was something that she wasn't telling him, not that it mattered in the slightest; she would tell him when she was ready. The bond between the two had built up over many years. In fact, he reflected, he had helped deliver her with Caenwen, Fran's mother. He smiled to himself, remembering the birth and the conversations with Josephine and John Tapper, her mother and father.

What Maisey and Gumshu didn't know was that when he had heard about little Katherine being so ill he had been many miles away, but he had walked *continuously* for nearly a day and a night to be with them. He had arrived within minutes of her death and had knelt in the middle of the cottage floor with his huge arms encircling them both, not in prayer but in pure love and comfort at the time of their grief. He had stayed with the family for nearly a week, sleeping on the floor in front of the fire, just being there when he was needed. To him, that was what being a man of God was about.

'Are you staying, Father?' Maisey had asked earlier. 'You know you can stay with us. We might even give you a mattress this time!' There had been a mischievous twinkle in her eye. 'Now you're getting older,' she added, ensuring she was well outside the reach of his huge arms. A playful cuff from the friar could send the recipient skidding for yards on their bottom in a highly undignified manner, as she had discovered quite regularly over the years.

'Thank you, but no, my child,' he returned. 'The abbot in the small priory about four miles towards Chepstow has been promising to show me round his newly repaired building and then to test the contents of his restocked cellars, and tonight's the night!' He paused and then added, 'And by the way, Maisey!'

'Yes, Father?' she replied, turning to him.

'The Lord believes in revenge!'

They both laughed, and she went up and gave him a big hug, whereupon he poured the remains of his mug of cold ale down her back, between her dress and her skin.

'Told you!' he said, retreating through the door with all the agility of a man of half his age.

All she heard as she dried herself was a loud chortle from the departing friar.

They had had ale and water fights many times before, and he always came off worse for some reason. He knew what that reason was, of course. It was definitely against his religion to waste the ale, so he would always drink it rather than throw it.

Maisey's curiosity was beginning to get the better of her. With Gumshu working at the mine and the children being entertained by Father Benedict, she was alone. She went to her secret hiding place, a large hole in the wall that was only accessible by removing two wall stones at the bottom of the wattle and daub. There she retrieved the big red bottle with the peculiar stopper in it, which she had found at the Richmonds' house. She put it on the table and sat looking at it. She managed to open the stopper and sniffed the contents cautiously. The smell stirred her memory of the thumping head that she had had the previous morning, but it also stirred memories of her lovemaking to her husband.

'Was it only yesterday?' she mused to herself. She promptly returned the stopper to the bottle and then, resting her chin on her folded hands, stared at the bottle once again.

'Mm,' she said out loud. 'I think Gumshu needs to be here before I do anything with that!' She giggled to herself and promptly returned the bottle to its hiding place.

Gumshu arrived home just before sunset. Maisey first became aware of his return when she heard their children laughing, and the dogs started to rush in and out of the cottage in their excitement. It was always the same when he came home; total chaos ensued.

She ran out of the door to greet him, and became rooted to the spot when she saw him. At least, she thought it was him. A grey and black apparition stood in front of her, dripping wet, the only recognisable features were his eyes and his mouth. When he raised his arms to embrace her, it was as if he had gossamer wings.

'You are definitely *not* going to give me a hug whilst you're in that state!' she said, hastily stepping back.

The children and the dogs ran round him, the children laughing and the dogs yapping.

'How is it', she continued with a broad smile on her face, 'that whenever you come home, the place descends into bedlam, both with children and the dogs, and that's after I've spent all day trying to bring calm and discipline to our home?'

'It's just my popularity, humour and charm, which is all coupled to my natural good looks!' he retorted.

Maisey decided that she had heard enough, and also the grey apparition was getting dangerously close to her, and she mistrusted his intentions. She caught hold of his hand and pulled him round to the back of the cottage, to where the crystal clear, whispering spring fed water to a small pool that was the beginnings of a Forest stream, a stream that eventually flowed into the River Wye.

She stood him beside the pool, saying, 'Right, off with the lot!' as she grabbed a wooden pail that was kept close by.

Filling it up with ice cold water, she took aim and fired it at the now naked Gumshu. He was just about to speak, but the cold of the water over his naked torso took his breath away, rendering him speechless. The first pail full was followed closely by a second, third, fourth, and fifth. As each one hit its target, there was a loud cheer from the children, who had followed them behind the cottage to watch the proceedings.

Maisey knew what she was doing, with her father having been a Forest miner. It had been Maisey's task to administer water to him on his return from work, usually in the same state as Gumshu, hence her being well practiced at the art.

She also knew where to aim the pail of water to get maximum impact should she receive any cheek from her victim.

Drying off in front of the fire after his ordeal by water, he told Maisey about the day. He discreetly omitted the details of Richard Owen's death on the previous day and also that Ralph was getting the blame for it because of lack of shoring timbers.

'How many deaths at the mine in the last ten days?' she asked.

Gumshu looked at her, a little taken aback by her directness. Then he suddenly remembered that her father had been a Forest collier, so she was well versed in mining life.

'Two,' he replied, not quite sure how she was going to react.

'Both by collapses?' she queried.

'No, only one by collapse. The other was a child crushed by a cart.'

'Probably about average,' she returned. She then went on to change the subject completely, telling Gumshu about Father Benedict's visit.

'Didn't he want to stay the night? You did invite him, didn't you?'

'Of course, I did,' she replied, 'but he was off to visit that small priory on the way to Chepstow.' She went on to tell him about the Lord's revenge after her remark about the mattress.

'You two always manage to start something between you,' he said, laughing.

That night Maisey lay awake, deeply worried about her husband's new job. She had not shown any reaction in the morning when he had burst into their room just as she awoke, beaming and full of enthusiasm about being offered work in the mine. Her heart had missed a beat and gone cold.

She had cried softly when he had left to catch Ralph up. Memories of the time of the accident that crushed her father's leg and had cost his friend his life came flooding back to her.

Despite the friar's visit, she had a sick feeling in the pit of her stomach all day. It had only stopped when she saw the grey apparition in front of her earlier in the evening.

Maisey knew she now had to come to terms with the change in their circumstances, just as she knew that the constant worry over Gumshu's safety would be a permanent feature of her daily life. Her husband needed the work, and his family desperately needed the money he would earn.

She prayed to the Lord that family history would never repeat itself.

# CHAPTER 7

Edward had been highly successful on his last buying trip into Herefordshire. The wool building's stores were now full of baled fleeces, as were the two large adjacent wooden buildings that he had rented on a long-term lease, rented because the owner wouldn't sell them. Although Grundwell and his men had managed to make them weatherproof, the only problem they had was trying to secure them against some of the town's younger population, who used the stored fleeces as a convenient, warm, and unobtrusive love nest.

One day soon after the arrival of several cartloads of fleeces from the north of Herefordshire, Grundwell had come across a young couple performing the age-old ritual, clothes flung asunder over the bales, totally naked as the day they were born.

Such was their concentration and their noises of delight, as well as the softness of the wool underfoot, they did not notice the coming of the warehouse foreman until he spoke, all be it a minute or so after his arrival.

He found himself admiring the curvaceous young girl, the prowess of the young male, and the ability of both of them to intertwine in various positions that even he and Sophie hadn't thought of. Eventually he said, in a rather husky voice, 'I'm sorry to disturb . . .' He got no further with his sentence.

He had chosen a bad moment for the youngsters, as they were intertwined in a particularly physically testing position. The girl tried to pull round to see who had spoken, whilst the boy, at that moment, was near to reaching the fulfilment of his intention. He gave out a loud scream of pain rather than of pleasure, Grundwell suspected, and rolled apart from his partner, clutching his manhood with both hands.

The girl in the meantime rushed to find her clothes, which was proving difficult as they had obviously disrobed with passion in mind and not tidiness. Eventually, after much confusion, they both found and donned their clothing. They stood in front of Grundwell like naughty children, the boy still clutching himself in a rather revealing manner.

'I would prefer not to catch you here again,' he lied, trying to speak in the sternest voice he could muster. 'You'll smell of lanolin for one thing, and this is someone else's property for another, and you just shouldn't be here. The fields and woods are yours, and there's no one like me to tell you that you shouldn't be there or complain about the noise!'

The girl looked at him accusingly, saying, 'Do you realise just *how* cold it gets out there?'

Grundwell smiled, not at her reply, but on remembering his own experiences in the surrounding fields, woods, and Forest glades, with wenches having flaxen hair and complexions of milk and honey, to black haired beauties with skins as smooth as olives. They had all been a party to the fun and frolics of his youth.

He remembered one particular flaxen-haired girl, a cabinetmaker's daughter if he remembered aright. They had been making love in a Forest glade when in their enthusiasm they had inadvertently rolled into a rather deep and fast-flowing stream. He shivered. He could still remember the cold on certain parts of his body. He could also remember his indignation that the wench wouldn't finish their lovemaking once they had extracted themselves from the icy cold water.

The noise of the young couple's departure broke into his thoughts and brought him back to the present.

'So don't let me catch you again,' he called after them.

· There was an inaudible response from the boy, which, Grundwell realised, was the only sound he had uttered other than the initial scream of pain.

Six months had passed since Grundwell and Sophie had completed their tour of the cottage that Edward had rented to them. They were now well settled and had added to their comfort by buying beds for themselves and the children. The animals and chickens that Mary had presented them with had multiplied, much to Mary's amusement. She swore that she thought that the lambs were both ewes, and that she had kept the chickens away from the cockerel for weeks before they came to Sophie. Sophie had learnt over the months that the twinkle in her friend's eye often portrayed the underlying mischief in some of her actions.

'Hmm!' had been her only reply, as Mary issued her assurances when a second clutch of eggs that a hen had been sitting on magically transformed themselves into five chicks. The children, of course, thought it was animal heaven. Grundwell had muttered but still carried on and made a second hen house and sheep shelter for the back toft of the cottage.

Both Sophie and Grundwell had been aware since moving from Forest to town that there would be a need to consider the education of their children. Alice was already showing signs of a thirst for knowledge. Grundwell reckoned she came out of the womb with the word *why* already formed on her lips. The last week had been particularly wearing for Grundwell, as he was extremely busy at work with the arrival of new wool stocks; the nights were beginning to draw in, and some of his outworkers had banded together to ask for a better rate of pay. All Edward had said was that it was his problem to solve; that's what he paid him for.

Then he came home to the incessant *why*. Alice had not yet learnt the age-old female art of tactical withdrawal, so she would persist with her questions, ending up in tears because her father became ill-tempered with her.

'She's only seven now. Just think what she'll be like when she's a teenager,' he commented to Sophie after one such incident.

Sophie smiled indulgently.

'Perhaps the time has come to try and find her some form of tutor,' she stated with obvious satisfaction, as she had been working up to the topic for some weeks.

'A tutor?' Grundwell gasped with a horrified look on his face. 'Can I just mention things like money, who would teach her, where it would be done, and small things like that?'

'Oh, that's easy!' Sophie retorted. 'The rector from the church would teach her. There are seven other children whose parents want their children to be taught, and he would take payment from us in eggs. The other children are all boys, but he's always had a shine for Alice because she's so bright, so he sees no problem. That will come later, I suspect!'

'I don't suppose that a room to teach them in has been forgotten?' Grundwell countered somewhat sarcastically.

'Actually no,' responded his wife, ignoring his tone. 'The nave in the church is quite wide enough to take the class without it hindering worship, or the general day-to-day activity of the church.'

He'd done it again. He'd walked into the feminine trap. He looked at his now smiling wife and shook his head as he walked towards the door that led to the back toft area.

'I'll go and lock the animals up and see if the hens have laid any golden eggs. As a matter of interest, when does she start?' He knew there would be a definitive answer before he even posed the question.

'Sunday, after matins,' Sophie replied swiftly, throwing the cushion that she had just been embroidering at her husband's departing back. 'He *never learns*,' she reflected.

Grundwell's day always started with a walk around the warehouse and work rooms, sometimes with Edward, but on that particular morning he was alone. He passed through the storage area, the washing and drying rooms, the carding and combing room, which they had just extended dramatically as the previous area had been too small, then passed on to the spinning and loom areas which were also part of the new extension to the building. Here he stopped short. The room was full of people. As he went through the door, a silence descended, and everyone turned to look at him.

He recognised most of the people who were standing; they were his outworkers. The others, who were seated, worked at the warehouse. There was some embarrassed coughing, and then one of the outworkers was pushed forward. It was Richard Beachwood, one of the best outworkers that he had.

Grundwell waited. He and Edward had discussed this moment since they had heard that their workforce were going to approach them for a better rate of pay for their work. The two had agreed a response that they both thought was effective and could well give them the upper hand in any negotiations.

'Well, Richard, what can I do for you?' he asked in a slow, slightly raised voice so that the assembled workers could hear him.

'Master Grundwell, sir, it's like this.' He looked away from Grundwell's direct gaze. 'We've talked, and all of us have agreed that we should be paid more for what we do.'

'That's fine,' Grundwell stated. 'How much were you thinking of? Is this increase to be paid for the finished items? Is it to be paid for the starting items? Is it to be paid for the quantity you produce? Does it take into account that we buy, supply, and maintain the spinning wheels and looms that you all use? Does it take into account the costs of bringing the raw materials to your houses and pick up the finished items? How are we going to work out the difference between an outworker and an employee who works here at the warehouse?' He paused and awaited a reply.

Richard looked absolutely dumbfounded. He turned away from Grundwell and looked helplessly at the assembled workers. No one spoke.

Grundwell continued, now warming to his subject, 'Could I suggest that you go away and think about what I've said and then *three* of you come back to see Master Edward and myself? Then I am sure we can come to a new arrangement!'

There was a groundswell of assent at the suggestion, and a relieved Richard Beachwood accepted the idea without further discussion.

'May I say one more thing?' Grundwell called out, again in a loud voice. 'Make sure you all agree what you are going to ask for. That way, everyone will be satisfied, and there will be no more dissent. Now please can we all return to work?'

There was a general shuffling, more talking, and then the crowd dispersed, much to Grundwell's relief. He beckoned Richard over.

'Richard, I meant what I said. Make sure you talk to everyone before coming back to see us, and bring two other sensible people with you.'

'Yes, Master Grundwell, sir.' Richard backed away from him and then headed for the door as quickly as he could.

'That', Grundwell thought, 'went extremely well!'

He then carried on with his tour of inspection with renewed vigour, peering into every corner, making a mental note of anything that was out of place.

Edward was at that time passing Saint Michael's Church, not walking with any particular purpose, but he appeared just to be taking the fresh air and observing the passersby. His mind, however, was as sharp and calculating as ever.

He had seen Sophie at Craven Street in the morning, leaving her three children with Mary, as she wanted to visit some of the shops in the middle of the town without the children dragging behind her. Mary had been delighted, as ever, when the request was made. He also heard Sophie tell Mary that she was going to go back home afterwards to collect some eggs and take them up to the cleric as an advance payment for Alice's tuition.

Sophie came round the corner of the High Street and turned into the lane where the cottage was. She failed to notice the man sitting on the grass bank, near the church's lych gate. She walked up to her front door, extracted the large key from its hiding place, and unlocked it, going in and leaving it open, just as she always did. She then went out into the toft and collected some eggs from the laying boxes in the hen house. She came back into the cottage and without looking up, carefully started to fill a small basket with the eggs, singing quietly to herself as she did so.

Suddenly becoming aware of someone else's presence in the room, Sophie turned, looked up, and then froze. Edward was standing by the open door.

She stared at him; her stomach turned over, and the terrible foreboding that she had felt the first time she had met him swept over her.

He quietly closed the door, and without a sound or a word, he came within a pace of where she was standing. He gently but firmly removed the basket of eggs from her grasp and put them on the rectangular oak table that was beside her. She was rooted to the ground, her eyes wide and her breasts heaving with fear and anticipation.

He looked into her eyes, and without a word, he undid the front lacings and belt of her outer clothes. He then circled behind her and gently pulled the garment back over her shoulders so that it dropped to the floor. He unlaced her bodice, letting it fall on top of the dress that he had just removed.

He then put his hands on either side of her hips and slid the last remnants of her clothing to the ground. Gently applying pressure to her now naked body, he pushed her so that she had to take a pace forward and was then standing clear of her clothes, with her legs slightly open.

'Please, Edward, no!' Her voice was barely to be heard. 'Please, please . . . no!'

He did not speak. She heard and sensed him remove his shoes, hose, and britches. She shuddered as she felt one of his hands pass between the cleft of her buttocks and then the top of her thighs, forcing her to open her legs to expose the depths of her womanhood. His fingers explored her, finding the most sensitive part of her organ. Her juices of passion started to flow. She began to moan with a mixture of fear, anticipation, and lust, her hands clenched by her side lest she be tempted to assist the man in his carnal exploration.

He slid his hand from the depths of her body and then, with both hands on her naked waist, turned her round to face him. As he did so, he slowly knelt down in front of her, first kissing her breasts and belly, and then pulling her to him with his hands now clasping the soft and shapely cheeks of her bottom. When she involuntarily opened her legs, he slid his face down further, exploring where his fingers had been with his inquisitive and invasive tongue.

She suddenly clasped his head with both of her now unclenched hands, pulling his head as tight as she could against herself, pushing against him with a pulsating movement that matched the delving of his tongue. He moved his hands from her buttocks, sliding them up across her stomach, and began caressing her soft, ample breasts and hardened nipples.

For several minutes, their positions remained unaltered—Sophie unable to speak, her mouth open with a low moaning, her head back and eyes rolling in ecstasy, with Edward drinking the fluid of passion that belonged to the woman he had coveted since he first saw her.

He pulled himself away, rising and moving behind her once again. She gently cried and sagged in his arms, still in ecstasy from his caresses but now fully aware of his final intent. He pushed her forward, bending her over so that she lay face down on the table, her feet on the floor. He opened her legs with his knee and then caressed the soft and swollen lips of her passion with one hand and her silken-skinned buttocks with the other, once again resulting in the sound of moaning from the semi-prone, full-bodied woman.

Pulling his hand and knee from between her legs, he pushed himself in as close as he could to her, feeling the softness of both of her buttocks against his groin, guiding his lust-enlarged manhood so that it penetrated deep into her organ of ultimate pleasure. Gripping both of Sophie's hips with his large and powerful hands, he began to achieve the climax of his desire.

He became totally oblivious to his surroundings, a total and uncaring driving force, thrusting and grinding his manhood into the sensuous cavern of the beautiful woman that lay in front of him, his hands digging into her flesh as he pulled her hard against him, intent only on one thing—his own full carnal satisfaction of his pent-up emotions of sexual desire.

After a brief period and with a final momentous thrust, accompanied by an ear-splitting yell, he filled the woman's passion with the fluid of his lust.

Edward stood behind her for several seconds, running his hands over her now shaking body, before stepping back and pulling his depleted manhood from between her legs. Sophie was moaning and sobbing in acute pain, total shame, utter humiliation, and consuming guilt. She tried to stand up; Edward stepped forward again and taking hold of her hair roughly pushed her down to her original position on the table.

'You stay there until I've gone,' he hissed into her ear. 'Just remember, you wanted that as much as I did. If you tell anyone, I will deny any wrongdoing. And I swear to you, you will lose everything that you treasure and much, much more. I will sow the seeds of doubt in Grundwell's mind as to your willingness so that you will lose him as well.'

Stepping away from her, he started to dress slowly, still casting admiring glances at the woman he had just abused. Occasionally, he went forward again, and he ran his hands over her, appreciating the sensuous and beautiful body. Sophie reacted with shudders of revulsion. Finally, she heard the door close behind him, as he left her in the same way as he had entered—in total silence.

Sophie raised herself from the table, sobbing and shaking.

Still naked, she went slowly into the back toft, the pain between her legs making it difficult for her to walk. She staggered over to the water butt, and taking a piece of cloth that was hanging on the line, she dipped it into the water and washed herself frantically, not caring if she rubbed herself raw, not caring if anyone saw her; she just needed to rid her body of his body scent. She rubbed between her legs until blood started to colour the pool of water at her feet, and even then, she continued the onslaught on her body.

All the time, she was sobbing and shaking.

When she could stand the pain no longer, Sophie slowly and painfully returned inside the cottage. Not bothering to dry herself, she made her way over to where her clothes lay on the floor, still in the same place where they were peeled from her body by her seducer. She dressed herself, and then with a slow, determined step, she passed through the cottage door on to the street. Without pausing to close it, she started the slow and painful journey to Craven Street, and her children. Her eyes portrayed the innermost hurt and revulsion she felt. Others stared at her, but when she looked back at them, her face was totally bereft of expression.

The young cleric from the church was walking along the High Street when he encountered Sophie. He smiled and spoke to her, as they had recently become friends. She neither spoke nor was there a flicker of recognition in her eyes. Recognising a person in deep shock and trauma, he fell in step close behind her so that he could safeguard her progress.

After a few minutes they arrived at Craven Street, where Sophie quickened her pace until she reached the door of the house. Without hesitating, she opened it and went straight in. The rector then turned and made his way towards the church, speculating as to Sophie's problem.

His mind went back some three years to when his elder sister had been abused and raped by their cousin. The looks and aura were so similar that a huge weight seemed to drop in the pit of his stomach and tears of sheer pity sprang to his eyes.

Sophie entered the big room of the house and stood for a few seconds before collapsing on to the stone floor. Mary and Estor were preparing to cook on the open fire. They looked round as Sophie came in, Mary's smile of welcome dramatically cut short by Sophie's collapse.

She rushed over to her, knelt down, and rested the girl's head on her lap. At that moment, all three children rushed in from the toft, as they had heard Mary's cry of '*Sophie*' when their mother had collapsed.

Mary immediately instructed Estor to take them back outside.

'Before you do, get me those salts from the cupboard!' she said urgently, indicating where the maid would find them by a wave of her hand.

Estor moved quickly to do Mary's bidding. Even Alice was shocked into unnatural silence by the sight of her mother's plight. Mary removed the top of the blue-coloured bottle and held the open container just under Sophie's nose, waving it to and fro.

At first, there was no response from the prone body, then as Mary was beginning to panic, Sophie stirred; her eyelids fluttered, and she opened her eyes, staring up at Mary like a terrified fawn.

Still cradling Sophie's head in her lap, gently stroking hair out of her eyes, and caressing her forehead, Mary softly whispered, 'My child, my child, what on earth's the matter? What's happened to you?'

Sophie was so traumatised she was unable to answer.

As Mary asked her question, Grundwell and Edward came through the front door, having a loud and lively discussion about their labour problems. Both of them momentarily froze on seeing the two women on the ground in front of them.

Grundwell rushed forward, throwing himself on to the floor next to his wife, and tried to envelop her within his arms.

'My love, what in God's name is wrong?' he cried, his face turning ashen.

Sophie clutched at Mary, drew away from him, and curled up against the older woman, as if seeking refuge from his attention.

She began sobbing and sobbing 'I'm sorry, I'm sorry, I'm sorry!' over and over again. Her body was racked with shaking, almost to the point of convulsion.

Edward meanwhile had shrunk back against the wall next to the door. His face, too, had turned white. His forehead suddenly showed the perspiration of panic and guilt. He said nothing. He pushed himself hard against the lime-washed wall, as if asking God to make him invisible.

Then Sophie noticed him. For several seconds, she stared into his eyes, looking at him as if he were the devil himself. She turned her head away and screamed and screamed and screamed. Mary and Grundwell both held on to her, wrapping their arms around her, trying to create a wall of protection. Eventually she fell quiet through sheer physical and emotional exhaustion, and a near total silence descended on the room.

Mary and Grundwell were now staring intently at Edward. Mary's face was becoming a mask of hatred, as grim realisation had started to dawn on her. Grundwell's mood was changing from that of panic to blind rage, as he too started to understand. He began to get up, but Mary reached over Sophie and caught hold of his jerkin. He looked at her, and she shook her head. He sank back on to the floor. They both turned their gaze to Edward.

The silence continued, broken only by the sound of Sophie's sobbing.

'Edward,' Mary's icy voice asked, 'what has happened?'

Sophie turned her head back to face him.

He started to reply, but his voice failed him. He tried again, but his lips and throat were parched with fear.

Yet again he tried to speak, and this time he succeeded.

'Earlier I went to the cottage. She was there. She was asking to be taken. She was asking for it! I could tell she wanted it as much as I did. I swear, I swear!' His voice trailed off.

Mary turned to look into Sophie's eyes. There were several seconds of unbroken silence. Then she gently asked, 'Sophie, did my husband take advantage of your being alone, seduce you, and then finally rape you?'

'Yes!' Sophie replied in a soft, shaking voice. 'And I didn't want him. I didn't want him. I promise you!'

Grundwell stared at his wife, totally confused, not knowing how to react. Words seemed to fail him.

Mary returned her gaze to Edward.

Speaking quietly, with a voice that was icy, flat, and expressionless, she continued, 'Do you remember just before we were married, you went to the Far East with the first shipment of wool that you had sold out there, and you were away for nine months?'

He didn't answer; he simply stared at her.

'I told you when you came back that I had been in child but had lost the baby?'

Edward was again silent, Sophie gazing up into the expressionless mask above her.

'The baby, a girl, was born early, but she lived. Because I was so ill and barren of milk, my parents and the clergyman from the church took the newborn infant away from me. They gave it to a most wonderful couple who were childless. The man worked as a charcoal burner in the Forest.

'Just before my mother died twelve years ago, she told me their names and that they lived in Cumdean.

'I watched from afar as my daughter grew up. I watched from afar on the day she married. I was close by her each time she had a child, and then I watched from afar as my grandchildren started to grow up.

'But I was there on the day she came out of the Forest into Mitcheldean, and on that day I brought her and her family into my life as well as my home.'

There was a terrible silence, followed by Mary's cold, penetrating voice.

'Edward! You have just seduced and raped your own daughter!'

He stood absolutely motionless, feeling the hatred in the look that she was giving him. Her calmness frightened him.

Eventually, Mary looked down at her daughter with tremendous tenderness and feeling, with tears now running down her face and her arms tightening around her, saying in barely a whisper, 'Can you ever forgive me? Can you ever forgive me for what he has done to you? I brought you into this house with love, and then he abused you with lust. May God forgive me!'

Sophie was unable to speak. She simply reached up and caught one of Mary's tears as it fell from her cheek and then buried her face into Mary's bosom, again breaking into low, long sobbing.

Grundwell was so shocked by what he had just witnessed that his initial reactions evaporated. His anger had subsided into pity—pity for his wife and pity for Mary—and a dawning of how his wife must feel.

Suddenly, Grundwell caught a movement out of the corner of his eye as Edward turned to open the front door. The sheer hatred he felt towards the man unleashed a surge of power that enabled him to reach his wife's seducer before he had a chance to escape. He smashed against the departing figure with a force that sent both of them crashing on to the street outside.

Grundwell fared worse in the fall, hitting his head on the street cobbles with such force that it momentarily knocked him out. Edward managed to get up and pulling himself free of Grundwell's now inert body, first staggered and then ran towards the wool warehouse.

Minutes later, he burst into the storage area, sweating, vomiting, swearing, and shouting. The loaders, who were dealing with an incoming cart of wool, scattered at the sight of their employer in such a high state of agitation. He yelled at them to get out.

His eyes were wild and bulging; his face was bleeding from the cuts he got when he hit the cobbles in Craven Street. His clothes were covered in spittle and vomit. He ran to the box where the unloading hooks were kept, wrenched one out, grabbed some cart traces that were lying on the floor, and then turned to face the door.

Grundwell smashed through the same door a few moments later, bent low in anticipation of Edward's retaliation.

The sight that met him transfixed him to the ground in absolute horror.

Edward was hanging from one of the gigantic wooden roof beams, with a leather cart trace wrapped around his neck, and an iron unloading hook driven into the underside of his throat.

His death mask showed the terror of his ending.

# CHAPTER 8

Gumshu straightened his back as he emerged from his tunnel. It had been a long and arduous day with little reward. The coal seam that he had been working had suddenly changed direction, leaving him with just earth, rock, and shale. He knew from his limited experience that he would have to start excavating a new tunnel once he had rendered that one safe. That would take two days, unless he could persuade Ralph to adopt it as a drainage heading so that he could leave it open, which meant he would be paid for his work.

He went to find his foreman, and they climbed up to the top gallery of the mine to agree about a new position. Gumshu did manage to persuade him to adopt the old working after much discussion, so at least he got some reward for his efforts, but he would still have to finish it so that it was effective for mine water drainage. Another day of digging and shoring would have to be completed before he could start the new heading.

It had been an uneventful few months since he had embarked on his new career. He worked six days a week, sometimes seven; as of late the demand for the coal that they extracted had grown ever stronger. Now understanding Ralph's words, he was counting the days until he had worked a year and a day in the mine, and then he would have the chance to start his own. It was one daydream that he had not shared with Maisey, as they sometimes had enough trouble finding money to buy food.

When he returned to the cottage that evening just before sunset, he knew instinctively that there was something wrong. The dogs were outside to greet him as usual, but the children seemed subdued, and when Maisey came out of the back door to apply the usual cold water treatment, he could tell she had been crying. She shook her head at him, and they carried on with the washing. Only when he was dry and sitting in front of the fire did she start telling him the story of what had happened to Sophie and Grundwell. The children were out of earshot in the bedroom, safely cocooned in their soft woollen blankets, gifts from their old Forest friends who now lived in Mitcheldean.

Maisey sat on Gumshu's knee with her head resting on his shoulder. He pulled the shock of chestnut hair to one side so that he could see her face. The flickering flames from the fire cast dancing shadows of light around the room whilst the steady light from the candles exaggerated the colour of the lime-washed walls. Maisey told him the story exactly as a devastated Mary had recounted it to her in the afternoon when she came to see her at the cottage in Cumdean. She left nothing out, even to the details of what Grundwell had found when he had burst into the warehouse storeroom.

'So let me get this right,' Gumshu said. 'Edward seduced and supposedly raped Sophie at the cottage. Afterwards, she managed to make her way to Craven Street and then actually told Mary and Grundwell what had happened while Edward was there in the big room. He managed to escape from the house and ran to the warehouse pursued by Grundwell, but by the time he got there, Edward had hanged and garrotted himself. And just to finish the story off, Sophie is actually Mary and Edward's daughter, not William and Lisa's?'

'Yes,' whispered Maisey, 'that's about it.'

Gumshu sniffed Maisey's breath.

'You haven't been taking that stuff out of the flagon hidden in the wall, have you?' he asked.

Maisey straightened up, indignation showing on her face.

'No, I most certainly have *not*! And how do you know about my hiding place, and more to the point, what's in it?' she demanded.

'I've always known where you hide things, Maisey, and I just happened to find the flagon a couple of days after we came back from Mitcheldean.'

He looked at her and grinned.

'Do you not remember how you felt a couple of days ago when we blew all the candles out and made love in front of the hearth?'

'I can remember how you yelled when that spark from the fire hit your bare bottom!' she said, laughing.

'And I can remember you yelling, and it certainly wasn't about a spark out of the fire!' he returned just as sharply.

Maisey blushed. She did remember that and other occasions too when she felt highly enthusiastic about making love. She had put it down to her passionate nature and a little too much mead, but now she suddenly realised what was in it.

'You haven't used it all, have you?' she questioned, a little sheepishly.

'No, certainly not,' he replied, dispelling her concern. 'Too much and you go to sleep or I can't handle the consequences, so I've learnt, just a little drop and . . .'

'That will do, Gumshu!' She cut him off in mid-sentence, but he noticed she was blushing again.

They suddenly realised they had got off the subject they were originally discussing.

Their serious looks returned, and then Gumshu asked, 'So what else did Mary tell you?'

'Well, Sophie, Grundwell, and the children are staying at Craven Street, at least for the time being. Sophie is still in shock from Edward's attack, if you can call it that, and she will hardly let Mary out of her sight. Grundwell is finding coming to terms with Sophie's seduction very difficult, and he now has to run the business as well, obviously with Mary's help. They have given the foreman's job to Richard Beachwood, one of the outworkers who Grundwell has always trusted.

'It was Sophie who actually asked Mary to come and tell us what had happened, so she came with John, their house servant. She had left Estor to look after the children and keep an eye on Sophie, who refuses to leave the house. And that's all I can tell you,' his wife replied, beginning to get upset.

'Maisey, what a dreadful mess it is. Let's pray she doesn't get pregnant,' he sighed.

'Ah,' Maisey said after a pause, 'the news is better there. Sophie and Grundwell were about to tell Mary and Edward that she was in fact pregnant, but were waiting until she had told her mother and father, well, the couple she thought were her parents, so at least *that* can't be blamed on the rape.'

'Let's hope that everyone believes her!' Gumshu commented.

Maisey turned and looked at her husband, and then she snuggled up close to him again. He put his arms around her as if he were protecting her from all the bad things in the world, and they remained silent for several minutes, both lost in their own thoughts, the only sound coming from the crackling fire.

Gumshu stirred. 'Did Mary mention any funeral arrangements for Edward?'

Maisey raised her head. 'Yes, she did, but only as she was leaving. She said that they have sent the body back to the village in the north of Herefordshire, where he was born. Whether the church there will bury him in the graveyard is up to the local rector.

'Edward's parents are buried in the same place, so she is presuming that he will probably be buried in an unmarked grave, close to them. She has sent funds up with the body, so she must be pretty sure. Obviously no one will be going to the funeral, at least not anyone from around here.'

The two returned to their original position, sitting with their arms wrapped around each other. The cottage became quiet again, save for the noise from the fire and the calling of a distant owl.

The following day was a day off for Gumshu, and as with every free day he had, he always tried to spend it with his four children and his wife. They usually walked somewhere in the Forest and tried to find the places where they had spent time with the charcoal burns, reliving old memories. The children had started to get bored with that type of outing, so Maisey was trying to think of other ideas, without a lot of success. But on that particular day, they were going to the annual market and fair which was held in Ross-on-Wye, some four miles from the Forest village.

Although it meant getting up at dawn, Gumshu had decided that he had a problem to try and resolve before they set out.

Since that fateful visit to Mitcheldean, he had had a pain in the lower part of his buttocks that kept coming back, especially when he sat in a certain position. He blamed the action of the dogs when they had inadvertently bitten him during his altercation at the Richmond's house.

Maisey kept saying that it was spark inflicted, especially after a session of their lovemaking in front of the fire. On inspection, all she had managed to find was a small scar from one of the dog bites, so she gave him no sympathy and told him to not be such a baby.

Gumshu, however, was not convinced and decided to do his own investigation.

He couldn't turn his head around enough to actually see his bottom, even with the aid of Maisey's small hand mirror, though he had tried on several occasions when he was alone.

Before any of his family stirred, he crept out of the cottage totally naked and stood over the pool of water that surrounded the spring. His idea was to look down at his own reflection in the pool and then see if he could identify the source of the pain.

Gumshu had not reckoned on two things. The first was that Maisey was a mother of four, and any unusual movement or sound in the cottage always brought her instantly out of her sleep, whatever the time of night. That reaction of hers had always slightly bemused her family because when morning came and it was time to get up, they could never wake her.

The second thing that he had overlooked was that it might have been *his* day off, but for others in the village, like his friend Ralph, it was a normal working day and they always passed by the cottage on their way to the mine.

That particular morning was no exception. As he tried to view the offending area, Ralph and several of his miners were, in fact, going past. They stopped and watched silently as Gumshu pulled, pushed, and twisted himself, totally oblivious to their presence.

In the end, his view was obscured by his manhood, so he got hold of it to pull it to one side. At that precise moment, the back door of the cottage opened and Maisey threw out a pail of some ice-cold water, which struck him at exactly the area that he was addressing. He let out a cry of what could only be described as anguish, whereupon he slipped on the wet stones around the pool and landed on his backside amidst some rather thorny briars, briars that Maisey had put there to keep the wild boars from soiling the water.

That all resulted in a loud cheer from his fellow miners who were still watching with total fascination. After a lot of ribald comments, they then happily went on their way to work, laughing and joking very much at Gumshu's expense. The last comment came from Ralph, who asked what the entertainment for the following day would be.

'What did you do *that* for?' Gumshu enquired of the hysterically laughing Maisey.

'I heard a noise, and I thought it was one of those wild pigs again that always makes a mess in the pool, so I thought I'd better move quickly. Little Emmy opened the door, and I flung the water,' she replied, with tears running down her cheeks.

'I noticed!' remarked the still naked Gumshu, as he extracted himself from the briars.

Little Emmy popped her head around the door to see what all the commotion and noise was about, but seeing her father's face and the look he gave her, she quickly thought of something else that she had to do inside the cottage.

'Could I dare ask what you were doing or is it a miner's secret that women shouldn't know about?' Maisey asked in a mischievous voice.

'Are we all ready to go out yet?' Gumshu enquired somewhat frostily, ignoring his wife's question completely.

'Yes, we're ready and waiting, waiting for you, my husband,' she replied with a grin.

As a large number of the villagers were going to the fair, four large carts had been organised, drawn by oxen. The previous year everyone who went had either taken their own cart or walked, carrying children, food, drink, and clothing for their family. The outward journey had been fine, but coming back had been a disaster, with tired children, exhausted mothers, and drunken fathers. This year, the mothers of the village had organised the transport, and as far as they were concerned, there was not going to be a repeat performance. The fathers had also had a stern warning as to the amount of alcohol that was to be consumed.

Gumshu and his family joined the other Cumdean families who were travelling on the carts, and off they set, wending their way through the country lanes, occasionally catching sight of the meandering River Wye. Gumshu's dogs had been dissuaded from joining them on that particular adventure, but a few of the village dogs had tried to follow them, but soon they grew bored and turned for home. The oxen plodded on through the hazy morning sunshine, the cartloads of chattering, laughing, and excited villagers shattering the peace and tranquillity of the beautiful river valley with the hubbub of noise.

Having travelled for some two hours, including stops for children's toiletry, the group finally arrived at the outskirts of the town, with dozens of others like them. The oxen were tethered on a grassy meadow, watered, and left grazing contentedly under the watchful eye of the landowner's son, who was doing a brisk trade in tending animals and their carts.

As they walked into the town, heading towards the square, they could hear the music of the pipes, the lyres, and the drums, all being played by enthusiastic musicians. They also could hear the booming voice of the town crier as he announced the programme for the day, rounding every announcement off with a resounding 'God Bless the King', which was followed by a loud cheer from his audience.

Street entertainers juggled everything imaginable; jesters pranced around performing cartwheels, backward somersaults, forward somersaults, and jumping on and off walls, carts, and anything else that was available. There was the smell of a multitude of foods being cooked on open fires to suit a multitude of tastes. There were the callings of the vast numbers of street vendors and stall holders, each one trying to outdo the other both in volume and content.

But above all there was the sound of laughter and chatter of the throngs of people—young, old, infant, and child, all intent on enjoying the day.

Maisey was definitely not in control of the situation. She had tied a red ribbon in each child's hair so that they could be identified in the crowd. The problem was that every other mother seemed to have had the same idea, and the crowd was now full of dozens of children all with coloured ribbons in their hair, making individual recognition an impossible task.

She also had the added responsibility of controlling Gumshu, who was determined to dance with every troupe of dancers on every street corner, and with every passing pretty girl who would let him.

Maisey was so worried about the children getting lost that in the end she bought some rope lengths from a street trader. She then tied a piece around each of her children's waists, thus enabling her to control them like hounds on a leash.

She was not so lucky at controlling her husband; he never stood still long enough for her to tie the rope. As they were made their way along the street that approached the square, an immense pair of arms encircled her from behind, and attached to the arms was a giant of a jolly friar, with a large copper cross hanging from a hand-woven leather thong around his neck. Maisey stood still and looked up.

'And how are you, my child?' he boomed in a deep baritone voice, slightly raised to be heard above the crowd.

'Dry!' Maisey replied, smiling up at Father Benedict's face that seemed to reach to the sky above.

The friar laughed a laugh that appeared to come from the depths of his more than ample stomach.

'And how were the prior's new cellars that you were bound for after our last encounter?' she asked, without changing her position.

'Somewhat depleted after the four-day sabbatical we took to ensure the standard of his wines reflected his station in life,' he replied, wincing slightly at the memory of the first day back in the ordinary world.

'Four days!' she gasped. 'I hope he fed you properly as well.'

'My dear child, never ever spoil good wine with food if it can possibly be avoided!' he responded, totally aghast. On reflection, he couldn't remember eating at all, but that was not for the ears of his young friend.

At that moment, the children noticed their mother's assailant and encircled them both with screams of delight. The friar released Maisey from the bear-like hug he was giving her and scooped the children up in his arms, all four together. He looked at the ropes with a questioning glance.

'Control!' Maisey said with a smile. At that moment, Gumshu returned from one of his dancing sorties. Seeing Father Benedict, he started cavorting around with him as well, the friar still clutching the children. The six of them twirled down the street, followed by a slightly exasperated Maisey, still trying to hold on to the children's ropes.

The dancing came to an abrupt end when the monk smelt a particularly strong odour of his favourite meat being cooked. The party moved to the side of the thoroughfare where a spit had been set up over an open fire, and they stood and admired the cooking beast.

'I do love a well-cooked pig,' the friar sighed as he gazed lovingly at the rotating and well-basted animal on the spit.

'Father, you love all food!' the stallholder replied, slicing off enough of the sizzling meat for all of them. Gumshu was about to extract some money from his well-concealed money bag when the stallholder held up his hand.

'No, no need. This pig was blessed by the father in early spring with a prayer and then sprinkling ale on it. I reckon its size was due to that blessing, so it's the least I can do.'

'You mean you actually *saw* Father Benedict waste ale by throwing it over your pig?' Maisey asked incredulously.

'Good Lord, no! The ale that I'd put in the mug ready for the blessing was consumed in one draught by the father, who then turned to me and said it was the thought that counted,' the stall holder replied, much to the amusement of the crowd that had gathered around them.

The friar returned the children to the ground, untangling himself from their ropes. He was laughing, his reputation still intact. The group then made their way into the square, where the town crier was still entertaining the crowd but with a slightly hoarse voice after nearly three hours of exercising his throat.

They paused for a moment, the three adults looking at the seething mass of revellers in front of them. They watched the performers, the tradesmen selling their wares, the musicians, and the dancers; they listened to all the sounds of enjoyment, and it couldn't help but make them laugh.

A thought passed through the friar's mind, and it must have showed on his face. Maisey looked up at him and smiled.

'Yes, Katherine was with us last year and *how* she enjoyed it all,' she said quietly.

Gumshu heard her and taking her hand into his gave it a gentle squeeze. Father Benedict said a prayer under his breath for the departed little girl and silently blessed her mother and father. The moment passed, but they all knew that she would never be forgotten.

'Right!' the friar said. 'It's time to go and visit other members of my flock!'

Gumshu and Maisey laughed. That was always the way their jolly friend declared his departure, usually to go and find further sustenance elsewhere. Maisey reached up and kissed him. Gumshu patted his arm, as he tried never to shake the father's hand because the crushing he got could usually be felt for a week. The children yelled goodbye, as they were presently gazing in awe at a street vendor's toys.

The couple were alone again with their offspring. This time things were more under control, as Gumshu had done enough dancing for the day, so each parent had two children. Maisey had Little Emmy and Richard, whilst Gumshu had George and Hannah.

They tried their hand at several games. The children's favourite was soaking rags in pails of water and then hurling them at their parents. The idea was that Gumshu and Maisey had to run the gauntlet of the rag throwers whilst navigating through some upturned logs as obstructions, and then reach a sanctuary behind a *pile* of logs. The course was very twisty and about thirty paces long, and designed to give the rag throwers a definite advantage.

Maisey had four rags that hit her, whilst Gumshu had none. He started to show off and run back, so Little Emmy promptly picked up her pail of water and threw it at full force at him as he passed her. The aim was perfect, and the water hit him in the exact spot that Maisey had caught him with her water earlier in the day.

That brought a cheer from the assembled onlookers.

Gumshu fixed her with an accusing look. 'Has your mother been teaching you to throw water again?'

'Yes, and she says I'm getting a lot better at it!' Little Emmy responded and immediately took flight, as that was the other thing Maisey had taught her—when to run.

The crowd was warming to the family battle, and they parted to let Little Emmy through and then closed ranks again when Gumshu tried to catch her. However, Gumshu cheated as he had a crafty little trick of his own up his sleeve. He produced some rather tasty morsels of sweetmeat from his pocket, sat down, and proceeded to eat them.

Unfortunately, Little Emmy loved sweetmeats, and seeing her father eating, she emerged from behind the crowd, throwing caution to the wind. Her father suddenly got up, ran, and caught her. She immediately burst into heartfelt crying, so much so that he forgave her the water indiscretion, and presented her with all of the remaining sweetmeats to stem her flow of tears. What he didn't see was the wide grin and wave she gave to the crowd when he put her over his shoulder. There was a loud cheer, which Gumshu thought was for him.

The day passed all too quickly with the family playing skittles, chasing lambs, buying food, and then playing even more games that the numerous stalls offered.

Walking round the fair, they came across several of the village men folk, who seemed to have completely forgotten the stern warnings given to them about alcohol consumption.

'Retribution will be swift and merciless!' Gumshu grinned.

The villagers assembled back at the oxen carts just as the sun began to sink in the sky, tired but happy, ready for the homeward journey. The return to Cumdean took about the same length of time as in the morning, but the toilet breaks were now mostly for the men as the majority of the children were sound asleep in their mothers' arms.

That evening in the half light, after the children were asleep and Gumshu was quietly dozing in front of the fire, Maisey slipped away to the churchyard and noiselessly made her way to the little grave under the oak tree. She had a small wooden toy in her hand. She knelt down and put it by the roughly carved cross.

She stared, a little taken aback. There, on the other side of the cross, was another toy. She picked it up. It was dry, so it was obviously a recent addition, and she recognised that it had come from the same stall where she had bought *her* toy that afternoon. She laid it back on the grave, got up, and looked around. No one was in sight, and she knew Gumshu had not been to the churchyard.

She knelt down again and quietly whispered, 'I think you have a guardian angel that looks after you, my darling.' Her voice was deep with emotion, and she was nearly at the point of crying.

She bent her head as the tears started to roll down her face, wetting the high white collar of the dress she had been wearing all that day.

Such was her position, she did not see the large figure dressed in a brown friar's habit that noiselessly slipped from behind the wall, and walked away over the fields.

Gumshu arose as usual the next morning, a little before dawn. He lit the candles in the big room of the cottage and rekindled the dying embers of the fire for when Maisey and the children got up. He washed in some warm water, a task he never understood why he did, especially when he came home at night covered in grey slime anyway.

There was a loud banging on the door. He opened it to find five or six of his fellow miners standing outside. There was a silence, and then one of the miners, Benjamin Travers, pushed forward and asked if they could talk to him.

'Of course you can,' Gumshu answered and opened the door wide so that they could all come in.

They stood around the now blazing fire, the light playing on their rugged features, and then Benjamin turned to face him, saying, 'You haven't heard, have you?'

'Heard what?' Gumshu replied, becoming slightly concerned.

'There was a roof fall at the mine last night.'

His blood ran cold. He wondered what those men were about to tell him.

'Was anyone hurt? Come on, man, for God's sake, was anyone hurt?' he demanded to know impatiently.

'I'm afraid Ralph was underneath the section that caved!' Benjamin blurted out, obviously relieved to offload his news. 'And he didn't survive. There were probably four or five tons of earth, shale, and rock on top of him,' he continued.

'What in God's name was he doing in there? We have all agreed that no one should go into the mine alone, especially at night!' Gumshu almost shouted in reply.

Maisey came into the room, still wearing her nightgown, awoken by the noise of the talking.

'What's happening?' she asked, taking her husband by the arm.

'Ralph's been killed at the mine,' he replied very quietly. Looking at Benjamin, he asked, 'Which section caved? Was it a side tunnel or part of the main chamber? Why was he excavating? Had he started a new tunnel?'

'It was the tunnel that you hadn't quite finished the day before your day off,' Benjamin explained slowly. 'Ralph decided that he was going to finish it himself so that you could start a new heading today. He reckoned there would be a good coal seam there.'

Gumshu felt the room spin. Maisey went very pale. The men were silent.

'But how can that have collapsed? I doubled up on the usual shoring timbers because the roof was so unstable. Ralph knew that because he made sure I had enough timber.'

'Yes, I know.' Benjamin nodded. 'But he removed half the timbers as he went in so that there would be enough supports for you to start the new heading. The timber gangs have failed to meet the demand again, I'm afraid.'

Gumshu went very quiet for a few moments, with no one breaking the silence.

'So now what happens?' he asked in a hushed voice.

'Well, one of the Cottrell brothers came to see me at about midnight last night after the accident was discovered, and has asked me to approach you to see if you will take over as the foreman,' Benjamin replied hesitantly.

'I haven't got the experience to run a mine, and if I did have, I'm not sure I would want to run this one!'

'You've got what it takes to do the job, Gumshu, even without the experience, otherwise the Cottrells wouldn't have asked you. I've only spoken to these lads so far because it's so early, but they all agree with me, you're the only one of us that can take it on. I've thought of nothing else all night. I've tried to think of somebody other than you who could do it, but I can't think of anyone.'

Gumshu looked at Maisey, who shrugged her shoulders and said, 'It's up to you, but could I suggest you go and talk to the Cottrells first before you decide? I think you could do it, but I'm your wife so I'm slightly biased.'

'Yes, that's a good idea. I'll do that because they're bound to be at the mine this morning. But first, gentlemen, we need to start to organise Ralph's burial. I know he wasn't married and that he lived with his uncle and family. I'll go and see them and see what funeral arrangements they want to make. I take it the body has been brought out of the mine?'

'Yes,' Benjamin answered, 'they brought it up from where the tunnel was within a couple of hours of the accident being discovered. I believe it's just by the entrance to the mine now. The Cottrells asked the pumping gang to go in and help them to bring him out. They also asked one of Mitcheldean's surgeons to have a look at the body as well, just to verify the cause of death.'

'They might be able to verify the cause, but I warrant that they won't give a reason behind it. The Cottrells and I have got to do some very serious talking. If they want me to run it, then they are going to have to do things my way because the mine is dangerous as it operates now. We all know that, and I won't have it.'

'This is why you need to be foreman,' Benjamin said quietly with a smile.

Later in the day, after he had arranged to return Ralph's body to his family, Gumshu met with the mine owners, and there followed a long discussion about the mine's future and the part that he would play as foreman.

# CHAPTER 9

Grundwell and Sophie now lived at Craven Street with Mary. It had been over twelve months since the terrible day that had changed all their lives so dramatically. Sophie had now become the daughter that Mary had always dreamt of, and the need had gone to watch her from afar.

The children had settled into their new home. Alice's menagerie had moved back with them, and the addition of a new sister was now no longer a novelty.

She had been baptised in Saint Michael's Church only a month previously. The ceremony had been conducted by the young cleric, the Reverend William Benson, who was now also Alice's tutor. There had been a small gathering at the church, including Gumshu, Maisey, their four children, Father Benedict, and Sophie's Forest parents, as they were now affectionately known.

Grundwell had faced the inevitable *why* from Alice about all her grandparents, but he had been ready for that particular question and answered it as casually as he could.

'It is because your mother has a town parent as well as Forest parents. It just depends on where she is,' he had said.

Alice had opened her mouth as if to question the reply, then she looked at her father's face and decided that one of the sayings that the Reverend Benson had taught his little class probably applied now—*silence is golden.*

She had asked the inevitable why at the time, but he had smiled at her and said, 'You'll find that time and experience will give you your answer, Alice.'

Mary, John the house servant, Estor the maid, Richard Beachwood and his wife, and Phillip Fletcher and his wife had completed the little group around the font in the Mitcheldean church.

The Reverend Benson was a little taken aback when he was introduced to the prospective godparents, Gumshu and Maisey.

Trying not to show a reaction, he thought, 'Wasn't this the man I fled from on the grassy slope outside the church last year?'

Father Benedict, who was doing the introductions, sensed the unease of the parish priest. As he knew the story from Maisey, he tried to make things worse, as was his wont.

'This man flattens parish priests, puts them on a spit, and then eats them for supper!' he declared without a flicker of a smile.

The young priest, however, was a match for the friar's mischievous humour.

'He would have difficulty with a certain rotund friar though. He'd have to cook him for months, and that's if he could even get him on the spit!'

'Your trouble is you are becoming too used to Forest ways,' the friar boomed, giving him a resounding slap on the back, which sent him flying into Gumshu's arms.

'I'm not sure which is worse, being flattened by a woodsman or slapped on the back by a particular friar,' the rector said, trying to get his breath back.

The humour of the conversation set the mood for the whole baptism and the celebrations that followed at Craven Street.

Acting in her new role as grandmother, Mary had secretly made an exquisitely embroidered baptismal dress, which was white with Honiton lace edgings, and a finely embroidered Valencian lace cap and shawl. When Sophie first saw it, she held the soft silk to her face, rubbing it gently against her cheek, and started to cry.

'That's an expensive handkerchief!' Grundwell told her unkindly.

Mary looked at him without speaking. There was still anger and resentment in him; it ebbed and flowed like the tide. The problem, she realised, was that the symptoms were not abating. At least there was no doubt who the father of baby Anna was. She had Grundwell's eyes, nose, and ears without a doubt, and she was obviously going to be tall. Mary had made that very public knowledge since Anna's birth, as there were those in the town who would have liked to believe it was Edward's child, just as Gumshu had predicted.

With the baptism behind them, Grundwell could now concentrate on the business. Although Mary was obviously still the owner, she left the day-to-day running to her son-in-law. Before that fateful day, Edward and Mary had done all the trading accounts themselves, but Grundwell now employed a full time bookkeeper, a man named Philip Fletcher, of Chepstow, who had been a shipping clerk on the docks.

That was until he met a girl from Mitcheldean and he moved to the town so that he could marry her. Grundwell had met him whilst on one of his trips to sell wool to a local trader. He had liked him straight away and immediately took him to meet Mary, who also approved and liked him.

He had started work for them within two days of the chance meeting.

Rather than have him use the house on Craven Street, Grundwell's men had built a special room inside the warehouse, which housed all the records like ledgers, shipping orders, sales and purchase papers, and this was where Philip now worked.

As always, Grundwell was doing his morning rounds with Richard Beachwood. The first place they looked in was the storeroom. Every time he went there, Grundwell felt his stomach heave, and momentarily, his mind went back to that fateful day when he had found Edward hanging. The flashbacks had become less frequent and easier, but his mind never completely shut out the fact that his father-in-law had seduced and raped Sophie. In fact, he had to admit to himself that the whole event preyed on his mind more and more.

'Why did she let him? Had she wanted Edward?' He could remember that there was always a certain spark between the two of them. 'Had she really been a willing partner and things just got out of hand, or had it actually *been* rape?'

There were so many questions that he really didn't have the answers to. Sophie refused to discuss it, simply saying she had been seduced, then raped. Grundwell then more often than not became aggressive and ended up storming out of the house, heading for the nearest tavern, coming home hours later, usually the worse for drink.

One particular night, Sophie thought she had smelt another woman's odour on him, but she had convinced herself that was impossible. It was rapidly coming to the point when neither of them talked to each other, other than to discuss day-to-day matters such as the children, the business, what was going on in Mitcheldean, and other somewhat trivial matters. The wonderful and lively discussions that they used to have had stopped. They now rarely kissed or even touched, and although now able to make love after the birth of Anna, their urges were negligible.

Mary, meanwhile, watched the agony that her daughter and son-in-law were going through with the greatest of concerns. Sophie had become so withdrawn that the three elder children now turned to their grandmother for all their comforts as well as their entertainment. Anna seemed to have become the centre of Sophie's world to the exclusion of all else.

Grundwell didn't appear to want to spend time with his offspring and was usually short-tempered with them when they approached him and would certainly never play with them.

Repeatedly, Mary found herself playing the lone parent role to the children. Time and again, she had tried to tell Sophie and Grundwell that they should be doing the parental role, not her.

Grundwell's character also seemed to have changed. He became a man totally obsessed by business, profit, and money to the exclusion of all else. He drove his workforce with an uncompromising approach to the quantity of output he expected. If a household did not give him the required output of yarn or cloth, he would remove the spinning wheel or loom, and they would do no further work. That happened so frequently that many outworkers had gone to see Mary to put their case to her. She decided that the time had definitely come to discuss the issue with him.

The first problem she had to overcome was his resentment at being told what to do by a woman. Mary was, however, not a lady to be ignored when she gave an instruction.

When she heard his reasons for the removal of the spinning wheels and looms from several of the houses, she looked him straight in the eyes, saying, 'You will return the spinning wheels and looms to them all tomorrow. You will then tell each family what you expect from them, and you will give them a month to achieve that output.

'You will instruct Philip to carry out a weekly check, to see if they can reach the target you have given them. If it is obvious that they cannot, you will reduce it to one that they can achieve. I will not have people in this town going hungry because of me. Do I make myself *very* clear?'

Grundwell was completely taken aback by the abrupt statement from Mary.

He drew breath to speak, but she continued after giving him a thunderous look.

'In two days' time, I will come to the warehouse to check my instructions have been carried out. Then you and I will go and visit every outworker that we have, and *I* will confirm exactly what we want from them and also check that they are now happy with the way we are treating them. As you have said in the past, they get well paid for what they do since the increase we gave them last year, but to get the output we have to treat them properly. That also goes for the workers we have in our own weaving rooms at the warehouse. Now that's an end to it, and I *never* want to have this conversation with you again.

'You and Sophie can't go on like this either,' she continued in a softer tone. 'It's affecting the whole family, including me. You have got to come to terms with what happened. What neither of you have given any thought to is how I feel about it all. *My* husband seduced Sophie and then forced her to have sex with him. The fact that it was his own daughter makes it all the more terrible. I brought you and Sophie into my home. My guilt is eating me up as well. But life must go on, and you have children to consider as well as yourself.

'I am sorry, Grundwell, but for everyone's sake, you must resolve your problems and then you must help Sophie. You have to show some strength and stop wallowing in your own self-pity!' Mary was shaking uncontrollably by the time she finished.

Grundwell stood still for a few seconds, looking at her, and then quietly said, 'I need to walk. I need to think!' With that, he turned and walked out of the house.

Instead of taking his now usual route to the nearest tavern, he walked through the centre of the town. He passed the array of small stores that Sophie had found so fascinating when they first arrived from Cumdean. He walked past the top of the lane where their cottage was and then on to the entrance of the church.

He stood at the lych gate, looking at the building.

There was not a sound, but a single candle lantern burnt in the porch, acting as a beacon to welcome all who needed guidance.

He softly opened the gate, walked up the short path to the porch, then stood and gazed at the entrance doors in front of him. For a moment he hesitated, not knowing what had drawn him there.

He walked forward, seemingly helped by an invisible hand, opened one of the heavy doors, and went inside. He stood for a few minutes letting his eyes get accustomed to the light in the dimly lit building; he knelt down beside the font, not daring to go any further lest his form be caught by the light of the candles burning in the nave and distant sanctuary.

His eyes became transfixed by the cross that stood on the altar, the flickering candlelight playing upon the body of Christ being crucified, breathing a life and a soul into the carved image.

He remembered the words that he had learnt from Father Benedict, when he was Alice's age, about forgiveness, about trust, and foremost, about love. He remembered but a month ago when the Reverend Benson had uttered those self-same words over Anna as he baptised her, and he was now kneeling beside the font where that baptism had taken place.

But the image that haunted him the most was the one of Gumshu and Maisey laying little Katherine to rest. He had seen two people's unbelievable grief been made bearable by their love and devotion for each other.

He bowed his head, tears running down his weather-beaten young face, and he prayed silently to the Lord, the prayer remaining the sole property of the man and his God.

The only sign that someone had come into the church was a slight movement of the candles that lit the inside of the building, as the draught from the open door suddenly influenced their task.

Just as silently as he had come in, William Benson closed the door as he went out.

As he stood in the porch, he raised his face to the heavens. 'Thank you, Lord!' he whispered.

Grundwell stayed in the church until dawn, eventually going to sit in one of the private pews in front of the sanctuary screen. As the morning light started to illuminate the inside of the church, his gaze was caught by the beautiful and poignant ceiling painting high above him, and yet again, tears began to roll down his cheeks.

It was only then that he became aware he was not alone in the awakening building.

As he got up to leave, he looked across into the widest part of the nave and simply said, 'I'm grateful, Rector!'

William's voice came out of the darkened corner where he had been standing. 'The Lord is a good listener, Grundwell, but he now leaves the remedy to you.'

Grundwell paused, glancing back towards the altar, still lit by the remaining candles.

'Yes, that is my part of the arrangement,' he answered, and with a smile towards the cleric, he walked out of the church, a man beginning to come to terms with himself.

He retraced his steps of the night before, but instead of going to Craven Street, he carried on to the warehouse. Dawn was now fully broken, and Philip Fletcher was already standing at his table, busily sorting papers. Richard had also arrived and was repairing a spinning wheel broken by an overzealous spinner. Grundwell called the two together and told them what Mary had instructed the previous evening. He gave Richard his orders for the day, and as he left, he told them, 'I'm going to be away for a few hours. Whether I'm back today depends on something I have to do at Craven Street.' And with that, he left them to their day's tasks.

He quietly opened the front door of the house and slipped in, gently closing it behind him. As the window covers had not yet been taken down, one candle was still burning, the rest of the room being lit by the flames of the fire, which cast its magical multicoloured lights across the darkened room.

Grundwell jumped as Mary's voice cut across his thoughts.

'I hope the church was not too cold last night?' she enquired in a low voice.

'How did you know I was there?' he asked, slightly taken aback.

'William Benson came to tell me. He was worried that we might not know where you were,' she replied, getting up from the oak settle to the left of the fire. She turned and faced him, enquiring, 'And your wild demons, are they any closer to being tamed?'

Grundwell looked at her, this woman of so many conflicting characters, a hard-headed business woman of considerable wealth, a woman who cared passionately about her family, a woman who always had consideration for the people that she employed. He began to feel deep admiration for her, and his resentments against her started to evaporate.

'My demons have nearly returned whence they came—back to the devil and hell.'

Only Grundwell knew how close he had come to befriending the devil whilst still living in his own private hell.

He moved forward and kissed Mary on the forehead, before taking a candle, lighting it from the one that was already lit, and going up to the bedroom where Sophie and baby Anna were sleeping. He sat quietly on the bed, the candlelight illuminating his beautiful wife and child, the light casting gentle shadows around the room as the light of the morning was not yet bright enough to penetrate the thickly woven window coverings.

Sophie stirred, opened her eyes, and once sleep had been brushed away like a spider's web, she reached out to her husband as a child would to its mother, seeking the reassurance of touch and warmth. Grundwell took her hand, raised it to his lips, and kissed the long fingers and the soft palm with a warmth and tenderness, the joy of which he had long forgotten.

'My love,' he said in a whisper, 'forgive me my doubts of love, forgive me my words of anger, forgive me my actions of hurt, forgive me my indiscretions, but most of all, forgive me my disbelief in the truth.'

Sophie looked into her husband's eyes and saw the depth of sincerity and love that he was now offering. She knew then that they were both beginning the path to recovery, and she prayed that nothing would ever stop it, not even the guilt of her innermost thoughts.

She sat up, opened her arms, and softly pulled his head to rest against her chest. She felt the warmth of his tears, which now mixed with her own as they fell from her cheeks in an outpouring of relief.

Anna stirred, as if she sensed that her father and mother were at the beginning of the journey of love once again. Her soft cry of hunger was answered by Grundwell, who raised his head from Sophie's breasts, gently wrapped the child in its soft woollen blanket, scooped her up from the bed, and presented the infant to his wife.

She cradled the baby for a second or two, then opening the front of her night dress, she placed the child against her bared breast, guiding its mouth to the source of her milk. She stared down at her daughter, giving her the look of love that only a mother can give as she looks upon her feeding child.

She raised her head and looked at her husband, giving him a smile that melted the core of his being. He seemed to have momentarily lost the power of speech and gazed at her as if she had magically bewitched him.

Mary stood outside her daughter's bedroom door, and hearing no noise, she softly crept to the children's room, where she had heard sounds of the children awakening. Estor, the maid, had also heard the children stirring.

She was aware of Grundwell's arrival back from the church, as she had been standing behind the storeroom door and had overheard the conversation between him and Mary. When she heard the children, she quickly went up the outside stairs of the house that led to the landing and thence to their bedroom. She and Mary met at the bedroom door, and together they went in to dress and wash the three children.

Alice was, as usual, in a *why* mode. Why *couldn't* they go into their parents' bedroom? Why *couldn't* she go and help feed the baby? The questions had been relentless, so much so that Mary took her to one side and implored her to be quiet, as she had heard enough. Alice was about to ask the *why* question again when she noticed the look on her grandmother's face, a look she had never seen before, so she made an instant decision to obey without question.

Once dressed, the three children, Alice, Elizabeth, and young Thomas, were escorted downstairs for their breakfast. It was Alice's day to go for her lessons with the Reverend William Benson, so there was panic whilst her books were found, and some Latin work that was supposed to be finished at home was quickly completed.

Alice was a bright child, and it was to her credit that she found such work easy. What she really loved though were the sums that William Benson did with his little class. She was fascinated by the answers that a combination of figures could give, and Mary noted that Alice's interest in such things matched her own.

Mary decided that she would take Alice to the church for her lessons herself, so grandchild and grandmother walked through the town, hand in hand. Mary seemed to have suddenly lost the burden that she had been carrying for the last few months. There was a bounce in her step once again; her pride seemed to have been restored, and one shopkeeper had remarked as she went by, 'Mary seems to have got her smile back.' Had she heard, she would have agreed.

The class of William Benson was made up of seven boys and Alice. They had set up the classroom in the corner of the wide nave of the church, leaving the rest of the church free to carry on its day-to-day functions. William could also keep a watchful eye on some of the more active members of his congregation as he taught. There always seemed to be some sort of friction between the groups, and he had mentioned to Grundwell one day that he seemed to spend a lot of his time mediating between the various factions of parishioners.

'And what has happened to the basic foundations of Christianity that you tell us about almost every Sunday, such as love, tolerance, and understanding?' Grundwell had said, with a cynical smile.

'Ah yes,' William replied, 'but that only applies if the mothers' group have got exactly what they want, the flower arrangers have the room where the light is best, the musicians have got total silence so that they can hear every note they play, and the choir master doesn't have to compete with the bell ringers!'

'And if there is a conflict?' asked Grundwell.

'The word *rector* becomes the most used word in Mitcheldean,' the young cleric had sighed.

As usual, William had started the day's class with Latin, a subject very close to his heart. It also stopped Alice asking *why* every time he drew breath; *quid ita* was something she was yet to learn. After about an hour, the little group switched to Greek, then after another hour, William switched to mathematics. He inwardly groaned.

'Here come the whys,' he thought to himself, 'Alice's favourite subject.'

'My grandmother says I have to stop asking *why* so much,' quipped Alice.

'Good!' replied William. 'It will help us to get on a little faster, although it does show you are interested and paying attention.'

He smiled at her, quietly thanking Mary for her intervention.

It was a delicate balance trying to keep her interest alive, while at the same time knowing that the others in the class also had to have some of his attention.

'I will have to know all about mathematics when I run the wool warehouse,' continued Alice, obviously not yet finished with him. William was a little taken aback. A girl of nearly nine declaring that sort of intention was indeed rare in the year of our Lord, 1614. It was more usual to be the beginning of the training period leading to marriage, not a life in commerce.

'And why should you want to run your grandmother's wool business? Your father runs it at the moment. He isn't that old, and I hear he's quite good at it!' William asked somewhat fascinated.

He suddenly realised he had partly answered his own question. Alice's grandmother was known throughout the area as a very astute lady. She had obviously been a driving force behind Edward, albeit he had been a very hard man in completing deals within the wool trade. Indeed, from what William had heard, he had been one of only a handful of traders representing others when buying and selling fleeces.

'I've been watching Philip Fletcher work at his table. He uses mathematics all the time, and he says it all comes down to money, and money is power!' Alice retorted.

William knew Philip was Grundwell's bookkeeper, so he had not been surprised by the remark.

'Be careful, Alice, money can make people corrupt, greedy, and jealous.' And as he said it, he knew the response.

'What's corrupt?' Alice asked.

William then explained and also told his little class the story of Jesus and the moneylenders.

The story was listened to by other ears within the building, as William's voice, although soft, had a certain penetration that could not be ignored. With the vaulting on the high ceiling being shaped as it was, his voice seemed to seek out all the corners within the building, telling every person and every crafted stone in the church the story of Jesus.

William noticed a heavily cloaked figure silently sitting close to the sanctuary screen on the far side of the nave. Although he thought he recognised the man, he could not be sure, so he carried on with his lessons. Occasionally he glanced back, his eyes searching the rest of the building as he talked.

Suddenly the figure rose from his seat and walked quietly down the aisle, then across the wide nave to where William and his pupils were working. As he came into the full light of the windows, William swiftly knelt down, took the man's hand, and kissed the large ring of office on his finger.

The man was William's archbishop.

His presence seemed to fill the church, a softly smiling and quietly spoken man, whose eyes appeared to look deep into the souls of all those who met him. His outer garments hid the clothes that heralded his office, but his demeanour and presence gave away the power that he wielded and the reverence in which he was held.

'Your Grace, what a wonderful surprise!' William beamed, having been called to his feet. 'It has been many months since we last met.'

The archbishop and William clasped hands such was their real pleasure at seeing each other again.

'William, I was passing but a few miles away, so I thought I would give my son a visit and hopefully share in his table this evening,' William's father replied, still holding his hand. 'I have two chaplains with me in attendance, but we have brought enough food in anticipation of our visit. And still being a bachelor, your mother also packed some things she has cooked. I have to admit, at one stage, this morning one of her pies was nearly sacrificed to the archbishop's stomach! The only thing that stopped me was that when I opened the wrapping there was a note inside that said 'No, Richard, this is for William.'

Both men laughed, as that was typical of William's mother. His father might hold one of the highest church offices in the land, but to his mother he was Richard Benson, the country rector from Suffolk, the man that she had fallen in love with and married over thirty years ago.

As they chatted, they walked over to where some of William's parishioners had gathered. The archbishop then talked easily and personally with every one of them. He didn't hurry; he just made each of them feel as important as he was, putting them completely at their ease. It was a knack that both father and son shared, and was one reason why William was so highly regarded within the parishes that he served.

The little group of William's pupils had also gathered by the adults. The boys looked slightly apprehensive, but Alice was simply impatient to meet the archbishop. She'd never actually met one before, and to think it was her tutor's father!

When Richard Benson finished talking to the parishioners, he walked over to the group of youngsters. William brought him a small stool from behind the screen in the nave, and his father sat down.

His son had seen him do that many times before. He gathered the youngsters around him and talked to them at their level, not looking down at them. The eight were soon chatting to him as if they were talking to their own father, telling him their likes, dislikes, what they liked to eat, what they had played when they were in the Forest, and what animals they had at home—just the talk of children.

Finally, he stood up, placed his hand on each of their heads in turn, and quietly chanted the child's blessing above each kneeling youngster.

He then turned, removed his outer garment, and laid it on the stool that he had been sitting on. By so doing, he exposed the full regalia of his office. He walked into the circle of parishioners who had knelt down with bowed heads. He stood quietly for a few seconds whilst his son joined him, and together they said the Lord's

Prayer. William then knelt in front of his father, who gave blessings for family, friendship, love, and church.

Early next morning, as he was about to leave the Mitcheldean rectory, the archbishop took his son to one side; William had been waiting for that moment. His father did not do things merely by chance, and so when he told William he was passing but a short distance away and thought he would call and see him, William had been on his guard.

'William,' his father said after a pause, 'yesterday, I sat in your church and listened to you teach some of the children of your parish. It confirmed what I and your bishop from Gloucester were already aware of. You have a natural gift for teaching young people. As you will know, the Church has been establishing cathedral schools, where we can teach scholastic subjects such as Latin and Greek, along with mathematics, the same subjects you taught yesterday. I now intend to develop such a school at my own cathedral. But I intend to offer more subjects of study and very controversially, a thespian class as well.'

William had looked quizzically at his father over his last comment.

Seeing his son's reaction, the archbishop continued, 'Well, how many boring and lifeless priests do you know who send their congregation to sleep during the first sentence of their sermon, or lose all meaning to the prayers and Bible readings that they perform?'

William had to agree that he knew many, whether they spoke in Latin or English.

'Well, thespians are taught to breathe life into words and passion into readings. If the Church is to hold its congregations into the future, we as priests don't just need belief. We need passion, conviction, realism, and above all, the ability to communicate the message of God to all the good people of this land in words that they *understand.*'

William found himself agreeing with his father again. He still awaited the reason behind all that the archbishop was saying, and he was about to find out.

'Having the funds and building in place for my school, I now need the right people in place to carry out the teaching. I have a headmaster, James Bowman, a brilliant scholar and also a good administrator. I have a fiery thespian tutor of whom all the young clerics are terrified called Estor Trotman.'

Again William waited, and his father continued, 'I now need four good tutors for my other subjects that we have just spoken about. I have found three. I now need to find a fourth.'

William looked at the archbishop. He now understood the reason behind the visit.

He said very quietly, 'Father, my parishes need me. I have only been here a short time. I replaced one of those boring and lifeless priests of whom you have just spoken. I have filled the churches with enthusiastic people again. But more than that, I have been able to give the pastoral care which you hold so dear. If you instruct me to come as my archbishop, then I will obey, but I ask you, as my father, not to take me away from my parishes and the people of the Forest.'

Richard Benson looked at his son, and he thought how close to his own values those of his son's were.

'The people have now gained confidence in me, and being the rural community that they are, that confidence together with their trust is not given lightly!' William continued.

He went on to explain what had happened to Sophie, and the pastoral care he had been able to give to her and her husband, Grundwell.

'And, Father, that help was based on personal experience as you well know from when my own sister, your daughter, was raped by our cousin. You always taught me that the pastoral care we give as priests is nearly as important as the religious aspect of our calling.'

Richard Benson turned away from his son, lest he saw the look on his face and the tears in his eyes. The memory of his daughter's rape would never fade, as neither would her trauma and suffering, all of which still haunted him.

He then understood exactly what William had meant. 'Perhaps', he reflected, 'it is I who have become too remote from my flock, and I need to heed my son's words.'

Turning back, he took his son by the hand and gently said, 'So be it, William. But I warn you, I will ask you again.'

'Yes, Father, I know that. But when you ask again, I might be ready to come to your cathedral school.'

The two men of God walked to the archbishop's carriage, and before he mounted into the leather interior, he turned to thank his son for his hospitality. William knelt in front of his archbishop and once again kissed his ring of office. The archbishop took his hands, gently pulled him to his feet, and gave him a father's embrace of farewell.

'I will tell your mother that you are well and happy. She will be disappointed that you do not join us at the cathedral, as am I. But I see you have your responsibilities to your community, and I respect and admire that commitment.'

Richard Benson paused again, and looking at his son, he quietly added with a smile, 'I feel that I am now starting to learn about the Lord from you, William, and that tells me that your tutors and life have taught you well.'

With that, the archbishop turned back and with his two chaplains, settled into the luxurious opulence of the carriage. The coachman applied his whip above his team of horses, and the parental visit was ended, as the coach and its mounted guards returned William's father to his cathedral.

# CHAPTER 10

Gumshu had learnt a lot about coal over the last twelve months.

When he had first taken over as foreman of Cottrells' mine after Ralph's death, he promised himself that his first priority would be the safety of everybody that worked in the mine and that profit and the commercial side would be a second priority.

'How wrong I have been,' he thought to himself, as he walked back from yet another meeting with the Gaveller's deputy, Thomas Sutton.

He and Thomas had got on very well from the outset, and during the first few months, Gumshu had found himself turning to Thomas for more and more advice.

Benjamin Travers's comment had been right when he had told Gumshu about Thomas.

'If you want to know anything about mines, go and see Thomas Sutton because he knows this industry better than anyone, and I promise you, you can trust him. He might work for the Crown and be involved in setting and collecting dues and revenues, but he realises the importance of the Forest miners because without them, he wouldn't have a job,' he had said.

After that particular speech, Gumshu had looked at him with a frown.

'If you know so much, why didn't you take the foreman's job?'

'I earn more by being an ordinary miner' was his simple reply.

Gumshu had noticed that. He seemed to be earning less now than when he was digging the coal out, but at least his pay was now consistent, and he had negotiated with the Cottrell brothers that he got an extra payment for good overall coal production from the workings.

All that added to his thoughts about having his own mine, but he had to admit to himself now that the profit created was as important as the safety of the colliers. The two went together; the problem was getting the balance right.

'It's no wonder Ralph was always torn between the two,' he mused as he walked. Gumshu had gone to see Thomas on that particular day to discuss the usual problems of availability of timber for shoring, and the Cottrell working's general safety.

They talked about the pressures on the natural resources of the Forest at some length, especially the lack of new plantings of trees to replenish the rapidly depleting stocks.

'The problem is', Thomas said, 'everyone wants the timber now, particularly the ship building yards, because our trees are so suitable, but they won't pay for replanting. They forget or they choose not to think about it. We have to plan for the future, and this area depends heavily on timber and *will do* for generations to come. That means we *must* replace the trees being taken now to allow for a decent growth period if nothing else.'

The meeting between the two men was held on the outskirts of the Forest because the miners didn't have a meeting hall, and neither did Thomas have a room anywhere where he could meet people like Gumshu. It was nothing to see a group of colliers sitting on a wall somewhere having heated debates about issues surrounding coal, and then retiring to the nearest tavern to lubricate their throats for further discussion.

After the meeting, Gumshu decided he would walk back to the mine, taking the track that wound through the woods on the hilltop rather than in the valley as had been his habit of late.

After Thomas's last visit to Cottrells some two months previously, he had shown considerable concern about safety. He and Gumshu had had an acrimonious meeting with the owners about overextending the excavations in the mine. Not only was the Deputy Gaveller worried about the depth and spread of the workings, he was also now concerned about possible gas accumulations, coupled with insufficient ventilation and water disposal. However, as there were no government regulations being broken, Thomas was powerless to intervene.

Gumshu, over the three months prior to official's visit, had also been expressing grave concerns about the same issues. In fact, it had been his suggestion for Thomas to make his visit because it was obvious that the owners were taking no notice of their foreman, and it was frustrating and worrying him.

As he walked, he pondered his problems over safety. He also wondered how he could possibly start out on his own because he felt that he couldn't carry on working for the Cottrells, unless there was a radical change in their approach.

He was now some 600 yards from the mine and its entrance in the valley.

He was about to turn on to the track that led down to the mouth of the excavations, when the earth under him began to shake and a sound like a never-ending roll of thunder emitted from the ground on which he was standing.

The trees around him began to vibrate with the branches and leaves moving as if every tree was being shaken by a giant's hand, and making the noise of a thousand rustlings.

One after another, tree after tree started to lean at a crazy angle and then disappear into the ground as if pulled under by a gigantic animal. Birds flew off in every direction, adding to the cacophony of sounds by screeching their alarm calls in their panic to escape.

Two foxes fled in terror from a hole under one tree, just before it crashed over and was swallowed up into the earth, leaving no trace that it had ever existed.

Gumshu was having great difficulty in keeping his balance, a task made even harder by having to avoid the numerous chasms that were opening up around him. The ever-increasing ground movements now began to push him into the valley, down towards the entrance of the mine.

The roll of thunder from underneath him had turned into an indescribable roar.

Then, as quickly as it had started, everything became still, and there was a fearful silence, save only for the cries of the circling birds high above the Forest.

The silence was suddenly shattered by the most horrific and spine-chilling screams of a dying pony, screaming in agony and panic, its back obviously broken.

Then there came the sound that every miner in the world dreads to hear—the sound of a *total* collapse when hundreds of tons of earth, clay, shale, and rock implode upon itself.

There was a terrifying crescendo of a final roar, like the death cry of a huge beast, followed by a resounding *thump* beneath the Forest floor.

That was followed by an all-engulfing cloud of dust and debris erupting from the entrance of the mine, pushed out by the pressure of the collapse inside the main chambers.

A huge crater then appeared in the ground above the workings, as if a giant had taken out a great shovelful of earth.

The pony's screams had ceased. There was once again a deathly and eerie silence; even the birds circling high above the Forest had fallen silent.

Gumshu froze in absolute horror at what he had witnessed. There was a group of colliers standing by one of the spoil heaps, close to where the tunnel entrance had been. They, too, bore witness to the collapse and were covered in a layer of filth and dust that had come from the final moments of the Cottrells' mine. They, too, appeared frozen to the ground, immobilised by the terror of the moment.

Closer to the tunnel stood a boy with his pony and cart, the cart full of coal. The child stared at where the tunnel entrance had been—the entrance from which he had emerged only seconds before.

There was no entrance now, just rubble. Beneath that rubble was the body of a dead pony, only the head visible. Attached to the pony had been a cart, with a child in attendance. There was now no evidence that either ever existed. Gumshu could still hear the screams of the dying animal in his mind, and it sent an involuntary shudder through his body.

It took several seconds for him to come out of his traumatised state. His reactions suddenly re-awakened. He urgently called down to the men by the spoil heap.

'Get your shovels and any picks that you have and go into the crater and start digging. See if you can find any shafts that lead down into the workings. Listen as you work. Listen for the slightest sound, so work in silence. Spread out, but keep in line so that you can cover the ground as thoroughly and as quickly as possible.'

The men seemed not to hear him at first, so Gumshu repeated what he'd said. Then they suddenly responded, as they too came out of their trauma of shock.

To the boy he yelled, 'We need help. We need more hands to dig. Run to the surrounding mines and tell them what's happened. Tell them we've had a *total* collapse!'

The lad didn't move or react in any way but stood and carried on staring at where the entrance had been, as if in a trance. Gumshu ran over to him and shook him by the shoulders. The boy looked up at him, eyes wide with terror.

He shook him again, recognising him as the young carter who had nearly run him down the first day he had been in the mine.

'Come on, boy. We need your help, and we need it now!' Gumshu yelled, his face only inches from the boy's.

Suddenly the youngster responded. He dropped the cart traces, turned, and ran, ran as fast as he could to the first of the adjacent mines. Gumshu could hear him yelling.

'Cottrells, there's been total collapse! There's been a total collapse!' he shouted at the top of his high-pitched voice.

But the sound of the earth imploding upon itself had sent its own deadly message out into the surrounding mining community; there were men and children, carts and ponies arriving from every direction of the Forest.

Gumshu directed the men with picks and shovels to the top of the crater, telling them to start excavating downwards, as he had instructed his own colliers. He prayed that they would find an air or drainage shaft that had not collapsed. That would give them access to the top of the workings, giving them the chance to search the adjoining galleries for any trapped miners. Excavating into the mine entrance would have been dangerous and pointless. If they couldn't find any shafts, he knew the rescuers would then have to start sinking their own rescue shafts, a dangerous and time-consuming operation. He then organised the carts that had arrived to wait in the valley close to the mine entrance so that any injured miners could be taken straight to the surgeons in Mitcheldean. He dispatched a boy to warn the two medical men in the town of impending arrivals. He sent another child off to find the rector, as he had no doubt his presence would be required. He wished he knew where Friar Benedict was, as he was sure that he would be needed as well as William.

He called one of his own miners down from where he had been digging.

'I want you to go to our village and warn people that there has been a mine accident. Anyone who has someone in the mine will want to come here, but they must know what to expect when they arrive. We will need cloth to bind any wounds or broken bones, and blankets to keep the injured warm. Find Fran and tell her we need her urgently. We will also need ale, food, and water for the rescuers.'

'Find Maisey. Tell her that I'm not hurt and then ask her to organise it all. She'll know what's needed. Then I want *you* to arrange the transport to get it all here. Someone will lend you a pony and cart. I'm sending you because you will be able to tell people what's happened and answer any questions better than anyone who didn't work at Cottrells.'

The man hurried away, repeating to himself all that Gumshu had instructed him to do and say.

Gumshu turned back and watched the rescuers. They had already divided themselves into teams—some digging, some bringing up shoring timber that they had found near the spoil heaps, some already framing and shoring out the rescue shafts their colleagues were excavating. Others had returned to their own mines to fetch ropes, more timber, and tools. All the time the numbers grew.

The rescue had begun.

Every so often, someone would call for silence, and every ear strained for the sound of movement or a call. Gumshu prayed that they would find someone who had been working in the top drift. There could have been just a possibility. He knew that those in the bottom galleries stood virtually no chance of survival; neither did those who had been working in the main hall. They would have taken the full force of the collapse. So far, of the seventy-six people who worked the mine only nine had survived, and those were the ones who had been outside the workings at the time of the disaster.

Gumshu desperately wondered if he had missed something when giving instructions to the rescuers. 'Was there anything I didn't think of? Was there something I didn't know?' He agonised as he dug, the agony of a man filled with guilt that he hadn't been in the mine, filled with guilt that his experience didn't match the task that was in front of him. His mind went back to the words of Joshua. He had never known his second name; he was just known as Joshua the Mole. On his first day in the mine, what *had* he said? Suddenly he remembered.

'When you come in the morning, also help check the shoring in the main chamber. If that caves, you're dead!'

Gumshu wondered if Joshua had survived, because he was as sure as he could be that lack of shoring timbers was the cause of the accident; nothing else could have started such a collapse of the magnitude that they were facing. He also realised that the two Cottrell brothers would have been in the mine that day as well, as they usually waited for Gumshu's return from seeing Thomas Sutton to hear about coal revenues or any cost increases by the Crown. Gumshu mentally added another two people to his list of missing colliers, becoming even more racked with guilt than before.

'I should have been in the mine. I shouldn't be alive. I should have died with my men,' he said aloud; such thoughts making him dig even harder.

Suddenly a shout went up from the rescuers on the east side of the crater. Gumshu ran over. A half-collapsed shaft had been found, cleared out, and a fresh one driven down some twelve feet further through the shale; it had been shored up to stop any collapse, and there, at the bottom, was the grinning face of Joshua the Mole. Two of the rescuers were frantically digging round him to release him from the grip of the earth. It was slow work, but eventually the Mole was lifted clear of his prison and helped out of the rescue shaft, completely unhurt.

Gumshu gave him a bear-like embrace in his relief at seeing the collier alive. The two men went down to where the mine entrance had been.

As he looked at the pile of rubble, Joshua sighed. 'I thought it sounded like a total collapse. That final *thump* seemed to have been the death throes!'

'But in that case, how did you get to where you were found?' an incredulous Gumshu asked.

'Do you remember when you and I first met? I said you had to *listen* to what the ground was telling you,' Joshua said as he looked at him.

'Well, yes, I do, along with "help check the shoring timbers in the main chamber",' Gumshu replied.

'Right, I helped check those shoring timbers this morning, and they were fine. You always kept us well supplied with any timber we wanted, Gumshu, always. But what you don't know is that the Cottrells, when you were not around, used to get the younger, less experienced miners to take timbers *out of* the main chamber. They would then use them to start new headings. That is what happened this morning. I watched them do it, and I was going tell you this afternoon after you had seen Thomas Sutton!'

Joshua sat down on a large piece of rock while he was talking, as he suddenly felt shock setting in.

Gumshu took his tunic top off and put it around the shoulders of the Mole, who then continued with his account.

'Anyway, as I have already said, you have to *listen* to what the ground is telling you. About two hours ago, I heard the ground. It was moving, and it wasn't doing it quietly either. I backed out of my tunnel and yelled to Benjamin in the next tunnel, asking him if he could hear anything.

'At first, I didn't get a response, and then suddenly he was beside me, yelling at me and asking if *I* could hear anything. We both agreed the signs were not good. To get back into the main chamber would have taken us about an hour because as you know, we were well in and deep. We both agreed the best thing to do was to find an air shaft or flood relief tunnel, then head upwards. I found one, and he found another a short distance away.

'I then found a coal box that I pushed in front of me so that if there was a collapse my head would be protected and the box would contain some air that might, just might, keep me alive until rescue.

'That is exactly what happened, thanks to you starting the rescue so soon and in a downward direction. I am sure Benjamin did the same. I've told the rescue gangs, so they are working in the right area to possibly find him.'

Joshua's was beginning to show the signs of total exhaustion as he finished his explanation and bent forward, burying his face in his hands.

'I'll give myself a few minutes, and then I'll go and join the rescue gangs up on the east side. I'm certain Benjamin made it,' he repeated, as he recovered his composure.

'I pray God you are right, my friend,' Gumshu commented, remembering all of Benjamin's help over the last twelve months, since the morning after Ralph's death.

News of the tragedy had arrived before Gumshu's messenger.

A silence had descended over the whole of Cumdean.

It didn't just affect the mining families; the whole community seemed to sense the impending doom. The men who were not at work were already collecting any shovels or tools that they thought would prove useful and making their way to the mine—a community responding to a disaster, a disaster affecting some of its own.

Most of the village women were standing in their cottage doorways, seemingly undecided what to do. Those who had family or friends working in the mine were collecting their children and making their way as fast as they could towards the scene of the accident.

Maisey was one of them.

No word was spoken and no look was exchanged; they all had but one goal—to be at Cottrells as soon as possible.

Maisey met Gumshu's messenger on the outskirts of the village. He carefully repeated everything he had been told to say, forgetting nothing, as he had repeated it to himself over and over again on the way from the mine.

Maisey only heard one part of the message. 'Gumshu says he is all right.' Beyond that, she heard nothing.

She leant against a cottage wall. She shook as tears of relief rolled down her cheeks, clutching her children around her. The messenger stood beside her, not knowing quite what to say or do. She looked at him, suddenly realising that her husband wouldn't have said just that; there was more she hadn't heard.

'What else did you say?' she asked, standing up straight and looking at the man her husband had sent. He again repeated word for word what he had been told to say.

Once she had got over her initial relief, Maisey's natural ability to organise sprang into action. She sent the messenger off to borrow a pony and trap from Samuel Longden, a yeoman farmer who owned a smallholding on the other side of the village.

'Ask him if he could drive it for me as I need *you* to go round telling people exactly what has happened. Tell Samuel to meet us at my cottage,' she added.

She ran back into the centre of the village, against the flow of other people, looking for helpers. She didn't want to stop anyone going to the mine or slow them down, so she asked the women whose men or children didn't work at Cottrells.

Maisey and her children raced from cottage to cottage, gathering everything they could think of that could be wanted. She arrived back at her own cottage with a small army of helpers. She went through Gumshu's list again in her head, to check that she had everything he had asked her to get. She even remembered the wood for the splints, something he had forgotten. Fran ran up to her with an armful of healing remedies. When Samuel Longden arrived at the cottage to meet Maisey, he had brought his own cart, as well as two driven by his neighbours. They loaded the first one with all the things that Fran said she needed to tend the injured, and with her on it, the cart sped off to the mine.

As Maisey climbed on to Samuel's cart with her children, he turned to check the contents.

'The rescuers will want to work into the night. Have we got oil, rags, and sticks to make torches?' he asked.

'No, we haven't!' she replied, looking desperately around.

Samuel suggested that they send the third cart back to his smallholding to collect the materials they wanted and also call on his other neighbours to ask for the same things. 'Hopefully,' he said, 'that will give us enough to make torches that will last the night.'

Mindful of her omission, she asked out loud if anyone could think of anything she had forgotten.

'The Lord's mercy' came a deep voice from behind her.

She turned round and there, as if by a miracle, was Father Benedict. She bent her head as if tears were about to flow.

'Come on, Maisey. No time for that now,' he said. 'Tears can be shed *after* the rescue.'

With that, he reached up and gently squeezed her hand, and the party of volunteers, together with Samuel's cart, swiftly set off for the mine.

Gumshu was once again on top of the crater formed by the collapse. He had now re-organised the rescue volunteers, splitting them into three teams. Each team dug for an hour, then swopped with one of the other teams, who were either resting or bringing up and placing shoring timber for the rescue shafts that were being driven down. That way he could keep the men as fresh as possible, and also hold a reserve team in case they were needed urgently in one particular part of the collapse.

It also meant he could regulate the number of people on the crater at any one time. Such were their numbers they had become a danger to themselves, and unintentionally started to hinder the speed and efficiency of the rescue operation.

He also sent some of the youngsters into the woods to cut thin saplings. The rescuers then used them to carefully probe into the earth and shale to feel for any evidence of a collapsed shaft, or even a man's body.

The biggest problem that they were facing was the quantity of trees that had been swallowed up into the collapse.

When they were probing, a tree had been mistaken for a man's body on more than one occasion, and precious time had been lost excavating down through the debris to see what the obstruction actually was.

A crowd had now gathered in the bottom of the valley—wives and children, mothers and fathers, brothers and sisters, sweethearts and friends, their sombre and strained faces portraying the fact that they had someone trapped underground. There were few tears and little conversation, just a terrible look of fear and anticipation. They waited, they prayed, and they waited, never taking their eyes from the scene of devastation that was once Cottrells' mine.

Maisey, Samuel, Father Benedict, and the volunteers arrived close to the mine entrance, where Gumshu had prepared carts to take any of the seriously injured to the surgeons. Fran had set another area aside to treat any of the miners who were less seriously injured. Her only patients had been Joshua the Mole, whom Gumshu had sent to her to check that he had no hidden injuries, and the child carter, whom she had wrapped in a woollen blanket to keep him warm until his parents arrived to collect him.

Seeing his family's arrival, Gumshu ran down into the valley, gathering up his wife and children into his arms to embrace them, turning his head away so that no one saw his tears. Maisey looked at him with tremendous relief in her eyes.

'The foreman's job has just saved your life, my love,' she whispered.

They had talked some nights earlier about the miners being able to earn more than him. He had said then that he might well return to being an ordinary collier again.

He half smiled and nodded, as he had been thinking the same thing she had.

Putting all thoughts of himself to one side, he asked Samuel Longden if he would organise the torches once the third cart arrived and take them up on to the crater so that they were ready when darkness fell. 'Something else I forgot!' he said to Samuel with a wry smile.

He then turned to the friar. 'I am glad to see you, Father. I think we are going to need both you and William tonight.'

'Looking at this, I would think so, Gumshu. I'll take water to the men who are digging, and that will keep me in the right place if I'm needed,' he continued with a meaningful look. 'But first let me go and talk to those who wait.'

Gumshu returned to the crater and started digging again, digging and organising the teams of men who now strove to save the lives of those who were entombed beneath them. Meanwhile, Maisey and her volunteers set about organising the food and water for the group of rescuers presently resting, and then she moved quietly amongst the people who waited. The friar donned a goatskin bag full of water and hung some mugs on his belt, going to each of the rescuers in turn to make sure that they had a drink. He was joined by William Benson, and the two men administered refreshment to all who wanted it.

They then walked amongst those who waited down in the valley, those who waited with immeasurable patience, with dignity, and now in near total silence.

'There are no words we can offer them that will relieve their suffering and heartache,' William quietly said to the friar. 'We can't even offer them hope.'

The searching questions about God's intent towards man would come later, but it was a question both men knew would be asked by many of those involved.

The procedure of silence, listen, and probe had now been established on a regular basis. The rescue had been in progress for nearly five hours, and only Joshua the Mole had been dug out.

A call then went up. Gumshu raced over to where the shout had come from. Joshua was already there, standing and looking down a rescue shaft. At the bottom, where two rescuers had been clearing, was the top of a box similar to the one under which he had been found. Very carefully, the two miners lifted it up and pushed it to one side.

There was the smiling and relieved face of Benjamin Travers.

There was a loud cheer, and the two rescuers very carefully cleared around Benjamin's body to release him from the grip of the earth. Once that was done, he was slowly brought to the top of the shaft. The friar and William took over from there, the friar lifting him clear and then gently carrying him down into the valley, laying him on some woollen blankets that Fran had laid out ready in one of the carts.

She and William slowly and purposefully went over every bone and every part of his body to find out the extent of any injuries. Just as they had nearly finished, Benjamin's wife and children arrived at his side. The emotion between the reunited family members would have cured any ailment, save the broken arm that his wife's hug had found. Fran and the rector bound the arm to a splint, and after some discussion between the two, they decided that the cart should take him back to the village, where Benjamin's wife could look after him herself.

The rescue continued throughout the night, with the torches surrounding the crater lighting up the sweating, drawn, and tired faces of the rescuers. They appeared to move around like grey statues that had come to life in the flickering lights, the grey coming from the colour of the mud and slime that lay in the crater.

Nine times through the night, a cry went up. Nine times the rescuers moved with care and hope. Nine times a village family's silent prayers were answered.

William and Fran did what they could for all who were found. Two of the nine had serious bone breaks to legs, arms, and backs, and they were immediately sent to the surgeons in Mitcheldean.

Once Fran and William had checked them for injuries, the other seven were sent back to the village in carts, wrapped in woollen blankets for warmth.

Each time a cry had gone up, each time there had been a call for quiet, the waiting faces on the floor of the valley had looked up with expectancy, with hope, and with prayer. Each time a family had been reunited, there was joy, there was laughter, and there were tears of relief.

For the families who were left, there was further prayer, there was despair, there was desperation, but there was always that forlorn hope that the person they loved would, by some miracle, be restored to them.

'No children have been found yet,' William said quietly to Gumshu, as he gave him some water.

'There will be none, William,' he replied, his voice shaking. 'They were all working in the bottom gallery of the mine.'

Tears sprang to the young cleric's eyes as he turned to look up at the crater.

The streaks of dawn began to appear in the eastern sky, and with the retreat of the night came the retreat of hope for those still entombed underground.

Full dawn then came.

The light was cold, the sky grey, and the morning without warmth or solace.

With the torches extinguished, the rescuers paused to take stock.

Gumshu was standing in the middle of the crater; beside him was Thomas Sutton who had arrived just before midnight, and he too had been digging alongside Gumshu and his teams. Joshua the Mole stood with them, as did Father Benedict and William

Benson. They looked around them at the rescuers, both the effort and the raw emotion now showing on their mud and sweat-soaked faces. They appeared both physically and mentally drained, but still there remained a grim determination to find anyone who might have survived the terrible accident. However, the rescue shafts themselves had now become places of danger, adding extra risks to the lives of the rescuers.

Gumshu looked into the valley, down at the families who waited, down at the souls who prayed. The greyness of the dawn seemed to exaggerate their features, stark and bereft of hope, fearful of his next words, knowing by instinct what he was going to have to say.

Suddenly out of the crowd, a little boy of no more than five came forward, crying and looking up into his face. He pointed into the ground.

'Please, please, Master Gumshu, find my father!' His mother then came forward and took the child's hand, and she too looked up at him, saying nothing, but the pleading was in her eyes.

Thomas Sutton said to him, very quietly so that only those within their small circle could hear, 'My friend, you are about to take the hardest decision you will ever take in your life. May God guide you.'

Gumshu looked at Joshua, who very gently shook his head.

'We now risk other lives, to add to the ones we have already lost,' he said, as quietly as Thomas.

The friar and William Benson looked at Gumshu, and they too nodded in agreement at Joshua's words.

He looked back into the valley again, and he looked for and found Maisey. Her face and her eyes pleaded with him to go on, pleaded with him to give the rescue more time.

'We dig for another hour, and then we must stop!'

His voice was not challenged, but hope once again showed on the faces below him.

For another hour, the men of the Forest toiled, sweated, listened, probed, and prayed. For another hour, the waiting families kept their vigil in silence, in hope, with their innermost thoughts calling to the Lord to be merciful, yearning for those that they loved.

At the hour's end, both William Benson and Friar Benedict went down into the valley. They walked amongst all those who waited and made the sign of the cross upon their foreheads.

They then knelt down in front of the families who joined them and all the rescuers, in a prayer for the dearly departed.

# CHAPTER 11

Time had passed on since that fateful day of the mine collapse. Bones had mended and tiredness forgotten. But the grief of the families would never pass; neither would the memories of those who were killed ever dim. The mine was sealed off on the instructions of the Gaveller, the crater filled in, and the trees replanted.

At the entrance stood a large wooden cross which had been erected by the Forest miners. No names were on it, but there were fifty-eight cuts upon the timber, a cut for every soul who had been lost. In a simple but emotion-filled service, William Benson and Friar Benedict carried out a blessing to the cross, a blessing that would remain for time immemorial.

The scars on the minds of the survivors had been a more difficult problem. They had to get over the guilt of living. Those who had been rescued also had to come to terms with their memories of the mine, the mine that could have become their tomb. All but two were now, so they said, ready to go back to their work as colliers.

The worst case of all the survivors had been the child carter. His memories seemed never to have dimmed. He had vivid nightmares, and his parents had asked William Benson for help, although so serious he had thought the problem to be, he doubted if the lad would ever improve and lead a normal life again.

The rector and Father Benedict spent many hours at the village, applying the pastoral care that they both passionately believed in, so much so that when Archbishop Benson paid another visit to his son, he never thought of mentioning the teaching post at the cathedral school. He and William talked into the night, talked of many things, but mainly of how to help with grief.

William finally looked at his father and asked the question for which he did not know the answer, and he wondered if his father would. The question was: *'What was God's intention to man?'* What answer could he give to those who had asked after such a disaster? His father looked into his son's troubled eyes.

'That is one question for which I do not have an answer, and it is the answer that I have been searching for since I found there was a God.'

Even though it had been nine months since the accident, those who had either lost loved ones or been injured were still being supported and helped by the Forest community.

'We'll be here as long as they need us,' Joshua the Mole had declared one evening.

The village community, however, realised that things now had to move on.

'It's easy to say but hard to do,' William Benson said to the friar when they discussed it.

'Pray to God that the mine owners learn something,' the friar responded with concern. 'Lessons have to be learned by everyone. Safety and the true value of a human life are the first priorities. Fifty-eight lives lost in one accident is too high a cost to pay.'

Those lessons were uppermost in Gumshu's mind as he planned the opening of his own mine. Now that he met the criteria for such an operation, his enthusiasm and impatience to start were beginning to have no bounds. With his contacts, he gained a licensed location for the mine; an extraction licence from the Crown, with rent and levies set; a small workforce; and with the help of a local forge, all the tools and mine transport he would need.

Now his friend, the smallholder, Samuel Longden, agreed to provide transport for the coal from the mine to any customer whom Gumshu sold the coal to. They came to an agreement on the rates; all that was needed now was the coal.

Gumshu looked at the side of the wooded valley and wondered. Joshua and Benjamin stood beside him, sweating and praying. All three were suffering from nerves. Gumshu took hold of the digging spade and marked the entrance to his first drift mine. Maisey stood behind him with the four children, and she wondered what the future would hold for them all.

Little did she know that that day was the beginning of a dynasty that would provide wealth and power beyond her imagination for her family now, and for future generations.

That day, there was but a small gathering. The three miners started to dig. Within an hour, the shape of the entrance was formed and the shoring timbers that were stacked beside them were started to be used. Then William Wheeler, together with two of the other miners who had been rescued from Cottrells, came down on to the valley floor. They looked towards Gumshu, who waved them towards the pile of newly forged tools, and they too started to do the only thing that came naturally to a collier—to dig.

Maisey and the children returned to the village. She didn't know whether to be happy or terrified when she saw Gumshu start their mine. But when she saw the look on his face, she saw the enthusiasm, she saw the sense of adventure in his eyes, and she witnessed a transformation in his character, back to the anticipation of his youth.

'I'll get the *very cold* washing water ready,' she said with a mischievous smile. She also realised they hadn't used the 'potion' for many months, so that night, she thought she'd put some in *his* drink for a change! The children had gone to play with their friends from the smallholding.

She walked over to her hiding place, pulled the two stones clear, and peered inside. The large red bottle with the peculiar stopper had gone. Instead, there was a pot of honey, with a note attached to it in Gumshu's terrible writing.

All it said was 'Far better for you, and at least I'll get some sleep tonight!' She was a slow reader, but the note made her giggle to herself.

'That's what you think, my husband,' she muttered out loud.

Luckily, Little Emmy didn't hear the full sentence, only hearing *'my husband'* as she came in through the cottage door. But she was now old enough to know that whenever she heard her mother refer to Gumshu as *her husband*, it was always worth pretending to be asleep then listen to her parents 'frolicking' as she called it. Gumshu and Maisey would have been mortified if they'd known, having had enough audiences to their passionate encounters.

Gumshu returned home from the mine, after walking the twenty minutes' journey with his now foremen, Joshua the Mole and Benjamin. Benjamin had been given the task of looking after the outside functions of the mine. He arranged the supply of timber for shoring; he ensured that the excavated material dumped was within the distances set by the Gaveller. He also organised the excavated coal into graded heaps ready for transport by Samuel

Longden. Joshua, meanwhile, tended to the mine's underground organisation and production.

The three men parted company in front of Gumshu's cottage, whereupon Maisey came out of the front door, took her husband by the hand, and led him to the spring at the back of the cottage, which she referred to as the washing area, but Gumshu referred to as '*Maisey's torture pit*'.

He stood over the little pool again, remembering the other miners' laughter on the morning they caught him looking at himself. He felt a sudden feeling of desolation; everyone of that group was now dead. His mood lasted only a few seconds, and then Maisey stripped him of his grey-encrusted working clothes, her hands lingering a few seconds more than they should have done over certain parts of his body.

Gumshu's manhood suddenly started to react to the encouragement. Maisey dodged clear of his large powerful hands, grabbed her first pail that she had already filled with ice-cold water, and fired it at the part that was beginning to cause him some embarrassment. The effect was truly amazing; his embarrassment disappeared within seconds. Then the second, third, fourth, and fifth pails of water hit their intended target with Maisey's expertise in water throwing. The sixth pail was reserved to wash the clay out of Gumshu's hair. That was Maisey's undoing.

As she reached up to pour the water on his hair and rub it to remove the bits of clay, he spun around, grabbed her, snatched the pail, filled it with water in one scoop, and discharged it down the front of her dress.

Father Benedict would have been proud of him.

There followed what could only be described as a brawl between the two. Luckily, the surrounding briars that Maisey had left around the pool to prevent the dogs and the wild pigs from soiling it had long gone, as had the pigs. To whose table the animals had actually gone had been a matter of speculation in the village for some time, but gone they were.

The two ended up fighting and rolling in the grass around the pool. By the time peace had been declared, *both* of them needed to wash themselves down.

Maisey stripped down to her undergarments, with some enthusiastic help from Gumshu. Luckily no one was around to see the two re-engage in close combat, or the successful conclusion of the collier's efforts to completely disrobe his wife. They were, however, heard by their children, and during one lull in the proceedings, Little Emmy was heard to say to the other children that Mother and Father were just having a little *'frolic'*.

Gumshu was pleasantly relaxed after the water fight. Maisey was changed and looked fresh faced *'and somehow radiant'*, he thought. The food simmering in the cooking pot over the fire was full of meat and herbal aromas, and the candles had been lit, casting their flickering lights into all the corners of the room.

Gumshu was attempting to start some paperwork for the coal production of the mine, and having little success. Maisey brought the meal to the table, and as the children were already in their night clothes, she served them first. Gumshu moved his papers, making room for the covered platter that Maisey brought to him. She lifted the cover for her husband. Underneath was a pot of honey and nothing else. Gumshu rested his chin on his hand, smiled, got up, and then chased his laughing wife around the room, much to the children's delight.

Some months later, the two lay awake discussing the mine. They talked of the future, which they had often done since the accident.

'Life can be very short, and who knows what tomorrow will bring,' Maisey said.

Gumshu nodded, reflecting on not only the mine accident, but also on the loss of his daughter.

He turned his mind back to the present and their new venture. Joshua had now got a total of seven miners working under him whilst Benjamin had three. Gumshu was either working where he was required in the mine, or out selling the coal they had won. That latter task he tackled with great relish and with such enthusiasm that there came a great deal of success.

The high sales were based on several factors, as well as his own ability to sell. He had a reputation brought from Cottrells of being fair on price; the coal was clean and of good quality, as well as being well graded by Benjamin and his men, and finally, the coal was delivered on time by Samuel Longden—all definite advantages over most of their competitors.

The combination had produced some extremely buoyant sales, and with the revenue created, Gumshu was able to richly reward his colliers for their labours.

He was extremely pleased with the result; even after paying for all his rents, levies, timber, and labour, there was still a princely amount remaining. The only problem he had to wrestle with was his bookkeeping, and he spent many long hours at night trying to resolve it, so much so that on many nights he got no rest at all, much to Maisey's concern.

In desperation, Gumshu went to see Grundwell to ask for advice, and together they talked to Philip Fletcher, Grundwell's bookkeeper. Philip suggested that Gumshu should approach his brother, Edmund, who was also a bookkeeper. He was presently working on the docks in Chepstow but wanted a change. He was also well acquainted with the coal trade. Gumshu had arranged a trip to Chepstow that week, so he took the opportunity to meet with Edmund.

'The trouble is', he said to Maisey, as they lay side by side in the candlelight, 'I am very well aware that he won't produce anything.'

'Yes, he will!' she responded sharply. 'He'll produce the figures on the paper, and they are nearly as important as the coal out of the ground. You've had good money from the mine over these last few months, but do you actually *know* if it's making a profit? Because there's cash left after paying all the costs doesn't mean it has done. For example, have you allowed enough for taxes?'

Gumshu rolled over and looked at his wife with a quizzical eye.

'Mm!' was all he said as he extinguished the candle and moved his hands underneath the bedcovers, trying to divert her mind from the commercial aspect of their life. 'You'd better go and warn Little Emmy we're about to "frolic",' he murmured.

The following day, Gumshu met Edmund at the mine. An affable sort of man, he toured the inside and outside of the mine workings and was impressed by the organisation of the man running it and that of his two foremen.

'I'll work for you part-time to start with, and then as the mine increases in size, I'll come to you full-time,' he offered as the two went to meet Samuel Longden, discussing payments and where Edmund would carry out his bookkeeping tasks as they walked.

When they met Samuel, he told them he owned a building that could well suit their needs. The three men visited the cluster of sheds beyond his cottage. One proved ideal, for not only was it spacious and watertight but also convenient. As Samuel was providing the cartage, the loads of coal being delivered to the customers could be counted out and checked, without the newly appointed bookkeeper needing to be at the mine; thus, he could calculate revenue. The quantity of items like shoring timbers, tools, hours of labour, and transport could be reported back to Edmund as they were utilised, enabling him to keep an accurate costing when added to all the hidden government costs.

Theoretically, deducting total costs from total revenue would give them the profit figure, the bookkeeper explained. Gumshu was extremely happy with the outcome of the meeting, especially as Maisey approved of Edmund when she met him later in the day. All that was needed then was to extract as much good coal as possible from the seams that they had struck, and then for the mine owner to sell it.

Within a month, Edmund had joined them full-time. Joshua the Mole was quite amazed. He had not seen such a rich seam of coal for many years, and it was so accessible the miners were actually standing up to extract it rather than lying on their stomachs. That was almost unheard of in such a new project.

Thomas Sutton visited the mine three times in the first twelve months, and he too was struck by the organisation that went into the running of the operation.

Unbeknown to Gumshu, there was another mine, a mile and a half up the same Forest valley and on the same seam as his; it was about to be taken away from the existing operators. One reason for the Deputy Gaveller's visits was to assess the capabilities of the new mine operator and his team, to see whether they were ready to start another project.

It, too, had a large coal reserve that was easily accessible. Unfortunately, the brothers running it had fallen out, so rather than give it to either one thus causing more friction, it had been decided that the best course of action was for it to be leased to another operator.

Gumshu gave an unreserved *yes* when Thomas offered him the mine. He, his foremen, and Edmund went to see it on the first morning it was available. It needed complete reorganisation, both inside and outside.

As Joshua commented, the miners who had decided to stay when the ownership changed also needed to be reminded that their purpose in life was to dig and extract coal, not to drink ale. The other issue that had to be addressed was that of child workers operating within the mine. Gumshu was adamant that he would not have any children working underground in *any* mine that he owned. Outside yes, inside *no* was the rule.

No one ever argued with him because everyone knew both the story of the child carter at Cottrells and that *not one* of the children working underground had survived.

After the mine's reorganisation, a cart track was constructed along the floor of the valley, linking the two mines together. That made communications much easier and the sharing of resources much simpler and cost-effective.

'The mines need to bear a name for ease of identification and costing,' Edmund suggested, after confusion had arisen over some materials that were incorrectly entered.

'So that we can tell which one is the most profitable!' Maisey countered.

Gumshu wondered where his fulsome wife had suddenly developed such a taste for commerce. When he mentioned it to her one evening as they sat by the fire, she looked at him with a demure smile.

'I've never had the chance before, Husband dear!'

On hearing that remark, Little Emmy wondered if that was a sign of a forthcoming frolic. As there were no further sounds from her exhausted parents, she eventually went to sleep, disappointed.

The following day at the mine, Gumshu collected his two foremen. After completing their usual morning tour of inspection, they walked to the converted farm shed where Edmund was standing at a table working on his journals.

'We need to name the mines, as Edmund and I discussed yesterday,' Gumshu said. 'Well, has anyone got any ideas?' Silence followed the question.

'Right, in that case how about naming them after large, black, or dark birds?'

'That's as good as anything,' Joshua replied. 'I like fishing myself, but I can't see mines named trout and pike. It doesn't sound right.'

Benjamin nodded, as he was in agreement with Gumshu's idea of the dark birds.

'How about Hawk for our first mine and Crow for our second?'

There was agreement from the two men, and as Maisey had already agreed, the decision was taken about the names the two mines would carry. Whilst they had been talking, Edmund had done a sketch of a hawk, as his drawing skills matched those of his bookkeeping.

'How about this as our mark?' he said, showing the colliers his sketch. The three were again in full agreement, Gumshu being particularly enthusiastic, as he was sure Maisey would approve as well.

'What a wonderful sketch, Edmund, and what a good idea!' she enthused when she arrived at the shed to join them.

'We have only one slight problem now. We can't keep calling this place *the shed*, so how about we call it the *coal building*?' she continued.

'Well, that's original!' her husband replied, laughing, but neither he nor the others could think of a better name.

Gumshu was now travelling further afield in his search for customers. He sold to the Forest forges; he sold to the limekiln owners; he sold to householders and landowners alike. He visited not only the towns of Gloucestershire but also Herefordshire and parts of Wales.

'I follow the rivers if I get lost,' he replied to his wife when she enquired how he found his way in strange areas. 'I wish I had a boat sometimes, not just a pony and trap!'

Samuel Longden had to buy two extra wagons and oxen teams, now having a total of six delivering the Hawk coal. He did remark to his wife one evening after a particularly busy autumn day of deliveries, that he could see an end to their farming days in the not too distant future. She replied that that time couldn't come soon enough.

Eighteen months later came the chance of yet another mine. That one, again, was on the same coal seam and in the same Forest valley, but a mile to the west of the original Hawk mine. Gumshu and Maisey agonised about taking it over.

Like their second mine, Crow, it was available because of an argument between the two men who held the present lease. Whereas Crow had been an easy decision, this one meant they would have to find a foreman who could be trusted to run it, and neither of them was of the opinion that any of their own colliers were suitable for such responsibility.

At the present, Joshua ran Hawk, Benjamin ran Crow, and Gumshu sold the coal, whilst Maisey and Edmund did the overall organisation and bookwork.

Gumshu decided to seek Thomas Sutton's advice.

'There's a miner I know called Elijah Cribwall, a Cornishman. He's mined everything there is to mine, but I'm not sure of his experience in our type of drift working,' Thomas said. 'It's the usual thing. He's met a Gloucestershire girl who lives in Mitcheldean, and having moved here, he can't find work! His last job was running a tin mine somewhere on the north Cornish coast from what I'm told.'

Gumshu decided to visit him the following day, as Thomas had told him where the lady and her Cornish miner were living. That was near the church, down a lane opposite the lych gate and a grass bank. The track had a thatched cottage at the end of it.

Thomas asked him if he knew the place and was surprised when Gumshu started laughing. He then told the deputy the story of how he had first met William Benson.

The collier and the Cornish tin miner had a long discussion, and Gumshu got the impression that the man could deal with all types of mining operation, not just those limited to tin. The *only* problem was that he lived so far from the proposed mine.

In the end, Elijah and Lisbeth, his lady, decided that if there was a cottage available to rent in Cumdean, they would take it and live in the village. At the moment, they shared the Mitcheldean cottage with Lisbeth's parents, which, in Elijah's words, could possibly lead to murder being done. As he had not elaborated, Gumshu hadn't asked.

The new mine was named Rook, and it seemed to have all the attributes of the other two mines, with the added advantage that it had been well run. It had sixteen miners, all hard working and not as fond of the ale during working time as had been the case with the miners at Crow. Gumshu and Elijah organised the working patterns to be similar to the Hawk and Crow, with a small team running the outside and a larger team excavating and cutting out the coal. They also linked it to the other Hawk mines by means of a cart track.

When Gumshu told Samuel about the new acquisition, the carter looked at him with a smile, saying, 'Now you'd better go out and sell a *lot* more coal!'

That was a point not lost on Gumshu.

With the approach of May, it was decided by the villagers that they would hold a maypole celebration, as had been the annual custom before the mine accident. There had been no heart for such partying the first two years after the disaster, but this year the Forest community was endeavouring to return to normal in as many ways as possible.

The Reverend William Benson had been a little dubious when told of the plans, because in certain parts of urban England the age-old custom was thought to be close to paganism and was frowned on by some Church authorities.

However, Friar Benedict took him to one side and explained that this was *rural* England in 1617, and dancing the maypole *they did*.

What he omitted to tell him was that the party that followed, especially when colliers were involved, was a gastronomic bonanza of wonderful proportions, washed down with copious amounts of ale and mead. That particular event was going to be held in June, as in many other country parts of England, because the weather was warmer than in May, with far more flowers growing in the surrounding woodlands, flowers that would play a very important role in the celebrations of the day.

There were also more hours of daylight to eat and drink, but that was only Friar Benedict's thoughts on the matter.

Maisey and Gumshu laughingly talked about all the previous village maypole days they had been involved with and how their pre-dawn frolics in the woods, supposedly gathering flowers, had caused some parental raised eyebrows as well as raised voices.

The two were sitting on the grass bank by the babbling Forest stream when the conversation had taken place. They were having a quiet stroll after their evening meal, one reason being to escape from the four children, whose main topic of conversation was the coming event. Little Emmy persisted in asking why she couldn't dance around the maypole.

'Because you're far too young! It's a fertility dance for the people who will be getting married soon,' her mother explained to her, and as soon as she said it she regretted it because she knew the next question before it was asked.

'Does fertility mean the dancing makes you have babies?' Little Emmy persisted.

'Well, it doesn't make you, but it just might help, so the stories say!' Her mother replied, trying to evade any more questions from her inquisitive eldest daughter.

Gumshu put his arm around her as they retreated out of the door and laughingly said, 'You asked for that, my love!'

The peace and understanding the two found in each other's company could only be described as something that appeared to be heaven-created, as there seemed to be no logical explanation. On many occasions, there was no need for speech between the two; a glance was enough to know exactly what the other was thinking. Even when they were apart, there appeared to be an instinctive bond between them.

'Being born on the same night, and in the same village, was a definite influence,' the friar had remarked knowingly one day when the three were talking about the subject.

This night was no exception. Their thoughts were as one.

Gumshu took his lover's hand and looked into her eyes, and with his voice so soft it could only just be heard above the quiet babbling of the stream, he asked, 'When is the next little one due?'

His wife's large brown eyes filled with tears, tears of joy, not of sadness. She leant against him and squeezed his hand, and in a voice as soft as his, she answered, 'In eight months, I would think.'

There were no words spoken between them for several minutes. The high-pitched calling of a passing bat, whose hunger had made it an early riser, a distant dog barking, and the constant murmur of the stream were their only companions in sound.

'How did you know?' she asked, breaking the silence.

'Do you remember that first day we started the Hawk mine, and we had a water fight in the evening when I came home?

'Yes, I do,' she answered. 'But, my love, that was about *two years ago!*'

'I know, but you had a certain radiant look on your face that night, and whenever you get that look, I know you want a child. It has happened with all the others, and you have always conceived within two years.'

She gazed into her husband's eyes, not quite believing him, but awaiting tender words of love and romance.

'But please, please, not twins again!' he begged, endeavouring to get away from her. Laughing, she managed to roll on top of him before he escaped, her long chestnut hair cascading down over his face.

'You know you're trouble, Master Gumshu, *too* much frolicking,' she said as she kissed him before slowly standing up, the most wonderful radiant smile on her face. Taking both his hands, she pulled him to his feet.

'Shall we go and tell Katherine?' she asked him, and without waiting for a reply let go of one of his hands, and the two walked silently towards the churchyard to tell their daughter the news.

# CHAPTER 12

Grundwell, Sophie, and their children had also been invited to the maypole celebrations in Cumdean.

Gumshu called at Craven Street with the news of their impending addition to the family, and at the same time issued the invitation to his two lifelong friends and their offspring. He also asked if Grundwell could tell Philip Fletcher, his bookkeeper, of a similar invitation from his brother Edmund.

'But *I thought* that such things were to influence and encourage youthful union and fertility, with the young of the village dancing around a foliage-bedecked, multicoloured maypole. That's *after* the boys scatter vast amounts of flowers around their true love's abode, flowers that they had gathered from the woods prior to dawn. Surely it's not supposed to be an excuse for a party for people of our age?' Grundwell enquired mischievously.

'Yes, you're quite right,' his friend responded. 'But when have we ever needed an excuse for celebrations? Anyway, we'll leave the first part of the day to the youngsters, as I really don't think that any of us are in need of any more fertility, do you?'

'Certainly not!' came the response from Sophie, with a sharp glance at her husband.

Trying to ignore the look that had just passed between his two friends, Gumshu explained, 'Well, Maisey and Lisbeth are organising the day, for both young and old. Their idea is that we'll watch the procession with the maypole in the morning, and then everyone has food at midday, outside if it's fine or in the church if there is rain. After the meal, we'll start our own dancing to music from two musicians that Maisey has found in Mitcheldean. William found them to be honest, and he says they are very good.

'Everyone is helping with the food, and I'm buying the ale and mead from that merchant beyond Saint Michael's Church, in case we haven't brewed enough ourselves by then. Oh, and whilst I remember, Sophie, Mary and your Forest parents are invited too!' Gumshu concluded, suddenly remembering Maisey's last words before he left this morning.

'Don't forget to ask Sophie's parents, *all* of them!' she'd said, and he nearly had.

'We'll bring food and drink with us as well. I'll call in at the merchant if you like and collect anything that you may be short of. I'll pay, and we can sort it out when we meet,' Grundwell offered. 'We'll be in the pony and trap, so we might as well. We can also bring William Benson, if he wants to come with us.'

Gumshu grimaced and dropping his voice answered, 'Ah, there we have a slight problem. I think he is still of the opinion that maypole dancing verges on the pagan and has reservations about it all, in spite of Father Benedict's *sort* of persuasion. The upshot being, I honestly don't know if he'll come.'

'I can imagine what was said,' laughed Sophie, knowing that the friar was not well known for tact and diplomacy.

'You're right. I think the words were "This is rural England in 1617,' and maypole dancing *we do*"!' Gumshu smiled as he continued, 'And yes, before you ask, the friar will be there on the day. Maisey and I were talking the other evening, and we can't remember one he hasn't been to. Do you remember, Grundwell, the first May celebration we went to?'

'Only too well! We went out well before dawn. The girls had told us where to go to gather the most flowers, and then they ambushed us,' Grundwell responded, taking hold of Sophie around the waist and giving her a kiss square on the lips. She giggled like a teenager. Gumshu smiled to himself. Perhaps his two friends were back on course again after all, in spite of the last three years, but Sophie's sharp look at her husband earlier troubled him.

As he guided his pony and trap out of Craven Street to go home, he noticed the large half-timbered house on the corner. With its faded paint, overgrown toft, and broken gate, it was obviously still not lived in, even after all the passing years, and a thought struck him.

After Gumshu left them, Grundwell and Sophie sat quietly by the fire, waiting for Mary. Grundwell had come home especially to discuss an idea with the two ladies, as his wife had now become as much a part of the business as Mary.

He had been going through some figures with Philip that morning, and the more he looked at them, the more he was convinced that there was now a need to look at fresh markets for the wool, fresh ideas for their products, and a complete revision of the business.

In the last two years, under his stewardship, it had expanded dramatically. More wooden buildings had been erected around the warehouse, housing not only areas specifically for the production of cloth, but also for the manufacture of a range of woollen goods. They were now one of the biggest wool merchants and manufacturers in southern England, mainly due to the fact that they took in a vast variety of fleeces in addition to those of the Ryeland sheep. Not only did Grundwell travel all over England buying wool, but into Wales as well.

Eventually Mary burst in through the door, carrying two large packages which she deposited on the floor in the corner of the room. 'No peeping!' she instructed her daughter.

She sat down on one of the oak settles and took a mug of ale from John, who always miraculously appeared when he heard Mary come home from an excursion. He also had a knack of managing to be absent when one of the other family members wanted him.

'Now, what do we need to talk about?' she said, removing her outer cloak when she had warmed up in front of the fire.

Grundwell briefly explained his idea to the two women, to which Mary replied, 'So let me get this straight. We've got three *fulling mills* of our own further up the county and in Herefordshire. We employ well over 200 people drawn from the surrounding area as direct workers within our own buildings, as well as countless outworkers who operate in their own homes, not only in Mitcheldean but other local towns as well.

'We have an English trade that goes beyond London and even as far as Yorkshire and across into Lancashire. We trade across most of Wales. We also have an overseas trade from Bristol, Plymouth, and Chepstow to both Ireland, Europe, and beyond for our raw wool, woven cloth, spun yarn, *and* woollen goods, which is second to none. The raw wool which we don't export or use ourselves, we resell to other cloth makers.

'We own two of our own *trows* for moving our goods around the coasts of the Bristol Channel, and we also transport other merchant's cargoes when there is space. We have a warehouse and rented buildings that can store up to twelve months worth of fleeces for our requirements. We have weaving sheds and finished product manufacturing facilities that even dwarf our warehouse, and now you want more?'

Grundwell cleared his throat and his mind and then carried on with his explanation.

'It's not the fact that I want more. I feel we need to safeguard what we have, by a switch in direction and diversification, and we also need to plan for the future.

'The biggest problem, at the moment, is that we have a heavy reliance on our overseas trade. With the ever-shifting political situation with France and Spain, and the fact that we seem to have upset the Dutch, our cargoes as well as our markets are coming under increasing threat. Losing some of our market is one thing, but I am not happy at the thought that our potential enemies could start plundering our cargoes as they are being delivered to our other overseas customers. It's bad enough that those vessels that transport our cargoes at the moment have to contend with so many privateers, without adding our enemies' ships.

'Edward always said that it was our overseas trade that allowed our expansion and safeguarded the business. Now, it would appear that policy could well *endanger* the business. What I'm suggesting is that we develop and substantially expand our manufacturing side with improved facilities and far better buildings. Pay far more attention to attaining a finer weave, aligned with being able to offer a bigger colour range, patterns, and very importantly, a vastly improved quality. All of these would give us the basis upon which we could develop and expand our home markets even more, as well as sustaining and improving our overseas trade when the shifting political situation allows.

'The increase in this type of production would mean we would have to all but cease selling raw wool to other cloth makers, both at home and overseas. I've always questioned the wisdom of selling so much of it overseas anyway, when we could have sold them more cloth, yarn, and finished products instead, giving us far more potential profit! As a matter of interest, the Government is thinking along the same lines, and I hear they are going to increase the tax on the export of raw wool quite substantially, as a way of regulating it.

'If we expand along the lines I've suggested, then we are going to need to employ more people in our manufacturing facilities, but it *will* reduce the number of our outworkers. This is obviously dependant on where we open these new facilities because my whole scheme is dependent on employing an experienced and available workforce.

'If we get this right, I calculate we will increase our profits threefold, and that will also increase the amount we can invest in product development. My ultimate aim is for woollen goods to compete against silk, but I must admit that time is some way off, but I'm confident it can be done. The whole package will also put us well ahead of our competitors, especially those from the northern counties, who have been responsible for the demise of much of Gloucester's woollen industry in the past, it has to be said!' He paused, enabling his audience to digest his words.

'Is that it?' Mary responded, somewhat overawed by it all.

'Not quite!' replied her son-in-law.

'So what *else* do we need to consider, for goodness' sake?'

'If we do start manufacturing on the scale that I have suggested, then obviously we are going to have to employ more selling agents throughout the country. Although I've said we *could* lose a large part of our export market, that is still only a possibility, so we must develop a trading policy that is versatile, and we can switch when, or if, the need arises. To do that, we also need more agents to lay the groundwork, nationally, for increased sales.

'I'm sorry to quote Edward again, but he was right when he used to tell me that diversified markets and a finer weave were the key to success in our industry. He was right, and you only have to look at the last two years since I've been running the business to see that. I've diversified, or rather we have, and we are presently reaping the reward.

'Now, we need to take it forward again. I would add one more thing. Transport is becoming more and more of an issue. Moving goods around the country overland is painfully slow and dangerous. In spite of privateers, waterborne transport is the key, as we've already proved by having our own trows. Even if we have to switch from exporting our goods to concentrating on the home markets, transport will still be an ever-present issue. Depending on our reserves, we should look at operating our own fleet of ships, if not on our own, then say in conjunction with Hawk Mines, although we'd have to keep the cargoes separate!' he concluded with a wry smile.

Mary looked at Sophie and then said in a slightly sarcastic tone, 'Can we fund all this out of our own reserves or do we need to find a goose that lays golden eggs?'

Sophie started to laugh, saying to her mother, 'Well, you did give us some hens once that you said would only lay barren eggs, and we had two clutches of chicks, so maybe we should look in the toft at the back?'

Mary smiled and pulled a face at her daughter. Then looking at her son-in-law, she continued, 'Ask Philip and his clerks to do some costing. You go and look for the site where you think it would be beneficial to establish new production buildings, and then let's talk again. I agree with a lot that you have said, but I think the fleet can wait till next month! As a matter of interest, how long will this plan of yours take to become a reality?'

Grundwell thought for a minute because he was not quite sure whether Mary was being serious, and then he answered carefully.

'About four years to get the full plan up and running, but we need to start going in the right direction now, to safeguard ourselves and to be ahead of any competitors. I have actually met the golden goose already. His name is Nathaniel Purnell, the goldsmith who presently holds our reserves.'

'As his father did before him,' Mary replied with a sigh of resignation. 'Another man of ambition. You two should work well together. Sophie, come and open these parcels with me upstairs before your husband gets any more ideas.'

The two ladies collected the parcels and disappeared upstairs, Sophie laughing at her mother's extravagance with her grandchildren. Grundwell returned to the warehouse, to have long and meaningful discussions with Richard and Philip.

The dawn of the maypole dance arrived. In the village, the young people had been out since well before dawn. Gumshu had been highly suspicious, as not one of the youngsters had complained about having to get up early.

Something had been arranged between them all, so he too got up early, curiosity getting the better of him. Maisey was sleeping deeply, and in her present state of motherhood, he was determined not to wake her.

He left the dogs by the cottage and quietly approached the outskirts of the woods. He stood and listened. He smiled, turned, and walked back to the object of his own dreams. They were not his children out there in the woods, so it had nothing to do with him. His worries would start when *Little Emmy* was old enough to become involved with the maypole.

Gumshu silently returned to his bed, and the dogs to theirs. Maisey woke up, smiled, and asked, 'Were they making love?'

'Oh, yes, with a lot of enthusiasm, judging by the noise,' he replied.

'It's a good job our parents didn't come looking for us! The last time we did the maypole dance before we were married, you grinned for a week afterwards!' she said.

Gumshu turned over and looking at her with a smug smile said, 'Yes, I remember!'

An hour after dawn saw the return of the young, carrying flowers to scatter outside their true loves' cottages and boughs of green leaves and blossoms to decorate the maypole.

The day had dawned fine with a gentle warm breeze and a cloudless sky.

William Benson arrived in the pony trap with Grundwell, Mary, Sophie, and the children from Craven Street. The youngsters poured out and raced off to join their friends. Alice and Little Emmy immediately linked up to go in search of the maypole, which was being taken around the village on a flower-covered oxen cart.

William stood a little awkwardly, watching the dancers attached to their ribbons on the pole twisting and turning, matching their movements to the music of the pipes, drums, and tabors being played by the many musicians all around them.

There were older dancers too, dressed as court jesters in multicoloured costumes, covered in bells and dancing in lines and circles, dancing and twirling around as attendants to the duly appointed Maid Marion of the day, who headed the slow-moving procession of rural enjoyment.

A jester upon his wooden horse cantered up to the young cleric, smiling, laughing, and singing to him, 'Come join us, William. Come dance and laugh. If in our spells and magic you do believe, your love to find you might well achieve!'

William recognised the mounted jester as Joshua the Mole. He looked around; he looked at all the village people, his people, and then he remembered what he had said to his father about being at one with his community.

With that thought in his mind, he dropped his coat on the ground and pranced off alongside Joshua to join the dancers and immerse himself in the revelry, laughter, and fun.

Grundwell, Sophie, and her three parents joined Gumshu and Maisey outside their cottage. Sophie had Anna on her lap as they all sat on the ground and watched the revellers go twirling past.

A fresh figure then joined the dancers, dressed in a large brown habit with a copper cross swinging from his neck on a lanyard made of leather. Father Benedict's dancing lasted but a few minutes before he collapsed beside Sophie,

'*Methinks* my time has gone by for such things,' he managed to gasp out. 'I'll just leave it to the youngsters.'

'*Methinks* I would have got ale down my dress if I'd said such a thing.' Maisey laughed, mimicking her friend's old-fashioned speech.

'*Methinks* you're right, wench!' the friar replied. 'But I will forgive you the thought for a mug of your best ale.'

Maisey leant behind her and passed an already prepared mug of ale along the line of friends to the friar.

'Thank you, my dear. God will bless you for such a kindness to an old monk,' he said, downing the ale in one draught.

'And he'll bless you some more, if more there *be*?'

Maisey struggled up and replenished his mug from a jug by the door of the cottage. She had put it there earlier, in anticipation of the friar's visit.

'This could go on all day,' she commented.

'Hopefully, yes' was the man of God's instant response.

The other man of God, being fit and a lot younger than the friar, was still dancing. He had not had so much fun since he was the age of Alice and Little Emmy, when he used to chase after the maypole in the Suffolk village where his father had been rector. He remembered the scent of the flowers, and he remembered the music, but most of all he remembered the laughter of everyone there.

The Maid Marion of the day was in fact Eleanor, the daughter of Edmund Fletcher who had now moved permanently into the village. He and his wife lived in a cottage not far from the coal building.

She came to see her parents on a regular basis, as she had kept her position in Chepstow when her parents had moved, living in rooms above the ladies clothing shop in which she worked. Barely in her twenties, she had long blonde hair, blue eyes, and a figure that was the envy of many a girl in the Forest and beyond. It also drew admiring glances from the men and boys—the men in sidelong glances, the boys quite openly.

However, her temperament was that of her father—quiet, determined, talented, and extremely single-minded. She loved books, she loved the outdoors, she was good with figures, and she was also becoming very attracted to William, and he noticeably to her.

As the army of young revellers moved around the village, the two often found themselves next to each other; both would smile and link arms, their hands starting to linger together a few seconds longer than necessary each time.

Two certain ladies watched the proceedings with a degree of satisfaction, glancing at each other whenever the dancers passed them by.

'What have you two been up to?' Gumshu enquired.

'Us?' replied Maisey, with a look of total innocence on her face. 'I don't know what you're talking about,' she continued as she levered herself up.

She took Anna from Sophie and helped her friend to stand up as well, giving her god-daughter a hug as she did so. 'Come on, Sophie. Let's go and help with the food!' And the two disappeared, laughing as only two female conspirators can.

'The man doesn't stand a chance!' Grundwell laughed.

'He was doomed the day Maisey and Sophie first met her!' Gumshu commented.

'I'm glad I'm a monk,' the friar stated.

The other two looked at him rather puzzled.

'Well, who do you think they might match me to if I were not?'

'Don't tempt me,' muttered Gumshu, rolling out of the way of a well-aimed kick from the man of God.

The day continued with a feast, everyone sitting at tables groaning with a multitude of foods, all prepared or gathered by the people of the Forest village. Sweetmeats, pies, meats and chicken, strawberries, nuts, and herbs were all in abundance. A whole pig was being cooked on a spit, with juices being lovingly poured over it by a dedicated friar. Copious amounts of ale and mead were consumed by thirsty dancers and onlookers alike. As Father Benedict had predicted, the day was a gastronomic bonanza of wonderful proportions.

After the feast came the dancing. But instead of it just being to the music of the pipe and drum, every musician and every dancer that had been in the village during the morning had decided to stay and join in the fun. Now, there was no distinction between young and old!

'Do I remember someone saying this day was just for the young?' Gumshu grinned.

'I'm sure our parents didn't act like this!' Grundwell panted, as he danced past his friends with a laughing Sophie.

There wasn't a man, woman, or child who did not join in, a village filled with laughter, music, dance, and song. But occasionally someone would slip away to be with their memories in a few moments of peace and tranquillity—to remember a loved one.

Father Benedict and William Benson were both on hand to watch over their flock. Both were well aware that they would still be wanted to offer care and words of comfort. They, too, would slip away when needed, two caring and dedicated men of God.

Fran watched them with a gentle smile on her face, thinking of her own father and of the values he held despite his advancing years and recent heart-rending loss of her mother.

With the coming of sunset, the festivities drew to a close. The maypole and costumes were packed up for another year, the remnants of the feast cleared away. The musicians returned home, as did Grundwell, Sophie, and the children, leaving Mary to stay the night with Sophie's Forest parents.

'Having three grandparents is wonderful,' Alice declared. 'They all spoil me!'

When Grundwell offered William a ride back to the rectory, he thanked him but declined. Eleanor was standing a short distance away with a contented and happy look on her face. William went over to her and took her hand, and they walked into the fading light of the Forest to find a place of privacy.

'What we have got to do first is move away from providing so much raw wool to making more woollen products, the finer the better. We must then ensure that we can switch from exporting to expanding our home markets without losing momentum. We have to put ourselves in that position sooner rather than later,' Grundwell murmured, deep in thought after more discussion with Philip. He repeated to himself what he had told Mary and Sophie.

'We have enough reserve to build two or more large buildings or perhaps . . . perhaps . . . perhaps . . .' His concentration evaporated.

'When we decide on the buildings, the next question is where do we build them, and *then* where do we get skilled workers from?'

Still muttering to himself, he started to walk round the warehouse. Then he decided to go through the town to clear his head. He reached Craven Street and had his hand on the latch when it struck him! He already had the workers. They were there. They knew him; they knew wool better than he did. It was simple—all his many outworkers!

He turned on his heel, went back to the warehouse, burst into Philip's room, beamed, and as one voice, they said, *'Outworkers.'*

The two put all the figures down on paper so that they could double-check the costing before showing them to Mary and Sophie. They could not afford mistakes.

'Well, not at this stage anyway!' Grundwell thought, as he returned to Craven Street.

He burst through the front door to be met by Sophie and Mary, both laughing.

'Are you staying this time, my lover?' Sophie enquired. 'Or does your mother-in-law frighten you that much?'

'Ah, yes, well,' he stammered, 'just as my hand hit the latch, I had an idea so I went back to see Phillip.'

'And the idea was?' Mary questioned, realising that this could take time. Sophie sat down next to her mother, the pair gazing attentively up at him.

'We bring *all* our outworkers into two or possibly three new buildings, which we erect next to our others in Mitcheldean. That way, we utilise people who know wool. We've got all our facilities and workforce in one place, making it easier for Richard and I to control. Our suppliers remain local to us, especially our loom maker who is all important.

'Our transport links are already in place, both overland and by water. We can also develop my idea of a fleet of commercial ships without going too far afield to get them built, with the ship builders of Chepstow and the Wye being so close.

'All we have to do is increase the number of agents we use so that our sales match the increase in the production of our woollen goods, as I've already explained. This will also give us the flexibility that I want to incorporate into the way that we operate the business.

'We save on the cost of equipment to the outworkers, and we also save on all the transport necessary to sustain those outworkers, especially outside Mitcheldean, a not inconsiderable sum according to Phillip. We also honour our employment commitment to the local community,' he said excitedly, smiling at Mary.

'The savings made can then be added to the investment we are intending to make out of our reserves and may reduce the need to seek out quite so many golden eggs! Should we require more funding than we have reserves, Nathaniel has already looked at my scheme, approves of it, and will make an advance to us, should it be needed. And, Mary, the fleet can be purchased the month after next!'

'Yes, all right, carry on and do it, but not the fleet, not yet!' the ladies replied.

'Have I missed something with you two? I never get away with it this easily. Where is the catch?'

'My dearly beloved, Mary and I both thought of the outworkers this afternoon, and we've been waiting to tell you.'

'I need a drink. Fetch me mead, woman!' Grundwell said, as he slapped her bottom.

She turned round to say something to him but realised Mary was still listening and thought better of it. She went out to the cool room and poured them all a drink of mead, but as she passed her husband on the way back, she accidentally kicked him.

'Now, my children,' Mary said, laughing. 'I'll send you both to bed if you don't behave!'

Mary wasn't quite sure who got to the door first, but a few seconds after it shut, Sophie opened it again, put her head round, and said, 'If Anna wakes up, could you give her tea? And I'll be down later, on second thoughts, a lot later.' She giggled as she closed the door. Mary heard her running footsteps go up the stairs.

She smiled to herself. Being a grandmother had definite advantages over being a parent. She loved her grandchildren, doted on them and spoilt them; she enjoyed being involved in their lives and loved playing and looking after them, as long as there was parental input as well. But she always had the option of giving them back and thereby lay the advantage.

Grundwell was very late into the warehouse the next day. He came in smiling. Richard whispered to Philip, 'I wish he wouldn't smile like that. I never know quite what to expect.'

'Come on, Richard. Have you forgotten the reason why men smile like that?' Philip returned.

'Yes, nearly! Have you met my wife?' The two men immediately dissolved into hysterics, as Philip had indeed encountered Richard's somewhat formidable lady.

Grundwell came back into the room some minutes later to find both of his most trusted employees with tears of laughter running down their cheeks and unable to enter into a sensible conversation with him.

Richard and Philip visited every outworker in the business over the next few weeks, to explain what they were going to do and why. Grundwell set about designing his buildings, discussing his ideas with first the town fathers, followed by a building designer, a stone mason, and a builder. He and Philip then worked out the price of the buildings. The two impressive units were going to have two floors, large galleried rooms, and importantly, an abundance of natural light.

The land adjacent to the warehouse and the other units belonged to the Church and had previously not been available for sale because of government restrictions. A shift in the political situation had freed up considerable areas of such restricted land for development, including in Mitcheldean. The Church authorities in Gloucester were quite happy to dispose of the land, although they found Grundwell a formidable negotiator on price.

The new machinery for the project then had to be organised. He travelled extensively to look at different designs of machines but eventually decided that his loom maker from Gloucester would build them. They were to be partly Grundwell's and Richard's design and partly the loom maker's. Because of their size and complex nature, containing a host of revolutionary ideas, the man would construct part of them in his workshop and complete them in the new buildings in Mitcheldean.

Not only were they able to give a finer weave, they were also capable of producing a coloured and patterned one, a revolutionary step forward in the production of English cloth. Such was their complexity that Grundwell had to engage two highly experienced weavers of Oriental origin to operate them. They were also going to instruct his own employees in the new technology, a move that intrigued his competitors as well as his own staff.

'If the Dutch and French can employ such people, so can we!' he said by way of an explanation to a concerned Richard. 'And these gentlemen certainly know their work.' It was a comment which Richard came to endorse with great enthusiasm after the two had been working with them for three weeks. Grundwell also provided two cottages for them and their families, in the lane opposite the church that led to Cumdean.

The one problem that Grundwell seemed unable to resolve was a product mark.

Then, one evening, he walked into Craven Street to find that Alice was still up. Mary and Estor were finishing the preparation of the evening meal; Sophie was trying to settle Anna upstairs, so Alice had her father's full attention for once.

'And how were things at the spinning wheel today, Father?' she enquired brightly.

Grundwell stood and looked at her; Mary turned and stared at him. Sophie had just come into the room and was standing by the door.

'Alice, how long have you called the warehouse the spinning wheel?' Sophie asked. 'Oh, I don't know, forever I suppose. How long till we eat, Grandma?' she demanded.

'Agreed?' Grundwell questioned.

'Agreed!' replied the two ladies, thus creating a mark that would be retained for generations of the family to come.

Two months later, the buildings were started, built of brick and stone unlike the adjacent wool buildings, which were all timber and of a somewhat temporary nature. Grundwell involved himself in every aspect of the construction, arriving on site before dawn and leaving at sunset. Craven Street hardly saw him, but the family forgave him, as even Alice knew how important all the building work was to the future of the Spinning Wheel.

She told her tutor she was going to be running the business in the not too distant future, a comment that made him smile benevolently.

The Reverend William Benson had a very special guest. She was young and beautiful, but of that he didn't care. When he walked back to Mitcheldean after the maypole party, his heart had felt like it had been singing and flying in the trees. He had never met true love before, never experienced the elation, and never experienced the heart-stopping excitement of meeting her again. Neither had he ever experienced the simple desolation of when they were apart. No one could tell him. No one could show him; those feelings were unique to each and every one who could honestly say that *they were in love.*

The evening was wet and extremely windy.

The rectory windows were all tightly shut, protecting the occupants from the wind and the rain. William's housekeeper had lit the fire in the main room and put up the window coverings, so all that could be heard was the tapping of the rain and the voices of the yew trees in the adjoining churchyard, as the wind howled through them. She then returned to her home, a cottage on the other side of the grass bank beyond the lych gate.

William and Eleanor stood in front of the open fire, looking into each other's eyes and holding hands as if the wind would blow them apart. Neither spoke, the fire casting its beams of light upon the man and the woman, lighting her hair as if it were summer golden corn and lighting his face to show a man being reborn.

Eleanor dropped his hands and very slowly started undoing his doublet, followed by his linen shirt; she lifted them over his head and dropped them to the ground. She massaged his chest and his shoulders, coming close to him so that her lips searched and kissed where she touched him, and then taking his face in her hands, she kissed him long and deep, her tongue searching and probing around his open mouth. He could taste and smell the passion that was rising in her body. It was as if he were in a trance, mesmerised and still, frightened to break the moment and frightened to even breathe.

Eleanor sank to her knees and first removed his boots and then his stockings, followed by his britches, so that the light from the fire displayed his complete nakedness in front of her.

He stroked her head, feeling her soft flaxen hair running through his hands. She caressed and explored his body with both hands and tongue. He moaned in pleasure, not knowing how to respond. She stood up in front of him, and not taking her eyes from those of her lover, she first removed her bodice and then her skirt. Very slowly, she then took off her shift, exposing the full glory of the youthful and naked body that lay beneath.

She paused to let him drink in her beauty. For minutes they stood, lost in a world of wonder, lost in a world of love. Then together they sank to the floor and lay on the soft floor coverings, consummating their love with passion, a physical passion bred from a deepening fulfilment to each other.

Afterwards, William lay alongside Eleanor for several minutes, holding her, kissing her, and whispering of his love and devotion to her. She pushed back his hair from his face and saw the tears that he shed, shed as her lover and shed as her life, and she knew then that this man would be hers for time immemorial.

William had no kin in the parish, so he returned to the Forest village alone to see Eleanor's father some days later to negotiate the marriage settlement. They talked of many things, but Edmund was already aware of the feelings between the young parish priest and his daughter; one would have to have been blind not to have seen it.

He also knew that to try and arrange a marriage for Eleanor would have led to such family conflict that he was quietly relieved and delighted that nature had taken its course.

Edmund laughingly asked if William had met Friar Benedict on his journey to see him. Assuring him that he hadn't, William smilingly remarked that he'd actually met a herd of goats belonging to Samuel Longden. The two concluded their negotiations and drank to each other's health in a way that Friar Benedict would have been proud of, which resulted in the need for William to spend the night at the Fletchers' cottage, much to Eleanor's delight.

The cleric told his intended sometime later, when she asked about her father's comment about the friar, it was considered bad luck to meet a monk on the way to negotiate marriage settlements and good luck to see a goat.

'I thought you didn't believe in paganism, William Benson?' she questioned accusingly, as she pulled him down and under the bedcovers so that she could snuggle up to his naked form.

'I don't, my love, but why tempt fate?' he replied with a grin, endeavouring to keep their lovemaking as quiet as possible so as to not wake up his future parents-in-law, asleep in the next bedroom.

Some days later, William and Eleanor travelled to see Archbishop Benson and his wife to tell them of their forthcoming marriage. There was delight and celebration at the archbishop's palace following the announcement.

Richard Benson asked them the inevitable question about where they were going to get married.

William and Eleanor looked at each other, and William gently replied, 'With your permission, Father, in my church, amongst my family, my friends, and my parishioners.'

Eleanor looked at Archbishop Benson, with her eyes pleading for a positive answer.

'As well as granting us your blessing, Your Grace, would you also marry us?' she asked in a soft voice.

Richard looked at his son and this slip of a country girl, and his mind went back to when the girl he was to marry asked the same question of *his* archbishop father. He looked at his wife, who smiled at him, knowing his thoughts.

Taking her hand, he kissed it and replied tenderly, 'Eleanor, you certainly have my blessing, and I would consider it a privilege and an honour to conduct the marriage service.'

# CHAPTER 13

The two men sat in the grassed toft at the back of Mary's house in Craven Street.

'Gumshu, do you remember some fourteen or fifteen years ago, I think it was, sitting in a hut in the Forest, watching one of my father's charcoal kilns burn, when it suddenly collapsed with the earth crust cover cracking and all that smoke, steam, and charcoal pouring out of the split?'

'Yes, I remember it only too well, and I can remember what your father said when he saw the result of his son and friend looking after one of his burns!' Gumshu replied, still obviously slightly embarrassed by the memory.

'I wonder what he would have said now, seeing us both,' Grundwell reflected.

The owner of the Hawk Mines frowned 'If I remember, he said we were both lazy, ale-swilling, womanising, no-good layabouts who would never make a living from charcoal.'

'He was right about that at least. We never did make much money out of charcoal!'

The two men often shared an evening drink now that Gumshu and Maisey lived in the house on the corner of Craven Street.

'You're crazy, you know that!' Maisey had said when Gumshu told her that he had bought the house.

She had stormed out of the cottage down to the place she always went to when she was angry. Her refuge was a tree just off the path to the small stream where she and Gumshu used to go and sit on a fine evening. The tree bore the carving that they had made when they were both fifteen. Although the lettering was now becoming obscured by the bark's growth, it could still be made out, announcing to the world that they loved each other.

She usually sat down at the bottom of the tree with her knees tucked up. This time, in her present state of motherhood, she leant against the tree and glowered. Gumshu came and stood some distance away and half smiled at her. She raised her head and looked at him. He wasn't sure whether to speak, be silent, or just admit guilt and go arrange for the sale of the house.

'Maisey, my love . . .,' he started, but Maisey cut him short.

'Don't grovel. You know I hate it when you do that!' she hissed.

Gumshu wished he had taken the second of his two options—silence.

He started again, endeavouring to justify his actions. 'We can't live in the cottage forever, my love. We need to move on. We are about to gain another son or daughter, and our children grow as does our wealth. I need to be more in the centre of commerce, like Grundwell. We now have three mines, soon to be four. We are outgrowing ourselves, and you and I always said that when that time came, we would grow with it, did we not?'

'Yes, I agree with all that you have said, but the words "you and I" usually means *we* talk about things together . . . *first!*' she growled.

Gumshu replied with a weak 'yes, my love.'

Maisey was not about to admit to him that she and Sophie had taken a secret look at the house some three months previously. She had thought then that with some alteration and some painting it would suit them well, especially being so close to their old Forest friends.

'So could you explain *your* thinking to me?' she asked, slowly walking towards him.

Threatened with imminent reprisal for his apparent misdemeanour, he very quickly blurted out, 'We keep the house. We alter it to suit our needs. We paint the outside to match the other black and white houses on Craven Street. We furnish it to your every taste. We buy our cottage from our landlord so that we always keep our links with Cumdean, and we repair the gate to the new house so that next time you and Sophie use it you don't leave it open like you did on your *last* visit!'

He finished just as she encircled his neck with her arms. Fortunately, their forthcoming child kept its father relatively cushioned from Maisey's next move, which was her knee in his groin.

'What did you do that for?' he gasped, holding the part of his anatomy that was hurting the most.

'Next time that will be a reminder to talk to me *before* deciding to buy things such as a *house!*'

Whereupon she turned, picked up her skirts, and regally swept up the path towards the village and their cottage.

'And,' she said, pausing to look over her shoulder, 'for trying to be clever . . . I saw it first!' And with that final remark, she departed the scene.

The painful incident had been some seven months previously. Since that time, they had moved from the cottage to the Corner House. It had been altered, refurbished, and painted; the gate had been repaired and the house lavishly furnished to suit Maisey's exquisite taste.

Little Emmy, George, and the twins Richard and Hannah now had a baby brother. Robert had been born in the Forest cottage as both Maisey and Gumshu had wanted. Fran had delivered him. '*A bouncing, demanding little lad,*' she had told an exhausted Maisey when she had presented the baby to his mother for milk.

'Just like his father then,' she had returned, smiling up at an ecstatic Gumshu.

Their children came bursting in shortly after. Little Emmy became very serious as she gazed at the baby, so much so that Maisey asked her what was wrong.

'Is that what you get if you *frolic?*' her daughter asked with a worried frown.

'Yes,' replied Gumshu without hesitation, 'and sometimes you get two of them!' He pointed at Richard and Hannah.

After a moment's thought, she returned with conviction, 'Well, when I get married, I'm *not* going to frolic at all, that's for sure!'

Gumshu laughed and looked at his daughter. 'I'll remind you of that in ten years or so,' he said, ruffling her long chestnut hair, wondering what the future would hold for her.

The baby's christening had been a Forest affair, with his godfather, the Reverend William Benson, conducting the simple service in the little village church. The weather being fine and warm for the time of the year, the baptism celebrations were held in the open, with music, much laughter, and dancing, as well as vast amounts of food and drink.

Father Benedict had remarked to William and Eleanor on the way back to Mitcheldean in the autumn sunlight that perhaps God was starting to smile on his Forest people again. The friar, too, had been asking the same question William had asked after the mine accident: *'What is it that God wants of his people?'* And he too still searched for an answer.

The day after the christening, the two proud parents took baby Robert to the village churchyard to meet his sister.

Maisey knelt with him in her arms and opened the soft woollen blanket so that she could see his face. Gumshu knelt beside them, saying very quietly, 'Katherine, meet your baby brother Robert. We've named him after my grandfather.'

The mother and father leant against each other, putting their heads together, remaining silent so that all that could be heard were the contented sounds of a recently born infant.

William and Eleanor's wedding took place shortly after the christening, so close together in fact that Father Benedict was reported as saying he would not drink so much at the wedding as he was still recovering from the christening. That he flatly denied when Maisey laughingly told him what she had heard.

The banns had been read at Mitcheldean and at the little Forest church. The bishop from Gloucester read them in the Church of Saint Michael and All Saints and the rector from St Briavels read them at Cumdean. William had declared that reading your own banns of marriage and those of your future wife was a little unusual to say the least.

With that in mind, he prevailed upon his bishop and fellow cleric to perform this service for him, including the preparation of the certificates of no objection. His father, on his arrival two days prior to the wedding, had agreed with his son and paid the two for their services, as was the custom.

The Tuesday of the wedding dawned bright and crisp, the church adorned in the greens and golds of autumn leaves, with late flowers covering every surface and twisting as if by magic up every column and colonnade within the building.

The rectory was a bustle of activity, the archbishop's wife in her absolute element, organising droves of church ladies in preparing the wedding feast. The archbishop and his son quietly withdrew to the nave of the church to find the peace that they needed for contemplation and prayer prior to the service.

The Corner House at Craven Street was the bride's refuge before the ceremony. In that household, too, the men had retreated to safer climes, but not for contemplation and prayer. The ale brewing shed at the rear was Gumshu's retreat, where he was joined by the bride's father. Edmund looked absolutely terrified by the whole event, and the two consumed not a little ale.

*'Purely to steady our nerves,'* they told an enquiring Maisey who came looking for them sometime later.

The bride arrived at the church lych gate in her flower—and ribbon-bedecked open trap, wearing a plain white silk wedding dress and a fine lace veil. Her bridesmaids, Little Emmy and Alice, were dressed in a similar style, all of the dresses being made by Mary and the mothers, all seamstresses of quality and great flair.

Eleanor had followed many of the age-old traditions, including that of wearing a borrowed item with her wedding dress. Mary had also left one dress stitch undone so that it could be completed just before the bride went up the aisle. She had then panicked because she couldn't remember where it was.

At last all was calm; the bride and her father, with attendant bridesmaids, processed up the aisle. Eleanor looked radiant, beautiful, and blooming, standing in front of the altar with her betrothed, who looked handsome but petrified.

Gumshu held the ring as well as supported the groom, in his role as the best man.

The church was full—full of Forest people, full of town's people, full of the parish's people, full of relatives and friends from far and near, all there to witness two people in love make the bonds and oaths of marriage in front of their God.

The archbishop guided them through the ceremony with sincerity, feeling, and love. After the placing of the silver wedding band on her figure, William's father raised Eleanor's veil, took the bride and groom's hands, and joined them together, placing part of his vestments over them, thus binding the two in the sanctity of marriage, as God and the King had empowered him so to do.

The rectory rang to the sounds of the celebration for many hours afterwards, with music and dancing, laughter and chatter, eating and drinking. No one wanted to leave; no one wanted to go home.

Children slept curled up in various safe places, watched over by attentive mothers, awaking again to start their fun and games and leaving their exhausted mothers to try and find a few moments' sleep before rejoining the celebrations.

Slivers of light appeared in the eastern sky, heralding the approach of dawn and the realisation to many that it was the beginning of another working day.

With the revellers gone, it left the two families who were now joined by the marriage of the two people who they loved to quietly sit and talk of many things; such was the affinity that had developed between them.

Father Benedict was out walking, but not for pleasure. He was suffering the most excruciating pain; he had a toothache.

He hated toothache, but he hated the cure almost as much as the pain, namely seeing the surgeon. He had been to see Fran in the Forest village. She had tried all of her remedies to relieve him of his suffering, but to no avail.

After the second visit, she eventually told him, 'Father, it's going to have to be the surgeon. I can do no more.'

She tried not to smile, but the friar caught the corners of her mouth about to expand into a grin, and he gave her a look like thunder.

He had tried a prayer to God, but that hadn't worked either. What really upset him was that drinking ale and mead just made it worse.

'I seem to have exhausted all things bar the final and worst possible cure, a visit to the surgeon. But really, does it hurt me *that* much?' he pondered out loud, trying not to breathe in as the cold air made him wince with pain when it came in contact with his tooth.

The friar endured agony all through that night, so he concluded reluctantly that it really *did* hurt that much.

The suffering monk walked up the lane into Mitcheldean, his swollen face well hidden in a woollen scarf, not for protection of his identity but to stop the cold on his tooth.

He arrived at the surgeon's shop and slipped inside, half hoping that the man of pain would be out. The friar's luck was not to be; the man of blood was in residence. The friar looked at his blood-soaked apron, and his stomach turned somersaults. Suddenly he felt that his toothache had been miraculously cured and made to turn for the door.

'Ah, the good Friar Benedict, seeing your face is all lopsided, it seems to me you must have a tooth that needs my tender loving care?' asked Joseph Hack, the surgeon.

The friar turned back, looked at Joseph, and rather than speak, he nodded. Joseph had taken Benedict's last troublesome tooth out. Then, it had taken five strong and burley men to hold him down to let Joseph look into his mouth, let alone to remove the offending molar.

Master Hack sent his assistant, William Blood, next door to the ale house to recruit help. Moments later, six extremely large gentlemen came back with him, and the friar later swore that there wasn't a Christian amongst them; they just wanted to see a monk suffer.

Within a short time, the deed had been done. The six gentlemen of the ale house collected their rewards from Joseph, and then with a laugh and a wave, they were gone. The friar looked at Joseph and paid him his dues, saying through clenched gums, 'I'll say a prayer for you tonight!' Joseph Hack wondered what words the prayer would contain, but he knew the friar of old, so he was aware that he didn't bear grudges.

Father Benedict returned to Cumdean to see Fran. She gave him some Forest herbs that she had prepared to clean the damaged gums left by the departed tooth. That done, he returned with much relief to Gumshu and Maisey's cottage, which they had lent to him. 'The friar now needs warmth and a proper bed, especially in the winter months. He really is too old to be sleeping in hay barns and under hedgerows,' Maisey had said one night.

'I think that covers all times of the year, not just autumn and winter,' Gumshu added.

Sometime after that conversation, the two of them persuaded the friar to use the cottage as if it was his own. He hadn't needed much persuasion and was soon enjoying the benefits of cottage life, as he had never lived in one place ever since becoming an Anglican friar.

To Benedict, the fact that he was in the middle of all the people he had served over the years was an added benefit to his new-found way of life. It also kept the abbot happy, as he too had thought the friar was becoming too old for a life of wandering and had suggested he come back to live at the priory, a thought that was definitely not to Father Benedict's liking.

The Hawk Mines were now four in number, the last being added a short time after Robert's christening. It carried the name of the Raven Mine, and was the largest of the four. It was located some two miles to the south-west of the other three, but still shared the same rich coal seam.

It had thirty-six miners extracting the coal, but as usual, it employed children to act as carters. Despite some opposition from the miners, Gumshu stopped them immediately.

'Children only work outside the mines that I own, as you well know,' he told one of complainants, and there the matter ended.

To compensate, he employed some older men who used to be colliers but were either slightly injured or considered too old to extract coal. The system worked extremely well in the other three mines. It had been Maisey's idea when they started Crow, when Gumshu couldn't find carters to replace the children.

After two weeks, the newly appointed foreman, Jonathon Cribwall, Elijah's brother, reported to him that the Raven Mine was functioning well, especially with the added workforce. In his opinion, he thought that not only did they make excellent underground carters, but their general mining experience rubbed off on to the less experienced miners, and they were a good source of advice. And their enthusiasm seemed boundless.

Gumshu continued his policy of linking the mines by a cart track. There was now a large stockpile of timber shoring supports at a central point, with each mine having its own smaller stock to prevent any unforeseen shortages. If any did occur, the mine foremen were under strict instruction to stop any further excavations.

There had been only one instance of a mine not doing so. Elijah, from Rook, had told the other foremen that when Gumshu had found out he was so angry he had nearly closed the mine. It never happened again in any of the mines that carried the Hawk mark.

Gumshu's greatest concern, however, was the volume of his sales. With all four mines running at their full capacity, the output of coal was far in access to the amount that he was able to sell. It was something that he and Maisey worried over on many evenings when he wasn't on one of his selling trips. However far he travelled and however many customers he saw, he still was unable to sell the amount that he needed to.

He talked at length to Edmund, who showed him the figures and assured him that Hawk was still making a substantial profit, even at the present level of coal being sold.

'But it needs to be more, Gumshu! We have to build up our income for the future. We need to be able to invest in more mines, as well as substantially increase our money reserves.'

Then it snowed.

It came down relentlessly for three days and three nights, leaving a strange and silent world, blanketed in a deep, thick covering of white. With the snow came a bitter north-easterly wind, freezing and immobilising everything in its path. From springs to rivers and streams, nothing or no one, was immune from the consequences of its icy blast.

In Cumdean, movement became impossible. That brought problems with work, with food, and in some cases, with life-threatening lack of warmth for both inhabitants and livestock.

Samuel and Edmund managed to deliver coal and wood, drawn from Hawk's surplus stocks, to every cottage in the village, using one of the oxen teams to help battle their way through the massive drifts. As they visited each home, they also did their best for those who were short of food, ensuring that neighbour assisted neighbour and collier assisted woodsman.

'Sadly, there's nothing we can do to help people get to work!' Samuel remarked to a shivering Edmund, as they returned from one of their delivery trips.

'Now our colliers have to dig snow instead of coal,' Edmund replied. 'But none of us earn money from that!'

That point was also resting heavily on Gumshu, because if his miners weren't able to earn money from mining coal, then neither was Hawk Mines.

The only good thing about the cold weather was that many more households in town and village alike were burning his coal. But if he wasn't able to mine it, he couldn't deliver it, and if he couldn't deliver it, he couldn't charge for it. The other point was that if families couldn't work, then they couldn't earn, which meant they couldn't pay even if he could deliver it.

The many businesses that he supplied to were also facing the same crisis—no workers, no production, therefore no revenue. They, as well as Hawk, were in total shutdown.

The Forest of Dean had ground to a halt.

That was Gumshu's first business crisis ever since starting Hawk Mines, and he became extremely worried. Maisey hated to see him so concerned and frustrated.

As they lay in bed one night, agonising over the multitude of problems that the snow had brought, Maisey suddenly asked, 'What about our coal stocks that we can't sell? Why can't we use those now?'

The owner of Hawk Mines fixed her with a beady eye, or would have done if he could have seen her.

'And just how do you propose to move it, may I ask?'

'Just a thought,' she replied, as she turned over to go to sleep.

He was not about to admit that he had had the same thought and had been trying, unsuccessfully, to solve the problem of transport as she spoke.

Gumshu managed to struggle across Craven Street to visit his friend. When he opened the door, Grundwell saw the haunted look on the collier's face. He knew what the topic of conversation was going to be as he ushered him into the big room, where the whole family had gathered to keep warm.

As in most other houses, mattresses and bedding had been brought from bedrooms and sleeping areas so that the household was functioning in the room where the fire was. Some of the smaller livestock had also been brought inside, as being a main food source there was a need to keep the unsuspecting animals safe, warm, and away from hungry predators.

Moving over to a quieter part of the room, Gumshu explained some of his woes.

'You're suffering in the same way we all are, I'm afraid,' Grundwell replied. 'I can only get *some* of my workers into the weaving sheds. Like you, although we have the new buildings that house all my production, the output isn't enough to cover my costs. You have to cover your Government charges. We have similar costs to cover, costs that never vary.

'This is where good bookkeeping comes in. The two Fletchers are expert at building up reserves from profits, reserves to be used in times such as these. What did Maisey once say to you, *"Edmund gives you production on paper?"* She was right, and now you will see the benefit.'

Gumshu guiltily admitted that neither he nor Maisey had looked at the ledgers for some time. That was one of the drawbacks, with the mines and the coal building being over three miles away from where they lived. He also admitted that he was away on his sales trips probably a little more than he should be, and certain aspects of the business had suffered in consequence. His lack of ability to actually check any bookkeeping was also a problem, and he was not quite sure how to overcome that particular hurdle either.

'In that case, may I suggest a rethink in the way you organise the bookwork and its preparation? I know you don't like paperwork and you enjoy the selling side, but you've *got to* check what your clerks are doing. The Fletchers are honest, luckily, but many aren't, I'm afraid to say,' Grundwell said, after a moment's thought. 'I take it that your money is lodged with a goldsmith in the town?'

'Yes, Nathaniel Purnell. He is the same one that you use. If you remember, it was you who advised me to use him, and Thomas Sutton also recommended him.'

'Good, he's honest too. I have to admit that not only is he my banker, Nathaniel also carries out certain of my bookkeeping tasks as well my own bookkeeper. This acts as a double-check on our work, helps Philip if he becomes too busy, and lets Purnells have an up-to-date picture of our finances should we need to make borrowings. Perhaps it might solve some of your problems if you did the same. Checking the cash ledger is probably one of the most important things in any organisation because at the end of the day money is why we are in business, as well as the power it brings, of course.

'I would advise that if that suggestion isn't acceptable, you ask Maisey to do the ledgers with Edmund on a regular basis, and then *she* always knows what's going on. She's a very astute lady, so give her the chance. Travelling around the country, I have noticed more and more wives are getting involved with the bookkeeping side of their husband's work.

'This does two things from what I can see. It puts family eyes close to the money. Also, if anything ever happens to the husband, the wife is in a position to take over the business. But always include Maisey in the running of the mines, as I know you already do, but *talk* before you decide anything. I hear that that has been a problem for you in the past!'

Grundwell was laughing as he spoke, knowing the story behind the house on the corner of Craven Street.

Gumshu blushed and said nothing, as he didn't know that anyone else knew the tale. Sophie and Mary were now listening to the conversation and were trying not to laugh.

'My wife has a habit of hitting the spot!' he eventually said, with a wry smile on his face.

Grundwell then continued in a more serious tone, switching the topic of conversation as he had begun to realise the collier's discomfort while discussing bookwork.

'The other thing I suspect you were going to talk to me about, judging by the way this conversation has gone, is about how you can increase your sales?'

'Yes, I was,' Gumshu admitted. 'I'm sorry. I seem to be burdening you with all my problems, but I am running out of ideas, and we are now producing more coal than I can sell.'

Grundwell smiled and took a breath. 'From what I can see, you need to spread your markets further afield, both in England *and* Wales. You also need to look abroad, to Ireland or even Europe, for example, for another market, and then one will always compensate for the other if one hits bad times. Edward used to call it the law of market compensation.

'Because the two are linked, you also need to look at your transport and the way that is organised. As an example, water-borne transport, either by sea or river, is easier and more cost-effective if you can organise loading and offloading efficiently. It's better than a horse and cart. It's far quicker. You can move a lot more coal, and as long as your distribution point is close to a waterway, it means your deliveries can cover a greater area. It's also safer.

'You have four good mines. Most other owners have only one, so therefore you have a far better chance of supplying the bigger users, maybe under a contract, with Hawk Mines guaranteeing the price and your customer guaranteeing their requirements.' He paused for a moment. 'Before you even think of setting prices, all the hidden costs must be taken into account, and that's on top of your direct costs like transport, labour, and timber. If you don't do it properly, you could easily end up losing money on every load of coal you sell. You've got a good bookkeeper. Now it's obvious to me you need a good general manager. To build a business, you need good staff!

'If *you* haven't enough experience, buy it is the golden rule. And going back to sales, why not appoint agents to do some of your selling for you? You can't be everywhere at once. In theory, the more people you have selling, the larger the volume you will sell. Just watch them for motivation would be my only warning. I'm actively appointing more agents at the moment because we too have to sell more. I was lucky. Edward taught me well.

'Whatever else he was, he knew the wool trade and the importance of sales, and strong sales are probably one of the most essential parts of any business like ours. I also have Mary, who knows as much as he did if not more, and as I've just said, wives are as good as, if not better than, husbands at running a family business.'

There was a round of applause from the ladies of the house.

Gumshu walked home with his head down, so deep in thought he was that he cannoned into another figure, struggling through the snow in the opposite direction.

Thomas Sutton was on his way to his new home, on the other side of William Benson's rectory. Both men fell in the snow and started laughing, then after a brief snowball fight, they got up and dusted the snow off each other, which resulted in them both slipping and ending up lying in the snow again.

'Will you come and have a mug of hot mulled wine with honey, Thomas?' Gumshu asked, Grundwell's words now ringing in his head. '*If you haven't enough experience, buy it.*'

'Now there's a good idea, Gumshu,' Thomas replied.

The two men struggled up, slipped, and slithered their way to the Corner House and one of Maisey's warming draughts.

Since the coming of the snow, she had become highly proficient at making the drink out of French wine that she had bought from the merchant by the church, adding her own mixture of honey, cinnamon, cardamom, and galingale. When she had first made it, Gumshu looked at her with deep suspicion and asked what else was in it.

'As if I would!' she answered, a look of pure innocence on her face.

At the Mitcheldean rectory, Eleanor and William lay on soft floor covers in front of the fire, their nakedness hidden by a beautiful thick woollen blanket, a gift from Grundwell and Sophie. William was lying on his side, one hand caressing his wife's long, silky corn-coloured hair, while the light from the fire and candles danced around the room, playing light and shade upon their tender, smiling faces.

William's other hand gently stroked the now obvious presence of their unborn child. Their smiles had been roused by the child's resentment at being woken, felt by the movement from within the warmth of its protective womb.

# CHAPTER 14

Gumshu talked at length with Thomas Sutton.

The two had now been friends for a number of years. Since the mine collapse at Cottrells and the development of Hawk Mines, Thomas had come to respect this woodsman turned collier, a man who would always sought advice when he needed it, and appeared as dedicated to the coal industry as he was.

To work for him, however, would be a totally different phase of their relationship, and the Deputy Gavellor was very unsure of his ground. He had had offers of employment from other mine owners over the years but had always declined, but this man was different; this man had success written on his face, and Thomas wanted some of that success. Working for the Crown was secure and fairly well paid, but it lacked the excitement of running a mine that was privately owned; but to have four of them, and probably more to come, was enough to whet anyone's appetite.

After he had heard Gumshu's offer and his plans for the future, he sat quietly for a few minutes, sipping his hot mulled wine.

'I must go away and have a think, then talk to my wife. Thank you for the chance, Gumshu. For that I am grateful!'

Thomas then took his leave and started to make his way through the thick snow, back to his wife, children, and his new home. As he passed the rectory, he saw the flickering light of the fire and the dancing lights of a pair of candles being carried up the stairs.

As he trudged on towards his house, he pondered what answer he was going to give to Gumshu.

His memory went back to that night at Cottrells' mine when the young cleric had toiled relentlessly through the night, digging, tending the injured, and giving comfort to those who waited for news of loved ones. He, like all of them there, had never faltered in his efforts to assist in the rescue.

The man had been a total stranger when he had first arrived in the Mitcheldean parish three years earlier, but the Forest community had accepted him; he was now a part of that community. Thomas had lived within the area for nearly eleven years and still hadn't been accepted; he was still an outsider, and one reason, he realised, was because he worked for the Crown.

'Other than the pay and conditions I've been offered, that's another reason why I shall accept the offer,' Thomas decided, 'subject to my Isabella's approval, of course!'

'Memories of the snow fade as quickly as it melts on the first warm day,' commented Thomas Sutton, general manager of Hawk Mines.

He was sitting in the newly constructed coal building on the site of Samuel Longden's smallholding in the Forest village.

Around the table with him sat Gumshu, Maisey, Edmund, Joshua the Mole, Benjamin, Elijah, his brother Jonathon, Samuel Longden, and goldsmith Nathaniel Parnell. Completing the gathering was Anthony Burrell, foreman of the fifth mine that carried the Hawk mark.

Some eighteen months had passed since the snows, and much had moved on with the mining business. Since Grundwell's talk with Gumshu, Thomas had joined them as had Samuel, who had sold his smallholding to Hawk Mines as he had ceased to work the land as a farmer. It had now become the centre of the extraction operation.

They had taken on a fifth mine, some little distance from Hawk and the other mines. Called Jackdaw, it was run by another Cornishman Anthony Burrell, a cousin of the Cribwall brothers, hence his seat at the table. He, too, had come to live in the Forest village with his young family, but as his wife had died at childbirth, his unmarried sister, Abigail, had moved from Cornwall with him to look after his three children.

The group around the table discussed the output from each mine: the men digging the coal, the safety in the mines, the markets for their coal, the performance of their growing number of agents, and, as always, ways of improving transportation.

They talked at length about the opening of new mining operations and whether Hawk should start investigating possible acquisitions of stone quarries, an idea floated by Maisey. Her reasoning being that as Hawk excavated and removed considerable amounts of rock to expose coal they had the experience and expertise, so why not put it to commercial use? One of her other thoughts had been to start test boring for coal at the proposed location of any new workings before actually opening the mine. It was an innovation that she had heard was being used in the coal fields of the north-east of England.

Gumshu smiled; his wife's aptitude for business never ceased to amaze him. After the foremen and Samuel had left, Edmund, Nathaniel, and Thomas reported on the full financial position of Hawk Mines. Even after buying the smallholding, erecting the new and enlarged coal building, the paying of annual lease charges to landowners, and all the many Crown costs by the way of levies and transport charges; the amount of money that Nathaniel now held for them was considerable and increasing rapidly.

'Perhaps the time is right to approach the Crown to negotiate a lease for a substantial part of the Forest so that we hold a sole mining interest. I'm sure they'd view it favourably, especially after the amount of money we have recently paid the King's treasury for taxes!' Maisey commented with feeling.

The others looked at her with some reservation, as this was a subject that they were all aware would cause much controversy, especially with other Forest colliers.

She continued, 'Well, we all agree that we need a bigger share of our local market, and one way to do it, without dropping our coal price, is to make it impossible for one owner and partnership mines to operate. They will have a choice. Either they don't mine at all or they mine under our mark and then sell their coal through us. That means *we* profit from *their* effort.'

Nodding at his banker, Gumshu took up his wife's theme. 'Nathaniel has already agreed a loan to us should we need it. Together with our own cash reserves, that gives us an extremely sound financial base on which to operate such a large undertaking.'

They had all known that this point would be reached as Hawk expanded, but due to the ongoing success of the business, it had come a lot sooner than any of them had anticipated, but that wasn't going to make such a decision any easier.

'What we decide now will affect Hawk Mines' future without doubt. We could keep the business the size it already is, but if we don't go for that lease, someone else will. We all know that. There is talk of it even now in Mitcheldean. If that happens, *we* could be the ones put out of business,' Maisey added with a worried frown.

There was a pause, and then Edmund broke in, 'You're right of course. I'll prepare some figures and then give them to Gumshu.'

'No, Edmund, if you could get them ready for Thursday when *I* come to go through the ledgers with you, I would be grateful,' Maisey said, giving her husband a sharp look in case of dissent. 'We also need to look at the idea of buying some trows. That would give us the means of moving our coal around on the local waterways or to ports like Chepstow and Bristol, where we could offload on to bigger ships for transport further afield. If we are going to sell our coal into cities like London, we need faster transport that carries vastly more coal than a horse and cart. And it might even give us the opportunity to think about the export market!' she added with another meaningful look at Gumshu.

'What's a *trow*?' Nathaniel asked.

'It's a cargo-carrying all-but-flat-bottomed boat that can navigate in shallow waters, like the rivers we have in Gloucestershire or in and around the Bristol Channel. Because they can float in so little water, any cargo they have can be unloaded, say on to a riverbank, like in Gloucester at one of our selling points.'

'Grundwell has two for carrying wool. I did ask him once if we could hire one of them, but he wasn't happy about a dirty cargo like coal being mixed with his good, clean fleeces!' Gumshu explained.

'You must have seen them, Nathaniel. You can see lots of them sitting on the bottom waiting for the tide to come in, especially around places like Chepstow where there is such a difference between high and low water. The mud is so soft that they don't do any damage to themselves either,' Edmund interrupted.

'Ah, yes, I have. I've often wondered what they were doing but never liked to ask.'

Maisey coughed, bringing the maritime conversation to an abrupt end. She thought for a moment.

'On reflection, Edmund, instead of my coming here on Thursday, could you bring those figures to us at the Corner House, please? I think we'd best do our talking in complete privacy. Could you both come as well?' she asked, turning to Thomas and Nathaniel.

They both replied that they would do so. Thomas offered to put some extra figures together as well, as he knew what the Crown would want in the type of application that Hawk was going to make.

Edmund told them that he had a shipbuilding friend with a yard on the river below Chepstow, and that he would make enquiries about the best size and design for the trows. He added that he would also find out about prices and the availability of men for crews.

Maisey looked at Thomas and Edmund. 'Could Gumshu and I have that information at the same time as the other financial papers?'

'Yes, of course you can,' they both assured her.

Maisey walked through the Forest village, meeting so many of the people she had grown up with, the people who had celebrated her marriage and the christenings of her children, and she wondered.

She met the people who shared her grief when Katherine had been taken from her, the people who had stood beside her and grieved at Cottrells' mine, and she wondered. Had Hawk Mines the right to dictate to these hard-working and genuine people, the very people who had left food in their cottage on that day when they came back from their nightmare experience in Mitcheldean?

Hawk Mines would prosper, of that she had no doubt, but at whose expense was the question.

She suddenly felt an awful weight on her shoulders. The responsibility of other peoples' lives never rests easily, especially on one whose shoulders had never borne such a weight before.

Were they right or were they wrong? She needed to talk; she needed to unburden herself, but secrecy was essential. The answer appeared out of her Forest cottage door.

'Such was the depth of your thoughts, my dear, I thought you were about to pass me by,' the friar said quietly.

She looked at him, not speaking; she took his hand and led him back into the cottage, closing the door behind them. She let go of his hand and turned to sit on the old oak settle by the fire.

The friar went to his ale jug and poured two mugs.

He had been down this path with Maisey on many occasions; he knew the signs, and he knew the part he would have to play—that of a listener.

Maisey talked; she talked for nearly an hour.

When she stopped, the silence that followed was only broken by the gentle noise of the flames devouring the wood and coal on the fire.

Benedict spoke softly, with an understanding that came from years of experience of dealing with the human mind.

'If you and Gumshu do not try for this lease, then others will, just as you've said. They could come from anywhere, or worse, they could even be foreigners from what I have heard.

'You have wealth, so do not be afraid to use it. By obtaining such a lease, you will have the opportunity of creating work, at the same time securing your own family's future. How you use the power it will bring, only you and Gumshu can decide.

'I do not have beliefs beyond my own vow of poverty, but that does not mean I cannot see the benefits to the community of what others may do. You must pursue this chosen course of yours with all the determination you both can muster, and then you must seek within yourselves for the answers to your other questions.'

Maisey got up, took her old friend's giant hand, and kissed it.

'Thank you, Father. I wonder how many times over the years you have sat and listened to my problems?'

'Many times, my child, many times, but that is one of the tasks that we men of God are supposed to do. You have repaid me in countless ways, so there's no need of thanks,' the friar replied.

Maisey looked quizzical.

'How have I done that?'

'By always being genuine, always showing your love, and always caring for others, just as you have done today. I would not have expected anything less from you.' He smiled as he hugged her. 'Now go and see Katherine, as you were going to do.'

'You look into people's minds as well?' Maisey asked, as she opened the door.

'Luckily no, not one of my attributes, but I have to say there are many more that I do have!' he replied, downing the last drop of ale from his mug and refilling it from his supply next to the fire.

Maisey waved before she closed the door, giving him a dazzling smile.

'Occasionally, just occasionally, I wish I wasn't old and a monk!' Friar Benedict sighed.

Quickly he grasped his copper cross that was resting on his chest.

'Sorry, Lord, a slip of the tongue!' he muttered, half expecting the wrath of God to descend on him.

As there was no bolt of lightning from above, the friar assumed he'd been forgiven for the remark.

Maisey sat by the tiny grave under the oak tree, talking to her daughter. She'd already explained to her why the family had all moved to Mitcheldean, but she told her that she would always come and see her. Even when she had little Robert as a babe in arms, she'd kept that promise. When she came, she always tended the grave with care, putting flowers by the rough wooden cross, when the seasons allowed.

Father Benedict had assured her that would she not be able to visit, he always would. During the snows of eighteen months ago, he had kept to his word. She had never doubted him, but on her first visit after the snows, one villager had told her that everyone thought that the friar had turned peculiar, as he kept digging a path to the churchyard, often with help from Joshua, Benjamin, and Elijah.

When she mentioned this to the three mine foremen, Joshua admitted that although they would have helped the friar anyway, it was also a penance for losing to him at cards. Elijah said that they always lost the game when the bet involved helping to clear the churchyard path, and they couldn't understand it.

'Perhaps he had a little help from above?' Maisey had questioned.

When she next met Benedict, she mentioned her conversation with the colliers.

He had smiled innocently, saying in a conspiratorially low voice, 'The Lord just helped my fingers move a little faster than their eyes!'

Maisey closed the conversation at that point. What she didn't know she couldn't tell!

The silence at the Corner House was deafening. The children, including young Robert, had been sent off with Joanne, the maid, to play with the Craven Street children.

Gumshu and Maisey now concentrated on all the papers and ledgers that were spread out on the large oak table in front of them.

It had been three weeks and two meetings since their first Forest conversation with Edmund, Nathaniel, and Thomas. Such was the volume of facts and figures required for the lease application that the amount of paperwork had been daunting. It had all taken considerably longer to read and understand than Maisey had anticipated.

The positive decision on ordering the trows had been very simple by comparison, but it had been decided that they would commission four to be built, not the two originally planned. They were going to be large and designed specifically for carrying coal.

Gumshu was already bored, but he felt it was not wise to show it, with Maisey in her *business* mood. He loved the practical side of the business; he excelled at the sales side, but he did not enjoy all the paperwork involved. He thanked the Lord for his wife, his staff, and his banker. He remembered the help that Maisey had always given him when Father Benedict was teaching them to read and write. 'The friar must have known,' he thought.

Maisey said, luckily, without realising her husband was thinking other thoughts, 'Based on these papers and ledgers, we have more than enough reserves to fund an operation of this scale, without any borrowings at all, and it still leaves a healthy balance for future expansion.'

Gumshu looked at his wife.

The previous night she had been in her *loving* mood. They both had added a small amount of the love potion to their drink of mead when the children and Joanne had gone to their beds, and it had weaved its usual magic into their mood and performance of lovemaking.

Such was their passion, they had not moved from the main room of the house, with its soft floor coverings and log fire burning in the large hearth. They removed each other's clothes and then indulged in exploration of their partner's body by means of hands, mouths, and tongues, lying in front of the dying embers of wood within the fire basket.

Gumshu got to his feet, picked his wife up, and held her in front of him with her legs wrapped around his waist, her arms encircling his neck, and her breasts tight against his barrel of a chest; his vast hands held both her ample, shapely buttocks. Their kisses had been passionate, long, deep, and probing. He carried her over to the table and gently sat her on it. She released her arms and legs and then leant back, her arms stretched out behind her head.

He took his hands from her buttocks and held her long, shapely legs open, resting them on his shoulders, whilst driving his desire hardened manhood deep inside her passion-moistened organ of ultimate sensations. He then began a momentous thrusting movement, to which Maisey had responded by pushing back against him as hard as she could, with vigour, noise, and enthusiasm. The final crescendo of sound that came from both of them echoed around the house, down the surrounding streets, and then out into the Forest.

Maisey gazed up into her husband's face with a smile of deep satisfaction, and with half-closed eyes and moist mouth, she softly murmured, 'That was *the* most wonderful frolic. Now take me to my bed, my collier lover.'

Gumshu looked at the table, now covered in papers, his memories of the previous night showing on his face.

Maisey kicked him under the table, saying softly, 'Your mind on now, please, my husband, not then. We have a decision to take!'

By the time Nathaniel, Edmund, and Thomas arrived at the Corner House, they had reached that decision. The three sat down around the oak table to join the owners of Hawk Mines, little realising that the table was a place of passion as well as business.

Maisey looked at them, then back at her husband. 'Gumshu and I have reached the decision that we *have to* apply for the lease, if we are to safeguard Hawk Mines' future.'

'We've been talking on the way here, and that is the conclusion that we have all come to,' Thomas replied, with assenting nods from the other two.

'We think the application should go in as soon as possible, as there are already rumours spreading about Hawk Mines' possible application. That could be dangerous. If anyone else who is interested thinks we are serious, they could well apply first,' he continued.

Gumshu looked at his wife. 'Right, gentlemen, then let's not waste any more time. Can we put the application down on paper now? Then Thomas and I will go and see first the Gaveller, and then the Surveyor for the Crown. After that, we will need to go to London to seek representation at the highest level.'

Maisey got up quietly, and calling Joanne, she started to prepare drinks for the group. She felt an excitement and anticipation that she had never felt before.

She looked at her husband sitting at the table, and she could see by his expression that he seemed to be sharing that same excitement.

Over the following two months, the Hawk Mines' lease application was discussed at length, both locally and in London.

Gumshu and Maisey appointed a London lawyer to handle their affairs and help them make representation in the right quarter. His name was Nicholas Milton, the brother of the Mitcheldean Justice of the Peace, Paul Milton.

He came highly recommended by the Gaveller, as a man who moved in the best circles and had influence in the right places.

As the mine owners knew Paul Milton to be a shrewd and trustworthy lawyer, they had no reason to believe that his brother would be any different.

'His fees make my eyes water' was Gumshu's only comment after first meeting him.

'I don't mind if they make them weep', replied his wife, 'as long as we get *that lease!*'

Gumshu and Thomas's travelling between Mitcheldean and London was exhausting, time-consuming, dangerous, and extremely uncomfortable.

If their coachman wasn't worrying about the state of highways, he started worrying about the number of highwaymen at large.

Thomas said during one journey, 'Travel by sea has never sounded so attractive.'

'Well, at least there would be no highwaymen or potholes!' Gumshu replied as their carriage hit yet another large rut in the road.

Finally, the Gaveller, Gumshu, and Thomas returned from London with a royal warrant for their mining extraction lease, a lease that would span a thirty-five-year period.

'How do you want to celebrate?' asked a jubilant Maisey of her husband.

'No frolics for a month,' declared an exhausted Gumshu.

'Really?' Little Emmy commented, joining the conversation from the next room.

As an attractive teenager starting to show her mother's looks and attributes, their eldest daughter had grown up quickly. Gumshu said that he thought she was also related to a bat, because she seemed to be able to hear any conversation in any corner of the house.

Father Benedict had once told her that if she wanted to learn about words she should listen to other people' conversations, the exact same advice he had given to Maisey many years previously. And Little Emmy always did as she was told!

'Well, at least with less noise from frolicking, we children should be able to get some sleep for the next month!' she continued, making a fast exit up the stairs before her still agile mother got the chance to catch hold of her.

Maisey blushed as her daughter continued, 'One of the best was about two months ago after we had all gone to bed and left you both in the big room. Even Joanne said to us that she wished she could find out what our parents had been drinking that evening because she wanted some of it too!'

Little Emmy dived under her bed in a vain effort to escape from her mother. The giggling fit that followed rather gave her hiding place away, as did the sound of her striking the earthenware pot that was kept under it.

Mother and daughter sat on the bed together, tears of laughter running down their cheeks. They were more like sisters than mother and daughter, and their friendship encompassed all topics of conversation, with few exceptions.

Little Emmy suddenly became very serious and said, 'Will I find a love like yours when my time comes, and will I enjoy it as much?' She looked into her mother's eyes, seeking the reassurance of an answer.

After some thought, Maisey replied, 'I don't know. All I can tell you is that when you find a man that stirs you in body, heart, and soul commit yourself to him without reservation, but you must always remember that you do so through good times as well as bad. If *all that* is returned by the man you have chosen, then true love will more than likely be yours.'

Her daughter quietly got up from the bed and giving her mother a dazzling smile, went down the stairs to find her father.

She found him in the big room, standing by the hearth and gazing into the fire. She went up to him, wrapped her arms around him, reached up, and kissed him.

'I love you,' she said quietly and then went out to find her friend Alice.

Gumshu was still in the same position when Maisey came back into the room.

He said thoughtfully, 'We have the lease. Now we decide the policy.'

She sat down on the oak settle and put her feet on one of the old dogs that lay in front of the fire, scratching its ear with her foot.

'Well,' she said, 'we've talked to a lot of the smaller mine operators, and they all seem happy to come under the Hawk mark, as long as we give them some degree of freedom. What's the worry?'

'The bigger partnership mines and the ones owned by the large landowners are the worry,' he replied, still deep in thought.

'That's easy. They stop operating in the area we have the lease on, close their mine, and start again outside our area. Or if that's not acceptable, they do the same as the smaller operators and extract coal under the Hawk mark. *Either, or*—that's it,' she stated.

'It may be that simple, but I know that *they* won't see it that way,' Gumshu said, frowning slightly.

'In that case, you and I need to visit every mine within our lease area. We explain and give them four weeks to comply, or we invoke the terms of our lease to the letter,' Maisey replied with a degree of finality.

Over the following week, Gumshu and Maisey visited all the mines affected, and true to her word, Maisey explained to every collier what Hawk Mines' intentions were. All but the two mines owned and run by a major landowner concurred to her requests. The two mines involved closed within a week, so Hawk took them over and started to operate them, re-engaging the miners and putting in their own foremen.

Edmund and Thomas had already drafted an agreement for all the independent owners to sign, which in simple terms allowed them to carry on operating, but any rents and levies they paid now went directly to Hawk and not the government. On their part, Hawk contracted to buy their coal. Most of the colliers thought the agreement fair, in that they had a guaranteed market for their coal at a guaranteed price.

The only stipulations Hawk made were about safety standards and *not* employing children underground.

The four trows built at Chepstow were now operating on the Wye and Severn Rivers and on the Bristol Channel, when tide and weather allowed. The specially adapted vessels carried their cargoes to areas hitherto inaccessible to Hawk Mines, and with the network of selling agents that Gumshu had appointed, coal sales soon became extremely buoyant.

The quantity of coal sold was now matching the amount extracted. That was with the new lease area running at full capacity and their first deep mine in production as well. The monthly Hawk Mines meeting at the much extended coal building now involved twenty of Hawk Mines staff, such was the increase in mine numbers. Maisey's idea of adding stone quarries to their mining interests had also been implemented, with two small Forest quarry units now being in production.

Thomas said to Gumshu at the end of one such gathering, 'It was one lucky snowball fight you and I had in Craven Street that night!'

The wool business was also thriving.

As there was still a heavy government tax on the export of raw wool, restricting sales, Grundwell's diversification plans had been well timed. He had constructed a third brick weaving building close to the first two, and that too contained the revolutionary new production machines.

He had also employed two artists to enhance the designs of the coloured cloths he was producing. Such was the demand for the Spinning Wheel products that he had gone back to a considerable amount of *outsourcing.* That became achievable because experienced *weavers* and *spinners* from other parts of the county were moving into Mitcheldean. The Spinning Wheel was more than able to provide employment for them.

Sophie mentioned one evening when she, Mary, and Grundwell had been talking, that perhaps it would be good for the Spinning Wheel business if they built their own cottages to rent to those who were seeking to work for them.

That remark was the result of a conversation that she had had with William Benson, when he told her that more and more of his parishioners were newcomers to the town, and one common complaint was lack of accommodation.

Grundwell thought for a few minutes.

'We already own two of those cottages on the lane out to Cumdean,' he said. 'But we've rented those to our Oriental families. If I have a word with the town fathers and see if we can build more cottages, maybe ten in that street and possibly more elsewhere, that may help to solve the problem.'

The next morning he and Philip went to see Nathaniel, and they began going through all the Spinning Wheel's finances. With substantial reserves, it was obvious that there was no need to borrow funds for the new project.

They decided, after a talk with Mary, that they would build twenty five and not the ten originally discussed.

Grundwell saw the town fathers, architects, and his builders; the project was going to be started six weeks later. He kept Sophie and Mary fully informed with all the details, as he was planning an extended trip. His idea was to see if he could expand sales even further by appointing more selling agents, and making some personal calls on his customers.

The plan was to visit Plymouth first, as many of his textiles were exported to Europe through the port, and then Waterford, in southern Ireland.

The new weaving buildings were producing finer items than ever before with the modern looms. With a dyeing and finishing section also within each of the buildings, Grundwell had succeeded in developing a finished product that was beginning to compete with the silk trade, as he had predicted to Sophie and Mary.

Although the political situation had worsened, his European market was still strong, and he was keen to maximise it whilst the opportunity existed, hence the need to visit Plymouth.

'Using agents is fine, but there comes a time when a personal visit is far more effective for promoting business,' he told Sophie when explaining the reasons for his trip.

He had also never been to Ireland before, and with Waterford being the gateway port for imports into Ireland, he felt that a personal visit there would also be beneficial.

Gumshu came to similar conclusions, after several discussions with his friend.

He wanted Hawk Mines to take advantage of the thriving coastal trade that was developing, as he was sure that he could match the coal fields of the north-east on price as well as quality. To do that, he too felt that he should go and meet the people involved on a personal basis. His ultimate aim was to be able to supply a lot more of his coal into London, which had a phenomenally high demand.

Thomas had also told him there was a continental market growing for quality English coal, news which whetted his appetite for the trip even more as coincidently the exporting port was Plymouth.

He had recently heard news that some Welsh-mined coal was being exported to Ireland from the ports around Cardiff and Swansea. As Hawk Mines were looking to Wales to expand their operation, he felt that an Irish trip could well be beneficial to their plans.

Like Grundwell, he had never set foot on Irish soil and thought the trip an opportunity not to be missed, especially as he seemed to share an affinity with several of the Irish people he knew. Their sense of humour and relaxed attitude always intrigued him.

Having talked to Maisey at some length about the need for the trip, she was enthusiastic though a little troubled that her husband would be away for up to three months.

'I'll be all right,' he said. 'I'll be with Grundwell.'

'That's what worries me,' retorted his wife. 'That's what really worries me!'

# CHAPTER 15

Grundwell and Gumshu stood on the quayside at Chepstow, opposite the high white cliffs, watching the hive of activity both on the dockside and the river. There were merchant ships of all sizes, loading and unloading, preparing and departing for sea, arriving back from voyages afar, as well as small trows and dinghies scurrying hither and thither, powered by current, wind, and oar.

The tide was on the flood, covering the mudflats and filling deep channels and ravines with grey swirling water. Boats that had been previously out of sight and mind rose up from the riverbed as if awakening from a deep slumber.

With both men now owning trows that plied the waters of the river with their cargoes of wool and coal, they were both well aware of the shortage of time before the tide receded, leaving navigation on the river virtually impossible for all but those boats with the shallowest of drafts.

They boarded the brigantine *Rachel* bound for Plymouth. They had booked passage sometime earlier with their shipping agent, Captain John Saunders, who had made all the arrangements for them. In fact, *Rachel* was loaded with some of Grundwell's woollen cloth that was being transported to Plymouth, eventually destined to be shipped to France and Portugal. Gumshu had also got a substantial cargo of coal on board that he wanted to show to the coal merchants of Plymouth, to give them an idea of the quality of his product.

On Grundwell's insistence, the coal had been loaded well away from his woollen goods and had been extremely well sheeted.

They intended to follow their plan of going to Plymouth first and then on to Waterford, appointing selling agents in both ports, who would in turn deal with the various town—or city-based merchants. That had been the arrangement that both men had set up in Bristol and Chepstow some twelve months previously, and that had proved successful and highly lucrative for both Hawk Mines and the Spinning Wheel. When they had planned their trip, the only loose end they hadn't tied up was whether to engage the agents on a commission-only basis or employ them directly. They were both concerned that, with the agents being so far removed from Mitcheldean, lack of motivation could well become a problem.

Their other thought had been to develop Grundwell's idea of buying their own fleet of larger ships for the transport of the goods by sea, as the use of the trows had proved highly successful and profitable. Lawlessness coupled with the slowness of transport using animal-drawn carts had become a major issue for both men, so they needed to seek alternatives.

They had actually got as far as instructing their bookkeepers to prepare costings, had been to see Nathaniel for his observations, and then approached ship builders in the Chepstow area to discuss suitable ship designs and prices.

They were shown down to a small cabin in the stern of the vessel, with two box sea berths, a small fixed table, and a cupboard that was supposed to take their baggage.

'Puts a new meaning on the word *small*, doesn't it?' Grundwell commented, trying to push past his friend whilst stooping down to avoid banging his head on the low deck head.

Gumshu looked at the sea bunks, which were some five feet long by two feet wide, constructed somewhat like an open-topped coffin, then glanced at Grundwell's six-foot frame which was similar to his own.

'We were always told when we were boys that we were the children of the Forest Giant, not of our fathers, if you remember.' The mine owner grimaced.

'Yes, and I can remember what my mother said by way of reply! I didn't understand it then, but I do now.'

'How the hell do I fit into that?' Gumshu replied, looking down at the bunk.

'Well, words to that effect!' Grundwell retorted with a grin.

The crew of the brigantine began to work their craft into the centre of the river to benefit from the last of the flood tide, helped by two small oar-powered pulling boats. The captain, a thirty-two-year-old native of Plymouth, was a regular visitor to Chepstow, so knowing the winds and tides, he started using the wind as soon as he cleared the cliffs that towered above his boat's two masts, setting his large stern sail first, followed by the three forward sails that were mounted on the bowsprit. He would leave his top gallants until he was clear into the Severn Estuary, as he was aware he had to navigate some two miles of bends in the River Wye before he reached more open water, so the less sail he carried the better.

The friends stood on the afterdeck of the *Rachel*, keeping well clear of the crew. The disgruntled looks on their faces gave away their feelings about leaving port and its many attributes and about having to manoeuvre a 110-foot-long, well-laden vessel around some of the river's tighter bends at the start of a voyage.

Gumshu felt the boat shudder a few times as she carved an unintentional groove in the soft grey mud, but with some deft helming, the captain corrected his errors without mishap.

The two turned to look back at the docks, as if there should have been someone there to wave them off. But all the tearful goodbyes had been already said in the privacy of their own homes in Craven Street.

Sophie had Mary's shoulder to cry on when her husband had finally left, but Maisey had no one. She had sat with Little Emmy by the fire, quietly praying for her husband's safe return, knowing that she would not see or hear from him for at least two months, possibly three.

Alice had said to William Benson in her class at the church the day before, 'I might be sixteen years old now, but I can still cry like a child.'

'Never lose that ability, Alice, because showing your emotions is never wrong,' William had replied.

He had cried uncontrollably when he had held both his firstborn and recently his second child. Eleanor had smiled at her husband with a radiance that had been very hard to describe, according to the midwife who attended to her for both births.

The *Rachel* started to pitch into the swell of the Bristol Channel as she cleared the coastal hills' protection from the brisk cold north by north westerly wind. The captain set his top gallants before he came out of the lee of the land, so she now caught the full force of the wind and heeled to the task in hand. She started to feel the beginnings of the ebb tide under her keel, which sent her speeding on her way from leading mark to leading mark, as her helmsman expertly followed the channel down towards the open sea and Plymouth.

The captain's aim was to get to Oxwich Bay, a small bay on the south facing coast of the Gower Peninsular, and lie to his anchor there. That would give him some protection from the wind and the ferocity of the Bristol Channel's incoming tide. They would then wait until the tide changed to the ebb again and then make all sail, crossing the Bristol Channel, leaving Lundy Island to their starboard, and heading down towards the Isles of Scilly.

There they would pass to the landward of the Isles, passing Land's End headland and giving a wide berth to the partly submerged Seven Stones, and infamous Wolf Rock. Captain Dickens would then set a course along the English coast, passing the Lizard, and then eventually arriving in Plymouth Sound.

His biggest concerns had been the activities of the privateers and the wreckers of Devon and Cornwall, both groups of which were active in the prevailing conditions of wind and tide. But the *Rachel* had a good turn of speed, sailed well to windward, and in fact had some cannon power of her own.

Gumshu and Grundwell were wool men and colliers, not seamen. As the boat entered the Severn Estuary swell when passing the mouth of the River Avon off Bristol, their woes began. Both retired to their bunks after depositing their previous meal over the vessel's portside rail, having taken the advice of a crew member about wind direction. They also turned the colour of green that only sailors can describe, when they refer to mal de mer.

The two entrepreneurs stayed in their bunks until the motion and angle of the vessel had regained some form of normality, when the captain laid his anchor in Oxwich Bay some eleven hours later. Although not still, the *Rachel* became a solid platform again, and the two got up and ventured on deck.

Sadly for them, the cook was in fine form, frying beef, vegetables, and spices on his cooking fire box, coincidentally heated by Hawk Mines' coal, and the aromas hung in every corner of the boat.

The point of origin of the coal was lost on Gumshu, as he had once again found it necessary to use the portside rail and then retire to his bunk. Grundwell, meanwhile, was confident that he would be immune to any further mal de mer, until he smelt the smoke from something disgusting that a sailor had put in his mouth and then set alight.

'They're gone for the night,' Captain John Dickens commented at supper, as he asked the cook for a second helping. He spoke very quietly to his five ship's officers, who were seated round the table in his cabin.

'Do not make a joke of our passengers' seasickness please, gentlemen. These two men are about to start commissioning ships to build up their own fleet, from what I hear on the dockside at Chepstow. I would like to be a part of that business, if possible. Pass the word to the crew as well. It would be better working for them than being pressed into the King's Navy.'

His fellow officers took the point, as nearly half the crew were absconders from the royal ships of the line and had no intention of returning, either voluntarily or succumbing to the press gangs of Plymouth.

Well before dawn, the *Rachel* weighed anchor and set her sails, bound for the channel between the Isles of Scilly and the headland of Land's End. With the wind still in the same quarter as the previous day, north by north-east, and the ebb tide gaining momentum under her keel again, she showed a turn of speed that would have been the envy of many a ship's captain.

Later in the morning as they left Lundy Island about three miles off to their starboard, Captain Dickens caught the outline of sails of a twin-masted boat coming out from behind the island, apparently steering an interception course with them.

His fears were confirmed by the lookout at the masthead a few moments later.

'Warn our passengers of the impending problem please, Mister Grey,' John Dickens said to his second in command, 'and then order the gun crews to attend to their cannon and run out both port and starboard side!'

Captain Dickens was a one-time naval officer, as were three of his ship's officers together with thirty-one of his crew. Gunnery practice was a regular part of the ship's daily routine, and although only carrying sixteen cannon, with her speed and agility coupled with a well-disciplined crew, she had seen off many a privateer who had attempted to cross her path.

Grundwell and Gumshu came on deck, standing well back in the stern to avoid hindering the crew in their work. The two seemed to forget their seasickness, instead concentrating on the unfolding drama on board the *Rachel.*

As a precaution and to add fire power, the captain broke out muskets and pistols to all his men. When he offered the arms to the two gentlemen of business, each took a pistol and primers, together with muskets, balls, and gunpowder. Both were good shots when shooting game in the Forest. '*Wild birds only,*' they assured the captain with a smile.

The two boats seemed to take an eternity to close on each other.

'If they think we are too strong for them, which they probably will, what they will endeavour to do is keep as close as possible on the *seaward* of our bow and try to push us, with the help of wind and tide, on to a lee shore where their wrecking friends will hope to finish us,' John Dickens told the two Forest men. 'What I will do is let them get their vessel into that position on our starboard bow and then at the shortest distance possible, swing *Rachel* sharply round across the wind to the stern of her so that as we turn, we can bear and fire our eight *port* cannon in one broadside. I'll then gibe our boat so that she comes completely about, enabling our *starboard* cannon to bear and fire, giving the privateer a full eight cannon broadside from *that* quarter. By manoeuvring in this manner, both our port and starboard gunners should find our friend's weakest point, his stern! That is the joy of *Rachel* being a brigantine, gentlemen, speed and manoeuvrability!'

John looked at his crew with a twinkle in his eye, as they had carried out this type of action many times before. 'Make ready, my lads!' he called, taking over the helm. 'Hold tight, gentlemen,' he warned his passengers. 'This is not going to be like shooting Forest game!'

The privateer held a course to close on to their bows, as the captain had predicted. Then just as it seemed that the *Rachel* would collide with her aggressor, John Dickens acted. He pulled the whip staff over as hard and quickly as he could, the sail crew swung on their rigging lines, and the *Rachel* sheared round across the wind, leaving her *port* gunners to bear their cannon on their intended victim. Mister Grey watched and watched and waited.

'Fire!' he eventually cried, and eight cannon roared their response to the order, with eight cannon balls finding their mark.

'Port cannon, reload!' he yelled, whilst turning to face his starboard gun crews.

John Dickens heaved his helm over again with all his strength so that the *Rachel* reacted with a near instant response to her master and sail crew, turning completely around, once again bearing down on the vessel and offering her *starboard quarter* cannon to the foe.

There was now much deck activity on the privateer. Her crew seemed to have been caught completely by surprise by the rapid manoeuvres and retaliation of their intended victim. With the considerable damage inflicted by the discharge and accuracy of *Rachel*'s eight port cannon into their stern, followed by the continual deluge of deadly small arms fire, the perpetrator of the attack was now making every effort to escape.

The cries of their wounded could be heard screaming above the sounds of the battle.

Unperturbed, Mister Grey calmly watched and watched yet again. His starboard gunners adjusted their gun elevations to bear upon the quarry, and then came his call.

'Fire!'

Eight cannon roared their response, with eight more balls of hell finding their target.

Ten seconds later, there was a massive explosion, and the privateer took a grotesque leap into the air, enveloped in a mass of fire and smoke.

John steadied his ship, the sail crew trimmed their lines, and Mister Grey yelled out yet again, 'Starboard cannon, reload!'

His captain quietly responded, 'There's no point, Mister Grey.'

The smoke had cleared from where the privateer had been to reveal only bodies, scattered debris, and a tangled mass of spars, rigging, and sails, all floating on the surface of the white-capped sea.

The captain helmed his ship to edge past the floating debris of wood, canvas, and corpses. Being a mariner, he seemed to check for life even in those who had threatened his. It was all to no avail as there was no one alive to bring aboard; there was neither life nor sound, except for the cries of the circling gulls.

'Their magazine must have exploded for her to disintegrate like that!' commented one of the portside gunners, running his cannon in and closing the gun port.

'Caused by an accurate broadside from our port and starboard cannon, let us not forget.' A very happy gunnery officer and second in command of the *Rachel* smiled in reply.

'That was something to behold!' Gumshu said in a rather shaky voice.

'They didn't even get to fire one cannon at us!' Grundwell responded incredulously.

The helmsman took the whip staff back from John Dickens, who with Mister Grey went and spoke to every crew member of the *Rachel*, congratulating them on a successful action.

Coming back to his two passengers, he smiled and said, 'How's the mal de mer now, gentlemen?'

'If that is what it takes to cure it, I swear I'll never suffer from it again,' Grundwell replied, laughing somewhat nervously.

The *Rachel* returned to her original course; the crew cleared the decks and then cleaned their cannon and weapons in preparation for the next encounter.

The captain resumed his constant watch on his ship, his crew, and distant horizons.

The two passengers conferred with the cook, who prepared a special celebratory meal for everyone on board, cooked over Hawk Mine coals.

'At least it's stayed where it should this time,' the owner of the mines commented sometime later.

'What has?'

'The food we've just eaten!' Gumshu said with some considerable relief.

With the onset of dusk and another change of direction of tide, John Dickens decided to lie to his anchor once again in a bay that offered shelter from wind and tide. Although the short encounter with the privateer had been successful, they had forfeited valuable sailing time to take them around Land's End. That had lost them a favourable tide and, importantly, the light to watch for the multitude of shoals that ran along the coast, as well as the lethal Wolf Rock that lay further out into the centre of the narrow channel they were to take.

Hence, they now found themselves safely tucked in within the curves of St Ives Bay.

Mister Grey posted armed guards on all points of the ship, including at the two mastheads, on his captain's instruction. John knew that there would be considerable interest in their presence, as he had no doubt that news of their action earlier in the day would have spread. Three other vessels lay not many cables from them, all out of Plymouth. Knowing their masters, John went to each of them in his dory, explaining what had happened and the need for diligence in case of reprisals.

Well before dawn, all four vessels weighed anchor, catching the tide and wind that would take them around Land's End headland and on towards Plymouth. It had been an uneventful night, but John Dickens speculated it was because all four ships had shown plenty of lights, and the presence of the armed guards could be well seen from the shore. There had also been a lot of banter between the watches of the different boats, so much so that Grundwell wandered up on deck to see what was going on.

He met with John Dickens, and the two fell into conversation as they walked around the deck. Grundwell explained something of his and Gumshu's idea about starting a commercial fleet of their own, telling him that neither he nor his friend knew anything of the sea or ships. He then asked if John would consider the idea of joining their joint venture to manage it for them.

The captain didn't mention that he'd already heard on the dockside at Chepstow that the two were considering commissioning several vessels to build up a small fleet of ships. He merely replied that he would be more than interested in such an offer.

'Once this trip of ours is over, we'll contact you through our shipping agent, John Saunders, and when your next trip takes you to Chepstow, we'll talk further. What would be the reaction of the *Rachel*'s owner if you came to work with us?

John smiled and said, 'The boat is mine.'

The following evening, they made their way up Plymouth Sound, heading towards the commercial docks of the port. With the aid of two harbour-owned pulling gigs, in addition to the skill of her master, *Rachel* was soon moored up and lying alongside her wharf.

Grundwell and Gumshu disembarked with John Dickens directing them to an inn not far from the docks. He told them that they were very welcome to stay the night on board again, if they so wished.

Gumshu thanked him for his kindness, but as he was still walking with a limp and a twisted back, he felt the urge for somewhere with a large bed and a lovely feather down mattress.

Morning found the two Forest friends talking with the merchant who dealt with the Spinning Wheel's wool and cloth, much of which was exported from the port.

Matthew James was an expansive man, with a loud, deep voice that announced his presence long before he entered a room. Being of a rotund build, a jolly face, and engaging smile, he had always told his closest friends that his secret with ladies of all ages was to replace good looks with good manners, charm, and wealth. It certainly seemed to work because although being unmarried even at the age of forty, he had a string of very beautiful ladies at his beck and call, much to the envy of all his friends.

Grundwell had met Matthew several times before, as he had stayed at Craven Street on numerous occasions. He had known Mary and Edward for a number of years, first meeting them on one of the wool buying trips made for his export business. He'd never asked the manner of Edward's death, neither had the family ever told him. However, as it had been the talk of the wool trade for months after it had happened, Matthew already knew. He sat and listened to his two visitors' account of the Lundy sea battle with great interest.

'John Dickens is a highly respected captain in this area and knows his job well. He has had several fights with the privateers and has always come out on the winning side, except once. That was when his wife and child were killed,' he said quietly.

Grundwell looked at him enquiringly, so after some consideration Matthew continued, 'As you know, the *Rachel* belongs to him, but at one stage, he had two boats. The second boat, the *Wayfarer*, was skippered by John's brother, Richard. Both vessels were given to him by his father, who was a very successful wool merchant. He had a fine house on the outskirts of town, as well as owning a weaving business and a huge dockside warehouse.

'From what I gather, Richard had been bringing a cargo back from London to the warehouse. This is the large building that stands back from the wharf where you probably berthed last night.

'As well as the cargo, he had also picked up John's wife and young son to bring them back home to Plymouth after visiting her parents, who lived in London. As they came round Bolt Head, off Salcombe, they were attacked by two privateers who had been hiding in the mouth of the river estuary. It was by *pure coincidence* that John had been coming out of Plymouth and sailing to Dartmouth with a cargo for the navy. He was less than a mile off the point where the attack was taking place, so obviously he went straight to Richard's aid.

'Very sadly, he didn't get there quickly enough to stop the *Wayfarer* from taking some fatal cannon shot from the privateers, as well as being boarded. John managed to drive the two attacking vessels off, sinking one and dismasting the other. When he returned to the *Wayfarer*, she was very low in the water and obviously sinking fast. He got his boat alongside, and then he and his second in command, William Grey, boarded her. What they found, I think, must be every mariner's worst nightmare!

'John's wife, son, and brother had been put to the sword by the privateers' boarding party. Most of *Wayfarer*'s crew had been killed by cannon shot, but any survivors or wounded had been murdered in the same way as their captain. The vessel was sinking so quickly, the only bodies that could be brought aboard the *Rachel* were those of his wife, son, and brother.

'Once clear of the stricken boat, John returned to where the other privateer's dismasted vessel was lying and raked it with cannon and musket shot until it sank. It is said, and I do emphasise that it is said, that there were still men alive in the water. John personally loaded the bow chaser with grapeshot and repeatedly fired into the floating wreckage where the remaining crew members were trying to hide.

'There were *no* survivors from either of the privateer's ships by the end of the action. John brought the bodies of his family ashore at the naval dockyard in Plymouth. His father and mother were on the dockside to meet him. As in all communities such as ours, word of such engagements spread like wildfire. The grief that the family suffered cannot be imagined.

'The joint funeral was probably the biggest event that this town has ever witnessed. All through that terrible time, John's face was a totally impassive and expressionless mask. However, after the funeral, he and his crew took *Rachel* out, and they went along both sides of the English Channel, flushing out and sinking another eleven privateers, leaving no survivors.

'His boat had originally been called *Gull*, but he renamed her *Rachel* after his wife. His father and mother died a few weeks after that fateful day of the action, some say from broken hearts, and how is anyone able to disbelieve that.'

There was a silence in the room after Matthew's revelations.

'But John took the *Rachel* through all the debris looking for survivors when we had that action off Lundy!' Grundwell said, looking a little shaken.

'If he'd found any, he would have killed them!' Matthew replied quietly.

Grundwell looked at Gumshu, and they obviously both had the same thought.

'Matthew, can I ask you a very sensitive and confidential question?' Grundwell asked.

'Yes, of course.'

'You know that we are thinking of starting our own fleet of commercial vessels?'

'Yes, you told me this morning, but I'd already heard the dockside chatter about it some time ago.'

'What you don't know, but have probably guessed, is that we've indicated to our Captain John Dickens that we'd like him to start work with us, setting the fleet up and then running it. The question is, would he be likely to set it up as his own private navy to eradicate all privateers that he can get his hands on?'

'In a word, *yes*,' Matthew replied without hesitation. 'You've seen how good his crew are at handling themselves. That only comes with training, and a lot of it. If you took him on, yes, he is a very good commander, he's a good organiser, the best you'll get. You're going to have to provide protection for your ships anyway, as these are lawless times on the high seas. But your cargoes would always come second to his revenge, to put it very bluntly.'

'As we've just begun to realise,' Grundwell replied somewhat testily, as he suddenly got the impression that they had been used from the outset of this trip and even before that. He remembered some of his conversations with John Saunders, their shipping agent in Chepstow. He had said how good the captain was and *by chance* his boat was in and heading back to Plymouth, just at the time Grundwell and Gumshu wanted to travel.

'This is something we need to sort out with Dickens now, don't you think, Gumshu?' Grundwell snapped, becoming extremely angry.

'Yes, but let's finish your business with Matthew first. Then we'll go and see Joseph Clerk who is one of the merchants for coal in Plymouth and whom Matthew has recommended. After that, we'll go back to the wharf where the *Rachel* is berthed and have quiet words with our captain!' Gumshu replied, endeavouring to calm his friend.

The culmination of the discussions was that Matthew would become the Grundwell's selling agent as well as his shipping merchant, whilst still retaining his independence to act as a merchant for other customers. Any items he sold belonging to the Spinning Wheel would be on a strictly commission-only basis for payment, although he would hold a considerable stock of their goods in his own warehouse.

It wasn't quite the arrangement Grundwell had in mind when he had first arrived, but he now thought it could well encourage Matthew to be more active in the selling of Spinning Wheel goods. Lack of enthusiasm over sales was a problem he was having with some of his other agents, and it was a problem that made him very short-tempered.

The fact he would have to stand the cost of Mathew's stock standing until it sold did not perturb him, as he was well aware that his product range sold extremely quickly.

Both he and Matthew shook hands on the arrangement and signed a contract that Matthew's clerk had drawn up on their joint instruction.

Joseph Clerk's coal merchant's buildings lay on the edge of the town of Plymouth. Joseph had reckoned no one liked coal dust, but everyone liked the heat that coal gave, so he was allowed to have the buildings just within the town limits.

'So that the coal dust won't spoil the taste of our town fathers' wine,' he had said on more than one occasion, when he was asked why his coal yard was so far out on the town's boundary.

He too, like his friend Matthew, was a jovial, rotund, and likable man, but that was where the likeness ended. Joseph was married, had six children, and did not have a lot of social life because he was rarely clean and tidy. Neither did he care what women thought about him, as he only had one woman in his life, Chantal, a lady of French origin who scared the wits out of him and everyone else she encountered.

'She was a slim, long-legged, long-haired beauty with a deep sexy French voice when I met her first!' Joseph told everyone.

Gumshu and he got on extremely well, in spite of never having met before. When they were discussing water transport, Joseph asked him if he knew that there were special boats called *colliers* that were specifically designed to carry coal around the coast. Built in Newcastle, they were designed to ship cargoes from the north-east coal fields into London.

He mentioned this to him because, in his experience, the unloading of coal from a brigantine was not an easy operation. His men had told him that unloading *Rachel* that morning had been no exception. There were three collier boats along the wharf from where *Rachel* was berthed, and if Gumshu liked, he would arrange for them to have a look at one.

'Why are the three together?' the mine owner asked. 'Surely that's a lot of unloading at one time?'

'They travel in numbers because of raids by privateers,' the merchant told him.

'Privateers again!' the wool man commented from the other side of the table.

Joseph and Gumshu came to a similar business arrangement as Grundwell and Matthew. As they left the building, Grundwell commented to his friend, 'Do you get the feeling that those two quietly manoeuvred us into an already discussed arrangement?'

Gumshu responded that he thought they probably had, but as it suited them all at the moment he really had no problem with it.

The two men then went to their inn for something to eat and drink before going to look at *collier* boats and find a certain sea captain.

# CHAPTER 16

After some thought and much discussion in their room at the inn, Gumshu and Grundwell decided that they would go and seek out John Dickens before going to look at the collier boats. The pair went down to the wharf where the *Rachel* was berthed and found the captain supervising the loading of a cargo before embarking on another trip.

John saw the looks on the faces of the two Forest men, and being perceptive, he immediately took them below to his quarters. They sat at the cabin table, and the ship's cook brought them some ale along with some oatmeal biscuits that he had made.

Sensing the atmosphere, he vacated the cabin as quickly as possible.

As soon as he closed the cabin door, Grundwell growled, 'John, the other evening you and I had a talk about the possibility of you joining us in a venture that Gumshu and I are considering.'

'Yes,' John replied tentatively, wondering what was coming next.

'We have been made aware of the horrendous incident off Bolt Head, and we are both extremely sorry about what happened and the ensuing deaths of your mother and father. We have also been told about your acts of revenge on privateers, which we fully understand, and although we don't endorse it, it certainly isn't our place to pass comment or judgement.

'But we now have a grave concern about your motives for joining us, and it's one that we both feel could affect the outcome of any discussions that we may have. Bringing it into the open now could well save us all a lot of time, expense, and possibly bad feeling.'

'Go on,' John said in a somewhat frosty voice, leaving the table and going to stand by the stern gallery lights that overlooked the river.

'We are not sure of boat numbers yet or the type of craft that we will end up buying. However, our investment is going to be substantial. It's going to be a long-term commitment and for a specific purpose, that purpose being to expand and complement our already fairly large business interests.'

Gumshu now took up the conversation. 'What we are not prepared to fund is a private vendetta against all privateers on the high seas, however laudable. We have a *suspicion* that could well be at the back of your mind when deciding whether to join us or not. As Grundwell has said, we are very sorry about your family and fully understand your motives, but that is as far as we go.'

John looked at both of them and realised that they were not about to accept any deception from him about his intentions. Those two were extremely hard men, who would not stand any nonsense from anyone. They were quite capable of sorting out any problem either by fist or by money, as long as the outcome was in their favour.

'You're quite right, of course. It was more than just at the back of my mind to be very honest with you,' he replied. After a pause, he continued, 'Having admitted my thoughts, where does that lead us?'

'Well, we expected you to give us an honest answer, and you haven't let us down,' Grundwell said, standing up and going to stand beside John, looking out at the busy port traffic as he did so. The Forest man looked down at the mariner and with a wry smile said, 'How come you're so short?'

'It's so that I can fit into the sea bunk on my boat without twisting and bending double. I also don't have to walk with a constant stoop when below decks!' he replied.

Gumshu, who was still sitting at the table, groaned as the agony of trying to sleep and move round in such conditions was still a very vivid memory.

The timely remark from Grundwell had the desired effect; it broke the ice and it also set the mood for the rest of the day that the three spent together.

The ship's cook made several visits to the captain's cabin with ale and biscuits, each time reporting back to the rest of the crew on how the negotiations were progressing. The rest of the time, the crew themselves tried to listen through skylights and cabin doors, without much success.

Eventually the three emerged into the afternoon sunlight and made their way ashore with the intention of having a look at one of the collier boats.

As he was about to go down the gangway, John Dickens turned to his crew, who were endeavouring to look busy. 'Well, gentlemen, what you couldn't hear by eavesdropping no doubt the cook has filled you in on, so I shall be brief.

'After our next trip, we will become part of the Spinning Wheel Hawk Mines enterprise. We are planning to have six brigantines built similar to *Rachel*, and subject to our visit now to have a look at a collier, we are going to have four of those built. Two brigantines will be built by the Dutch, two here at Plymouth, and two in Chepstow. Their crews will be drawn from where the boats are built, with the exception of the ones built by the Dutch as they will be based in Waterford, subject to Grundwell and Gumshu's visit there when they leave Plymouth.

'The *Rachel* will remain under my ownership, and if we undertake any little "*trip*s", it will only involve her. We hope to start the building programme within the next three months. Oh, and one more thing, I shall be running the new fleet. Are there any questions?'

'For my own safety, can I join one of the other brigantines, please, Captain? I fancy the chance of a long life and grandchildren bouncing upon my knee!' the ship's boatswain asked, amidst laughter from the other crew members.

'Careful, Ben! If I let you join another boat, her captain might make you work. And as for grandchildren, you've enough of them to make up a brigantine's crew. You've just forgotten which port they're in!'

With that, Captain Dickens turned and walked down on to the dockside, amidst a loud cheer and much hilarity from his ship's crew.

Gumshu and John talked at length with the collier's captain, who was from Newcastle. He had brought that particular cargo of coal from Cardiff, in company of the other two collier boats. They plied the south-western coasts of England and Wales when they got bored with their regular delivery trips, which were from Newcastle to London and back.

He said that their main worry was *always* the privateers who harassed them, hence the sailing in company.

The captain showed his three guests around the boat, although there was not a lot to see. John murmured to Gumshu when the collier's captain was out of earshot.

'And you think my boat's cabins are small and cramped!'

'The *Rachel*'s are palaces by comparison I agree, and unlike these, they're clean! Look, John, everything on the boat is black with coal dust, including the sails!'

Grundwell decided that he'd seen enough of collier boats, so he went off on his own to investigate the smell of fish that was more than noticeable in the air.

He turned a corner of the docks and in front of him stretched a fleet of large fishing boats, the like of which he had never seen before. Sitting on one of the bollards on the quayside was a lone figure who he thought he recognised.

It was Joseph Clerk, the coal merchant.

'Joseph, what are you doing here?' he asked.

'I was hiding, actually. I've finished all my work and was in danger of having to go home!'

Grundwell sat on the next bollard, and the two talked at length about everything and obviously coal. Joseph also explained to him the importance of the fishing boat fleet to Plymouth, its growth, and what he thought the future held.

'I suspect you're going to become part of that future, Grundwell.'

Grundwell looked at him sharply, not knowing quite how to respond to him.

'What? With a coastal fleet of some six, maybe ten ships? I don't think so, Joseph, unless you know something I don't?'

'No, there's going to be possibly more than boats, my friend, and if you've got a few moments, I'll take you and show you something.'

'Let me just go back and tell the other two I'm going off with you for a few minutes,' Grundwell replied.

'No need. We're going back to where the *Rachel* is berthed, and we'll need John with us anyway,' Joseph said, getting up from his bollard.

The two walked back to where John and Gumshu were coming off the collier brig and saying their farewells to its captain. Joseph went up to John, put his arm around his shoulders, and led him to one side.

Gumshu looked at Grundwell, who shrugged his shoulders.

The two returned from their confidential talk a few moments later.

Joseph smiled and said, 'First, what we haven't told you is that I'm John's uncle. His mother was my elder sister. Now, as Matthew the wool man may have told you, John's father was a wool merchant, the business dealing mainly in exporting as well as weaving his own cloth, much as I understand you do, Grundwell.

'What he didn't tell you is that the business belonged to me and my sister's side of the family, and John's father only ran it for us. When my sister and brother-in-law died, the business reverted to one owner by a series of wills of previously deceased family members. Bit complicated, but that's what lawyers do to keep us paying. Anyway, that person is, quite simply, me!'

'And it wasn't my father who bought the two boats for me. It was in fact my uncle Joseph and my mother,' John added. 'They did that to get me out of the navy because they thought it was *too dangerous!*'

'Really!' Grundwell commented with a wide grin, as they arrived outside a substantial stone building with a rough slated roof, standing back from the wharf where the *Rachel* was berthed.

'This is the building that the business operated from, and I want to sell it,' Joseph continued. He undid the locks with a large set of keys he carried and opened the heavy doors, and the party went inside.

Grundwell, for once in his life, was speechless.

Gumshu turned and looked at him, saying, 'This could be your weaving shed in Mitcheldean. It's so similar. The machines are older, but basically, as a collier, I'd say it was the same, only a lot, lot bigger!'

'And look at the storage space. I've even got separate buildings for mine, and there's still not as much,' Grundwell said before he lapsed back into a stunned silence.

Joseph took over the conversation again. 'To date, I have not been able to sell it because there is a clause in the will of my grandfather that states the property must only be sold to a member of the wool trade. This was to stop speculators buying it, which it most definitely did! I could have sold this building ten times over, if it hadn't been for that clause. Matthew wanted to buy it at one time, but as he already has a substantial building on the other side of the docks, I guessed he was going to sell it on. He lost interest once I told him about the restriction on the sale.

'I did say to John that if you two offered him the opportunity to run your fleet, however small, I'd give you a chance to buy this. I must be honest. The reason I was sitting on that bollard by the fish dock was because I was trying to work out how I could afford to buy a small number of fishing boats. I can foresee a time when it will be the biggest industry in Plymouth. It will also give me an excuse to stay out of the house.'

'Oh, come on, Joseph,' Gumshu replied. 'She can't be that bad!'

'Um, I'll remind you of that statement when you meet her,' John said, laughing.

Grundwell was walking around the building without comment. Joseph made a sign to the others to leave him alone, so they went outside the main doors and sat down on some old timber that had been left there, leaving Grundwell to his tour of inspection on his own.

About half an hour later, he came out and sat down without speaking.

Then, staring vacantly at the *Rachel*, he said, 'I came here to buy ships and set up agents to work for me to deal with the merchants in the town. What *actually* happens is that I get attacked by privateers, sleep in a bunk designed for a dwarf, suffer trial by mal de mer, appoint an agent who is really a merchant, get dragged on to a black floating coal bucket with a captain who talks the hind leg off a donkey, and because of his accent, I can't understand a word he says. Then I'm asked if I want to buy a wool facility that is immense, even compared with the one my family already own!'

The other three waited for his next pearls of wisdom.

None came, so Gumshu commented with a grin, 'Really, he's had a good few days. Just gets a bit emotional about things. It's his age, you know!' With that, he moved quickly out of range of his friend's arm because the fist on the end of that arm was something best avoided.

Grundwell turned to look at Joseph and John. 'Gentlemen, I will be honest. Until I contact Nathaniel, the goldsmith who holds my reserves, I can't give you a direct answer on whether I can afford to buy this building or not. I will also have to discuss it with my wife and mother-in-law because, unlike my friend here, I do not take decisions without first talking to them about it. I am interested, very interested, but can you give me say a two-month option on it? I also take it that you closed the actual business when your brother-in-law died?'

'Yes, it closed. Your offer on a two-month option on the building sounds like a reasonable request, Grundwell. I'll say a tentative "yes", but I will need the offer documented, then perhaps I can get a loan for the purchase of the fishing boats. I don't want to use the coal business as a security, in case anything happens to me, as it will always support my family.'

'Even the French connection?' Grundwell joked.

'Really, I do love her. But she does get very bossy. I always joke about it, but we've been through some bad times together, as well as some good, and have always pulled through because we've stuck together. The one thing she always says, though, is to please tell her if she ever gets like her mother because she actually doesn't like her,' Joseph admitted.

'Having six children is really the proof of how they feel about each other!' John said, laughing.

'Yes, I know. It's when she rolls those gorgeous great eyes at me and calls me her "cherie" in her husky French accent that I become a totally lost cause!' Joseph sighed with a faraway look.

'I have a similar problem. Maisey only has to drop her voice, roll her eyes and gently toss her hair, smile, and I'll do anything for her. Then she cheats and I get a flash of a thigh or breast, and I become a gibbering wreck!' Gumshu's voice trailed off, and he too gave a deep sigh as he remembered just how much he loved and missed her.

'Beautiful, but can be lethal when annoyed!' Grundwell added, 'She and my wife are the best of friends, and they are often taken for sisters. Sophie's got a smile that can break a heart at a hundred yards. The trouble is, my eldest daughter has got the same wonderful looks and smile, but she's got a fiery temperament with it. When she's older, she's going to be hell on two legs for some poor man!'

John smiled, remembering his own wife and the way she had always got what she wanted.

'I'm sorry, John. I shouldn't have started that conversation,' Joseph said apologetically.

'It's all right, Uncle. The pain dims but not the memory. It's good to listen to husbands being enthusiastic about their wives. You don't often hear that on board ship,' John replied.

The following day, Grundwell, Gumshu, and John Dickens met with the boat builder who they had decided would construct two of the brigantines for the new venture. His shipyard was further along the waterfront from *Rachel*'s berth; he and his team of shipwrights had actually built her some years previously.

The owner of the yard, Walter Symonds, was a thoughtful, third-generation craftsman, who had a passion for his trade, wood, and boats of any type. His premises gave away his character and his reputation, being tidy, well organised, and importantly, always busy.

The three visitors passed an area where three naval brigantines were being built. As they walked, they couldn't help but breathe in the intoxicating smells of newly worked timbers, glues, and hot pitch, all mixed in with the essence of the sea. There were also a multitude of sounds created by the men of the yard, as they engaged in their various tasks.

After three hours of discussion, the four men came up with a slightly revised layout to that of the *Rachel* for the new brigantines. There would be more cargo space, less accommodation, and a modified sail rig so that crew numbers could be reduced.

They also agreed a reduction in cannon power from sixteen to ten, a point that John Dickens wasn't happy with, but as Grundwell reminded him, the vessels were being built for carrying cargoes and not for fighting wars.

When all the details had been agreed, including prices, payment schedules, and delivery dates, Grundwell looked at Gumshu, and they both nodded.

'John, we would consider it a great honour if you would let us name the first boat off the stocks *Wayfarer* and the second *Gull* in honour of your family,' Grundwell asked in a quiet voice.

'Gentlemen, that would be a tremendous compliment, and I thank you both for the thought,' John replied, quietly leaving the table and walking outside the building to lean against a wooden rail beyond the door.

The others could see that his shoulders were shaking, and so they carried on with their discussions, leaving him to his private thoughts of those who were still so very dear to him.

When he came back to join them, the two Gloucestershire men looked at each other, and this time Gumshu spoke, 'Walter, how would you feel about building four brigantines for us instead of two?'

'The only problem I could foresee is how quickly I would be able to finish them for you. I have some good seasoned timber for hull and spars and the men to do it, but I can only build one at a time because of my other commitments,' he concluded, after some thought.

'Well, that would not be a problem for us, as it would ease our cash flow if the boats were not all ready at the same time. It would also ease John's task of getting crews for them, especially around here with the press gangs being so active.

'After our talk with him this morning, we decided not to have two boats built by the Dutch as we had originally intended, hence our request that you build four here, even though their prices are lower than yours. In spite of that cost difference, we all feel that the political situation between Holland and this country is not particularly good at the moment. Therefore, we could be risking capital. And we'd rather have English-built boats, if the truth be known.

'Not that it affects you, but we've also decided not to base any vessels in Waterford as we had originally planned. Again, we feel that to keep most of the fleet based where John can keep a watchful eye on it is by far the best plan. We're still going to have two built in the yard below Chepstow, but they can be watched over by John Saunders, our shipping agent there.

'The fact that he's also a friend of John's actually *helps* in this case!' Gumshu said, giving a blushing John Dickens a playful nudge before continuing. 'As far as the four collier brigs are concerned, rather than have them built on the north-east coast, we are going to have those built at the Chepstow yards as well.

'Our Newcastle-based captain friend is taking his little fleet to Chepstow docks to pick up a cargo of my coal and bring it back for Joseph Clerk. We're sending a message back with him for our shipping agent, asking him to take the captain to the shipyard that built our trows, and could possibly build the other two brigantines, to show them the design of the colliers. They appear to be very simple in hull construction and sail plan, and therefore should pose no problem to construct.'

'Let's hope that our boat builder in Chepstow can understand the captain of the collier better than I could. I still have no idea what he was saying to me yesterday!' Grundwell repeated with a grin.

The keel of the *Wayfarer* was laid the following week. As Captain John Dickens had embarked on another trip to Brest, it was only Gumshu, Grundwell, and Walter Symonds who watched the keel timbers being laid into their stocks, and then the boatyard team of joiners starting work with their adzes.

'So this is what happens to our Forest timber when the boat builders get hold of it,' Gumshu observed. 'I hope someone is going to replant all those trees that we are cutting down, otherwise we are all going to be very, very short of timber in years to come,' he added, returning to an old theme.

'Amen to that!' Walter Symonds commented, who had the same concerns.

He frequently visited forested areas all over the southern part of England and Wales, searching for prime timber for the boats he was building. It was now becoming harder and harder to find the right trees, especially for the masts and spars.

The two residents from Craven Street stayed for another three weeks in Plymouth, visiting various agents and merchants who dealt in the commodities that they offered.

They sent a horse-mounted messenger to Mitcheldean with extensive letters for their families and their managers, as well as for Nathaniel the goldsmith.

In their banker's lengthy correspondences, they explained the change of plans for their fleet of vessels, as well as the Spinning Wheel's possible acquisition of the dockside buildings belonging to Joseph Clerk. Grundwell asked for his comments on that latter idea, asking if Nathaniel would make funds available for the purchase if required.

They also told him of other changes in their financial arrangements that they had decided to make.

Hawk Mines and the Spinning Wheel had already lodged letters of credit with a Plymouth goldsmith, Richard Wynne, who was well known to Nathaniel.

However, that had initially been to pay for the construction of two brigantines as well as to deal with any expenses of establishing their business interests in the town, in particular with their newly appointed agents.

They then explained to their banker that there was no need of further letters of credit to be sent, in spite of the change of plans. That was because there had been a substantial income created not only by the cargo that had arrived with them on the *Rachel*, but also by those carried by seven other ships that had arrived recently from Chepstow and Bristol.

The resultant income was now being lodged with the Plymouth goldsmith, and had created an extremely positive cash flow for all three accounts that had been opened: one for each business and one for the fleet.

They also explained that they had engaged a bookkeeper and clerk to watch over their Plymouth interests, a gentleman of figures named Edrich Willerby, with an assistant named Paul, who was his son. They came highly recommended and were based at premises that the two Forest men had rented on the commercial docks.

Edrich would be sending a monthly trading statement to Hawk, the Spinning Wheel, and Nathaniel as well as to their Plymouth banker. Richard Wynne had now become effusive in his welcome every time the two called to see him.

'I wonder if he would be so pleased to see us if times ever got hard?' Grundwell was prompted to say after one particular visit when they had introduced Edrich to him.

One evening, they were sitting in their lodgings and sharing a mug of wine with Joseph Clerk, the coal merchant, when he warned them to be extra vigilant when out and about in Plymouth.

'Word has spread throughout the town about the two wealthy gentlemen from the border counties who are having ships built in the docks. If the business community is discussing you, then sure as hell the rogues are too, and with your height and build, you can't exactly hide in a crowd, can you?'

'Those Forest giants have a lot to answer for, don't they Grundwell?' Gumshu commented with a grin. Joseph looked slightly puzzled by the remark, so his friend explained, with a smile playing on his face.

'Well, there is a way round it, you know,' Joseph remarked.

The two Forest friends looked at him for an explanation.

'A lot of the local rogues in the town loiter around the dockside fish warehouses during the day, so if you invested in them as well, they might just leave you alone!'

'Not likely!' they both said in one voice.

But the warning was noted by both of them, as they were well aware of the power of a gang of men with knives over two individuals, whatever their size.

The two men then waited for the return of their horse-mounted messenger before they embarked for Waterford. He returned within ten days.

They both settled down in front of the inn fire to read the various letters, firstly from their families, then from their employees, and finally from Nathaniel.

Sophie and Mary agreed with Grundwell about buying Joseph Clerk's building, and Nathaniel agreed that it made good business sense. He also thought the Spinning Wheel could meet the cost out of reserves now that the shipbuilding programme was to be better phased. Added to that, with the finer wool products selling so well in both home *and* overseas markets, the constant revenue in itself was building a substantial reserve. This was a point that Phillip Fletcher also made in *his* report to his employer.

Richard Beachwood, now the Spinning Wheel's general manager, told Grundwell that their weaving units were running at full capacity, with all the outworkers extremely busy as well. He also reported that sales of raw wool were as busy as he'd ever seen them, despite the heavy taxation on exports, and the need for them to retain more than usual in their warehouse to satisfy their own needs.

Grundwell thought of his four-year plan and wondered if raw wool sales were the only thing he had got wrong.

'We need extra capacity, both for storage and manufacture,' Richard continued in his letter. 'And your ideas at Plymouth would help.' He went on to bemoan the slowness of their transport as well as the increasing lawlessness on the highways.

Grundwell smiled at that last comment, thinking that sixteen cannon on each cart would sort that problem out.

He then settled down to read the letters from his family. He smiled contentedly after reading Sophie's; Mary's had been about business as she and Sophie paid daily visits to the warehouse buildings.

He read notes from his youngest children; even Anna had managed a letter with a drawing of her father on a boat.

Then he started to read Alice's beautiful, neat handwriting in her letter.

'Boyfriend!' he exclaimed, leaping up from where he was sitting. 'Boyfriend!' Papers scattered everywhere. 'She's not yet seventeen years old, for God's sake!'

Gumshu leapt up to calm his friend. He sat him down again and called for more drinks. The landlord came over with two jugs of ale for them.

Having heard Grundwell's outburst, he said sympathetically, 'Yes, it does happen! My daughter is only thirteen and she announced the other night that she now has a boyfriend. I went off searching for a musket to demolish him before it started, but my wife calmed me down!'

Grundwell sat, glowering into the fire and muttering all sorts of threats under his breath.

After first helping his friend pick up his papers, Gumshu also sat down and carried on reading his own letters.

Maisey's letter was poignant and emotional, and it was obvious that she was missing him dreadfully. He read it at least five times before folding it up carefully and putting it in the top pocket of his tunic.

He then read each of the children's letters, looking at the different drawings of himself on a boat, obviously a theme that had been declared by Maisey.

He read Little Emmy's letter, checking carefully to see if there were any references to boyfriends. She was one of Alice's best friends, and usually where one went, the other followed. He was quietly relieved when he reached the end of her chatty letter, but he was also aware that his daughter was not as open as Alice, so he made a mental note to carry out a double-check when he got back to Mitcheldean.

The letter from Thomas Sutton was positive, full of news of mine openings and their financial performance and who had said what to whom. Gumshu smiled, as it was all typical of Thomas.

Edmund the bookkeeper's letter was full of figures, but the underlying results looked extremely good, with an increasing market share at home and a developing coastal market. They had also started shipping more coal into London, thanks to a very active agent whom Thomas had appointed in the south-east. Edmund also told him that demand was developing in Ireland, thanks to a contact of their shipping agent, John Saunders.

'That's even without me going to Waterford,' Gumshu reflected. 'A lot seems to have happened in a very short space of time,' he murmured, slowly re-reading some of his letters.

Thomas had already said that he actually had to buy some coal from Wales to satisfy one order, such was the strength of demand. He got a brief letter from Samuel Longden, bemoaning transport levies, bad transport routes, and as in Grundwell's case again, lawlessness on the highways.

Gumshu, too, reflected on the use of cannon, similar to his friend's thoughts. Finally, there were some scrawled notes from his mine foreman, full of humour and collier's chat.

Anthony Burrel asked him if he could find a wealthy husband for Abigail, his sister, because she was nagging him worse than a wife and driving him demented.

The two men completed their letter reading, then sat back staring silently into the fire.

'Those two are homesick!' commented the landlord to his wife.

She smiled. 'Just like someone else I know when he used to be away at sea before he crushed his leg.' The landlord gave her a hug because he had always hated being away from his family, unlike many of his fellow mariners.

'Have we really only been away eleven weeks?' Gumshu asked, breaking the silence.

'Just about. I told you that this little trip would take us at least three months, and it looks more like being four at the moment.'

Gumshu sighed. He was missing his family more than he cared to admit.

The following day, they went in search of Joseph Clerk, the coal merchant, with the news of the impending sale. He beamed when Grundwell told him he could now go ahead with the purchase of the dockside warehouse.

They also collected Walter Symonds, the boat builder, and the four then went to Richard Wynne's work building. The banker was going to instruct lawyers on the Spinning Wheel's behalf, and then transfer monies from the wool business's account to Joseph Clerk's, to pay for the building once the property contract was completed.

Gumshu and Grundwell also instructed him to make stage payments to Walter Symonds for the building of the *Wayfarer*. However, John Dickens was to verify that the work was satisfactory, and the stage completed, before any payment was transferred, a point that was accepted by the boat builder.

They also discussed at some length when, and in what order, the ten vessels were to be built, covering both Plymouth and Chepstow boatyards. Richard's clerk took all the details of the meeting down in writing so that he could prepare a document recording all that had been said. The idea was that a copy would be given to the absent John Dickens on his return, Edrich, and the two bankers, thus ensuring there could be *no* misunderstanding of any of the instructions given by the two Forest men.

Master Wynne was once again effusive as they left and even rubbed his hands together, an action that made both Grundwell and Gumshu grin.

When they had appointed him, Nathaniel had told them not to be put off by some of his mannerisms; it was just his enthusiasm about money that made him like that. The two now saw what he had meant.

From Richard's building, they strolled down to the Hoe with Joseph and Walter, where they sat on the lush green grass and looked out to the Sound and the wave-capped sea beyond.

'So where are you heading next, gentlemen?' Joseph Clerk enquired.

'We leave tomorrow on the brigantine *Sara Jane* bound for Waterford and more work,' Gumshu replied with a sigh. 'And we've checked her out, and very kindly, the ship's carpenter and the sailmaker have altered two sea berths for us.'

'Aye, she's a good ship, with a competent young captain. It's his first command, and he's done some good long trips, so you're in safe hands.

'The sky looks like it's got some wind in it though, but it's coming up from the south-west, so you'll get a swift but bumpy ride,' Walter Symonds commented, looking up at the scudding and somewhat threatening cloud formation above them.

# CHAPTER 17

Gumshu and Grundwell boarded the *Sara Jane* before dawn the following morning. The wind was blustery and strong, and as Walter Symonds had predicted, it was from the south-west.

They were welcomed aboard by second in command Richard Edriwch, brother to the captain, Thomas Edriwch. Both were young but full of enthusiasm and eager to please. After showing them down to their cabin, Richard apologised for his brother's absence, explaining that he was down below decks, sorting out a small problem together with the ship's carpenter.

'That comment should have rung some alarm bells,' Grundwell commented in later years.

The ship's joiner had done what he had promised and modified the two berths to all but fit the frames of the collier and wool men. They returned on deck as streaks of dawn started to break up the darkness of the night sky.

The boat was straining on her warps, seemingly in anticipation of the voyage ahead. Her cargo had been safely stowed and secured. On enquiring what her cargo was, Grundwell was told it was grain, brought from eastern England into Plymouth and destined for the Irish markets.

He commented to Gumshu, 'I wonder how you secure a load of grain.' He just assumed that that was what the ship's captain and carpenter were doing down below, and he thought no more about it.

A few minutes later, the captain reappeared on deck, looking slightly dusty but confidently smiling at his two passengers, saying, 'Welcome on board, gentlemen. Good to see you again.' He had met them when they had booked their passage and been shown around his boat.

She was an older brigantine than the *Rachel* but was only carrying ten cannon and was clearly not as well maintained. But she and her crew came well recommended, and it was, after all, only a short trip of some four days to Ireland.

For the passage back to Chepstow, they had arranged for the *Rachel* to pick them up from Waterford, along with a paying cargo. The only proviso of the two Forest men had been that the ship's carpenter was to alter their sea bunks, as in the *Sara Jane*. There had been much hilarity when both Grundwell and Gumshu had lain on the deck to be measured by the *Rachel*'s carpenter, who joked with them that he would keep the figures for when they needed a coffin.

Daybreak saw the *Sara Jane* making her way down the Plymouth channel with the ebb tide, with only her royals set. She tacked out into the Sound and began setting her top gallants so that she had all her sails set well before reaching the open sea. As soon as they were able to put Rame Head squarely on to their starboard quarter, the captain laid a course off that would put them clear of the Lizard by some five miles, safely leaving the Eddystone Rocks to his port. That gave him the advantage of making the best of the ebb tide whilst still keeping his sails full.

*Sara Jane* heeled to the brisk south-westerly wind, punching through the white crests of the waves and riding the underlying swell, showing the quality and speed of her breed to all who were watching. Her crew worked with enthusiasm and vigour so that the vessel made the best of both wind and tide. Grundwell and Gumshu stood on the stern deck with their cloaks pulled tightly around them, protecting themselves from the sea spray and wind whilst appreciating the sight of the sails above them and the smell of the sea that engulfed them.

'You don't carry as many crew as the *Rachel*?' Gumshu questioned the second in command, Richard Edriwch.

'Yes, we *did*, but the press gangs have been very active in the taverns and houses of ill repute over the last few days and have depleted our numbers somewhat,' he replied with a concerned look on his face. 'We should have no problems though. This wind seems to be set steady, and so there should be few changes of direction needed before we get close to the estuary of the River Suir. As long as we catch a flood tide, going up the river to Waterford should be relatively easy. It's only when we have to tack or manoeuvre in a confined space that we need a lot of hands.'

The two Forest men looked at each other and wondered what John Dickens would have made of that remark. In his opinion, full crews were essential both for the safe handling of a vessel and her continued maintenance.

'Perhaps,' Grundwell reflected, 'that was why *Sara Jane* seemed to lack care, and the press gang activity was just the excuse.'

The two men of Mitcheldean went below after three hours or so, as their stomachs were beginning to show small signs of a forthcoming upset. Thomas Edriwch smiled, as he too always suffered a little at the beginning of a passage.

'Just go and lie down completely flat for a couple of hours and you will usually find that helps. Keep warm. Have a small tot of rum when you get up, and you should be fine. I'll tell the cook to bring you a couple of tots when you are ready to come back on deck.'

'Sounds like good advice to me,' Gumshu said, as they made their way down to the small cabin that had been set aside for them.

As they lay in their berths, Grundwell said, 'This boat doesn't ride the sea with the same ease that the *Rachel* does, and neither does she sound the same.'

'I was thinking the same thing,' Gumshu replied. 'A good friend of mine once gave me some very sound advice on my first day down a mine. He said always to listen to what the ground was telling you. Never ignore it. That knowledge saved his own life in that collapse at Cottrells. I wonder what this boat is trying to tell us, my friend.'

The two men fell into an uneasy broken sleep, making several appearances on deck over the next few hours until darkness fell. Then dim lamps lit the deck, and the only noise other than the wind, was the eerie sound of the unseen waves as they surged past the hull of the ship, like disturbed spirits of the night. Soon not even that sound could be heard above the howl of the rising wind, a noise made even more threatening by momentary appearances of the ghostly moon from behind breaking clouds, only for it to disappear again and leave an impenetrable darkness of the unknown.

The cook provided a scanty cold meal in the captain's cabin, which the officers hardly touched before returning to the deck, the captain not even coming below at all. The Forest friends could hear the sounds of the crew, as they reduced sail to match the rise in the wind.

The noises of a vessel under strain were now becoming unmistakable, and they seemed to be coming from within the boat herself. However, with the warmth of their bunks and the rum in their stomachs, the collier and the wool man drifted back into an uneasy sleep.

Some hours later, they both awoke with a start, not knowing why. There were now noises coming from the hold that definitely hadn't been there when they went to sleep, and the whole motion of the *Sara Jane* seemed different. They could also hear water slopping around on their cabin floor. Grundwell lit a candle lamp, and they both looked down.

'That doesn't look good!' snapped Grundwell as his feet hit the floor at the same time as Gumshu's. 'I'll go and tell the captain. If you could go and have a look at that cargo hold bulkhead down the passage,' he continued in a worried voice, leaving his companion struggling to light the other candle lamp.

Grundwell bounded out on to the deck to find Captain Edriwch and tell him what they had seen. As soon as he got topside, he knew that there was something drastically wrong. The whole aspect of the ship seemed crazy. The wind had increased yet again, screeching through the rigging, but the *Sara Jane* remained virtually upright, with the breaking seas surfing over her side rails and across the decks. The moon showed a scene of utter chaos, worsened by the sounds of the flogging sails whose lines had been abandoned by the petrified crew. Grundwell span round and ran back down the companionway steps leading to their cabin, colliding with Gumshu who was scrambling up. He turned round, and the two raced out on to the deck, cannoning into a horror-stricken Richard Edriwch as they did so.

'Right, Edriwch, tell us exactly what's going on!' Gumshu said, as he grabbed the man by his tunic and pinned him against the side of the stern cabin. Just as he did so, there was the explosive sound of splintering wood from below, as one of the cargo bulkheads collapsed, spilling vast quantities of grain into the passage where their cabin was.

'The grain has got wet from a leak near the keel and has expanded, bursting out of the hold!' the second in command yelled, trying to get loose from Gumshu's grip.

'Have you taken the top covers off the holds to try and release the pressure?' Grundwell shouted above the noise.

'We can't because of the sea washing over the decks. If it gets into the hold and mixes with the grain, it will make the situation even worse!' Edriwch screamed.

'How long has she been leaking for God's sake for her to be so waterlogged and low in the water?' Grundwell yelled back.

'It started two days ago, but we thought we'd contained the cargo and stopped the sea water from coming in!' came the man's near hysterical reply.

The *Sara Jane* suddenly started to pitch and roll violently, lurching from side to side, and at the same time they heard a terrifying, thunderous roaring noise that cut short any further conversation.

The three staggered over to the starboard rail, joining most of the other crew who were trying to stand, clinging on to anything that they could. They stared in terror at the now visible mountainous surf, glistening and hissing like a vast monster from the deep.

'Where are we?' Grundwell yelled.

'We think we're somewhere off the Isles of Scilly, but the wind and tide having taken us way off course. We've been unable to steer for the last hour. Oh Lord, help us!' Edriwch cried as he sank to his knees in prayer, a look of absolute terror showing on his face.

The roar of the breakers had become deafening. The seas stood high above the decks of the *Sara Jane*. It wasn't just the surf that could be seen, but there were huge rocks towering above them, standing up as if they were the jagged teeth of hell.

Gumshu seized hold of Grundwell and pulled him over to the stern mast, which had been denuded of its sail and spars by a vast wall of water. He grabbed some rope and started lashing them both to it. Grundwell realising what he was trying to do managed to snatch some more loose rope and did the same. After a minute or so of frantic work, they had made themselves as secure as possible. It was useless trying to speak as the noise of the surf, the wind, and the screaming men made it impossible to hear the sound of their own voices. The two men looked at each other, smiled, and then bowed their heads, linking arms as they did so, putting their trust in the Almighty.

Other members of the crew followed their example by lashing themselves to different parts of the boat, in the belief that they stood a better chance of being taken through the surf by the *Sara Jane* rather than trying to survive by leaping into the sea. Those who did jump into the surf were first smashed against the rocks by the gigantic seas, and then disappeared completely as their bodies were dragged under the surface by the waves' undertow, their frantic cries for help lost forever in the turbulence and noise of a violent and angry ocean.

The *Sara Jane* rose up on a moving mountain of hissing water and was dashed against the first of the towering jagged rocks, flung on to her side by one wave, snatched up like a rag doll by another, and then smashed on to the rocks again, the power of the water spinning her round as it did so. All the time there was the persistent deafening sound of thunder made by a multitude of gigantic Atlantic breakers, crashing into everything that was in their path.

The boat's foremast and bow were ripped off as she turned, her stern momentarily disappearing under the surf. She seemed then to recover, her stern section intact with its mast still in place, only to be picked again and thrown into the air by another gigantic wave.

A mountain of boiling surf then hit what was left of the brigantine, pushing the remains of both hull and mast high over the rocks for it to come crashing down again, only to be swept up by yet another wall of spume and water that took the remains of hull and stern-mast into the bay beyond, rolling it over and over and then discarding it as a tangled mass of unrecognisable wreckage high on the white sandy beach, before receding in an ever-moving thunderous white wall of ocean.

After what must have felt like an eternity to any who had survived, first light dawned. With it came the clearing of skies and a dying of the horrendous storm-forced winds.

The terrifying anger and violence of the sea had abated, but there was still a massive Atlantic swell, powering past the islands and on towards the mainland beyond. Within the sandy cove lay a multitude of items of wreckage, interspersed with many corpses from the *Sara Jane's* crew.

Two tall figures went from body to body, seeing if any life existed except their own. Richard Edriwch and his brother Thomas were both dead, as was the ship's carpenter, who had been so helpful to Gumshu and Grundwell. They never knew his name. The two friends looked at each other, wondering how they had survived when so many others had perished. So far, they hadn't found one soul from the *Sara Jane* who had lived. Silently, they both went and sat on an outcrop of rock halfway along the beach, looking at the scene of devastation and death that lay all around them.

'We need to find some fresh water. My thirst is terrible. I seem to have swallowed a complete ocean,' Gumshu said.

'Well, when you find some, will you bring some back for me?' pleaded a voice from behind the outcrop, a voice that both of them recognised instantly.

They leapt up and ran round to the other side of the rock, to find the ship's cook lying on the sand, still with his arms tightly tied around a barrel.

'Could you also possibly find a knife to cut this rope? The boson's made such a good job of his knots, I can't untie them!'

Grundwell managed to release him fairly quickly and then helped him to his feet.

'Has anyone else survived?' the cook immediately asked, carefully rubbing his arms where the rope had dug into his flesh.

'Not that we've found, sadly,' Gumshu replied. 'Have you any injuries, Will?'

'Only fright. My old mum was right. "Don't go and be a cook at sea," she said. "Find a nice country inn."'

'So why didn't you take her advice?' a slightly bemused Gumshu asked.

'Fancied a wife in every port, I did.'

'And?' the two friends said together.

'Every other!' Will replied, grinning.

'I can't believe we're having this conversation. Wrecked God knows where, the rest of the crew drowned, and we're talking about Will's love life.' Grundwell laughed.

'Well, Will's love life was always the most interesting on the *Sara Jane*. I can tell you that' came a retort from behind the next outcrop along the beach.

'It's Monty!' exclaimed Will, running round the rocks and nearly falling over his crewmate as he did so.

Monty was the sailmaker on the brigantine and had helped the ship's carpenter alter the bunks for the two offspring of the Forest giant. He, too, was firmly tied to a barrel.

'Don't tell me, the boson again?' Gumshu enquired, as he untied the rope.

'The self same,' Monty replied, rubbing his wrists. 'He insisted on making sure I was tied to something before he sorted himself out. He said that as I was no good at knots he'd better do it. No good at knots indeed, and me a sailmaker!'

Gumshu remembered the mariner because he had sat watching him make a Turk's head splice.

But that hadn't been the main reason he remembered him.

As they had talked Dick Tatton, the boson, had suddenly said, 'You were the foreman at the Cottrells' mine, near Mitcheldean, weren't you, sir?'

'Yes, I was. Why do you ask?' he had answered, completely taken aback.

'Do you remember a little lad coming forward when you were standing in the crater after the collapse, asking if you could keep digging and find his father?'

'Yes, I do as a matter of fact. I also remember the pleading look in his mother's eyes when she stepped forward to take his hand. There is not a second of that night I don't remember, even though it's a long time ago now. The memory will live with me forever. How do you know all this, Dick?'

'The woman was my sister, Jane. She told me about the whole night and what a nightmare it had been. It hit her badly, losing her husband like that. She also told me how you and a lot of the people in the Forest village helped all those who had lost loved ones, and are still doing so.'

'Yes, we are. I still feel a degree of guilt, whatever anybody says. Not only that, but I strongly believe we have to look after our own, in good times or bad.'

Dick smiled at him and said, 'The rumour is you're one hard man, and people are scared of you.'

'Don't tell them the truth, Dick. It'll spoil my image,' Gumshu replied, grinning.

There had been no opportunity for further conversation.

'As a matter of interest, what's in those barrels that you were tied to? They've still got the tops on, and they feel like there is something in them?' Grundwell asked Monty, cutting across Gumshu's thoughts of his previous day's conversation on board the *Sara Jane*.

'Don't know, sir. It could be rum because there were some rum casks on the deck as well as some salted meat . . .'

Monty was about to continue when there was the sound of a faint voice from further up the beach.

'There is no way I'd have secured either of you to a barrel of rum. You'd have drunk the lot before getting ashore!'

A dark shock of hair appeared above the top of a rock, followed by the beaming face of Dick Tatton as he got up, undoing the last of the rope he'd used to tie himself to a barrel.

'Morning, gentlemen!' he said, touching his forelock to Grundwell and Gumshu and then turning to his two shipmates. 'Where the hell's my morning ale and biscuit? Just because we've been wrecked is no excuse for not looking after the boson!' he complained.

Monty sat down on the sand and put his hands over his face as if he was crying. Dick came out from behind his rock and walked over to him, putting his arm around his greatest friend.

'Come on, you didn't think you'd get away from me that easily, did you?' he said.

'No, it wasn't that. I thought you were dead, and you still owe me two shillings!'

The two friends rolled over on the sand in a mock fight, but the relief that each showed was obvious.

'They've been shipmates a long time,' Will explained to the two others.

After finding a small spring in the side of a low rocky cliff to quench their thirst, the five survivors spent the next three hours checking everywhere along the shoreline that was accessible, looking for more survivors, but finding none.

They buried the bodies that they found, scooping the graves out as best they could above the high water mark and then putting a pile of stones on each one.

Dick Tatton assumed responsibility for the little group and started organising the collection of useful items, taking them above the tideline. Finding a prayer book, they returned to the graves and said a prayer over each of them.

Gumshu and Grundwell insisted that no one should refer to them as 'sir'. They were now a group of survivors, and Dick was in charge.

They dragged timber to the top of a small rise on the seaward side of the bay to build a beacon so that they could draw the attention of any passing vessel they saw.

Dick collected some dry flints and tinder that he had found and made sure that everyone knew where they were.

'There's no point having a beacon if we can't light it,' he said.

'My friend here is good at lighting things with a flint, aren't you?' Grundwell said, laughing at Gumshu, who didn't see the humour of the remark and scowled by way of reply.

Despite the conversation that Grundwell and Gumshu had had with Richard Edriwch before the ship struck the rocks, none of them knew where they were.

Although they suspected that they were on one of the Isles of Scilly, Dick's reckoning that it was St Agnes was the most likely.

They built a timber shelter and covered it in sail cloth retrieved from the various bits of wreckage of the *Sara Jane*. Will found some of his cooking pots washed up in one corner of the bay, which they utilised to carry and store water from the spring.

Food was the next essential, and the barrels that the three seamen had come ashore on were broken open. They were less than half full of salted meat.

'How did *those* float?' Gumshu queried, taking up Grundwell's original question.

'I saw two or three washed off the deck sometime before we were wrecked, and they bobbed up again after they hit the water, don't ask me why. I think that they were watertight and had got air in them, which made them float.

'As you can see, they were less than half full of meat anyway, so I suspect the supplier only gave Thomas Edriwch half what he paid for,' Dick commented with a frown.

'But what if you'd tied me to a full one?' Will asked with an apprehensive glance.

'Well, we'd have more food now, but one less mouth to feed!' Dick replied with a grin. 'Do any of you get the feeling we are being watched?' he continued in a more serious tone.

'Yes. And for about the last half hour! I think there are three of them. They are lying on that small bluff above the spring,' Gumshu answered. 'What if Grundwell and I wander off for a walk, then try and come in behind them?'

'Good idea. Take a sword each, just in case you need to defend yourselves. Sadly, we haven't found any firearms up to now,' Dick replied.

The two Forest men sauntered along the beach, chatting and singing to themselves as they went, trying to appear casual. They made their way slowly up a track on to the top of the low cliffs that bordered the bay on two sides, with the sea on the third and the rocks on which the *Sara Jane* had floundered on the fourth.

As they came up the track, Gumshu said quietly to Grundwell, 'I wonder who created this track and why? I think we are on an island that has people, my friend!'

'I wonder if they are friendly.'

'I think we are about to find out,' Gumshu replied, doubling down into a concealed run.

With very little effort, they got behind the clifftop watchers and then crawled up the earth bank that was immediately behind them.

Peering over and thinking that they hadn't been noticed, the two men sat openly on the top.

One of the watchers rolled over, looked at them, and turned back to her companions, saying, 'That was very good, don't you think, girls? It was a little noisy over the final approach, but generally, quite a good effort.'

'That was brilliant, never mind quite good. We were as silent as ghosts!' Grundwell retorted indignantly.

'You've obviously got noisy ghosts where you come from.' The girl giggled.

'Could I just ask why have you brought swords?' one of her companions inquired, looking somewhat puzzled.

'You might have been unfriendly,' Gumshu replied self-consciously.

'Well, we've never been accused of *that* before!' the third girl commented, in an accent that the two men couldn't quite place.

'Would you like to come and take a look at our living quarters, ladies? They're even better *close to*!' Grundwell asked, a little lamely.

The five of them walked along the top of the low cliff, to where the track led down to the survivors' shelter. On their arrival, they found that the other three had noticed that they were about to have female visitors and had prepared something that was not dissimilar to mead to drink. Gumshu wondered where Will had conjured it up from, but now wasn't the time to ask. He also saw where he had got his romantic reputation from, as he became very attentive to their lady guests.

The girl who had originally spoken to Grundwell appeared to be the leader and was genuine when she said that they were very sorry for the loss of lives from their boat. She looked at them and asked how many men had died.

'Sixty-five souls,' Grundwell replied softly.

'Sometimes the sea can be very cruel. We could see you coming towards the rocks, but could do nothing for you as the boat seemed to be out of control, and the seas were so wild. The sad thing is that another fifty yards to seaward and your ship would have missed the rocks, come into the bay, and been driven aground on what is mostly sand, as you can see,' she said sympathetically.

Gumshu stared at the girls and wondered what their origins were. They spoke with what he now recognised as a Cornish accent, as it was not unlike that of his three Cornish mine foremen in

Mitcheldean, but their looks were those of foreigners. They were dark, with long black hair, and stood well over five foot tall. He put their ages at about twenty or thereabouts.

The girl who had been doing most of the talking turned to him and said, 'Excuse me, but have you finished your inspection of us yet?' She then flashed him a dazzling smile.

'Sorry, I was just fascinated by your foreign appearance, with a Cornish accent,' he replied with some embarrassment.

'I could say the same about your appearance, with you being so tall,' she returned, repeating the same flashing smile. 'Anyway,' she continued, 'what makes you so sure my accent is Cornish?'

'Three friends of mine are Cornish miners, now working in Gloucestershire, and I had trouble understanding them to start with,' Gumshu replied, slightly teasing her.

'Cornish is the only way to be, long shanks!' she retorted, tossing her hair back to reveal her beautiful, smooth, and olive-coloured skin. 'Anyway, what's this Gloucestershire?'

'It is the best, and only, place to be,' Gumshu mimicked. 'And do you know why?'

'I have a feeling you're going to tell me.'

'Because there is no sea! There are no rocks, no storms, and no isolated islands to get marooned on, that's why!'

'Ah, but there's no me!' she flashed back.

'And I thought I was good,' Will said quietly to Grundwell, as he watched the undoubted flirting between the two.

The other two girls were talking to Dick Tatton, telling him their names and which of the Isles of Scilly they were on.

As the survivors had suspected, it was St Agnes. They told him that they were sisters named Petrina and Rebecca and that they lived on the island with their parents. They also told him that the other girl was their cousin Nadine, who lived with her mother and father on the Isle of St Mary's, a short distance away. She had been visiting them, but couldn't get home because of the gales.

When Dick asked how long it had been since she had first arrived, the sisters told him that it was over a month ago.

Dick turned to Grundwell and commented, 'This is going to be the problem, not just getting to St Mary's, which is the main island, but then getting back on to the mainland at this time of year. This area is renowned for the ferocity and number of its gales.'

Petrina smiled at Will, who suddenly couldn't see that being a problem at all.

When Dick asked how the girls' father made a living on such a small island, there was an awkward silence from the two girls. Nadine was still chattering to Gumshu about the best place to live and Grundwell was talking to Monty, so no one other than Dick saw the reaction to his question.

'Oh, he picks up bits and pieces from the high tide mark around the islands, does a lot of fishing, and we keep a few animals and fowl, just like the rest of the villagers on the island, really,' Petrina eventually answered.

Dick suddenly realised why they hadn't found anything valuable washed up from the *Sara Jane*.

'Were these people opportunist beachcombers or should I be thinking wreckers?' he wondered.

He noticed that all three girls wore clothes that really didn't reflect their island living. They were all finely made, and Nadine's skirt, he suspected, was pure silk. That all pointed to one thing, but at present he decided he would keep his thoughts to himself.

The three girls decided it was time to go back to their village as dusk began to settle. Dick suggested that the survivors escort them, to ensure their safe arrival home.

Nadine told him that there really was no need as the island was only about a mile long, so she couldn't see them getting lost. The island wenches took their leave, but with a promise to return the following day.

'Hmm,' Grundwell commented. 'I wonder what the real reason is for not wanting us near their village.'

'The same reason we are all thinking,' Monty replied. 'I think we may find that the islanders are not averse to a bit of wrecking.'

'Did you notice the silk skirt that Nadine was wearing, Grundwell?' Gumshu asked.

'It's a wonder you noticed anything but the dazzling smile, long hair, flashing eyes, and fantastic body, my friend!' Grundwell returned with a knowing look.

'There'll be some activity in that village tonight,' Will said. 'And I don't mean of a romantic nature either. I suspect our presence will cause considerable discussion!'

'I think, gentlemen, we'd better post a watch tonight,' Dick suggested.

# CHAPTER 18

It had been twelve weeks since the messenger had brought the news that the *Sara Jane* was missing, twelve weeks in which prayers had been said every Sunday in the Forest village church and every Sunday in the Church of Saint Michael, but twelve weeks of *constant* prayer in the two houses on Craven Street.

Maisey and Sophie faced the potential outcome with dignity and strength when they were in public. However, within the privacy of their own homes, they showed the personal grief that the magnitude of the loss would really have should their husbands never return.

It was the strength of their children that both Friar Benedict and William Benson found truly amazing. Little Emmy and Alice seemed to have taken their fathers' mantles of family leadership and power, stepping into their shoes as if by a God-given right handed down to them by past generations. Both showed a power of leadership and resilience that could only be attributed to their inheritance of personality and character from their fathers. The friar privately mused about their bloodline, realising that now was an appropriate time to update the document he had written for Bishop Robert Galbraith so many years ago.

Little Emmy took to visiting the coal building every day, looking at the figures, helping Edmund Fletcher, and asking nearly as many questions as Alice. And as Edmund said, her thirst for knowledge of figures was quite phenomenal. When she wasn't with Edmund, she was out with Thomas Sutton, going down the mines, listening to the day-to-day problems, and then watching Thomas solve them.

As her father had once told her, 'If people do have difficulties, always listen to them. As often as not, they have the answers themselves. It's just that they are standing too close to see the solution.'

Thomas smiled at her after one particularly gruelling day and said, 'You listened to your father and you've now listened to us. You are your father's daughter. You have *got* to carry Hawk Mines forward with that knowledge. Many people will depend on you, and that is not a responsibility to be taken lightly.'

Alice was doing much the same at the Spinning Wheel. She would arrive at the warehouse well before dawn, as her father had done. When Richard Beachwood and Phillip Fletcher had their regular early morning meetings, she was always there, attentive and asking the inevitable *why* that she was now famous for.

She toured the weaving sheds, watching the spinners at their wheels and the weavers at their looms. She watched the designers with their sketches and the dyers with their colour swatches. She asked question after question on every aspect of the manufacturing process, from start to finish, gleaning all the information that she possibly could, but always highly attentive of the detail.

When she told William Benson that she could no longer come to his classes, she reminded him of her comment about her still being able to cry like a child, even at the age of nearly sixteen.

She said very seriously, 'Now, a few months later, I have to cry and act like a woman. Fate seems to have taken a hand a little earlier than I could have anticipated and in a way I would never have dreamt of!'

Like their fathers, they tried to meet most evenings and talk through what had happened during the day. Most sixteen—and seventeen-year-old girls in Mitcheldean would be talking of marriage, boyfriends, and other teenage pursuits, but those two would be talking commerce. Alice would have pleased her father as she had now dismissed her boyfriend due to the yoke of the family business on her shoulders.

Maisey and Sophie gave their daughters every encouragement in their desire to work. They were still too emotional about the disappearance of their husbands to be fully effective in the administration of the two fast-moving and expanding businesses. They depended on their staff, their daughters, and Mary.

Far from slowing down, Mary now found herself being more and more caught up in both the wool and coal trades.

As she had said to one of her friends, 'I thought you just put coal on the fire, but now I'm learning how to get it there!'

Her greatest joy was to see her granddaughter become so involved. However, they used to have some very serious arguments, but they usually ended up as friends again afterwards.

'It's a good job those two aren't husband and wife, because there would be murder done,' Richard Beachwood remarked one day.

Captain John Dickens arrived at the Corner House in Craven Street to discuss the forthcoming launch of the *Wayfarer*, the first brigantine off the stocks at Plymouth.

He had travelled to Mitcheldean twice before, once to bring copies of the instructions that Gumshu and Grundwell had left with banker Richard Wynne and the second time to update Mary and the families on the progress of the search for survivors from the *Sara Jane*.

The only area that he and the *Rachel* had not covered was around the Isles of Scilly. Because of the continuing gales, it was impossible to get close to the islands without endangering both his ship and his crew.

Although storms were a regular feature of the weather in autumn and winter around the south-western tip of England, this year they had been particularly frequent and ferocious, causing heavy seas and a continual threat to the safety of ships using the English Channel.

Although the captain had nothing new to add to the search news on this latest visit, he did say that the winds would start to die down, probably towards the end of March if they followed the usual pattern. He assured the families that at the first opportunity he would take the *Rachel* and carry out a search in and around the islands off Land's End.

'It would appear that this is the last hope, John, if I'm reading the situation correctly?' Mary said to him when they were out of earshot of the families.

'I think so, Mary. I can't think of anywhere else to look. The weather on the night the *Sara Jane* disappeared was horrific, and a lot of ships were lost. But I am still sure that those islands hold the key to what actually happened to her. That's unless she was blown further to the west, but I've searched *that* area and found nothing. I'm positive that this is where we'll find the answer.'

Endeavouring not to show the gravity of their discussion, John and Mary quietly returned to where the wives and their two eldest daughters were sitting.

Once seated, John explained to those around the table that the *Wayfarer* would be ready for sea in approximately a month, and once ready, he would set about engaging a crew. He had already appointed four officers and her captain, and they would supervise the completion of the vessel. The next ship to go on the stocks would be the *Gull.*

The question that he wanted to ask of the ladies was whether they still intended to carry on building the fleet of six brigantines and four colliers. John Dickens was slightly taken aback by the response to his question and from whence it came.

The two girls glanced at each other, then Alice retorted with a frown, 'Yes, Captain, we most certainly do. But there is one big problem. They're not being built fast enough!'

Mary looked at Alice and quietly asked, 'When was this matter discussed and agreed?'

'Little Emmy and I have been talking about it quite a lot recently. When you talk to Richard Beachwood and Thomas Sutton, the biggest complaint you hear from both of them is the speed of transport. We've been to see Nathaniel the goldsmith to ask his advice, and he confirmed what we thought. With all our ships ready, we can cure their problems and start to transport larger cargoes, thus reducing our unit costs. Speed is essential!' Alice countered.

'Don't you think you should have talked to the rest of us before reaching such conclusions?' Maisey asked, directing her question to her daughter.

'Thomas Sutton told me I was my father's daughter not so long ago, as I told you. Did Father always talk to you before he did things?' she said, laughing.

Maisey grinned. 'Yes, Little Emmy, but this about a joint business decision, not about buying a house!'

'It was a joint decision. Alice agreed!' Little Emmy replied triumphantly.

'I agree with the girls, and I think what they have said is right,' Mary conceded after getting a long, hard look from her granddaughter.

'Alice and I would also like to go to Chepstow to see how the ship building is progressing, as the completion of those four collier boats is now very urgent. We need to be selling more coal, and to sell it, we have to transport it,' Little Emmy continued.

'We've actually put the brigantines on the stocks first,' John Dickens admitted.

'That's not what our fathers wanted! Read the instructions that were discussed at Richard Wynne's!' Alice snapped, glowering at him. 'You've given preference to the brigantine fleet. May I suggest that doesn't happen again, and you follow the orders you've already been given?'

John Dickens was about to answer, but then thought better of it. It was bad enough taking orders from women, but when he was expected to take criticism from two teenage girls, he was beginning to doubt the wisdom of his involvement with the scheme at all.

Sophie spoke for the first time. She looked pale and wasn't really concentrating, but she said, 'John, it would be easier for you, I think, to take your instructions from Mary. That would stop any inquisition having to be conducted by two teenage girls!'

The two girls turned to her with looks that could have frozen hell over.

Mary was quick to step in and rescue the situation. Maisey, too, looked taken aback by Sophie's remark, but it was Mary who was first to speak.

'I think both Alice and Little Emmy have been right in what they've said, and they have obviously checked all the facts, just as their fathers would have done. But I think if John is to carry on being part of this business, then he must realise that at present it will be female led. As to whom those females are, whether it is me or my granddaughter or Little Emmy is immaterial.

'All they've got to do is remember to talk to the older generation before taking decisions that will affect either of the businesses.' She looked pointedly at the girls as she spoke.

'In that case, you won't need me! Just tell me what you've agreed occasionally, so I know what's going on,' Sophie exploded, as she got up and stormed out of the door.

Alice rose to follow her, but her grandmother shook her head, indicating for her to sit down again.

'Your mother needs time to adjust to life without your father, Alice. Don't get impatient with her. I'm not saying it's any different for you, Maisey, but Sophie isn't as strong as you, and all this worry is hitting her in a different way, that's all.'

She turned to John. 'You still own the *Rachel* and so can return to your previous way of making a living if you don't want to stay with us. You've been paid for your ship's time up to now, and we will go on doing that in the way that Grundwell and Gumshu had decided.

'So you have a decision to take. You either work with all of us, and give us the benefit of your experience or to be blunt disappear over the horizon, to put in maritime language.

'If you do decide to stay, and I hope that you do, then I want you to teach these two girls about running a ship and then about operating a fleet of them. It's up to you. Decide now, and then we can all get on with running the businesses.'

Alice smiled, saying quietly, 'The essence of a decision is . . . !'

Mary looked at her sharply, remembering that Edward had always said that.

John Dickens hesitated and was about to explain his thoughts, when Alice interrupted. 'My grandmother just wants a simple yes or no!' she said sharply.

He looked at her and replied, 'Just to annoy you, I'll say yes and I'll stay.'

'And I promise you, Captain, you will not leave us until you have taught Little Emmy and myself all there is to know about running a fleet of ships, whether they be large or small!' she said by way of reply, flashing him one of her dazzling smiles.

'Oh, no,' thought her grandmother. 'He's too old, Alice!'

'Chepstow, here we come,' Little Emmy muttered under her breath.

Maisey quietly thought to herself that it was a good job Sophie had left them after all.

'There is one thing that bothers me,' Mary said. 'The *Sara Jane* was lost before she got to Waterford, where is irrelevant at the moment. What is important is that our two Forest men did not establish any business links with either wool or coal merchants in Waterford. So how are we achieving so much trade there?'

'John Saunders, our shipping agent, has contacts in Waterford that we are using. I have checked the figures with Edmund, and the prices we are getting for coal are as fair as they can be,' Little Emmy reported.

'My grandfather's contacts are still trading with us in all the woollen items that we offer, and Phillip tells me the returns are good,' Alice told her grandmother.

'Is that wise?' Mary asked her, wondering if Grundwell's four-year business plan was still an option that could be worked to, or whether the circumstances had changed too much.

'They're glad of the trade, so who we are doesn't matter. The fact that the Spinning Wheel is now one of the biggest exporters of raw wool in the southern England again thanks to the easing of government export tax, and is fast becoming one of the biggest exporters of yarn and finely woven goods in the country is what impresses them. The *Rachel*, amongst others, has taken six full cargoes out of Chepstow for us. One of which was late I might add, judging from the message we got back two weeks later.' She turned accusingly to John as she finished.

'But there was one of the strongest gales we'd had for months, and we were forced to take shelter in Milford Haven on the Welsh coast. We were also searching for your father along both coastlines of the Irish Sea,' John protested, looking at Mary for some clemency.

'Excuses!' Alice muttered, giving him one of her withering looks.

'Well, what about the wool facility we bought in Plymouth, what's happened there?' Mary quizzed, trying to rescue John by changing the subject.

'We are only using it for wool storage at the moment, as I told you a few weeks ago. Richard and I haven't had the opportunity to go and look at the manufacturing side of it yet,' Alice answered.

'Fly by broomstick?' John Dickens muttered under his breath, which earned him a kick under the table from Alice.

'Right, you two, Chepstow tomorrow with John. I want to hear all about what's going on there by Sunday, so no lingering,' Mary instructed the girls. 'John, could you also bring them back please? I'm worried about highwaymen, as there appears to be a growing number of them along that road, if what I hear is correct.'

'Of course, I will, Mary,' John replied, and then muttered under his breath,' The thieves wouldn't stand a chance anyway!' A remark for which John got a glare and another kick from Alice.

Mary smiled to herself, as she perceived great-grandchildren in the offing.

Maisey watched all the activity going on in the big room of her house, and her mind went back—back to the cottage in the little Forest village, back to their simple life when Gumshu had just been a charcoal burner, back to when she never got away from the smell of smoke, and she wondered if it had all been worth it.

They were a tremendously wealthy family now, achieved in a short space of time. She thought of Friar Benedict's words to her when she and Gumshu had been agonising over the taking of the Forest lease.

'There is no sin in wealth', he had told her, 'as long as that wealth is used wisely.'

She thought of Katherine's little grave in the village churchyard. There had still been pain and grief when they were poor, so what difference wealth? She got up and stood by the window, looking at the gate that had been repaired. She giggled when she thought of the time when she had put her knee in Gumshu's groin.

She suddenly turned round and said in a loud voice, 'They're alive! I know they are! I know they are!'

John Dickens looked at her, remembering Grundwell's description of her after he had heard the story of the Corner House being bought. He looked at Little Emmy, he looked at Mary, and then he looked at Alice—young, beautiful, and fiery.

He was glad he had taken the decision to stay. Then he glanced back at Alice, who caught his look.

'I'm too young for you, John Dickens!' she said in a soft voice.

'But young women grow older,' he replied quietly, a twinkle in his eye.

'Maybe, but one certain brigantine captain won't if he's ever late with one of my cargoes again!' And she said it without any sign of humour.

'How had her father described her?' he thought. 'Something like "she'll be hell on two legs for some man when she's older." A fair description,' John reflected.

Three weeks later, the gales started to ease around the coasts of Cornwall, and the *Rachel* set sail from Chepstow to continue her search for the *Sara Jane*, without the hindrance of any cargo from the Spinning Wheel.

It had been a little over five months since the wreck. It had been five months of nearly constant storm force winds, heavy seas, and vast Atlantic swell. The sea and the spume had constantly lashed the island of St Agnes and all that stood on it, seemingly in a never-ending effort to tear its life and soul apart.

Petrina's and Rebecca's father, if father he was, said that he could never remember such winds over an autumn and winter period.

'This is a windy place. Even in the summer we have a lot of storms, but I can't remember anything like this,' he said one morning, as he tried to mend a fishing net that he'd snagged on some rocks.

Not being able to use their boats, he and the other fishermen on the island had resorted to fishing from the shore, using nets and lines as best they could.

Food and boredom had now become a serious issue.

Grundwell became increasingly aware that some of the islanders were starting to become somewhat resentful of their presence, even more so than when they were ship-wrecked.

On the second day after their dramatic arrival on the island, as promised, the three girls arrived back in the cove where the survivors had built their somewhat flimsy shelter. An increase in wind strength again was now starting to endanger the temporary abode.

'There's a cottage that hasn't been lived in for some time, which is fairly close to the other cottages in our village. After talking to the other islanders, my father has suggested that you use it until you are able to leave us. It is at least weatherproof, which is more than can be said for that!' Rebecca laughingly said as she pointed to the shelter.

Dick gratefully accepted the offer, at the same time reflecting that it was probably made with the thought that the islanders could keep a better eye on them if the survivors lived close by.

'Well, at least we don't have much luggage to take with us,' Will joked, picking up his pots and pans to walk up the track, followed by the others.

'Are the swords to fend off unfriendly island wenches?' Nadine asked Grundwell as he picked them up.

'No, they're to keep the wenches' boyfriends away should we get too friendly,' he replied with a smile.

'Bu I haven't got one,' she said very pointedly, walking ahead of him while swinging her hips.

'Neither have we,' the two other girls said together, helping Will and Monty with the half-full barrels of salted meat.

'Oh good,' Will said under his breath, as he accidentally brushed against Petrina's breasts.

During the first few weeks, in an effort to establish some form of friendly relations with the islanders, Monty repaired the sails of their fishing boats and taught them better ways of making new fishing nets.

Dick Tatton showed them how to cast their lines and nets from the shore in a way that he'd learnt in far distant lands. He showed them new ways to repair damage to their boats, to make lighter and stronger oars, and to do a variety of rope splices and knots, including his favourite of all—the Turk's head.

Will showed the women how to cook differently, using herbs that grew in abundance on the rocks and grasslands of the island. He taught them how to prepare certain shellfish and seaweed, things that they'd never dreamt of eating before.

Grundwell and Gumshu showed the men how to make charcoal from the pieces of wood that were washed up in vast numbers on the beaches surrounding the island. Then they showed how to use the charcoal for heating, cooking, and working metals, metal that would make fish hooks and spearheads.

'Let's not teach them too much about making spearheads. The way some villagers look at us, they might well use them on us,' Grundwell commented one day. 'And where's all the metal coming from, or shouldn't we ask?'

'I wonder what the reaction will be when we've taught them everything we know!' Will had remarked on a different occasion when the castaways were together.

'I think the ones who would cut our throats at the first opportunity are probably the wreckers. The others are what they say they are—simply fishermen, if there's a difference!' Gumshu said, as he remembered a remark by John Dickens about Cornish wreckers. He hoped that on this occasion John had been wrong.

'I think as a precaution we must make sure we're never alone with any of the doubtful ones, and try to stay together at night,' Dick Tatton warned.

'If you think I'm giving up my present sleeping arrangement to sleep with you lot, think again,' Will replied with a grin. 'If they get me, at least I'll die with a smile on my face!'

Will's present sleeping arrangements suited him fine, as he and Petrina had their own tiny bedroom in her parents' cottage.

At the time of this particular conversation, they had been on the island for three months, and Will's attraction to Petrina had been consummated within four nights of the wreck of the *Sara Jane*.

'Anyway, I think it'll be Petrina's father who will probably do for me before the wreckers, because it looks as though I've given him a grandchild,' he admitted, looking slightly embarrassed.

Dick looked at Monty, who had become besotted with Rebecca, and she with him. The two had been inseparable from about a month after their arrival. As with Will, he shared a tiny bedroom with his love in her parents' cottage.

Monty returned Dick's questioning gaze and said, 'Not yet, I'm still practicing!'

'She hangs on his every word when he's talking, and they actually sew together. It's unnatural,' Dick had said to Gumshu one evening as they were battling across the island. 'It's love!' Monty had confided to Dick Tatton on another night. 'I've had a lot of women in my life, but never felt like this. And at my age too, you'd think I'd know better.'

'There are going to be some broken hearts when we leave here,' Dick commented the night they had been told of Will's parenthood.

Will had simply said, 'I won't be leaving, Dick. I've found something that I've been looking for all my life, and now with a little one on the way, that's settled it.'

'Me neither!' Monty had added. 'I've always laughed at shipmates who have said that they just wanted to be with their wife and family. Thought they were daft. Like that chap with a crushed leg who keeps an inn not far from where the *Rachel*'s berthed in Plymouth. He was a pain in the neck talking about his family when we were away on the *Louise* together. I know what he meant now.'

'Yes, we've met him. We lodged at his inn when we stayed in Plymouth,' Gumshu replied, giving Grundwell an enquiring look.

Back at their own cottage that evening, Gumshu broached the subject of babies again and said to him, 'I have the feeling you have something to tell me.'

Before Grundwell could answer, Nadine came in and kissed her lover before going into the bedroom which they had shared from a week after they had first met.

'Are you coming to bed, my lover?' she asked.

Gumshu had commented to Dick on a previous evening after the three lovers had settled down with their respective girls, 'Do you reckon it's something in the air or in the water from that pool, or is it something in the food?'

'Well, whatever it is, we don't seem to be getting any of it!' Dick replied with a grin. He then added, 'We all thought it would be you and Nadine, not Grundwell.'

'No, she's great fun and has a great body, but it's like Monty said about missing your family. I miss Maisey like nothing on earth. Yes, I'll always flirt, but it stops there. 'Grundwell has a problem with his marriage, not his fault, but I think he covered the damage up, although it has always been there. Nadine is not the cause, more the solution, if you see what I mean.

'Anyway, you've never spoken about any family, Dick, or am I out of order?' He was very aware that Dick never mentioned anyone else other than Jane his sister, and he wondered why.

'No, you're not out of line. I lost my wife and children in the last plague in Plymouth, six years ago. It happened when I was away, as I usually was. It wiped out our whole family, except Jane, who had luckily married her Gloucestershire miner by then and had moved to your Forest village. She didn't hear for two years that our family had all died. It obviously hit her very hard.

'Then to go and lose her husband in Cottrells' mine that night. The poor girl doesn't know the meaning of "good fortune". But there are some good people in the Forest and they look after their own, as we've talked of before.

'There's a mad friar in the area, she told me. The first time she met him he was having a water fight with your wife. Anyway, she says that he and a clergyman, I can't remember his name, were wonderful with her both when she heard about the death of the family and when she lost her Will,' Dick concluded.

'Yes, the friar is crazy. He and Maisey are always trouble when they meet! But he's a man to have around at times of strife and grief. We lost our little daughter, Katherine, and I don't think we could have coped with our grief without his help.

'At the mine, on that fateful night, he was there when I had to take a decision that I will remember for the rest of my life. He and William Benson, the clergyman you mentioned, they make a good and caring team,' Gumshu quietly replied, lowering his head.

Dick got up and pretended to make sure that their cottage was secure, giving him a few minutes on his own.

'When we get off this island, what are your plans, Dick?' Gumshu asked him, having regained his composure.

'I haven't really made up my mind yet. I've lost my ship, and all my worldly possessions were on her. But I think I've had enough of the sea. That was a very close thing this time. That's the fourth time I've been wrecked. I think it's a safe shore-based job for me now,' he replied.

'In that case, come and work for me and live with your sister while we sort it out,' Gumshu offered.

'Thanks, Gumshu, I'd like that,' Dick responded. 'I've no money, well, nothing as I've said, and it was beginning to worry me a lot!'

Later in the week, Grundwell and Gumshu were alone again, walking across the sand bar that joined the next tiny island of Gugh to St Agnes, where they had been collecting more driftwood.

'Well,' Gumshu said, 'what were you about to tell me the other night?'

Grundwell paused for a moment. 'Nadine is in the same condition as Petrina!'

'Ah, I thought something was amiss. Dick and I haven't been subjected to as many sounds of passion as usual just recently,' Gumshu replied with a grin.

'You couldn't hear all that, could you?' Grundwell asked, looking horrified.

'Well, you are both, shall we say, enthusiastic over the act of making love, and it is a small cottage,' Gumshu answered, revelling in his friend's embarrassment.

Dawn was about to break, heralding the beginning of another day on the island of St Agnes.

Grundwell turned over, pulling the covers off the beautiful olive-skinned girl who lay beside him. Nadine softly chided him, pulling them back whence they came, and then cuddled into his back, letting the warmth of his body warm the extremities of her own.

They lay quietly, gently caressing and touching each other before finally slipping back into the magic land of Morpheus.

Grundwell awoke sometime later and kissed Nadine gently on the forehead.

He lay back with his hands behind his head and listened, listened to the silence.

Then he suddenly realised what he was listening to. Silence!

Throwing off the bedcovers, he sprang off the mattress and raced out of their bedroom into the main room where Dick and Gumshu were sleeping, unbolted the door of the cottage, and then in one bound he was outside.

The silence was deafening.

He stood totally naked, laughing and jumping around, yelling time after time, 'The wind has stopped! The wind has stopped!'

Gumshu and Dick came out and joined him, both draped in blankets, followed by Nadine, wearing a flimsy nightgown but still managing to reveal all her attributes.

The four danced around, encircling each other with their arms.

'The wind has stopped! The wind has stopped!' they chanted.

Monty and Rebecca appeared, followed shortly after by Petrina and Will.

All eight ran round and round the water pool, carrying on with the chant of 'the wind has stopped, the wind has stopped!' at the top of their voices.

The rest of the islanders peacefully slumbered on, being blissfully unaware of the momentous act of nature.

One day followed with no wind.

Two days followed with no wind.

Three days followed with no wind.

On the fourth day, the white sails of a brigantine were seen approaching St Mary's Bay.

The *Rachel* had arrived to continue her quest as to the fate of the *Sara Jane.*

# CHAPTER 19

Maisey knelt by the tiny grave in the Forest village churchyard, talking to her daughter.

Even when Gumshu was missing, she came every week. This time she was smiling as she cleared some strands of grass that had grown around the base of the little wooden cross.

'He's been found, he's alive, he's safe and well, the horse messenger says, and he should be back in about ten days,' Maisey recounted to Katherine.

'The *Rachel* is bringing him home, and Little Emmy and I plan to go to Chepstow with Sophie and her family to meet them, as Grundwell has been found as well.'

Then Maisey broke down, letting go all of her pent-up emotions that she had kept to herself for so long, and she wept—wept with relief, wept with joy, wept with exhaustion.

A deep voice spoke, 'You had faith, and you kept it, thank the Lord!'

Friar Benedict stood behind her, leaning on his staff, with tears in his eyes.

Maisey got up, and taking her old friend by the arm, she looked up at him, saying, 'I knew he was alive. I just knew. Don't ask me how!'

'The Lord will know the answer to that, my child. He's pretty wise and has been around a long time!' the friar said with a wide grin.

'Nearly as long as you have, Friar Benedict,' Maisey teased, tears of joy running down her cheeks, earning herself a gentle cuff from the ageing friar.

When the brigantine was first sighted arriving in the bay between St Mary's and Gugh, Gumshu excitedly asked Rebecca and Petrina's father if he would take them round to meet the *Rachel* in his fishing boat.

'No need,' he replied. 'They're making their way here!' And he pointed at the direction that the brigantine was sailing.

As he spoke, a plume of smoke, followed by a rush of flames, leapt into the sky from the small headland of Pidney Brow at the other end of St Agnes, opposite to where the *Sara Jane* had met her untimely end.

Dick had lit the beacon that they had built when they first got wrecked and which he and Gumshu had tended religiously ever since.

Luckily, that had included checking the tinder was dry enough to light with a spark from the flints.

The *Rachel* set more sail, carefully manoeuvring around the ledges that were visible with the low tide. They could make out two linesmen on the bow of the boat, taking soundings as she moved slowly forward towards their island refuge.

'That'll be John Dickens at the helm,' Dick Tatton reported. 'He doesn't trust anyone else when he's in a tight spot.'

About half an hour later, the *Rachel* came slowly around the headland, then swung into the wind and sent out her anchor so that she lay about two cables off the bay where the survivors were gathered. John Dickens launched his gig, and six skilful oarsmen sent her skimming across the glass-like oily sea.

A short distance off the shore, they backed their oars, and the gig gently slid up the white sand of the beach, with John Dickens stepping dramatically out of the stern sheets with the broadest of grins.

'I presume, gentlemen, you've been waiting for me?'

Laughing, grabbing him by the hand, and then hugging him, Grundwell and Gumshu greeted their rescuer with boundless enthusiasm before introducing him to the remnants of the *Sara Jane*'s crew and the three island girls.

Dick he already knew, as well as Will, who made the best seaweed wine in the Royal Navy according to John.

'So that's what it was,' Gumshu said, referring to the drink that had been made for the girls on their first visit to the shelter. Will gave a conspiratorial grin.

Monty, Rebecca, Petrina, and Will stood and said their goodbyes to those who were leaving, the two men assuring Dick Tatton that they were doing the right thing by staying. The girls clung to their men, in case there was a change of heart. But they needn't have worried; both were totally committed to their island sweethearts.

Their father had been heard to say, 'I now have a sailmaker and net repairer, together with a man to cook what I catch. Added to that I have an imminent grandchild, so what else could a man want?'

There had been many and varied answers to that question around the island village, most of which he had ignored and put down to envy.

Nadine stood apart from the others, not knowing quite what to do. She had her travelling bag with her, but it lay on the ground between her feet.

Grundwell took both her hands and looked into her eyes.

'We've talked at length about this moment, Nadine, and never really come to any conclusions. There are two options. We take you home to your parents in St Mary's. I explain who I am, you have our child with them, and I will support you from afar. On the other hand, you can come back to Mitcheldean, and I set you up in a house somewhere close by. That means I would be able to visit you any time, and you can have our child there.'

Nadine had always disliked her father, wasn't very keen on her mother, and didn't like St Mary's, so the latter of Grundwell's suggestions was really her only option for escape from her island existence.

She was very fond of him, and knowing of his wealth, she realised that neither she nor her unborn child would ever want for anything. So she picked up her bag, took Grundwell's arm, and said in a broad Cornish accent, 'So be it, my lover. Let's go and see this place called Gloucestershire that Gumshu thinks is the place to be!'

Gumshu looked at Dick. 'I see tears ahead!' Dick nodded in full agreement.

John Dickens looked at Gumshu with a question written all over his face.

'Don't ask!' he said, climbing into the stern sheets of the gig, alongside Dick, Nadine, and Grundwell.

With John at the tiller, the oarsmen pushed off from the beach with help from the two newest residents of St Agnes and then sent the gig skimming back to the waiting brigantine.

The island incarceration for three of the survivors of the *Sara Jane* was ended.

Back on board the *Rachel*, they were met by a concerned William Grey, John's second in command. He greeted the survivors of the *Sara Jane* enthusiastically, then turning to John he said, 'Captain, the wind has backed to the north over the last ten minutes, and it's started picking up with short gusts. Looking at the sky, I think we have another blow due.'

John Dickens was already aware that the weather signs had changed; he had noticed that the *Rachel* was now lying differently to her anchor, and he too had read the sky and seen the change in the cloud patterns. He quickly issued orders to his officers.

'Right, swing the gig aboard, get it lashed down, and let's make ready to get underway. We'll head for Falmouth, the closest place to find shelter if it is going to blow from the north. Have your sails set, Mister Grey, and prepare to weigh anchor. We'll have those two linesmen up on the bow again, if you please. Once clear, kindly set a course for a few points off the Lizard, and we'll show off our new Cornish lighthouse to these Forest gentlemen of leisure. It should take us about twelve to fifteen hours. Looking at the sky, we should be just ahead of what the good Lord is about to throw at us again.'

Turning to the survivors, he continued, 'I think, gentlemen, knowing how much you enjoy a bumpy ride and a lot of movement in my boat, we'll amend our plans and head for shelter in Falmouth. If the weather is going to do what William and I suspect, we may have to shelter there for several days. I just thank God I am not carrying a cargo from the Spinning Wheel!'

'What's the problem with Spinning Wheel cargoes?' a puzzled Grundwell asked.

'No problem, but your daughter was not best pleased with me for being late into Waterford with a cargo of woollen goods. The fact that we had to take shelter from a particularly strong gale and had been looking for you did not impress her at all,' John said in a somewhat wounded voice.

'Why is Alice concerning herself with such things?' Grundwell pressed.

John immediately realised that he'd started a topic of conversation that he would have been wiser to avoid, but having got so far, he thought he might as well tell the two men from Mitcheldean a little of what had been going on in their absence.

'Well, since you both disappeared, she's been running the Spinning Wheel with Richard Beachwood and Phillip Fletcher. Little Emmy, Thomas Sutton, and Edmund Fletcher have been running Hawk

Mines. Mary, with Nathaniel's advice, has been making sure that both businesses perform properly, while your two eldest daughters have also been making my life hell over the construction of the new fleet. They've been saying I'm too slow at getting the boats off the stocks, I've given preference to the brigantines over the colliers, and I wasn't following your instructions. Those two work well as a team. If one doesn't get me, the other does, and they are both very good!'

'What about Maisey and Sophie?' Gumshu asked, beginning to look very concerned.

John felt somewhat awkward and thought for a moment before replying.

'Both of your wives took your disappearances extremely badly. I've never met either of them before, but I remembered your description of them, Grundwell, when we were in Plymouth. If you remember, you were telling me of the consequences of Gumshu not consulting with Maisey over buying the new house on the corner of Craven Street?'

'Yes, I do remember,' Grundwell said with a smile.

John continued, 'When in public, they have been marvellous, but in private, they haven't been coping, Sophie particularly, according to Alice. She has become very withdrawn and doesn't seem to be able to concentrate on anything or want to do anything, in spite of Mary's encouragement and support.

'Maisey has had a lot of help from a Father Benedict, and from what Alice has told me, she has coped a lot better than Sophie, although it has hit her very badly and she's very shaken. Alice also told me that the Rector of Mitcheldean and his wife have been towers of strength for both families.

'I'm sorry, I have probably spoken out of turn, but it is perhaps better if you hear these things from me rather than from someone else. I've made three visits to Craven Street since your disappearance over five months ago. Alice and Little Emmy have been taking more and more business responsibilities and doing it very successfully. They're not afraid to ask questions and listen to advice, especially from your general managers.'

John turned his attention to his ship once again, making sure she was making a safe passage into open water and using that as an excuse for ending the conversation with Grundwell and Gumshu.

The *Rachel* eventually cleared the jagged tooth-like rocks and hidden ledges of the islands, with Mister Grey laying off a course for Falmouth as his captain had instructed. The brigantine settled to her new heading, heeling to the freshening northerly wind, with all her royals and top gallants set.

Gumshu, Dick, and the captain stood on the stern deck, looking forward to where Grundwell and Nadine were leaning over the ship's rail, talking and watching the dolphins playing in the bow wave of the boat.

'Are you going to tell me a bit of what happened now?' John asked Gumshu, more relaxed now that *Rachel* was in clear water and he didn't need to be close to the helm.

Gumshu explained all that had happened from when they embarked on the *Sara Jane*: about the lack of crew, the keel leak in the grain hold, and how they had lost steerage and been blown off course, ending up in the horrific surf on the lethal Lethegus Rocks off St Agnes.

He told him of the wreck and how just five of those on board had managed to survive, five out of so many.

John shuddered, knowing the Isles of Scilly was like a mass grave for so many good seamen and their ships.

'I've lost countless friends in the area,' he told them with a very sombre look. 'You are very lucky to be alive, gentlemen, very lucky!' he added softly.

Gumshu continued by telling him of their existence on the island, how they occupied themselves, and of the relationships that developed, especially the one between Grundwell and Nadine.

'They've been lovers since shortly after our arrival on St Agnes, and the result is what you see. She's expecting his child, he's besotted with her, and she with him, I think.'

'Not sure about the *she with him* bit, Gumshu,' Dick commented, looking a bit doubtful, 'but I hope that I'm wrong.'

'Whichever way it is, I don't think Grundwell has taken a wise decision in bringing her home. I think he's walking into a lot of trouble,' Gumshu said.

'Then I don't think I'll add to his woes by telling him that I would like to marry his eldest daughter,' John added with a wry smile.

Gumshu looked at him and laughed. 'You're not serious, are you? She's not yet seventeen, and you ought to have seen the reaction when she wrote to him and told him she actually had a boyfriend! It wasn't you, was it?'

'Regretfully not, but she got rid of him because she was too busy. No, it's just that I might live a little longer if I'm married to her.

'As I've just told you, I was late delivering a cargo of wool to Ireland for her, and you'd have thought I'd committed high treason by her reaction. I couldn't help being late. There were some awful gales, and I had to take shelter *and* I was looking for you. All she said was "*excuses*"!' John repeated in a rather hurt voice.

'Well, we can vouch for the gales,' Dick said, laughing.

'Have you mentioned marriage to her yet?' a fascinated Gumshu asked.

'No, I haven't. I'm not that brave! I'd rather face a couple of boats of privateers than ask her. It's just that I find her totally bewitching. She's beautiful, fiery, and oh that smile! I'd sail a thousand miles to be on the right side of that. The way she and your daughter have been driving the businesses forward in your and Grundwell's absence, I find totally amazing, as do a lot of other people.'

'You remember what we were talking about some time ago about all this romance, with you and me missing out?' Gumshu said, turning to Dick.

'I do, and we reckoned it must be in the water, food, or air,' replied a smiling Dick.

They both turned and looked at John.

'It must be in the air, if *he's* got it as well,' Gumshu joked. 'And, Captain, I would offer you two bits of advice. Firstly, I wouldn't approach your future father-in-law just yet. I think he has enough problems of his own! And secondly, don't keep mentioning Alice quite as much when you're talking. It really does draw attention to how you feel about her,' Gumshu continued.

'Does it show that much?' John sighed.

'Yes!' came the resounding response from Gumshu, Dick, and also William Grey, who was standing by the helm. William had suffered his captain being lovelorn for several weeks now, but hadn't felt that it was his place to say anything.

The *Rachel* sailed into Falmouth harbour some fifteen hours later, having fought the last of the conflicting tidal stream setting around Lizard Point. She had been carried round by the strengthening of the wind in her sails which John had not reefed in, thus allowing his ship to maintain her speed and power through the water.

The following morning, William Grey went ashore in the gig to dispatch a horse-mounted messenger with the news of the survivors' rescue to the two families in Craven Street and to Dick's sister in Cumdean.

Meanwhile, John Dickens moved the brigantine further up into the River Fal to find better shelter from the northerly storm that was building in ferocity. William arrived back sometime later, after his successful trip ashore, to find Grundwell and Nadine on the deck awaiting his return.

'Mister Grey, will you take us to the town dockside please and then await my return to bring me back to the ship?' Grundwell asked.

William Grey looked at his captain, who inclined his head slightly.

'Yes, of course, sir!' he replied.

Nadine said her goodbyes to Dick and Gumshu, who were still mystified at the sudden change of plans of their friend and his mistress. She thanked John Dickens for bringing her to Falmouth, then she and Grundwell settled into the stern sheets of the gig to be taken ashore by William and his oarsmen.

Some five hours later, the gig and her crew returned. They brought the lone Grundwell back with them. Without saying a word to anyone, he retired to his cabin, closed the door, and took to his bunk.

For four days, the *Rachel* swung and strained on her anchor, even in the sheltered stretch of the river that John had found. They could hear the storm raging over the top of them and could feel the wave surges that powered up the river on the incoming tide.

By the fifth day, the storm had blown itself out, and they were able to start making preparations for the passage to Chepstow.

Grundwell appeared on deck as they awaited a favourable tide to take them round Land's End and then up the north coast of Cornwall. He had not spoken to anyone but the cook since going to his cabin, and as the cook had told Gumshu: much wine had been consumed, but little food.

Grundwell quietly asked John if the gig could take him ashore and that as he wouldn't be returning aboard, it could come back straight away.

'I have one other request. Would you lend me some more money? As I told you yesterday when I borrowed some to give to Nadine, all that I had when the *Sara Jane* was wrecked has obviously been lost. When you get to Mitcheldean, ask Phillip Fletcher to repay you in full.'

John was more than happy to comply with the request, especially the latter part, as the amount of borrowed funds was now substantial.

Grundwell took Gumshu quietly aside to explain about the alteration to his plans.

'Nadine has changed her mind about coming back to Mitcheldean with me. One reason was that she heard all that John told us of what had been happening in our absence. She made me take her to her aunt's house, which is right at the top of the hill in Falmouth. The two of them talked at length, and she has now decided to stay here to have our baby.

'All Nadine has asked of me is to send her some money occasionally and to visit when I can. The trouble is that's not enough for me because I honestly can't live without her. Having thought it through, this is what I intend to do.

'I'm going to go to Plymouth from here, buy a house as close as I can to the dockside building, and then set Nadine up in it with her aunt acting as housekeeper. The aunt's husband has recently died and she doesn't want to stay in Falmouth. She would prefer to be close to her three children, all of whom live in Plymouth.'

'There's a surprise!' Gumshu said with heavy sarcasm. 'I find that all a bit convenient. You don't know these people, but they know you are very wealthy, especially after all Nadine has heard of late.

'Could I just remind you that you're already married? Could I remind you that you already have four children? Could I remind you that you have a business to run? Finally, could I remind you that it's not your business, but Mary's, and that could be important, not only for your future but for that of your mistress and unborn child!'

'The business would be nothing without me,' Grundwell returned testily.

'I beg to differ. From what John was saying when he rescued us, Alice and Mary are making a fine job of running it without you,' Gumshu responded, equally as testily.

Captain Dickens was reminded by William Grey that if they were to catch the tide they should be making ready. John shook his head as he couldn't help but overhear the conversation between the two friends.

'I think what is happening between these two is more important than catching the tide, William. Just stand the crew down, and let's see what happens. We'll catch tomorrow's tide if need be,' he instructed in a quiet voice.

'Yes, Captain,' William responded, turning to order the crew to stand down.

'John, could we use your cabin for a few moments, please? Grundwell and I have some serious and private talking to do,' Gumshu asked.

'Yes, of course,' John replied.

The two men went into the captain's cabin, closed the cabin door, and sat down at the round chart table in the corner of John's quarters.

Grundwell glowered at Gumshu.

'Do you remember when I came to see you, worried out of my mind, during that heavy snow that closed my mines and stopped all the transport?' Gumshu asked.

'Yes, but what's that got to do with my present situation?' Grundwell snarled.

'Everything! You gave me a lot of sound advice that night, both as a friend and someone whose business experience far outstripped my own. Can I ask you how many people work both directly and as outworkers for the Spinning Wheel now?'

'Seven hundred and twenty-eight, including the trow crews and agents, the last time I checked with Phillip, which was three months before we got wrecked.'

'That makes you one of the biggest woollen goods manufacturers and raw wool traders in the country?'

'Yes.'

'All those families rely on the Spinning Wheel for their livelihood, and you've even started building cottages for some of them to rent?'

'Yes.'

'And you and I are setting up a fleet of vessels to enlarge our businesses even more?'

'Yes.'

'Employing say, another 600 people?'

'Yes.'

'So between us, we employ over 2000 people, or will do if you include Samuel Longden's transport men and all our agents?'

'Yes.'

'You're probably right. Well, you are right when you say the business would be nothing without you. I don't say that lightly because I am as reliant on you as any of your employees. I always have been, even before you pulled me out of that hut fire when we were six years old,' Gumshu said quietly, looking straight into his friend's eyes.

'Your point being?'

'My point being is that you are going to put all that at risk for the sake of a twenty-year-old girl that you hardly know. Yes, she's carrying your child, but she's already given you the solution. You've just seen the common sense of the girl in refusing to go back home with you. Look beyond your own feelings, and if nothing else, at least think of hers. She doesn't want to be saddled with being the mistress of an ageing businessman, however wealthy. At twenty, she has a life to live. She doesn't want to be put on a collar and lead!'

With that, Gumshu went back on deck, leaving Grundwell to his own counsel.

'John, we stay put tonight!' Gumshu instructed the captain of the *Rachel* as he strode past him to stand in the bow, leaning against the bowsprit and gazing down the river at the town of Falmouth, hoping that his words to his friend had cut good and deep.

'Yes, sir!' John replied without hesitation. William Grey raised an eyebrow as it was the first time he'd ever heard his captain respond like that to anyone giving him a direct instruction on the *Rachel*.

The following morning the brigantine set sail shortly after dawn, catching the last of the tide that helped bring them out of the lower reaches of the River Fal. Thanks to John's timing, they were able to reap the benefit of the tidal streams created by changes of tide as they began their journey round the Lizard, through the passage between Land's End and the Isles of Scilly, and then up the north Cornish coast as far as Hartland Point. They would then cross to the South Wales coast, leaving Lundy Island some ten miles to port, and thence into the Bristol Channel.

With only a moderate southerly breeze blowing, they would then use the Gower Peninsular anchorages to await the tidal changes to assist their passage up to the River Wye. *Rachel*'s captain's reckoning was that they would reach Chepstow in about five days, taking account of the now settled favourable wind but allowing for some conflicting tides.

On the fifth day of the trip from Falmouth, the *Rachel* nosed her way up the two-mile stretch of the Wye towards Chepstow, swept along by the flood tide and the wind in her royals.

The captain lowered his gig with six oarsmen and his boatswain, Ben, at the tiller so that they could help the *Rachel* turn on the tighter bends. The day was fine, the breeze light, and for once on his entry to this port, it was coming from a favourable quarter.

On the final bend before the docks came into sight, Gumshoe felt the *Rachel* slow and then dip forward, as her keel started to cut a groove into the grey mud of the riverbank, much as she had done on their outward journey all those months ago. John Dickens gently adjusted his helm so that the *Rachel* turned to her starboard, coming free of the mud with help from the incoming tide, the breeze in her sails, and oar power from the gig. Once clear, he waited a few moments and then pulled his whip staff hard over so that *Rachel* turned sharply to her port and swept regally around the bend.

Gumshu was unable to resist it and said in an exaggeratedly loud voice, 'Alice is probably watching on the dockside, John. Carefully does it!'

William Grey suppressed a smile, but John Dickens replied with a voice like thunder, a voice that echoed around the wooded slopes and high castle walls, 'If one of my crew even dare smile, I'll keelhaul him!'

Sixty-eight seamen and five officers looked resolutely ahead with a look of total concentration on their faces, trying desperately to ignore Ben and his oarsmen in the gig, all of whom were making as many silly faces as possible to try and make them laugh.

Then, however, there came a lone voice from somewhere deep in the bowels of the *Rachel*.

'Thank God that there are some straight bits on this river!'

The captain never found out who the culprit had been, but the cook's name was mentioned more than once!

Half an hour later, the boat was safely at her berth, with her mooring lines in place and her gangway in position and secured. Grundwell, Gumshu, and Dick Tatton looked along the busy dockside, each searching for members of their own family who might have come to meet them.

The *Rachel* had flagged her time and day of arrival in port as she passed the Swansea Relay Tower on Mumbles Head. The post messengers that were dispatched should have reached all the families, and Captain Saunders, well before *Rachel* reached Chepstow.

Gumshu turned to Grundwell as they were berthing and asked how he felt.

'I'm not sure,' he confided quietly. 'You were right in everything you said to me in Falmouth, but it isn't making it any easier just at present.' He walked away to stand and gaze, unseeing, at the hustle and bustle on the dockside.

He had been so preoccupied as they came up the river that he hadn't even heard Gumshu's remark about Alice when John Dickens had touched the mud bank, which probably had been as well.

Maisey and all the children came running along the dock towards *Rachel's* berth, with Dick's sister and her son following close behind. Gumshu and Dick raced down the gangplank, where Gumshu grabbed his sobbing wife and lifted her high into the air before enveloping her in his arms and kissing every inch of her face.

Tears of joy ran down his cheeks as he let go of his wife and hugged the children. Little Emmy, although carrying her brother, was bouncing up and down with the others, trying to draw her father's attention. All of them were screaming at the tops of their voices.

'I think I ought to get shipwrecked more often!' Gumshu yelled, nearly suffocating under the onslaught from his family.

Dick was hugging his sister Jane in a similar way, with his nephew wrapping his arms round both of them. They were the remnants of a large family, a family which had been reduced to just three by the dreadful ravages of the plague.

Grundwell stood on the deck of *Rachel*, by the top of the gangway, and watched his two fellow survivors and their families, wishing he was back in Falmouth with the girl he loved.

Then Alice came into view, hurrying along the dockside, waving and laughing up at him, pushing past the families at the bottom of the gangplank. She came running up on to the deck, hugging her father for several long moments, Grundwell temporarily putting Falmouth out of his mind.

Alice managed to fit five *why*s in before the end of her first twelve sentences, much to the delight of her father, who suddenly felt that he was home again.

Taking her by the hand, he led her to the opposite side of *Rachel's* deck so that they could hear themselves speak above the screaming and shouting of Gumshu and his family.

'Where are your mother and the rest of the family?'

'Well, I'm here' came a voice from behind them, as Mary took hold of him and gave him a big hug and kiss.

Behind her, Elizabeth, Thomas, and Anna came romping across the deck, throwing their arms around their father in a somewhat more restrained way than the other Forest family, but equally as enthusiastic.

'No Mother?' Grundwell enquired.

'She felt she wasn't up to the journey, so she's waiting at Craven Street,' Mary answered, a look of concern crossing her face.

'Is she all right?'

'Yes, she is, but she has been out of her mind with worry, and it has taken its toll on her health,' Mary replied.

'Yes, I heard that from John Dickens when he rescued us.'

Alice reluctantly but gently let go of her father, saying softly, 'There is something that the captain and I must sort out.'

Knowing where he would be, she went below to his cabin to speak to him.

She knocked on his door and entered on his quiet, 'Come in.'

John was sitting at his table, completing the log of the *Rachel*'s passage from Falmouth to Chepstow.

He stood up when Alice entered and smiled broadly.

'What a lovely surprise!' he said, hoping that it was actually going to be lovely.

'You and I need to talk, John Dickens,' she said sternly, walking round the table so that she stood about a foot away from him.

'I have just heard on the dockside that you are supposedly in love with me and you've been acting like a lovelorn teenager for the last few months.'

'Where have you heard that from, if it's not a rude question?' John countered defensively.

'I heard William Grey and Ben talking about it when they were checking the mooring lines as I walked past them. That's why I was a little later than the others getting to the boat, because I stopped and listened.

'They didn't know what to do with themselves when they saw me! They also admitted that you hit that mud bank on the last bend before the docks. I already knew that because I was standing on the grass bank by the castle entrance and saw *Rachel*'s masts dip forward. I also heard what you thundered at your crew!' She laughed in a way that lit up her face and in a way that John had never noticed before. 'Anyway, you still haven't answered me. Are you in love with me?'

'Well, if you mean by love that I can't get you out of my mind, you totally bewitch me in every way possible, I think you're the most beautiful woman I've ever met, and you have a smile that reduces me to a gibbering idiot, I suppose that I must say it, yes, I am!' he admitted with a sigh.

'And how long have I had this effect on you, remembering of course that I'm only just seventeen and I told you I was too young for you a couple of months ago when we were at the Corner House?'

'The first time I met you,' he admitted again.

'Well, Captain, I fell in love with you the *second* time we met, so you've moved quicker than me,' she said, putting her arms round his neck and kissing him hard on the lips.

He was so taken aback that he failed to respond to his love's first kiss, something he remedied with passion the next time.

Alice withdrew from their second kiss, slightly breathless, and rested her hands on his shoulders.

'Next time you need to ask or tell me something, will you promise to speak to me and not let me hear it by dockside chatter?' she pleaded in a rather husky voice.

'Yes, I promise, but *there is* something else that I need to ask you.'

'Well, ask me then,' she sighed, 'but make it before I have the urge to kiss you again.'

'Alice, will you marry me?'

'I'll think about it, John Dickens,' she murmured, succumbing to her urge with considerable enthusiasm.

At the end of the kiss, which was a long and passionate one, she drew back saying, 'I've just thought about it, and the answer is *yes*. I would like nothing better, my love!'

She nuzzled and kissed him for a few more minutes, her arms wrapped round him, and then she whispered softly in his ear, 'But just because you will be my husband, don't think that will give you the excuse to be late with one of my cargoes again, Captain John Dickens!'

# CHAPTER 20

Grundwell walked through the front door of the house on Craven Street, wondering how he was going to react to seeing Sophie again.

It had been nearly nine months since he had left, five months of which he had been living with a twenty-year-old girl whom he loved and who was about to bear him a child.

Going into the large room, he smelt the wood smoke, the coals, and the food cooking with Estor standing over the fire as usual, preparing the evening meal.

She turned round with a big smile on her face.

'Welcome home, sir. It's wonderful to have you back and looking so well. The mistress is upstairs in her room, lying down.'

After quietly thanking her, Grundwell walked up the stairs and into the bedroom.

Sophie was lying on the bed asleep or he assumed that she was. He sat down on the edge of the bed, took her hand, and looked at the beautiful woman that lay in front of him. Her hair cascaded over the covers where she laid her head, which was slightly turned to one side. He bent down and kissed her forehead, and then he noticed that tears were rolling down her cheeks and he realised that she was awake.

'Sophie,' he said quietly. 'Come on, look at me. I know you're awake.'

She opened her eyes, wide and slightly fearful, and looked directly at Grundwell. It was as if he wasn't there; there seemed to be no recognition at all.

He held on to her hand, gently stroking it. He leant forward again to kiss her forehead, and she seemed to suddenly realise who he was because she let out the most fearful scream, flung her arms around him, and started to weep like a child.

She clung to him, saying over and over again, 'I've missed you. I've missed you. I've missed you!'

He wrapped his arms around her as if to protect her, as he had done all those years ago when Edward had raped her. He smelt her hair as he held his head tight against hers, he smelt her familiar body scents, and he heard her voice, heard her pleading with him never to leave her again, and he knew in those few seconds that he probably never would.

By the time Mary and all the children arrived back at the house, Sophie and Grundwell were sitting in front of the fire in the large room, holding hands, with Grundwell relating *some* of his adventures on the Isles of Scilly.

His graphic description of the actual wreck of the *Sara Jane* held his family spellbound for many hours that evening, but then Anna said, 'Father, the rest of the time must have been very boring, just stuck on a small island with nothing to do. How terrible!'

'It certainly was, little one, it certainly was,' he said and then started to ask Mary and Alice about the Spinning Wheel.

That night when they went to bed, he stopped Sophie from putting any night clothes on and held her, lying beside her under the covers, talking to her, caressing her, and eventually making love to her before they fell asleep in each other's arms.

Suddenly, St Agnes seemed an age away, and it was the next day that really mattered.

The following morning, he and Alice were at the wool buildings well before dawn, as Grundwell had asked her to show him everything before anyone else arrived. She took him round, explaining every aspect of production: for whom the orders were and what wool reserves they held. She also showed him some brand new weaving equipment that she and Richard had designed, equipment that produced even finer woollen fabric than ever before.

'Father, we need more room. With this new equipment, as well as getting a brilliantly finer weave, we could, if we had the space, increase our production twofold as well.'

'Why didn't you start to construct another weaving house then, if you were that sure?'

'Richard Beachwood and I put it to Grandmother, but she wouldn't let us. I even asked Nathaniel Purnell what he thought, and he agreed with me. In his opinion, we had enough reserves to pay for it, installing new looms throughout, and *still* be able to honour our share of the ship building costs. Even then, we would still have had *substantial* reserves left.'

'How many people work for us at the moment, including outworkers and agents?'

'Seven hundred and twenty-eight, the same number as when you decided to go living the life of a castaway.'

'If that's supposed to be funny, it's not!' Grundwell snapped.

'One subject to be kept away from,' Alice muttered to herself.

'Why not take on more outworkers then?'

'Because we can't control the quality properly, and quality is one of the most important things we offer. The new cloth is so fine the tension of the yarn has to be absolutely perfect to achieve the consistency of the weave. Any mistakes and the cloth is ruined, and we obviously can't use it. The other problem is that we can't take these new looms to the outworkers because they are too big and far too complicated, and so can only be assembled in our weaving sheds by our loom maker's men.

'We can still sell the cloth that is made on the outworkers' handlooms, but the market is becoming very limited because our customers want items of the finer weave. Also by using these larger looms, the production of the cloth is vast by comparison, thus reducing our item labour costs drastically,' Alice explained.

'Don't tell your grandmother that technology is replacing people. She will not be impressed!'

'She already knows, and it's the one thing we really argue about,' his daughter responded. 'She was not happy at all when I said that by using this new type of loom we could reduce our labour force, but increase our overall production dramatically,'

'Yes, I suspect that may have been part of the reason she refused to let you build another weaving house! She and I were disagreeing about that subject before my extended voyage,' her father replied. 'So if I say we build another facility, you could increase our overall production twofold, but with a significant decrease in the people we employ?'

'Yes,' Alice replied, 'but we would *have* to use these brand new looms to achieve it.'

'But if we do that, we would then need more production workers making our woollen goods to match the increase in the amount of cloth you say we could produce. One follows on from the other. So where are we going to get *them* from? We already employ most of the people of Mitcheldean who aren't involved in working leather or brewing ale,' Grundwell countered.

'The weavers that we replace by the use of these looms can move over to our production side. We also have experienced workers moving into the town from other areas looking for work, just as they were all those months ago before you went off on your trip. The completion of the cottages has helped. Word has spread that we may be able to offer accommodation to our employees. There are another six to build, and we've let twelve of the nineteen completed ones, so that's an added attraction when or if we take more people on, remembering we will need additional spinners for the increase in yarn that we will use.'

'All right, I want to see some figures within the week for another new building, and utilising these new looms. Talk to Richard and Phillip and then go and see Nathaniel to work out any funding requirements. You and I will put some costs together for setting Plymouth up to weave again, using all new looms, *and* manufacture woollen goods. That means we will be *producing* in one of the ports that we export from, thus reducing our item cost on transport. We can move the raw materials in by using one of our own ships. It can bring those items in, and then the same vessel can ship our finished goods out,' he answered, already starting to plan the future in his mind and wondering how close his original business plan was to reality.

'Welcome home, Father!' his daughter said with a broad smile.

'Welcome to the business, Daughter!' Grundwell replied. 'But one other thing. I don't mind you marrying John Dickens, but definitely no babies yet. You have work to do.'

Blushing, Alice queried, 'I didn't know John had spoken to you yet?'

'He hasn't, but when I saw both of you coming up from his cabin on *Rachel* after we docked at Chepstow, you were both, shall we just say, "*glowing*". Your grandmother then muttered something about great-grandchildren, and Anna went "Yuck, they're in love". I rather gathered there was something I'd missed. He's a good man, far too old for you, but anyone younger probably wouldn't be able to control you. I take it he's told you that he had a wife and son who were murdered by privateers and why his brigantine is called *Rachel*?'

'Yes, he has. He told Little Emmy and I when we went to Chepstow to see how the boat building was progressing. He also told us of your forthright talk with him about his revenge trips on the *Rachel*. Don't worry. He won't be doing any more of that, just as he won't be late with any more of my wool cargoes.'

'Who says?' her father asked.

'I do!' replied his daughter, as she went out to see if Richard Beachwood and Phillip Fletcher had arrived at work yet.

'I wonder if our brave captain quite realises what he's letting himself in for,' Grundwell said out loud to himself.

'Yes, he does!' Alice said, sticking her head back round the door. 'I just have to smile at him, and I get exactly what I want.' And with that comment, she departed on her mission. She came back some minutes later, with both Phillip and Richard.

Grundwell wasn't quite sure whether they were genuinely pleased to see him or whether it was a case of relief from taking instructions from Alice. With that in mind, he decided that he'd better explain to them how things were going to change.

'From now on, Alice will be running the Spinning Wheel, obviously with your help, but everyone answers to her and she in turn answers to me. John Dickens will take over responsibility for the fleet, as Gumshu and I had planned. We need to start it trading properly as soon as possible, but again, that is down to John, and he will answer to Gumshu and me.

'I, in the meantime, will go back to Plymouth and set up that part of the business, using the new looms that Alice has shown me. That will leave you three free to get a new building sorted out, which I will discuss with Mary tonight.'

'I'm giving Alice a week to work out figures and to check funding with Nathaniel. I want prices for the new looms in the proposed weaving house as well as at Plymouth, as I've said. I'm impressed with this finer weave and the increase in volume of production of cloth they can give. If we're going to increase our exports by using the Plymouth facilities as well as an increase in manufacturing from Mitcheldean for the home market, then we must organise things quickly. We also need to appoint more selling agents, re-organise our weavers, and make sure our loom maker is ready to supply these new looms once the new building is completed here and I've organised Plymouth to start production. Let's just hope that the political situation remains stable, both at home and abroad!'

Richard and Phillip assumed that was the end of the meeting and left to start work.

'I trust that suits what you've always intended, young lady?' Grundwell asked his daughter.

'*Why* can't I work with John as well?' she questioned.

'I knew there'd be a *why* somewhere! Because I want you to marry him, not scare the life out of him. You've got what you wanted, now leave it at that and don't push for that final bit that isn't there. I can remember saying to your mother years ago you were going to be a handful when you were a teenager, and I wasn't wrong.'

'Yes, Father!' Alice conceded. And she thought to herself, 'And you're up to something too, Father dear.'

Similar conversations had been going on at Hawk Mines. Gumshu and Little Emmy had arrived early at the coal building in Cumdean, but the atmosphere was very different.

Thomas Sutton and Edmund were already there when father and daughter arrived by pony and trap. They gave Gumshu a rapturous welcome, and had he felt a little less under the weather, he would have appreciated it.

The previous night had been one total celebration at the Corner House on Craven Street. Mead and wine had flowed like never before, starting when they all arrived home from Chepstow until not long before Gumshu and Little Emmy left for Cumdean.

'Not even time to indulge in any '*frolicking*' tonight!' Little Emmy had teased her mother and father. 'And certainly no time for a little mixing of the mead with the liquid out of the large red bottle with the peculiar stopper,' she'd carried on.

'What have you told her?' Gumshu accused his now blushing wife.

'Nothing at all, nothing, I promise you,' Maisey answered. 'How on earth did you know about that?' she asked her daughter, somewhat horrified.

'I've known about it for years, Mother, but never dared mention it. There's still quite a lot left, isn't there?' Little Emmy replied, a wide mischievous grin on her face.

'Yes, there is, and I shall mark the bottle too!' Gumshu retorted, as he encircled his wife in his arms. 'We don't need that tonight, do we sweetheart?' he murmured in her ear.

'Now look what you've made him think of,' Maisey laughingly accused her daughter.

'It's all right, Mother.' Hannah, one of the twins, grinned. 'We'll just sing like we usually do!'

272

'See what we've raised, children who know too much about the woods in May,' Maisey just managed to get out before Gumshu swept her off her feet to take her to their bedroom.

'And, children?' Gumshu said, about to close the door with his foot.

'Yes, Father?' they replied together.

'Make sure the songs are long as well as loud!'

'Gumshu, behave yourself!' they heard their mother say, just before she started giggling like a teenager as she was carried up the stairs.

Before he and Little Emmy left for the Forest village before dawn the next morning, Maisey said to him, 'You won't forget about Katherine, will you?'

'No, my love, I won't. That's one reason we are going so early,' Gumshu said, taking her face into his hands and kissing her tenderly on the lips.

'I love you' were his only departing words as he and Little Emmy mounted the trap and urged the pony on towards the lane with the thatched cottage at the end, the lane that led out to the Forest.

Dawn was breaking as Gumshu and his daughter walked through the churchyard gate, to go to the tiny grave by the wall. When they got to it, Little Emmy knelt down with her father standing behind her.

Like her mother, she had the habit of pulling out any long grass strands that had grown around the small wooden cross at the head of the grave.

Then she quietly said to her sister, 'Look, Father's back, all safe and sound.' Her voice trailed off with a gentle sob. Gumshu rested his hand tenderly on her shoulder and squeezed it.

'Hullo, my little one,' he said, with a shake in his softly spoken voice. 'We're all together again now.'

He took out two tattered pieces of paper from the top pocket of his tunic. He bent over and put them by the cross, weighting them down with a stone that he had taken from the churchyard wall as they came in.

Little Emmy looked up at him.

'That's the letter your mother wrote to me when we were in Plymouth, before we were wrecked. I kept it in my pocket, and it was the only thing that I didn't lose that night. I read it so many times during those months on St Agnes. I swear that sometimes it was the only thing that stopped madness setting in. All those months on a tiny island, it just doesn't bear thinking of.' Then he said softly, 'I used to close my eyes when I was alone and imagine I was with you all, sitting on the bank by the stream, the one where your mother and I used to sit and dream.'

Little Emmy looked at her father and took his hand as she stood beside him. She reached up and put her arms round him, giving him a hug. She then smiled down at her little sister, as did her father, and then the two turned and walked silently back towards the gate.

Gumshu now put his hangover behind him and concentrated on the business in hand.

He, Thomas, Edmund, and Little Emmy sat round the table and talked over what had happened in his absence. The one thing he couldn't get used to was his daughter working with them. What impressed him was her understanding of the figures involved and the way the mines operated.

'The way you are talking makes me think that you've been down some of our mines and have actually been down the tunnels and up to the coal faces?' her father said, looking at his daughter.

'Yes, I've been to all of them, including the deep mine, but Thomas wouldn't let me crawl down *every* tunnel there,' she announced. 'I've been regularly covered in grey slime as well, and it usually took ages to get it out of my hair. And it *always* had to be on one of the days when I was due to go out with . . .' her voice trailed off, and she looked down and blushed.

'Little Emmy!' her father said, starting to laugh. 'I knew it. I knew it! When Grundwell and I got those letters from you all when we were in Plymouth, Alice told her father she had a boyfriend, and he went mad. I looked at your letter to me. It was full of chatter, but not a mention of a boyfriend. I thought to myself then that where Alice went, you usually followed! So who is it then, Daughter?'

Thomas Sutton and Edmund started to smile.

'Don't say a word, you two!' she threatened.

'Us?' Edmund laughed. 'Our lips are sealed.'

Little Emmy looked at her father, took a deep breath, and told him. 'It's Cornelius Purnell, Nathaniel's son.'

'But he's twenty eight, and you're fifteen!'

'Sixteen!' she corrected him.

'Does your mother know?'

'Well, sort off. She thinks we're just good friends.'

'Does anybody else know, other than your two co-conspirators here?'

'Yes, William Benson does. He caught us having a bit of a kiss behind one of the gravestones in the churchyard in Mitcheldean.'

'Why in the churchyard, for goodness sake?'

'Well, no one ever goes there at night because of fear of ghosts, so it's nice and quiet. And anyway, we were behind a miner's headstone, so we thought that would be all right. We thought that he would look after us.'

'What did William say or isn't it repeatable?'

'No, he was fine about it and said to call in when we'd finished, and Eleanor would make us a warm drink. So we did do! But he was rotten. He hadn't told us that Friar Benedict was having supper there, after both of them hearing the deathbed confessions of an old lady named Martha. So you can imagine, he teased me like nothing on earth, and I've been doing penance for his silence ever since!'

By that time, Thomas and Edmund were in tears of laughter because Little Emmy had told the censored version of the story to her father, and everyone else involved, including them, were sworn to absolute secrecy about what had really happened behind the miner's gravestone.

'And was it worth getting cold for, Daughter?' her father questioned in total innocence.

'Ooh yes!' his daughter replied enthusiastically.

Gumshu wished he'd never asked.

'Now we've discussed my love life, can we get back to the coal business?' she requested with an angelic look on her face.

What she had not told anyone was that prior to the churchyard, she and Cornelius Purnell had tried to make love in a field. But what they hadn't noticed, until it was too late, was that the field had a bull in it, and the bull had given chase. In the panic to escape, they had had no time to put any clothes on, so they had fled out of the field totally naked. It had only been by sheer luck that no one saw them.

'Good job the friar hadn't been around then,' she mused to herself.

The coal business seemed very tame after the discussion of Little Emmy's love life, Thomas and Edmund decided, but they continued to give all the information to the Hawk Mine's owner that he wanted.

They then discussed at length the Crown's insistence on the alteration of transport levies and random increases being sought on extraction royalties. Emmy told her father that she and Thomas had been to see the Gaveller, but he had seemed loathe to help either Hawk Mines or any of the other independent mine owners that were still operating outside their lease area.

'Little Emmy has had a good idea, Gumshu, but she said that we should wait until you came home,' Thomas said.

'What is the idea?' Gumshu queried.

'Hawk Mines should make representation to London on behalf of all the mine owners in the Forest, both large and small. We ask government to set all their charges that they make to us for a *definite* period rather than alter things on a whim, as they do now. We include in this any official transport levies as well.

'This would mean that we could set the coal price to our customers, including *all* our own costs, which can be for a fixed term as well. As long as that charge is within the price limits of coal set by the government, everyone is happy, and we will know *exactly* what profit we make on every load sold,' Thomas concluded.

'I'll agree with that,' Gumshu said. 'But one thing, Emmy, how did you know that I wasn't dead?'

There was a silence in the room, and everyone looked at her, as Samuel Longden had also joined them.

'Like my mother, I just knew. I never had any doubts,' she said simply.

'And you were prepared to hold on with an idea as important as that?'

'Yes, Father, I was.'

'And we backed your daughter completely,' both Thomas and Edmund said without any hesitation.

'Your daughter is a natural at this business, Gumshu, and she won't be put off either,' Samuel said. 'The Gaveller wasn't going to see her, in spite of her running Hawk Mines in your absence, because she's a woman.'

'That was the worst decision he'd made for a long time,' Thomas said, taking up the story. 'She went blazing into the room where he was lurking at St Briavels Castle and gave him his character, and then some. She finished by saying she was quite prepared to go to the court in London, to put her complaints about him to the King in person. One was about his attitude towards women and then her suspicions on his honesty. She gave him five minutes to make his decision and told him she'd be waiting outside. She waited, and he came out grovelling. She got her meeting with him and has had several since, I might add.'

'Little Emmy,' her father asked, 'now that you are fifteen, how would you feel about becoming part of Hawk Mines on a permanent basis rather than just when I go off and get shipwrecked with dusky maidens?'

'Sixteen!' Little Emmy corrected.

'Even at the age of sixteen,' her father repeated, 'you seem to have got everyone on your side, including, I suspect, all the miners, you seem to know what you're doing, you listen to the advice you're given, and finally, your boyfriend is the son of a goldsmith.'

'Yes, please, Father,' she said, ignoring the last part of his remark.

'Good, this is what you've to do. You go and work under Thomas for six months, then you work under Edmund and your mother for six months, you work under Samuel for six months, then you come and work with me for six months. I expect you to go down the mines with Thomas, I expect you to get dirty, I expect you to get tired, I expect you to do as you're told, and finally I expect you to work longer hours than anyone else, is that clear?'

'Yes, Father.'

'And, Daughter?'

'Yes?'

'No babies!'

'No, Father!'

Little Emmy came around the table and gave her father a hug and a kiss, which sealed the arrangement, then she gave them all one of her dazzling smiles.

'Do you think everyone could just call me Emmy from now on? I'm nearly as tall as my mother, and really, our attributes are becoming very similar!' she pleaded.

'Attributes? Oh yes, I see what you mean!' Gumshu said after glancing at his daughter and laughing. 'You don't realise how quickly your children grow up, do you?' he continued, directing his remark at the other three.

As he spoke, Dick Tatton walked in.

Gumshu was delighted to see his fellow castaway again. After introducing him to the other three and his daughter, he then told them that Dick was coming to work for Hawk Mines.

Dick, he explained, was going to look after the four trows and four collier boats once they were all operating. Although the fleet was to be a joint venture with the Spinning Wheel, Dick would look after Hawk's interests, just to ensure that there was no repetition of the brigantine fleet getting preferences. Emmy gave her father a quizzical look.

'It was something I guessed had happened, Little Emmy, when I listened to something John Dickens said on the trip home. Although when I promised Dick a job when we were still on that island, I didn't know what it was going to be, not until I heard that remark. It's all right, Dick, no long trips again, but you, Samuel, and I will talk about it later,' Gumshu said in reply to his daughter's look.

'Yes, Father, that's quite right, but that was down to John Dickens, and it was one of the things that Alice gave him hell about,' Emmy replied. She then continued, 'Little Emmy?'

'Sorry, life without the *little* is going to take some getting used to,' her father replied, smiling.

Dick walked out of the Hawk Mines building sometime later with a satisfied grin on his face. He was thinking to himself that it wasn't everyone that could get wrecked on the Isles of Scilly, spend over five months as a castaway on a small island because of terrible weather conditions, and then come out of it with a job looking after four collier boats and four coal-carrying trows.

With his head slightly bent forward, he didn't see a tall, good-looking woman walking towards him until it was too late, and he cannoned into her.

Looking up, he said, 'I am so sorry. I was many miles away. I hope I haven't hurt you?'

Abigail Burrell said with a smile and a Cornish accent, 'No, it's all right. Luckily, I saw you were preoccupied, so I was nearly out of your way!'

Dick looked taken aback; he thought he was finished with Cornwall.

'But you've got a Cornish accent!'

'Probably because I'm from Cornwall!' came the Cornish reply. 'I'm Anthony Burrell's sister, Abigail, but everyone calls me Abby.'

'Who is Anthony Burrell?' Dick asked, somewhat puzzled.

'Oh, I'm sorry it's my turn to apologise! You're obviously a stranger to the village. Anthony runs the Jackdaw mine.'

'The Jackdaw mine?' Dick asked, even more puzzled.

Abby looked at that man who didn't seem to know anything at all and thought she had better start from the beginning. She explained how she and her brother came to be in Cumdean and how his two cousins ran other mines for Hawk.

Dick then explained who he was, how he came to be living in the village, and what he was going to be doing for the business.

'Ah, so you're Jane's brother. She has told me all about you!'

As they were talking, Gumshu walked out of the coal building.

'Dick, I thought you'd had enough of Cornwall and hearing the Cornish tongue?' he joked.

'Aye, skipper, but that was before I found out that a Cornish tongue could be attached to such a lovely lady!'

Abby blushed unashamedly and turned to walk back towards Anthony's cottage, hoping that she could give a clue as to where she lived. She suddenly stopped, thinking, 'Nothing ventured, nothing gained.'

'We have our evening meal around seven o'clock. If you can stand three children and a mine foreman, it would be good if you could join us?' she asked over her shoulder.

'I'd love to, Abby!' Dick replied, trying to catch up with his castaway friend.

Gumshu smiled to himself, thinking about Anthony Burrell's letter to him before he had been wrecked and wondering whether he ought to give Dick a bit of the liquid out of the large red bottle with the peculiar stopper.

He needn't have worried.

Nature had taken its course in a very definite direction by the end of the evening, much to Anthony Burrell's delight, especially when Abby actually stepped outside to say goodnight to her guest.

Gumshu carried on to see Father Benedict once he had finished talking to Dick. As he approached the friar's home, Dick's sister Jane came out.

Knowing the friendship that existed between Gumshu's family and the friar, she said, 'Gumshu, I don't think he's at all well. He's had some herb remedies from Fran, and she's coming back with some more in the morning, but there doesn't seem to be any improvement. He won't have it though. He says he feels a lot better, and I am to stop fussing. My lad was sitting with him earlier. The friar is teaching him to read and write just as he's taught a lot of the other village children, but he said that the friar kept going to sleep and was sweating a lot.'

Gumshu went inside to find his old friend sitting in front of the fire, quietly snoring. He put his hand on the friar's forehead, and he was indeed sweating just as Jane had said. Beside him was an untouched bowl of herbal juices that Fran had obviously made for him.

'And it's not too much ale, before you start thinking it is.' The snoring had stopped and there came a deep voice from the oak settle.

The friar opened his eyes and turned towards him. 'It's good to see you, my son, it's good to see you!' he said, clasping Gumshu's hand as he spoke, his eyes filling with tears.

'Maisey and your family knew you were alive. They and the good Lord knew, and they never lost faith,' he said, struggling unsuccessfully to get to his feet. 'The old legs are a bit stiff you know, lad, a bit stiff. That's what old age does for you.'

Gumshu sat on the raised hearth of the fire, facing the ageing friar. They talked of many things: of happy memories and of sad ones, of laughter and of tears, of weddings, christenings and of funerals. But most of all, they talked about the families of the Forest.

As he left, with the friar covered by a soft woollen blanket, nearly asleep again in front of the fire, he heard his deep voice saying, 'Goodnight, my son. Bless you both, you and Maisey, and may God be with you.'

Gumshu knew then that he would never see his old friend alive again.

Remembering the words he had spoken just before he left him, when the friar had said there were certain things that must be done alone and one of them was meeting the Lord God on High, he quietly closed the door and granted him his last wish.

He prayed that when the time came, the friar's spirit would soar to heaven without any hindrance from any earthly forces.

The bell in the little church in Cumdean tolled nine times the following day to announce the death of Friar Benedict. Although no one really knew how old he was, William Benson tolled the bell a further seventy-six times, one for every year of his life, remembering something that the father had once told him.

Maisey and Sophie followed an ancient funeral custom by covering the inside of the cottage with black cloths and boughs of willow. Fran laid Benedict out in his plain serge habit and used a finely woven woollen shroud that Grundwell and Alice had made especially for him that morning.

Candles surrounded the open-topped, black-painted oak coffin that lay in the centre of the main room of his home. His friends then kept a vigil throughout the night, through the next day, and into the following evening.

As the time set for the funeral approached, the village thronged with mourners from far and wide, as news had spread on the wind of the friar's departure from his earthly body.

The funeral left the cottage with the man of God borne upon the shoulders of some of those he had loved, followed by so many of those who had loved him, with flickering torches to guide their way to the village church.

William Benson and the Abbot led the quiet and grieving procession, with two torchbearers in front of them lighting their path, whilst they intoned the words of the prayers from the books that they held.

Following the emotional burial service, Father Benedict was committed to the earth of the Forest with all the due reverence and respect belonging to a true man of God. He was laid to rest in the churchyard amidst the people he had served and loved over the generations, the people who had loved him and simply called him, '*Our Friar*'.

# CHAPTER 21

It had been over two years since the time of the friar's death, time which had seen both families prosper, their business interests flourish, and their fleet of commercial sailing vessels increase in size twofold.

It had seen the wedding of Alice and Captain John Dickens, which had been a social event the like of which Mitcheldean had never seen before, and it had seen personal problems for Grundwell which had never existed before he was wrecked on the Isles of Scilly.

Nadine bore him a son, called Louis, a bouncing healthy child with a pair of lungs to match. When he set up the weaving and manufacturing facility in Plymouth, he made the fatal error of ignoring the advice that Gumshu had given him and moved Nadine into a house that he had bought on the outskirts of the port. Not only did he move his mistress in, he also moved her aunt in as housekeeper. That had also been another serious error of judgement, as she had three children living in the town, and judging by the bills, Grundwell soon came to the conclusion that he was supporting all three of them as well as their families.

For Grundwell, 1625 was not proving a good year.

Not only was Nadine demanding more and more money from him, but she also became pregnant again. This time she had a bouncing baby girl, and she had also formed the opinion that he should now be living with her and not with his wife. It was the worst kept secret in Plymouth, and as time went by, he was very aware that news of his second family would soon arrive in Mitcheldean.

He was sitting in the house one evening, trying to contemplate the future, when Nadine's aunt came into the room. When he had originally met her in Falmouth, she had been fairly pleasant and always helpful. Now she had become a total harridan, always making demands on him, always asking for money, usually based on some lie that she had concocted.

This time she was demanding more money to run the house because the price of fish had risen. Grundwell looked at her, waited for her to finish her tirade, and then said quietly, 'The price of fish has *not* gone up because I was talking to William Clerk this afternoon, who owns five fishing boats, and he was bemoaning the fact that the fish prices have fallen!'

As he awaited her reply, he got up quickly from his chair and faced the woman. Being considerably taller than she was, he actually looked as if he posed a physical threat to her. Thinking he was about to strike her, she screamed and took a step back.

Nadine came running in, and seeing his stance, she assumed the same thing.

'Don't you dare hit my aunt!' she yelled.

The two children in the next room awoke, and both started to cry. There was a moment's silence, broken only by the noise from the children. Grundwell looked at both women and decided he really didn't like either of them anymore. Some of his doubts began to crystallise in those few seconds of silence, doubts that had troubled him for some time. He thought suddenly that now was the time to bring everything into the open.

'I know the boy is mine, but I'm now sure that the girl is not. I was a fool. I should have worked out the dates. I wasn't here during the month when you told me that she was conceived. In fact, I was away for four months to be exact. Her hair is not the colour it should be, she's too small, and she has none of my looks or features at all.'

Nadine looked totally taken aback, then started to cry, trying to take hold of Grundwell as she did so. He was having none of it; he pulled back and gave her an accusing look, a look that was full of hatred.

'All right, so she's not yours. So what? The boy is,' she sobbed at him, with her aunt yelling at her to shut up and not say any more lest she got them both into serious trouble.

'I take it the girl belongs to one of your sons?' he asked the woman with a voice so cold and threatening that she went pale and stepped away from her niece.

'Yes, she does belong to one of them!' Nadine answered before her aunt could speak, aware that the truth was now out. 'But we only did it the once,' she continued, trying to justify her action in a whining, grovelling voice.

'I don't believe you. Which one of your cousins was it?' Grundwell asked.

'I don't know!' Nadine said, dropping to the floor, sobbing, 'I don't know. I don't know!'

'All three have had you?' her aunt said with a shocked look on her face. 'But you told me that . . .'

'I know what I told you, but I lied. All three did have me,' Nadine screamed.

Grundwell went cold. This was the girl he loved; this was the girl for whom he had been prepared to give up everything. Suddenly, Gumshu's words rang in his head,

'*You don't know these people, but they know you are very wealthy* . . .' What a fool he had been!

Grundwell made a decision.

'You both leave this house first thing in the morning, and you take the children with you. Where you go is your problem, but I never want to see either of you again. I will give you money to look after the boy, and I will make an arrangement that you can collect a weekly allowance from Richard Wynne, the goldsmith. Now get out of here and make sure you're both gone in the morning.'

He then retired to his bedroom, listening to the two women whispering, every so often becoming loudly abusive with each other.

He awoke in the morning to a silent house, except for one thing—the crying of an eighteen-month-old child outside his bedroom door.

Opening the door with some trepidation, he was greeted with babblings from his recently abandoned son.

Nadine had had her revenge, and now he would have to pay the price.

Although travelling between Mitcheldean and Plymouth usually took about a week overland, Grundwell preferred it to travelling by sea, as he now had his own carriage and team. It meant that he could be on his own without the need to talk to anyone, as his coachman was also a man of few words.

So it was by carriage that he made his journey back to Mitcheldean with his son and a children's nurse named Sara, whom he had engaged in Plymouth. She had been quite happy to travel to the Forest of Dean, as some members of her family lived in Chepstow. Her brother was also an officer on one of the Spinning

Wheel brigantines, which was where Grundwell had found out about her, the day following the start of his hands-on fatherhood.

A week later he arrived back in the Gloucestershire town. He decided it would be better if he went straight to Alice's house rather than Craven Street, hoping that she would be at home.

When he arrived, complete with nurse and child, Alice opened the door. The look on her face showed that she already knew of the existence of her half-brother, but the shock of actually seeing him with her father was very obvious.

'Oh, Father, what have you done?' was all that she said by way of welcome.

'I need your help, Daughter, and I need it badly!'

Once the group were inside the house, Alice took charge of both nurse and child, showing Sara into a bedroom where she could organise Louis's bedding and feeding arrangements. She came downstairs to find her father gazing into the fire in the main room of the house.

She sat down and waited for him to speak, which he did at some length.

Knowing that John Dickens would have told her the full story of what he knew, he told her everything, from the shipwreck on St Agnes right up to the morning when Nadine had left him with the child.

Alice was quiet for several minutes; she also had her father's habit of staring into a fire when she needed answers to a problem.

Finally she said, 'I always thought it strange that you gave me the running of the Spinning Wheel so quickly, especially at the age of seventeen. It shook me, along with everyone else! It was lucky that I had Mary, Phillip, and Richard to help me because there were times when I just didn't know what to do, but they've always been there for me, including John of course, but he's a mariner.

'I couldn't ask you because you were usually in Plymouth or rushing to get back there. What did you say to me when you told me to run the Spinning Wheel? "*No babies*" if I do but remember. I also remember thinking you were up to something, but until John told me the full story a few weeks later, I had no idea what that *something* was!'

Grundwell smiled at the irony of what he'd said to her. His mind went back to that time, and he remembered his reasoning for letting Alice run the Spinning Wheel. Being honest with himself, it had all been to do with Nadine and his obsession to be with her, the same

Nadine who he could now see had probably used him right from the start.

'So what now, Father? What are you going to tell my mother and the rest of the family? What are you going to do with baby Louis? How does this affect the rest of us? There are a multitude of questions that I'm afraid you're going to have to find the answers to and quickly.'

'Yes, I know' was the only answer she got. After another few moments, he asked, 'Can I leave Sara and Louis here with you for a couple of days? Sara knows about the circumstances surrounding my visit. The reason that I was able to persuade her to come here with me is because she has family who live in Chepstow, as well as the fact that her brother works for us on one of our brigantines. She can also have the use of my carriage as long as she looks after Louis.'

Silence followed his question, as Alice thought carefully about her reply. She felt that she would be betraying her mother if she agreed, but this was her father asking, the father of whom she had always been slightly in awe.

Alice looked at him with a frown, as she knew John would be back within the week from his trip to Ireland, and then she had a visit to Wales planned with Richard Beachwood to buy fleeces.

'Just for two days then, but for no more.' She wasn't sure whether to feel sympathy or anger for him. Either way, she knew that she had to help him.

Grundwell went upstairs to see his son and explain to Sara what was happening for the next couple of days. Sara looked at him, and came to the conclusion that wealth didn't always seem to bring happiness. She had heard his story from her brother some months previously and still hadn't decided whether all his troubles were self-inflicted or not.

'It is time to go to Craven Street,' he concluded out loud. What he was going to say, he had no idea. His coachman took him the few streets' distance between the two houses. Grundwell told him to wait again, not quite sure what would happen after his visit.

He went through the front door of the house and into the big room.

The layout of the downstairs had changed drastically over the last two years, as Mary had now built a dedicated kitchen at the back of the house, with coal cooking fires and a bread oven as well. Mary had called it progress; John the house servant had called it something else as it now involved him in more work. Estor, who now did all of the cooking, thought it wonderful as the family could no longer interfere in the way she prepared food.

Mary and Sophie were both reading, sitting in front of the fire, whilst Anna was doing what appeared to be some homework for William Benson. He had taught, and was still teaching, both Elizabeth and Thomas as well.

Grundwell stood quietly for quite some time before Sophie looked up.

She smiled and said without any warmth in her voice, 'We heard that you had arrived in Mitcheldean and had gone straight to see Alice. Apparently there was a woman and a child with you, so I presume you have brought your Plymouth whore and your bastard back with you.' She added, 'Why go to Alice's? Why not back here and then we can all meet them?'

Grundwell looked at her with a cold stare, realising that the last two years of their decaying marriage had obviously reached an all-time low. There seemed to be no feelings at all between them now, except dislike. 'Nadine has gone her own way, but left me with our son. The woman with me is his nurse. Perhaps it might be better if you and I discuss this in private, not in front of Anna and your mother.' With that, he took off his coat and went to sit by his daughter at the table.

Mary got up and came over to where he was sitting; she looked at him with total disdain, then taking Anna by the hand and pulling her up, she said, 'Come on, Anna, let's you and I go somewhere and leave your mother and father to talk.' At which the two of them went out to the toft at the back of the house.

Grundwell eased himself from the chair by the table and went over to sit where Mary had been sitting, on the other side of the fire from Sophie.

'How long have you known I had a mistress?' he asked, looking at his wife.

'I sensed something was wrong when you got back from being rescued, but I wouldn't admit it to myself,' she said. 'It was all so traumatic at the time, with Father Benedict dying, then his funeral. Then Alice took over the running of the Spinning Wheel, and I suppose it all got lost in the passage of time,' she concluded with a sigh of inevitability.

She looked at him, this man whom she had loved so much, and still did if the truth were known.

'Please, I want you to be completely honest and tell me the full story, from the very beginning on the island, and miss nothing out.'

For the second time that day, he recounted all but the finer detail to his wife, as he had done with his daughter. She listened with an impassive face until the point when he told her how Nadine had left their child outside his bedroom door.

'No true mother would ever leave her child like that, no matter what the circumstances,' she commented.

He then told her how he had found Sara and everything up to his arrival at Alice's.

'Have you told our daughter what you have just told me?'

'Yes, I have.'

'Have you told me the whole truth? Do you promise you haven't missed anything out?'

'I promise you,' he replied with considerable sincerity.

'Now I'm going to be as honest with you as I pray you have been with me,' she said quietly. 'When Edward seduced me that day in our cottage, he didn't rape me. I wanted him as much as he wanted me, and he was right when he said that. Do you remember he was leaning against the wall by the door when he said it?' she asked in an ice clear voice.

Grundwell nodded; his stomach turned over, and his head begun to throb.

'I enjoyed every second of what he did to me, every second. If he'd offered more, I would have taken it! I'd wanted that man since I'd first walked into this room and he came out of that corner covered in rabbit's blood. My passion used to stir whenever I saw him, and he knew it. He also knew what I wanted, as I knew what he wanted!' Sophie breathed a deep sigh at the memory of those stirrings.

Her husband's head was spinning at the revelations; he didn't know how to reply.

'The greatest burden that I have had to carry is the guilt—the guilt that he was Mary's husband, the guilt that I was your wife, the guilt that I hadn't tried to stop him, and the guilt that I enjoyed it so much. The horror that he'd treated me like a whore in the way that he took me, with sheer lust, with no feeling. And that was on both our parts, not just his. That was the humiliation of it all.

'But then to find out he was my father, *my father*! How could I live with that? But do you know something, Grundwell? I didn't feel ashamed about that at all. All I remember is the lust and the utter pleasure involved!' She then fell silent for several minutes.

'And Anna?' he whispered.

'Oh, don't worry. She is yours. If you remember, we were about to tell Mary and Edward I was pregnant before he had me. The only thing that stopped us was that we were going to tell the couple I thought were my parents before we told anyone else.'

There was a long silence between them whilst each took in the other's confessions.

Grundwell broke the silence. 'So where do we go from here?'

'I tell you where we go, Husband. We both accept what the other has done, and try and put our lives back together, yet again, as much as circumstances will allow us to. I've lived with my guilt and deception for over ten years, and do you know, I feel better than I've felt for years now that I've told you!

'I couldn't cope when we all thought you were dead, not from grief, although that did have some bearing, but *actual* guilt that I'd never been able to tell you. It was similar to when you stopped talking to me because you thought I had consented. But how could I tell you that I all but had? And so the distrust grew between us, and our marriage disintegrated.'

'I remember. Does Mary know any of what you have told me?'

'No, and she must never, ever, get an inkling from either of us,' his wife answered, looking at him with a frown.

'Go on with your idea of a solution,' he said with a flicker of understanding.

'Your child, with his nurse, can come and live here, and you and I will bring him up as if he is one of our own. That will be my penance for what I've done. Your penance for what *you've* done is accepting and living with my guilt.'

'How will Mary and the family accept that arrangement?' he questioned.

'With great difficulty I suspect, but if they see that I can accept it, then so will they. Mary will be the only one we might have a problem with, but I'll deal with that when it happens. Bring them here in the morning, and in the meantime, I'll tell John to get rooms ready for Louis and Sara. I think it would be better if you spent the night at Alice's so that we can both get used to the idea, don't you?'

'Yes, that's fair. Tell me, how long have you been thinking like this?' he asked.

'Well, obviously about the child only since you told me a few minutes ago, but about forgiving you your mistress? Well, shall we just say quite a few months. I just wanted to see how long it was before a nubile twenty-something guttersnipe got bored with her much older lover, wealthy or not.'

He smiled as he bent down and kissed her forehead, and without saying anything else, he went out to find his coachman.

The following morning, the carriage carrying baby Louis, Sara, and her employer arrived at Craven Street.

Alice watched them as they left her front gates, wondering what had transpired between her parents to end up with this agreement. Mary was wondering much the same thing on seeing the arrival of her son-in-law in Craven Street moments later.

The only comment she made to her daughter when Sophie told her of the new arrangement was 'Are you sure?'

'Oh yes, Mother, absolutely positive!' her daughter replied in a voice that seemed to contain no doubts whatsoever.

Mary accepted the situation, although she obviously had her own grave doubts, but she felt that now was definitely not the time to air them.

Whatever she thought of her son-in-law however, she considered his arrival back in Mitcheldean was more than timely.

She was very much of the opinion that the Spinning Wheel was fast becoming too large a business for Alice to run on her own, even with the help that she, Phillip Fletcher, and Richard Beachwood could give her.

'It's a pity that Sophie no longer wanted to be a part of the Spinning Wheel and suffered those awful mood swings,' Mary said to herself. 'She too could have been a great help to Alice, and it might just have taken her mind off whatever has been consuming her for so long.'

Baby Louis settled into his new home with Sophie acting the part of a surrogate mother and Grundwell acting the part of a devoted father and husband. The rest of the household stood back and watched with some scepticism, with John complaining that he was too old to be working in a household that had babies in it, but as he was having an old man's lusting for nurse Sara, he decided that he would stay, not that he had anywhere else to go.

Two weeks later in Craven Street, Grundwell sat down with Alice, Mary, Richard Beachwood, and Phillip Fletcher. They set about reviewing the complete business structure of the Spinning Wheel and the performance of the fleet of brigantines.

It was obvious from the outset that he had something very serious on his mind.

Prior to the day of the meeting, Nathaniel Purnell and Grundwell had spent some considerable time checking the cash ledgers that showed the reserves of the Spinning Wheel.

The two men were extremely worried.

'It just doesn't match up!' Nathaniel said. 'The amount of business you are doing, and we both know it's very profitable, should have generated nearly twice the amount of reserve that it has done, even after paying the royal taxes. Mary looked after that, as she always has done, and she's meticulous in the way she does it.'

'So where is the money?' Grundwell asked, stretching back in his chair. The two had been looking at the figures most of the day, and he was getting tired as well as worried.

Nathaniel looked at him and could see a realisation dawning that there was something seriously amiss.

The ledgers that the Purnells held balanced to the amounts of money that had been brought to them; what didn't balance was the value of business that the Spinning Wheel was doing compared with the amount of money that was being deposited.

'Other than Alice, who has been bringing you the money and promissory notes?'

'Phillip is the only one,' Nathaniel replied after a pause.

'That's what I was afraid of. What about Plymouth? Edrich takes any money and promissory notes generated straight to Richard Wynne. What state are those accounts in?' Grundwell questioned.

'I've sent messengers down to Richard, and I've double-checked his ledgers to your bookkeeper's ledgers of business. They are perfect, as are all his monthly trading statements.'

'So it's definitely here?'

'Yes, it can be nowhere else, I'm afraid, as you've now seen for yourself. It would appear that small amounts disappeared to start with, building up to the vast level of funds that seem to be involved now.'

'So the question is which of them is taking it, my daughter or my bookkeeper?'

Nathaniel remained silent for a few moments before replying. 'I wish I could answer that, my friend, but I honestly don't know.'

'How long has it been going on is another question. Looking at these ledgers and comparing them with our amount of business, I would think for about a year and a half, wouldn't you?' Grundwell asked his banker.

'Yes, I think so.'

'In fact, it appears to start just a few months after I gave Alice the task of running the business!'

'Do we still keep all our papers in the old wooden warehouse, or have we moved them into one of the newer stone buildings, as I asked to be done some twelve months ago?' Grundwell enquired at the meeting, knowing full well what the answer was going to be.

Alice responded, somewhat guiltily, 'No, we haven't moved anything yet, Father.'

'In that case, I want a small stone building constructed that will take all our extensive papers, where Phillip and his clerks can work and where we can meet. I don't want to have to do this in someone's house again, however hospitable they are!' he said, turning to Mary and giving her a smile.

'I also want to be able to check the last two years' business ledgers please, Phillip. Since I've been mostly in Plymouth, I've lost touch with what we've been doing, so I need to put that right.'

'Why, is there anything wrong?' Alice asked immediately.

'I'll tell you when I've seen the ledgers. Is that all right, Phillip?

'Yes, I'll get them ready so that you can see them next week,' the bookkeeper replied.

'This week, please,' Grundwell said, looking down at some papers in front of him. 'I want that small building started within three months, please, Alice, and finished within another two.' He looked at her as he spoke, and she gave a confirming nod. She realised that her father was not in the best of moods, so it was better to do as she was told. Phillip came to the same conclusion.

'Once we've moved all the ledgers and paperwork, we must then look at building a large stone warehouse to replace the existing one. That timber building is a fire risk, especially now that we keep it so packed with fleeces. I want a properly designed building which is less of a risk and has a bigger storage area. We can do nothing about the two rented buildings, unfortunately.

'Knowing that the timber warehouse carries about nine months of wool stock and is presently full, we'll aim to replace it within twelve months. And don't forget, we need to be able to make the replacement secure, especially against our teenage lovers!' He smiled for the first time that morning.

The reason for the smile was that a few days earlier he had related the tale of the teenage lovers using the wool store as a love nest to one of the new loom department foremen. He had said to him that he couldn't remember how long ago it had been since he had caught two particularly ardent lovers, who had impressed him with their enlightening performance on a variation of positions.

'Eleven years to be exact!' Liam, the foreman, had replied.

Grundwell gave him a long, hard look, then with a grin, he had said, 'Dare I ask about the wench you were with?'

'She's now married with three children,' Liam answered, with a rueful smile.

'Married to you?'

'Sadly no. Her husband's a sheep farmer over Gloucester way. I married her sister, and we've got four children.'

At that point, Grundwell thought it better to change the subject. But just out of curiosity, he did wonder whether they bought fleeces from the wench's husband.

'Now we need to talk about our brigantines,' Grundwell continued.

'I'd have thought we ought to have John Dickens here if we're going to talk about our fleet,' Mary cut in.

'We have Mistress Dickens here' was her son-in-law's cutting reply. 'And she should have the answers that I asked for from John, as he is presently on his way back from a trip to France and Ireland.'

'Yes, I have,' Alice said simply, more than worried about her father's tone of voice when he spoke to either Phillip or her. She continued in a quiet voice, 'You asked how many brigantines were in the fleet. John says twelve, plus the *Rachel* which is his. They all carry sixty-five crew and five officers including the ship's captain. No, he can't cut the crew numbers down, as each vessel is maintained by the crew as well, so they are always needed, and each boat needs a full complement when manoeuvring in confined waters.

'The fleet is constantly busy with a mixture of our goods and other similar cargoes on the way out and always full with a mixed cargo on the way back. Privateers seem to keep away when they see our pennant at the masthead, but over the last twelve months, he has had to deal with three that didn't.'

'What do you mean, *deal*?' Mary asked.

Alice looked at her father before answering.

He nodded, so Alice continued, 'When we have trouble from a privateer, John will take the *Rachel* out and try and find them. If he does, he will sink their boat and kill any crew who resist.'

'That was a good answer,' Grundwell thought. 'Best not to tell Mary he kills the crew irrespective of whether they resist or not, and that's why we have little trouble when our pennant is seen. It was the one thing that Alice had not been able to stop him doing, smile or no smile!'

'You also asked whether we need any more vessels. John thinks that we have enough as it's not the number of boats causing the problem. It's getting and keeping the crews. The press gangs are getting more and more active around naval dockyards, to such an extent that he has only been using Chepstow and the other Bristol Channel ports in an effort to keep our crews away from them.'

'Have any of our ships been late delivering their cargoes for any reason?' her father then asked her.

'No, they haven't!' was her humourless reply.

After the meeting, Alice sat at the table without moving. Mary had left to find Sophie, as she sensed that father and daughter needed to talk alone. Grundwell came and sat down beside his daughter and waited for her to speak.

'What's wrong, Father, because I know something is? Is it something that I've done or not done?'

Grundwell sat in silence for a moment or two, considering what to say. Finally he said, 'Nathaniel and I have found out that over the last year and a half or so, only about half the funds that the Spinning Wheel has earned has been taken to him to be put into our account. Sadly, only two people take that money to him, namely, you and Phillip.'

Alice looked at her father with a look of absolute horror, tears springing to her eyes, something he hadn't seen since she was a little girl.

'And you suspect me?'

'Well, Alice, unless I'm very much mistaken, it's one of you!'

Alice sat completely still, not moving a muscle; the colour drained from her face.

Grundwell asked very gently, 'Was it you?'

Alice didn't answer; she just stared at him in total disbelief. Then she said in a voice barely above a whisper, 'No, Father, it was not me!'

As she finished speaking, there was a knock on the door. Grundwell opened it to find Phillip standing with one of his clerks, both holding the many business ledgers that Grundwell had demanded.

'Come in and put them on the table.' Phillip did that without saying a word. The young clerk did the same and then went out, closing the door behind him.

'Sit down, Phillip, please,' Grundwell said, sitting down at the table again.

Phillip went and sat on the other side of Alice, taking her hand and giving it a squeeze of encouragement.

Grundwell looked at both of them, and then looking directly at Phillip, he said, 'You obviously know what this is about?'

'Yes, I've guessed.'

'So I'll ask you the same question as I've just asked Alice. Is it you who's taken all this money?'

'No, Grundwell, it's not. Whether you believe me or not is up to you, but it's not me, and it's definitely not your daughter,' he said emphatically, opening a small ledger. 'Now let me show you something. Alice and I had a suspicion some year and a half ago that there was something wrong with our account. We *both* tried to tell you there was problem at the time, but you would *not* listen.

'We did talk at length about telling Mary, but both agreed that we needed to be able to prove our suspicions before telling *anyone* else. We also agreed that our first loyalty was to you, and we would have to find a way to make you listen to us. Luckily, events overtook us!

'Anyway that aside, as you are aware, we have *always* kept a running check of what the account should stand at. When we first noticed there was a discrepancy, the differences were very slight, but of late the amounts have become substantial. So we decided to keep a ledger that only Alice and I ever saw. In fact, there are two. I have one. She has the other, and we both keep them at home.

'Every time we pay anything into Purnells, we enter it into our ledgers, and each of us countersigns the other. This way there can be no error. We do the same if there are withdrawals, so our ledgers always bear two signatures to every transaction, whether in or out, and there is always a running total which is the same on both ledgers, obviously. This running figure should always agree with Purnells, but it never does!'

'I take it this was your idea?' Grundwell asked him, referring to the ledger that Phillip was now showing him.

'No, it was Alice's!' Phillip replied with a half smile. Looking at her still sitting like a stone, he said, 'Come on, Alice, I told you when your father discovered that this was happening, he would look to us to blame. It would only be natural.'

'But I'm his daughter. To accuse me!'

'This is about theft, so there is no such thing as family,' Phillip replied. 'We now have to tell your father what we suspect, who we suspect, and why we have such suspicions. Alice, I need your help to do this, so please . . . ?'

Grundwell leant over and kissed his daughter on the cheek. Getting up and going to stand behind Phillip, he put his hand on his shoulder and said, 'I believe you. To accuse you without letting you defend yourselves was a bad error of judgement on my part, for which I apologise to you both.'

'That's two things you owe me for, Father!' his daughter said with a watery smile.

'I'll add it to the account!' her father replied with a nervous laugh, as he had just come to the cold realisation that his obsession with Nadine could well have cost him considerably more than just his marriage. He brought to mind the several occasions that both Phillip and Alice had tried to speak to him about their worries, but he had always been too taken up with getting back to his mistress in Plymouth to listen.

He shuddered at the thought of having to tell Mary.

The three then started poring over the ledgers, with Alice and Phillip explaining their suspicions of who was doing it and how the fraud was being perpetrated.

This time, Grundwell was extremely attentive to what he was being told.

# CHAPTER 22

Emmy had worked with her father for the last six months, been away with him on his selling trips, and travelled up to London with him to negotiate with the Crown over leases and extraction levies. She had argued about transport with the other coal mine owners, been on her own to negotiate coal prices with the Gaveller, and even represented other colliers at stormy meetings with the royal mining agents who tried, and failed, to take certain concessions away from the Forest miners.

Gumshu was beginning to get used to arriving somewhere on his own, only to be greeted with 'Where's Emmy?' or 'Oh, you're Emmy's father. How is she?'

She had worked with Thomas Sutton, crawling through tunnels to get to the coal faces of drift mines; been lowered down shafts to look at some of Hawk's deep workings; had got wet, cold, and very scared; and been covered in grey slimy mud on a regular basis.

She had worked with Dick Tatton and his crews on the collier boats, delivering coal to Plymouth and London, and on the trows taking coal along the Severn and Wye Rivers. She had been seasick and constantly coated in black coal dust morning, noon, and night, not knowing when her next bath would be.

She had worked with Samuel Longden on his carts, delivering coal to houses, forges, and foundries in the Forest and beyond. She saw how to organise transport so that there was a load each way, in and out of the depots; she was kicked and trodden on by horses and oxen, and bitten by horseflies and mosquitoes on an hourly basis.

She'd been bored to distraction for six months working for her mother and Edmund Fletcher on the ledgers and paperwork that it took to run a very large coal and stone extraction business, as well as being taught what to look for if someone was trying to steal from the business, either through paperwork or out of a mine.

But in spite of working for a copious amount of hours, she had still managed to have six boyfriends and made a lot of love, but as instructed, she hadn't had any babies.

For Emmy, 1628 was about to be a good year. She had finished her business apprenticeship and she had met a man she had fallen deeply in love with, again.

William Benson and Eleanor had decided to succumb to the archbishop's gentle persuasion to come to his cathedral school so that William could take up the teaching position he had been offered. However, it was no longer the Reverend William Benson; it was Canon William Benson, thanks to his bishop and the laity of the parishes that he served.

Of course, Gumshu, Grundwell, and families now referred to their friend and tutor as the 'big gun', but that was to be expected, and it secretly flattered William.

One insistence that he made was to approve his replacement at Mitcheldean. That had been a condition of him for taking the new post.

'Most unusual,' his bishop had commented when he read the archbishop's instruction about obtaining William's approval of his replacement. But the bishop had been the first to admit that his archbishop and his canon son were both unusual men.

William turned down two applicants as being dull and uninteresting and then met the third by the entrance of the church.

'Well, I actually "cannoned" into him on the top of the grassy bank as I came out of the lych gate!' he told Eleanor and his two young children that night at the rectory when they were having their evening meal.

'Does this one meet with your approval then, my love?' she questioned, laughing.

'Oh yes, very much so, and Emmy approves too!'

'How did Emmy meet him?'

'Well, we nearly knocked her over when we rolled down the bank,' the canon replied somewhat sheepishly.

'I know this might sound a silly question, but why were you rolling down the bank in the first place?'

'Ah, I knew you'd ask that. Well, when I "cannoned" into him, he grabbed my coat to stop himself falling over. Unfortunately, I lost my footing, so then we both ended up by rolling down the bank to the bottom, just as Emmy and Maisey were walking past. They very kindly helped us up!'

'And what did Maisey and Emmy say to these two clerics romping around in front of the church?' Eleanor queried, trying to keep a straight face.

'Maisey asked me if I remembered the first time that she and I ever met! Emmy asked Richard if the next time he wanted to meet her, could he do it a bit more formally. She then asked him why he was rolling round with her friend, the canon, to which he replied that he was hoping to become Mitcheldean's new rector. She looked him up and down, covered in mud because it had just rained, and told him that she hoped that he'd impressed me. As she and Maisey left, she whispered in my ear that she'd kill me if I rejected this one!'

'Richard? What did you say his full name was?' Eleanor asked.

'Oh dear! I didn't say, and I don't think I'm going to tell you either!' William replied.

'Come on, Benson, spit it out!'

'Richard, Richard *Rolland*, the Reverend Richard *Rolland*!' With tears running down her cheeks, Eleanor had to retreat into the next room in hysterics, leaving the two children with a canon who couldn't speak for laughing.

The hardest thing for William about moving from Mitcheldean was to leave the parishioners of his little Forest church. He also included the Craven Street families because they had been such an important part of his life for so many years.

He was kneeling on the floor in their bedroom packing a box while he was having those reflections. Eleanor came in quietly behind him, knelt down, and put her arm round his shoulders.

'We'll be coming back, to see my family and all our friends, William,' she said gently, looking into his face and seeing the tears in his eyes. She kissed him tenderly on the cheek, got up, and left him to his deliberations.

William stood in front of his friend's grave, hearing the village children playing and laughing nearby. He smiled to himself, remembering how the friar loved the sound of children's laughter.

He knelt down at the foot of the grave, crossed himself, and spoke with his God, asking him to bless the spirit of the friar and all who rested within the churchyard.

Standing up, he walked round, looking at the graves and remembering—remembering the people as well as the times.

He then went into the church to say further prayers.

When he came out, there was a pony and trap waiting for him with Emmy at the reins. She took him to the site of the Cottrells' mine, where he spent a further few minutes kneeling in prayer in front of the cross that marked the entrance.

She then took him back to the village to say his farewells to the villagers, and to pick up Eleanor and the children who had been saying goodbye to her mother and father.

They all then returned to the rectory, calling at Craven Street on the way.

Emmy didn't talk much during the journey, as she felt that William and his family would prefer their own reflections to her continual chatter.

William said to her before he and his family got down from the trap. 'I've never known you be so quiet, Emmy. Are you all right?'

'Yes, I'm fine, thank you. I just thought you'd prefer your own thoughts to my constant nattering,' she replied with a smile.

William looked at her and grinned. 'Is there a cost for your being so quiet?'

'William, I am hurt by such a remark!' she replied, tossing her hair and laughing. 'But now you ask, please could you tell me when the new rector is due? Purely on religious grounds, you understand!'

'But of course, Emmy, I wouldn't think anything else. Tomorrow!'

'Time?'

'Midday coach!'

'Well, there's a coincidence. I shall be around here at that time!'

'Be gone, girl, and thank you,' said a laughing William.

'No, Canon, the thanks are all mine. We'll miss you an awful lot!' she declared as she cracked the whip above her pony and was gone with a wave and another toss of her hair.

Dick Tatton now lived at Gumshu and Maisey's cottage in the Forest village.

For a few months after the friar's death, neither of them had felt that anyone else should live there. That was not until nearly dusk one fine evening when they had been walking back from the churchyard and paused by the cottage door.

On impulse, they decided to go in. It was all neat and clean, with the fire laid in the hearth. The grass had been cut at the back of the cottage, with the spring and its pool still clear as crystal. They sat on a rough wooden bench that Gumshu had made many years before and enjoyed the peace. They were surrounded by the sounds of the babbling of the spring, the sharp evening voices of the finches, and of one skylark who was announcing to the world that he was going to the moon.

There was tranquillity about the cottage that was difficult to explain.

'It needs life again,' Gumshu said quietly, looking at his wife.

'Yes, it does. But there is also an unsolved puzzle,' she replied, frowning. 'No one has ever found Benedict's cross!'

'Did the abbot not take it with him?'

'No, definitely not, because he asked me about it,' Maisey said softly. 'He did say that friars usually gave their crosses to someone close to them so that they entered the kingdom of heaven bereft of any worldly goods. He was surprised that he hadn't given it to either you or me . . . I wonder!'

Maisey stood up and went into the cottage. Gumshu followed her and watched her remove the stones from her hiding place. She put her hand in and brought out a large copper cross on a twisted leather thong.

There was also a folded document, a small package, and a note, all of which she brought back outside to read, as it was starting to get dark inside the cottage. After looking at them in the evening light, she slipped the document and package into her skirt pocket, and opened the note.

It simply said, 'A gift to you both for all the happiness you brought me.' And it was initialled FB.

Maisey clasped the cross to her chest and began to cry—cry for her friend, cry for the man who had always been there for her and her family, cry for his kindness, cry for the love he bore for others above all else, and she cried for a true man of God. Gumshu held her tight, suddenly realising that she hadn't yet grieved for her friend, so he let her grieve in the way that she wanted—with tears.

The following day, Gumshu went in search of Jane to see if she knew where her brother was, as Dick was still living with her.

'He should be back tonight. He is only on a short trip in one of the trows, going up to Gloucester.'

'Could you ask him to come and see me? I'd like to offer him our cottage if he'd like it.'

'I'd like him to like it!' Jane replied with a laugh. 'I now have a boyfriend, Dick's still stepping out with Abby, and now my lad has got a girl, so we draw straws as to who uses my cottage, and the others have to go out.'

Gumshu laughed because he remembered a similar situation before he had married Maisey; it could get very cold waiting for other lovers to finish their acts of friendship.

'I'll be at the coal building from early till late tomorrow, so if you could ask him to meet me there, we'll see what we can arrange. And our thanks for looking after the cottage so well,' he added.

'We all loved Father Benedict, you know. Hearing him talk, there must have been such a strong tie between him and your family,' Jane said with compassion, as she and most of the village had heard Maisey weeping the previous evening, and everyone had felt nothing but heartfelt sympathy for her.

'Yes, there was a strong bond, a bond that, as far as Maisey is concerned, even death won't break.'

Twelve months later, Dick was happily settled into his new home, content with his life and with a cottage that had a peace and serenity all of its own.

Abby was spending more and more time with him, much to Anthony Burrell's delight, as his sister was never best pleased when he had a lady friend to visit.

'I wouldn't mind,' he told one of his friends, 'but it's my cottage!'

Gumshu, Maisey, and Edmund started checking the ledgers. They checked and rechecked and still could find nothing wrong.

Emmy came into the coal building just as they were finishing and was worried to see her parents and Edmund so concerned.

'Are you going to tell me what's wrong?' she asked.

'Of course,' Gumshu said. 'Grundwell told me two nights ago that a lot of money has disappeared from the Spinning Wheel's reserves that Nathaniel Purnell holds for them. We have just been checking our own ledgers to see if the same thing has happened to the Hawk Mines account.'

'And has it?'

'No, not that we can find,' her mother replied. 'We have all been through the ledgers and found the figures to be exactly right with everything balancing. What we intend to do now is go to Purnells to ensure that the physical money count is correct because that is something that Grundwell hasn't checked yet.'

'May I come with you?' Emmy asked, with a frown.

'Why the worried look?' Edmund asked her.

'It's only a suspicion, but let's see,' she replied, whereupon she went to get the pony and trap ready for the trip into Mitcheldean.

Their arrival at Nathaniel Purnell's building caused great consternation amongst the clerks who worked for him and also to Nathaniel. Grundwell, Mary, Alice, and Phillip had arrived there as well.

There was a considerable amount of shouting taking place, mostly coming from Grundwell. Nathaniel was standing beside him, looking totally mortified while wringing his hands and saying 'I'm sorry!' over and over again.

'It looks as though Grundwell and Mary have found what they were looking for,' Gumshu said to Edmund. 'And your brother and Alice look somewhat relieved.'

'The trouble is, Gumshu, that it's all right finding out what was done and who might have done it, but it's the matter of finding out where the money is now that could be the real problem,' Edmund commented. Obviously he and his brother had talked at some length about the problems facing the Spinning Wheel and possibly Hawk Mines.

Emmy sat in the trap, with a haunted look on her face.

Maisey turned to her daughter. 'Emmy, it's just you and I now. Please talk to me because I know there's something bothering you. This could get very serious for both businesses unless it's resolved, and if you know something, now is the time to tell us.'

'I know. I think father and Edmund had better hear what I've got to say as well,' she replied. Maisey went to bring the two men back to listen to what Emmy had to say. The two stood beside the trap whilst Maisey remounted, sat back down, and prompted Emmy.

'When I went out with Cornelius Purnell whilst Father was lost, we used to walk for miles, talking about what we were going to do with our lives. Cornelius always said he was going to be richer than anyone in the town, and that included my family, the Spinning Wheel, and his own father.

'I thought it was just male bravado to start with, but he used to go on and on about it. I asked him how he was going to do it, and all he would say was that his future was in his signature and his digging ability. He would stop talking when I pressed too hard for an explanation.'

Peter R. Hawkins

As she finished, Grundwell, Mary, Phillip, and Alice came out of Purnells. They walked over to the trap, all of them looking extremely worried.

Grundwell was as white as a sheet. 'It's as Alice and Phillip suspected. There *are* two receipt ledgers in existence. The first one was the one that we actually signed when we deposited money, gold, or promissory notes. We would bring the money in and sign it into the ledger with a joint signature from Purnells.

'Afterwards, the forger would produce a second *identical* journal and forge our signatures on it for a lesser amount. He would then remove the now excess funds for himself. Both ledgers bore his signature for Purnells, so that was the easy bit.

'The ledger with our forged signatures would then become the official one that Purnells used for their entire bookkeeping exercise, including the notation of any withdrawals that we made.

'The forger then hid the original ledger until we came again. This he would produce for any further deposits, and the whole procedure would start all over again. It's very, very simple, but so very effective!'

'And who was the forger?' Emmy asked quietly.

'Nathaniel's son, Cornelius,' Alice replied to her question. 'Your old boyfriend!'

'As we suspected,' Edmund said. 'What about the physical reserves that are left?'

'They appear to be intact, but I think you'd better check yours. Luckily, Nathaniel has worked in conjunction with other goldsmiths in the area and has been issuing promissory notes. He has kept the bulk of the gold and coins in other secret and secure locations, secret even from his son,' Phillip answered his brother.

Gumshu took Grundwell on one side and quietly asked, 'How does this leave the Spinning Wheel financially?'

'Exposed, but we don't know yet how seriously.'

'What about Nathaniel? Won't he help?'

'Yes, up to a point. He's got enough reserve at the moment to tide us over should we need it. The problem is that we are such a large business, we would require substantial funding. He is concerned as to how long he could actually sustain us. Luckily, the fleet account is held by Richard Wynne in Plymouth, so at least our joint venture is safe.'

'I hate to say this, Grundwell, but thank God you had your mistress in Plymouth. That's the only reason we hold that joint account there, we both know that.'

'Looking at the ledgers for the Spinning Wheel, our own account *there* may be our salvation for survival. I thank the Lord we employed Edrich when we did.'

'It was lucky that Alice and Phillip recognised that something was amiss when they did, otherwise I suspect Cornelius Purnell would have bled you dry. Where is the despicable little pilferer by the way?'

'He's not been seen for two days. I think he got wind of our arrival,' Grundwell muttered. 'This could be a very bad day for Mitcheldean if I have to start laying off any of my workers,' he added out loud to himself, walking back to the carriage where his mother-in-law, Phillip, and Alice were waiting.

The Hawk Mines account was safe and intact, Edmund, Maisey, and Gumshu decided after carrying out several checks, watched over by Nathaniel and some of his clerks.

Nathaniel hadn't known what to say to his two biggest customers, who were also his close friends. He stood, guilt-ridden, looking through the window, staring into the distance.

'What do I say to people, most of whom have done business with me for many years and also with my father before me? What do I say to the rest of my family?' he questioned of his chief clerk.

Having heard what he had said, Gumshu quietly took his banker on one side. 'Nathaniel, at the end of the day, this is only about money. This is not life and death. You stood with me when William Benson and Friar Benedict consecrated the cross outside Cottrells' mine. You stood and saw the pain of the people around us. That's the really important thing in this world, my friend.'

Gumshu hoped that his friend would take heed and prayed that he wouldn't do anything rash. He still had a wife and family who needed him.

'Is everything all right?' Emmy asked her father from the trap.

'It is for us, Daughter, but I suspect there are going to be hard times ahead for the Spinning Wheel, and the word is going to be "survival". This may affect a lot of people in this town, very sadly.'

Later that evening, John Dickens arrived home to find Alice missing. Guessing where she might be, he put his horse in the stables at the back of the house and continued up to Craven Street on foot. He knocked on the door and went into the big room.

He was slightly taken aback by all the activity. His wife was there, as well as her grandmother, Grundwell, Sophie, Phillip Fletcher, and Richard Beachwood. They were all sitting round the candlelit table, poring over stacks of ledgers, books, and papers, obviously brought from the warehouse. Alice got up and ran to him, throwing her arms round his neck and giving him her usual ecstatic kiss.

He was about to tell her something of his visit to Waterford and an intriguing meeting that he had had with an Irish wool merchant, a man who lived next door to one of the biggest churches in the city, but looking around, he gauged that it was not the time.

So as to not disturb the others, she led him over to the fire and quietly explained to him all that had happened and what they were now trying to do. He removed his top coat and joined the six people starting to work through the night to see what could be salvaged from the consequences of one young man's greed.

Across Craven Street, Gumshu heard Emmy moving about downstairs. Donning a warm robe, he went down to see his daughter.

'Sleep eluding you, my love?' he enquired.

'Thoughts have taken over from sleep, Father,' she responded.

'And what are those thoughts, or can't you tell me?'

'It's what Grundwell said to himself as he walked past the trap this afternoon, and it's what Cornelius Purnell said to me. I can't get any of it out of my mind. I'm sure that I somehow hold the key to the mystery.'

'Emmy, what are you talking about?'

'Do you remember what I said to you this afternoon about Cornelius bragging to me about how he would be richer than us, the Spinning Wheel, and his father, and it would be his signature and his "*digging ability*" that would make his fortune?'

'Yes, I do, so what are you thinking?'

'Don't you see? He has started with his signature, forgery, and now it will be his "digging ability". That is what I have been trying to think of all afternoon. What does the "digging" bit mean? Digging in the earth, digging amongst papers, which is it, if any? If he's stolen all that money and gold and if there's a lot, and from what Phillip has told Edmund there is, then where is he going to hide it?'

'In the ground!' his daughter stated triumphantly, answering her own question.

'And if he's going on the run, he'll want to take some of it now. Come on, get dressed, and over the road!' Gumshu shouted with some excitement.

Father and daughter bounded upstairs and told Maisey what they intended to do.

'You two are a nightmare in the mornings, do you know that? You're both the same, always have been!' Maisey groaned, pulling the covers over her head. 'What do you mean in the ground?' came the muffled question to Gumshu's enthusiastic explanation, as Emmy disappeared into her room to get dressed.

'We think young Purnell has buried his haul, hence his reference to "*digging*" that Emmy told us about this afternoon. If he's going on the run, we think he'll try and dig some of it up to take with him!' Gumshu continued, throwing on some clothes.

'I don't want to put a dampener on your early morning excitement, but you could be wrong, and anyway, I don't know whether you've noticed, my collier husband, but there are a lot of places he could be "digging",' continued the muffled and sleepy voice.

'Emmy thinks she knows where it might be. When she and Cornelius were going out together, they always used to use the same field, the one that is beyond the church . . .'

'What do you mean *used to use*? . . . Emmy!' came a very loud call from a suddenly wide awake Maisey. 'She was only fifteen for goodness' sake,' she concluded, throwing back the covers.

'Sixteen!' Gumshu and Emmy said together, as his daughter had just responded to her mother's summons.

'Sorry, we really do have to go,' he said, bustling his eldest offspring out of the bedroom door. 'Oh, by the way, sweetheart, it's not morning, so you can't complain about us,' he called out as they departed.

'Well, if it's not morning, then what is it?'

'The middle of the night,' he answered, not quite understanding the reply she gave him, as he followed his daughter down the stairs and out on to Craven Street.

The two banged on the door of their friends' house to be let in by a surprised Sophie, who was still helping the others go through the figures. Gumshu quickly explained to them the conclusions that he and Emmy had reached.

Grundwell agreed and immediately went out and woke the coachman, who slept in the new stable building at the back of the house so that he could be near his beloved horses.

'Get the carriage ready as quickly as you can. Bring some candle lanterns and some shovels if you can find any,' Grundwell instructed, not pausing to give any explanations.

He then roused John, interrupting his grumblings with a wave of his hand and a harsh word, telling him to hurry and wake the constable, whose house was at the end of Craven Street.

'Tell him I want him up, dressed, and ready to be picked up in ten minutes!'

Grundwell had called to see Constable Marcus Watson earlier in the day and had explained to him about the disappearing funds and where the blame probably lay.

'I'll let the Justice know when he comes back from London, and then we can send the details into other areas. I don't think Cornelius Purnell is going to stay locally, do you? I'll also go and see Nathaniel and start an official enquiry. The Justice will want as much information as he can from me so that when we catch Master Purnell we can get him to trial as quickly as possible. You know what our Justice of the Peace Milton is like. He thinks he owns Mitcheldean and takes every crime committed as a crime against him personally,' Marcus had said with a grin.

He then continued with a very serious look on his face, 'Grundwell, I know this is a serious situation for you, and I can't start to imagine how you must feel, but please don't be tempted to take the law into your own hands, and keep that son-in-law of yours in check. Mitcheldean isn't in the middle of the ocean where our captain seems to have his own laws.'

John Dickens's retribution on privateers was well known over most of southern England and well beyond.

Grundwell knew Marcus well, as most of his family worked for the Spinning Wheel, and as parish constables went, he was one of the best there was.

It was decided that the ladies should remain behind, much to Mary's disgust, apart from Emmy who was needed to give them directions. The carriage stopped to pick up the constable, and then they set off to try and catch the thief. They pulled up a short distance from the field so that their arrival would not be heard.

'I hope the bull's not around!' Emmy muttered, as they made their way along the track, climbing over the rough field boundary as they went. They stood and listened in the darkness, as it was a pitch-black moonless night with very little breeze.

John Dickens spoke quietly, 'There's something happening on the far side of the field. You can see a very faint light.'

'Emmy, can anyone get away from us if we head towards that light from this direction?' Marcus asked quietly.

'No, there's a high bank that is very awkward to climb,' she replied in a soft voice.

'If it is Purnell, he must have a cart or something similar with him to move his haul because it's going to be heavy,' John commented.

'Grundwell, could I suggest that Richard, Emmy, and Phillip go back to the carriage and wait for us there? I think it would be safer, in case things get a bit nasty,' Marcus whispered.

'Yes, you're right,' Grundwell replied.

'Be careful, all of you,' Emmy said quietly, as the constable led her father, Grundwell, and John Dickens off across the field.

There was the sound of two flintlock pistols being cocked as they disappeared into the night.

'I hope that wasn't what I think it was,' Marcus muttered.

'Just a precaution,' returned the voice of John Dickens through the blanket of darkness.

Marcus whispered, 'We'll stop some thirty yards from them first to see what they're up to. Once there, we'll keep low and slowly move forward to about ten yards and then lie down so that they can't see our silhouettes. That also makes us smaller targets should they be armed and decide to take a shot at us. John, you stay next to me, and you only discharge those pistols on my instruction. Is that clear?'

'Yes, Marcus,' John's voice replied from the dark. John had forgotten that Marcus had been a sergeant in the Sovereign's Yeomanry and had a reputation for very strong discipline, one of the reasons why the Mitcheldean Justice of the Peace had appointed him a parish constable.

Their approach to the source of the light was both cautious and silent. With near total darkness, none of them could see the other but relied on their sense of touch.

Some thirty yards short of the light, Marcus signalled to the other three, and they stopped. They could make out two people, one digging a hole and the other holding a shielded candle lantern. Every few minutes, the person digging would stop, straighten up, and appear to listen before carrying on. The person holding the lantern was also holding the reins of a pony that was between the shafts of a small trap.

The party moved forward on Marcus's instruction and then stopped again some ten yards short of where the two figures were working. The four lay down on the ground as arranged, with John next to Marcus. John brought his pistols to bear on to the two dark shapes in front of them, and then they waited.

There was the noise of a shovel grating on something solid. In the faint lantern light, they could make out that the figure who was digging was a man.

He stopped on hearing the noise, bent down, and manoeuvred a large heavy chest up from the bottom of the hole, pushing it on to the grass at the side, sweating and quietly cursing with the effort. That was repeated a further five times before the figure in the excavation threw the shovel to one side and started to lever himself out from the hole.

As he was about halfway out and totally unbalanced, Marcus called out in a loud voice, 'Good evening! Master Cornelius Purnell, I presume?'

There was a moment's silence, and then the figure holding the light screamed. It was a girl.

The male conspirator half turned to look in the direction of the voice before suddenly making a lunge towards a pistol that was lying on some freshly excavated earth at the side of the hole.

'That would be unwise, Master Purnell, as there are two fully primed pistols already pointed straight at you!'

'Who are you?' the now motionless figure asked, his hand having fallen well short of the firearm.

'I am Constable Marcus Watson. The gentleman who has two pistols pointed at you is Captain John Dickens, and I also have with me two other gentlemen, one of whose property you are trying to steal.'

The girl started screaming again, and her hood fell back as she dropped the reins of the pony.

'Elizabeth!' Grundwell exclaimed.

Marcus turned round and looked in his direction.

'She's my daughter!' he said in an incredulous voice, leaping to his feet.

Then, on Marcus's instruction, Gumshu knelt and striking two flints lit the lanterns that he was carrying whilst John stood up, now bearing both his pistols on Cornelius Purnell to ensure that he didn't make a bid for freedom.

'Captain, if he tries to run, please feel free to shoot him!' the still prone constable said in a loud voice, as John Dickens moved cautiously forward.

Grundwell ran to where his sobbing daughter was trying to hide her face with the hood of her cloak.

# CHAPTER 23

The Reverend Richard Rolland's induction into the Mitcheldean parish had been a very solemn and religious ceremony, with official attendance from far and near. Laity numbers at the Church of Saint Michael and All Saints were severely restricted because of the clerical influx. This had been his first mistake as it had not gone down well with his parishioners.

The second mistake that the new incumbent had made was preaching a sermon on forgiveness on the Sunday following Cornelius Purnell's arrest. This was in spite of a warning from his new-found friend Emmy that he was treading on very thin ice by doing so, when he told her the content of his first address.

'I should have a few words with that young friend of yours before he empties his churches completely' had been her father's comment to her as they left the church.

'Yes, Father!' was her terse reply because she was now beginning to feel that her love was not being returned by the new resident of the rectory.

News of Cornelius Purnell's arrest had spread like wildfire through the town and the surrounding counties. The main problem for Nathaniel was the understandable reaction of his depositors as well as his own terrible worry about what was going to happen to his son.

'We want to see our money and gold!' had been the repeated demand of the people who queued outside his premises from morning till dusk for days following the news.

The hours after that fateful night when his son was arrested had probably been the worst of the goldsmith's life, but he had remembered his friend's words, and unbeknown to Gumshu, those words were probably responsible for saving Nathaniel's life.

The day following the arrest had also been a bad day at the house on Craven Street.

Marcus bound Elizabeth over to Grundwell's custody, on the strict understanding that they report to his home night and morning and that she did not leave the Spinning Wheel house other than for those visits to him.

The question everyone asked her was *why,* but it was a question she resolutely refused to answer.

Grundwell asked Marcus what he thought her fate would be, to which he replied that it was a court decision. However, he knew of no precedent for such a crime, so he had absolutely no idea of the type or scale of her punishment.

'She was an accomplice, whichever way you look at it, and was caught actually committing the crime for which she will be tried,' he said as they watched some of Gumshu's miners dig up further boxes of money and gold from the location at the top of the field.

Phillip, as well as Nathaniel's chief clerk, was also present, opening and counting the contents of each box before it was returned to Nathaniel's secure premises.

'We may need all of it as evidence,' Marcus said. 'So it must not be spent or moved once it is returned to Nathaniel's. I will put a seal on all the boxes to ensure that happens,' he continued with a wry smile.

'The total balance of the contents of the chests is exactly the balance we have missing from our reserves,' Phillip reported to Grundwell, after many long hours of digging and counting. The same balance was also confirmed by Nathaniel's chief clerk.

The figures were also given to Constable Marcus Watson, who raised an eyebrow, saying, 'I can't even begin to imagine that amount of money!'

All the carts taking the haul away had armed guards posted on them, including John Dickens, who still regretted the fact that Cornelius Purnell hadn't made a bid for freedom the previous night.

Master Cornelius Purnell now languished in a prison cell in a building that doubled as Mitcheldean's town hall. Here he would stay until the return of Justice of the Peace Milton from his visit to London.

'At least once the trial is over, we can return to normal,' Richard Beachwood was saying to Phillip Fletcher some days later at one of their early morning meetings when Alice walked in.

'I don't think anything will ever be normal again in my parents' household, especially after Elizabeth's involvement,' she commented.

'Is there any hint as to why she did it?' Phillip asked.

'None whatsoever! She stays in her room, comes downstairs to eat, and then goes back without a word to anyone,' Alice replied, starting to look through some ledgers that Phillip had prepared for her. 'Now we can get on with that ledger building Father wanted. I didn't think it was wise to mention it whilst all the drama was going on.'

Looking down at the papers, she suddenly felt sick, so she turned, ran out of the door, and deposited the contents of her stomach on to the ground with some relief. Phillip came to check that she was all right; this had been the third time she had been sick in as many days. On her return to the table, there was a bowl of warm water and a cloth to dry her face.

She smiled her thanks to the two men without comment and sat down to continue with her work.

'Stop smiling at each other, you two. It's just a stomach upset.'

'Yes, Alice!' they responded in one voice. Both of them were fathers and could well remember their wives' morning problems when first expecting a baby.

After her first tour of inspection around the wool buildings, she thought the time had come to tell John the wonderful news.

Her husband couldn't stop smiling when she told him about the expected boost in numbers to the Dickens family. He started fussing over her straight away, about how she shouldn't do this, why she shouldn't do that, and how they probably shouldn't be making love.

On the latter point, she put her arms around his neck and said in a husky voice, 'If you think you're going to have a rest from that, Captain Dickens, you are very, very mistaken.' Whereupon, she gave him the type of kiss and caress that made his toes curl and blood rush to the extremities of certain parts of his body.

After their passionate embrace, he drew back from her and in a voice that betrayed the effect that she had had on him said, 'I only go to sea for a rest, dear heart.'

That remark had probably been a mistake on the captain's part because an hour later they were in their bed, John sound asleep and Alice lying alongside him with an extremely contented look on her face.

Grundwell sat with Sophie, a deafening silence between them, a silence generated by the guilt that both of them felt.

Grundwell and Elizabeth had returned from Marcus Watson's house after fulfilling yet another day of the bail conditions, and yet again, Elizabeth had refused to say anything about why she was involved with Cornelius Purnell. On their arrival at Craven Street, she went straight to her room. Marcus had told them that the Justice was due back the following day, so if she wanted to escape being held in jail until the trial it would be better if she gave her version of events if not to her parents, then at least to him.

About half an hour later, Elizabeth came downstairs into the large room and sat close to her parents.

'I'm frightened. I don't want to go to jail!' she said in a tearful voice.

'Then talk to us,' Grundwell said. 'In your own time, please tell us what this is all about.'

Elizabeth started tearfully, 'Whenever you all talk, it's always about Alice, it's always about Anna, it's always about Thomas. Now it's always about baby Louis, but it's never about me. I know I wasn't any good when William used to teach me mathematics or Greek or Latin, but I hated them. I just love drawing. I love to paint all the birds and the animals around us. I love colours. I love the greens of the Forest. I love the blues and reds in the flowers. There's so much I want to paint and draw.'

Grundwell and Sophie didn't speak.

'The only three people who ever listened to me were Grandma Mary, Friar Benedict, and Cornelius Purnell. I'm eighteen, but it is as if I don't exist for anyone else. I want people to notice me. I want to be like Alice or you, Mother. Every time you walk into a room, you're noticed, and people turn round and look at you. I'm good looking. I'm everything you and Alice are. Why don't they notice me?'

Sophie knelt in front of her daughter, took hold of both of her hands, and looked up into her face, saying, 'We're all different, we all have different talents, we all have different characters. You're quiet. You love doing quiet things like your painting and sketching, watching the birds and animals. That doesn't make you any less of a person. We can't all be the same. When you walk into a room, the people who notice you are the people who love you. That's the most important thing. Nothing else matters. Now come over here and look at this.'

They both went over to a chest that was against the wall opposite the fire hearth.

When Sophie opened it, Elizabeth looked inside and gasped, 'Mother, those are all my drawings. Look at them all, even my sketch books from years ago. There are even some that I did on the paper that Father brought back from Plymouth. I did some for Father Benedict, and look, I did those for William. Where did you get them from? Why have you kept them?'

Her mother smiled as Grundwell walked over to where his wife and daughter were talking.

Putting his arm around Elizabeth's shoulders, he said, 'We have kept every drawing, every book, and every sketch you have ever done, well, nearly every one. Father Benedict gave us those that you drew in Cumdean around the church and in the village.

'You did one of Katherine's grave with flowers on it. We gave that to Gumshu and Maisey. Gumshu put it on a backing, and it is now in their bedroom. William gave us some he thought we'd like because they were so good. But he kept several that you did of the church and some of the flowers that grew in the churchyard. He thought them wonderful.'

'But why? Why didn't you tell me?' she asked.

'We did, as did William if you do but remember, but you'd either hide them or tell everyone they were no good and then try and destroy them. Your father used to try and find them or flatten the ones you'd crumpled up, then we'd put them in this chest.

'We thought that one day you would realise how good you were, and we'd give them all back to you. It looks like today's the day,' her mother said softly, before giving her a big hug.

At that moment, Alice came in and laughingly said, 'Now you've found some *real treasure* in a chest!'

'You knew too?'

'Of course, we all knew. Anna knew as well. She's been trying to copy some of them, but she lacks your natural talent,' her sister replied, realising now was definitely not the time to break her own news.

Elizabeth sat down again and started to cry. 'What have I done? What have I done? Father, I think I need your help.'

'You've been very silly, and we've been very thoughtless, but it's nothing that we as a family can't try and put right,' her father said, giving his daughter a kiss, at the same time wondering to himself whether he could actually put it right 'Elizabeth, I need to ask you a very personal and private question and I want a truthful answer, do you understand?' he continued.

'Yes, Father.'

'Did you and Cornelius Purnell ever make love?' her father asked in a very low voice.

'Most certainly not!' snorted his second eldest daughter. 'He tried on a couple of occasions, but I wasn't going let him get me pregnant. I don't love him anyway, and I'm not going to let any man have me till I'm married, and then it's got to be to someone I love.'

'We are two of a kind, after all,' her elder sister commented from by the fire.

'Now tell me exactly what happened. I want to know everything if I am going to be able to help you. Give me every detail. Don't miss anything out,' her father said, taking her to sit at the table with him.

'Do you want your mother and sister to stay, or should they go?'

'No, I'd like them to stay, please.'

Elizabeth then related the full story of her friendship with Cornelius Purnell to her family, from when he had first befriended her some two months earlier up to the fateful night in the field. She missed nothing out, not even when he had tried to put his hand up her skirt on two occasions and how angry he had been that she wouldn't let him touch her.

She told them that even when she'd been quietly sitting watching the birds and sketching them, he had sat with her, obviously not interested in what she was doing, but constantly talking when she had wanted to be quiet.

'He was always there. He always knew where I was. It was if he was watching me all the time,' she said with a shake of her head. 'Sometimes I'd try and hide from him, but he'd always find me.'

'Did he ever mention money or wealth at all when you were out walking?' her father asked.

'Yes. He'd say he was going to be richer than us, richer than Hawk Mines, and definitely richer than his father.' She gave her father a quizzical look. 'How did you know that?'

'Oh, it's just an idea,' Grundwell replied, thinking about what Emmy had told them. 'Did he ever tell you how he was going to gain such wealth?'

'Yes, but I never understood him. All he would say was by his signature and digging, and whenever I said that I didn't understand, he would smile and change the subject.'

'How did you come to be with him in the field that night? Elizabeth, this is probably the most important answer you will give me today, so please think carefully and be completely honest.'

His daughter looked at him, then at her mother, and finally at her sister.

She replied, looking down at the table so that she didn't have to look at anyone, 'I'd told him the evening before how unhappy I was and how I wanted to leave home and go somewhere, anywhere as long as it wasn't Mitcheldean. All he said was to meet him by the church the following night and he'd take me to wherever I wanted to go, as it was time he left as well.'

'He knew we were coming to look at the Purnell ledgers, so it was obvious that we'd found something,' Alice interrupted.

'Exactly!' her father agreed, getting up from the table and going over to stand in front of the fire.

'The following night, you were all busy. You had Phillip Fletcher and Richard Beachwood here, and you were all looking at ledgers and papers that were stacked on the table, so you didn't notice me slip out. I met him at the church just after dusk. I actually bumped into the new rector before I met Cornelius, but luckily he didn't recognise me. He apologised and then went on his way.

'A few minutes later, I met Cornelius in his father's pony and trap. He said that he had something to collect and it would take a few hours, but we'd be on our way before dawn. I got into the trap, and we went up to the top of the field where you found us.

'We were there an awful long time. I was frozen and kept walking round, but he got angry with me because I was supposed to be holding the lantern so he could see what he was doing. I didn't know why he was digging, and he wouldn't tell me. All he said was to keep quiet and to keep still. The pony then took fright at something, so I had to go and calm her as well.'

'The pony would have heard us coming up the field,' Grundwell commented.

'The next thing that happened was the voice out of the darkness that made me jump, and I screamed. He said who he was and who was with him, and I panicked and screamed again.'

'I noticed!' Grundwell said with a grin.

'Didn't you leave us a note?' Sophie asked with tears welling up in her eyes.

'Yes, Mother, I did, but you didn't find it. It was on my bed,' Elizabeth replied, looking up at her mother. 'It was still there when Father brought me back from the constable's house.'

Grundwell glanced at his wife with a terrible look of guilt on his face, then went over to his daughter and kissed her on the forehead.

'It seems that your mother and I have let you down very badly, Elizabeth. We didn't even notice that you'd left us a note, and I suppose that really says it all,' he said quietly.

Alice looked at her parents. She felt they needed some support, so she said softly, 'The last few years have not been the best of times for either of you, whether self-inflicted or otherwise, starting with the wreck of the *Sara Jane*. It has also seen our business interests grow well beyond anyone's wildest dreams, even yours, Father, and that has taken its toll on both of you.

'Think of that time when our first stone buildings went up. We never saw you, Father, but that didn't mean you loved your children any less. It just meant we had to get on with our lives without you. Elizabeth was doing just that, with her drawings. The only thing that you two are guilty of is that you stopped talking to us and more importantly, to each other!' she concluded with some finality.

At that moment, Mary came in and went to stand behind Elizabeth.

'Have you told them everything that you told me?' she asked her granddaughter.

'Yes, Grandma, everything,' Elizabeth replied.

'Has she already told you the entire story, Mother?' Sophie asked, taken aback.

'Yes, she has. She told me the day after she was arrested, but she made me promise not to tell you, as she said she would tell you when she was ready,' Mary replied, her hands resting on Elizabeth's shoulders. 'You were always too busy for her, both of you. I tried to tell you years ago that there are four children in your family and you needed to give time to each of them, but neither of you listened. Think back. Who was there for them when they fell over? Who was there for them when they couldn't do the work William Benson had set for them? Who was there for them when they got in trouble? Who did they come to when they needed comfort or needed to talk? It was always me, never either of you two. It used to be so different, but sadly, things changed drastically years ago.

'It's starting to happen again with Anna and also with your son, Grundwell. I suspect we as a family are now going to pay the cost, unless you can think of something, very, very quickly!'

At that she stormed out, with a thunderous look at both her daughter and son-in-law. She had already voiced her opinion to Grundwell about him not listening to Phillip and Alice's concerns over the account at Purnells. Luckily, they had been alone at the time.

'Grandmamma does not mince her words, does she?' Alice commented.

'I can assure you she doesn't!' her father replied, with considerable feeling.

'I seem to have caused trouble right through the family,' Elizabeth murmured.

Later that night, Grundwell lay awake, aware of every hour of darkness. He was up well before dawn and walked over to the Corner House to see Gumshu.

The two men then went to see John Dickens.

The following day saw the return of the Justice of the Peace Milton.

The first thing the Justice asked his constable was to bring him the report on the Spinning Wheel attempted theft. Marcus had already been to the Purnell's building and had been given a full account of the way in which the crime was perpetrated by the accused's father, Nathaniel. Marcus was then able to give the Justice a full review of the crime, a description of the arrest, and how the missing funds were recovered.

'How much money was involved?' he asked Marcus as he read the account.

Marcus showed Justice Milton the figures given to him by the Spinning Wheel bookkeeper, with the signature of verification by Purnell's chief clerk.

'I knew that the Spinning Wheel was a big business, but that amount is eye-watering!' the Justice commented. 'And you think the reason why it wasn't noticed earlier is because it was only taken in small amounts . . . to start with?'

'Yes, sir. They did have a suspicion and started doing checks some eighteen months ago, but it was difficult to prove.'

'Who found it eventually?'

'The eldest daughter, Alice, who actually now runs the business with Phillip Fletcher, the chief bookkeeper.'

'Did Purnell have no idea that his son was stealing such vast amounts from one of their biggest clients?'

'None, sir. It was a clever fraud, clever and very simple.' Marcus explained how the theft was done and how it remained undetected.

'And what part did the daughter Elizabeth play in all this?' the Justice asked.

Marcus repeated what Elizabeth had told him the previous evening when she and Grundwell had come to see him.

'Do you believe her?'

'That, sir, is not for me to decide. That's up to a trial jury,' Constable Watson replied.

'Do you have an opinion then?'

'I've reported what she has said to me. That's all I can do.'

'Come on, Constable, you must have an opinion.'

'No, sir, I don't!'

'Well, what does Grundwell think? It was his money after all.'

'No, it's not his money. The business belongs to Mary Kingscote, his mother-in-law. He and his daughter just run it for her.'

'You know what I mean, Constable!' the Paul Milton replied testily as he was becoming tired of the constable's slight belligerence, which he suspected was caused by a degree of envy about the amount of money involved.

'Yes, sir, he believes her, as does Mary Kingscote.'

The Justice asked for Cornelius Purnell to be brought before him. With Marcus standing slightly behind the prisoner, Justice of the Peace Milton questioned the accused at length about his method, his motive, and what had been his ultimate goal in the taking of such a huge sum.

'It was all about the money. It was about being richer than those two families who own the Spinning Wheel and Hawk Mines, and I would have ended up being richer than my father as well.'

'Yes, but you only stole from the Spinning Wheel and then only half their wealth, so you did not achieve what you set out to do,' the Justice pointed out.

'I was about to start doing the same to the Hawk Mines account, then I would have started stealing from my father's secure reserves,' the young Purnell bragged.

'But a lot of your father's reserves hold property belonging to the ordinary people of Mitcheldean and the surrounding counties. Wouldn't that have bothered you?' Paul Milton queried.

'Not in the slightest!'

The Justice just about held his temper. 'The young girl with you, what part did she play in all this?'

'Play? Her? She hasn't the wit. She was there to hold the lamp and the pony. She's dumb that one and she wouldn't even let me have her either. I needed someone in the Spinning Wheel household who would say if there was any trouble brewing. She hardly spoke anyway, just wanted to draw birds and flowers.'

'So who warned you that there was *trouble brewing* in the end?'

'Grundwell did. He sent a message to my father to say that he and other family members were coming over to check our ledgers as soon as possible. That was when I knew they had found something, so I wasn't going to stay around and find out what it was.'

The Justice of the Peace looked at his constable, shook his head, and looking back at the accused said, 'You will be tried by a judge and jury at the assizes for your crime, and they will decide your fate.'

With that, the parish constable removed the prisoner to the cells for the night, Master Milton saying that he was to be taken to a more secure jail to await trial as the facilities in Mitcheldean were not designed for long-term prisoners. The constable said that he would arrange transport as soon as possible.

Grundwell and Elizabeth were summoned before the Justice the following morning.

Addressing Elizabeth, he said, 'Young lady, from what the constable and prisoner have told me, I am satisfied that you had no part in this alleged offence whatsoever. Your only crime is that you accepted the friendship of an arrogant and dishonest man. It is to your credit, however, that you rejected his advances outright. May I suggest you are a little more careful with your choice of male company the next time?'

'Yes, sir!' Elizabeth said with a look of utter relief on her face and then turned and hugged her father.

'And to you, sir,' he said, looking at Grundwell, 'would you convey my thanks to your eldest daughter and your chief bookkeeper, whose diligence has saved you a considerable amount of money, and may have stopped a lot of hard-working people from losing their savings? However, I do have one suggestion.

'Tighten up your ledger work so that if anyone tries to steal from you again, you get to know about it a lot quicker!' It was a remark that struck home to Grundwell, after all his past preaching to both his staff and his greatest friend.

He simply murmured an unusually contrite 'Yes, sir, and thank you', as he and Elizabeth left the town hall building.

'I think this has been a very good day, Daughter,' Grundwell said to Elizabeth as they mounted their carriage to go back to Craven Street. 'Even your grandmother smiled at me this morning!'

'Are you sure it wasn't a snarl, Father?'Elizabeth replied, as she curled up against him for the short trip home.

Grundwell was quietly relieved that the plan that Gumshu, John Dickens, and he had devised was now not needed, as it appeared that justice would be served after all.

Some days later, Alice felt she was able to break the news to her family that she was expecting her first child, but it didn't happen quite as she had planned.

The whole family were coming out of the church when she inadvertently said something to her grandmother.

They had listened to a sermon from the Reverend Richard Rolland on honesty and how riches were not the way to heaven, a point which Grundwell and Gumshu had a vague feeling had been aimed at them, when Alice and Mary passed the font.

'I hope that gets a good clean before it's needed again' was Mary's innocent remark as one of the flower arrangers had inadvertently dropped some oak leaves into it.

Alice responded without thinking, 'Well, they've got about eight months before *I* do, so it should be all right.'

'What did you say, Alice?' Mary asked sharply. 'I didn't quite catch that!'

'She said it could be months before they do!' Elizabeth giggled, as her sister had told her the news three days before.

Mary looked at the two of them, then grabbed Elizabeth, and started to tickle her under her arms.

'Grandmother, that's not fair,' she said, going into uncontrollable laughter.

'You are going to be a great-grandmother is what I meant,'Alice said, taking pity on her sister.

'I told you!' Maisey said to Gumshu, as they watched Sophie and her family gather round her eldest daughter and her husband, everyone making a tremendous fuss of them.

'How did you know?'Gumshu asked, somewhat puzzled.

'Woman's intuition' was his wife's instant reply.

Gumshu looked sceptical but refrained from further comment as they had just approached the rector, standing in his usual place by the church doors and wishing his new flock a fond farewell.

The first time he had done it, Gumshu had whispered to Maisey that it was to check that neither he nor Grundwell had taken the poor box to further their fortunes.

That comment had earned him a kick from both his wife and his eldest daughter, which resulted in his limping past the young cleric, who was most concerned about his welfare and hoped he would soon be better.

On this occasion, Gumshu walked slightly apart from his wife and daughter for reasons of safety.

Their other four offspring thought this highly amusing whilst their eldest daughter was not at all amused at being rejected, yet again, by the reverend gentleman.

Her brother, George, had said that in his opinion she ought to look for someone normal and not of the clergy, advice for which he had also got a kick, much to Gumshu's delight.

George suffered Emmy's revenge for the remark some days later when she sent him on a particularly filthy collier boat delivering coal into Bristol Docks, with instructions to Dick Tatton that he was to stay working on that vessel for the rest of the month, and depending on his behaviour, it could well be for the following month as well.

'Younger brothers should be seen and not heard,' she'd told Thomas Sutton at one of their meetings.

Some days later, Emmy decided that George had probably been right because she met a man who would change her life forever, with no effort on her part or help from a potion from the big red bottle with the peculiar stopper.

She had finished one of her now famous shopping outings into Gloucester, having exhausted the local shops. The carriage had just returned to Mitcheldean and was passing the building that was being used as a temporary town hall. The fact that it was next door to a busy inn had not influenced the town elders at all in their choice of location, or so they said. When questioned, they said that they felt duty bound to support one of the local industries, but the fact that it was the brewing industry had been purely coincidental.

Emmy was thrown forward by the violent stop that her carriage driver had been forced to make. Her purchases were scattered all over the floor and on to the seat opposite. Her driver, a retired Hawk Mines collier, was loud and forthright in his condemnation of the culprit, a well-dressed man in his late twenties who had come out of the town hall building without looking where he was going. After apologising to the driver, who was still muttering, he opened the carriage door to apologise to the occupant.

At that precise moment Emmy had been kneeling down, trying to pick up her parcels from the floor of the carriage, so the view that the gentleman got was that of a well-dressed and extremely shapely bottom.

His apology had been accepted with a muffled 'That's all right as long as it doesn't become a habit.'

'Mistress!' he'd replied. 'Do I get the chance see the other end of the lady that I have so badly inconvenienced?'

Emmy stood up and turned round, her dishevelled hair cascading down around her shoulders, covering one of her ample breasts that had broken loose from her dress top. She smiled whilst brushing her hair back from her face, an action that exposed her naked breast to the full view of the apologetic young man in front of her.

Keeping his eyes looking straight up into hers, he said, 'If my hands were warm, I would replace the part of you that seems not to be where it should be, but very sadly they are freezing cold, so it is not a task that I feel I can perform without giving you great discomfort!'

A week later, as they lay in his bed at his father's house, it was obvious that his hands were now at the required temperature because she lay on her back without protest as he ran them first over her two breasts, then over her stomach, and down to explore the hidden depths of her thighs and moist organ of passion.

Her moans were also certainly not those of discomfort, and when they reached the pinnacle of their climax, her final cries had definitely not been ones of pain.

# CHAPTER 24

The trial of Cornelius Purnell had been set for the assizes within the month.

'Let's hope that punishment is swift and harsh,' Grundwell commented to Gumshu and Phillip Fletcher when they were on their way to the court on the day of the trial.

'I don't believe this is happening!' Grundwell said some two hours later. 'I just don't believe it!'

Cornelius Purnell had been bound over to his father's custody on a 2000-pound bond that two strangers had paid into the court, and was now about to walk free.

'Who are those two men who have posted the bond? I've never seen them before!' he continued, aghast at what had happened.

Justice of the Peace Milton, sitting on the side benches alongside the assize judge, looked incredulous as did Constable Marcus Watson, who was waiting to give evidence.

'What do they mean, no case to answer, but to prevent any further criminal intentions, we consider a considerable bond appropriate? What do they mean, sir?' the constable asked, a look of total disbelief on his face.

'It means that there has been a bargain struck somewhere along the way, Marcus, and a clever lawyer has made a lot of money,' a totally sickened Justice of the Peace responded. 'But I still want to know who those men are.'

'I should have let Captain Dickens shoot him!' his constable said in disgust.

'No, Constable, you have done your duty to the letter, even after pressure from me. It's not you who's let everyone down. It's the due process of the law, I'm afraid' was the reply from the disgusted Mitcheldean Justice.

The assize judge turned to look at Master Milton and was about to remonstrate with him for his remark when Grundwell and Gumshu came up to speak to Justice Milton themselves.

Grundwell met the judge's eyes and said in a very loud and clear voice that hushed the court, 'My lord, I suspect that there has been a travesty of justice in this court today, the reasons for which are unclear at the moment. But I make you this promise, if I ever find out that there has been any interference with the due process of law by any person in this courtroom, either known or unknown, I will take it to the highest level in the land to seek honest justice, and I will demand the severest punishment possible for those involved by way of retribution!'

The judge was about to respond when he realised the identities of the men who were talking to Paul Milton and the power that they both wielded, so he decided to remain silent.

John Dickens, who was in the body of the court with Alice and Elizabeth, swore that the judge and the prosecuting lawyer both turned pale on hearing Grundwell's words.

He told his father-in-law that the two bond providers must have been known to the judge because as they left the courtroom they had both nodded to him and he to them.

Nathaniel Purnell was as totally shocked as anyone at the outcome of the trial.

When his son was released to him by one of his two jailers, he asked him, 'How has this happened? Who paid for your lawyer? Who agreed the terms of your release? Who are those men who paid that tremendous bond?' He had had no involvement whatsoever in anything that had happened.

As far as he was concerned, his son had been guilty of a crime against him as well as against the Spinning Wheel, and in spite of his initial feelings, he felt that he should be punished for it.

'Well, at least someone knows my true worth,' Cornelius replied in answer to his father's questions.

As the two Purnells were about to mount their carriage, Grundwell and Gumshu came up to them.

'Both of our businesses will leave their accounts with you, Nathaniel, for the time being at least. But it is on the strict understanding that your son does not work for you anymore and that we be allowed instant access to your ledgers and secure areas, on demand.' Grundwell said.

'I can promise you that my son will never set foot on my premises again, and you can have access to my ledgers and secure areas any time you wish,' Nathaniel responded.

'I also need to know the identities of those men who posted Cornelius's bond,' Grundwell continued.

'Even if I knew, I wouldn't tell you. I don't even know who to thank myself!' Cornelius interrupted sarcastically.

'I just wonder whether you were robbing the Spinning Wheel alone or had accomplices,' Gumshu growled at him.

'Well, if I did have accomplices, one of them was definitely not your friend's frigid and stupid daughter' was Cornelius Purnell's sneering reply, as Elizabeth walked over to them with her sister and John Dickens.

Had Grundwell been able to catch hold of the arrogant young man, Gumshu thought that there would have been a reason to call the surgeon, but John Dickens was able to step in between them, and pushing Grundwell off, he turned to Cornelius. 'You and I will meet again in the not too distant future, sir, and you will not enjoy it!' With that, he escorted Elizabeth and Alice back to their carriage before taking them home to Craven Street.

Nathaniel looked at Grundwell and shook his head, and as he mounted his own carriage he turned to say, 'I am sorry, gentlemen, so very, very sorry!'

'You needn't apologise for me, Father,' Gumshu heard Cornelius say. 'These are glorified Forest peasants at the end of the day, so you needn't bother!'

Three nights later, Cornelius Purnell disappeared whilst on his way home from one of the more disreputable taverns in Mitcheldean.

The professional lady who had accompanied him later told Constable Watson that as she leant against a wall in a dark alleyway, with Master Purnell trying to lift her skirts, two men came up behind him; one had hit him over the head, and then the two carried him off between them.

Because it was so dark, she couldn't see their faces, and neither had spoken.

When the constable asked her why she hadn't screamed, she replied with a demure smile, 'I didn't want to wake the people who were asleep in the houses around us. You always tell me not to be so noisy when you and I go for our little evening walks!'

The following day, the *Rachel* set sail from Chepstow bound for Plymouth, with a gift for His Britannic Majesty's Navy on board or so rumour had it.

Whether the rumour had been true or false, the two strangers who had been in the assize court on the day of the trial forfeited their massive bond to the royal coffers, as Cornelius Purnell was never seen again in Mitcheldean or anywhere beyond.

The Reverend Richard Rolland had started off very badly in his new parish and was beginning to regret his move from his hometown of Bristol, as his mother and father had predicted he would.

'You're a city person, not a country person, Richard,' they had warned him on several occasions when he had discussed the move with them.

'But I am a man of God, and God is everywhere,' he had replied.

He now realised what they had meant. He was having such thoughts as he walked around the Forest village one evening. People were pleasant enough with him, but there seemed to be no warmth or depth in their welcome.

Emmy was the only person who really showed him any warmth, but he didn't think that was for the right reason. She was beautiful, youthful, and hungry for life; he also suspected that you couldn't hold an opinion that she didn't agree with. Richard had seen her reduce two of her more hardened and verbose colliers to a resigned silence after five minutes of heated discussion one morning.

He thought her family wonderful, but he had also unintentionally insulted her father when he had included a part in one of his sermons about wealth not being a key to heaven.

The rector liked her but as a friend and not a potential wife. They had nothing in common. He enjoyed the peace and tranquillity that he had now found in the countryside. He loved books; he loved drawing birds and animals. He was also becoming very fond of Elizabeth, not only because they shared so many interests but also because they were developing a mutual physical attraction for each other.

He also had a passion for bare knuckle fighting, at which he was extremely proficient and very well practiced.

Reaching the churchyard, he strolled around, looking at the headstones and markers. He stopped in front of one, and reading the inscription, he realised it was the grave of Father Benedict, of whom he had heard so much from so many people.

Quietly he said, 'Friar, what am I going to do? I can't make these people like me. I'm not like you or William Benson. I was brought up in one of the poorest parts of Bristol, but thanks to a wealthy benefactor, I was able to satisfy a dream and go into the church. But now I'm alone with no one to turn to, and I don't know what to do.'

He knelt down and pulled out some strands of grass that had grown around the bottom of the headstone. Still kneeling, he turned round to the tiny grave behind him and removed some more from around the rough little wooden cross against the wall.

He read the inscription, 'Katherine'.

He realised it must be a child's grave, so he said in a very gentle voice, 'Hullo Katherine, I'm Richard. I wonder if I might be your friend?'

He stood up, and as darkness had fallen, he could only just make out the graves. He wondered if the two had ever met, the friar and the little child.

As he retraced his footsteps along the pathway that led towards the churchyard gate, he glanced back at where he had been kneeling.

The full moon was emerging from behind a dark curtain of clouds, the moonlight suddenly bathing the two graves in a soft and white light, as if purely for his benefit.

At the same moment, there came the sound of an unseen songbird, its pure and vibrant voice rising to fill the whole of the night.

'I think I might just have had my answer,' Richard murmured, silently closing the gate so that no sound would disturb the bird or his song.

The parishioners of Mitcheldean noticed a very marked change in their rector, so much so that one of the church's sidesmen was heard to remark some weeks later that their incumbent seemed to be developing the humour of Friar Benedict, together with the sincerity and diplomacy of William Benson, and all he needed now was the love of a good woman.

One evening, Maisey walked quietly down to the little churchyard with some summer flowers for her daughter, and to have a talk with her friar. She had been slightly puzzled of late because whenever she visited, both graves were weed free, with either a little sprig of freshly gathered forest leaves or a small posy of flowers on each of them.

As she walked through the gate, she heard someone talking. Looking across to where Katherine and the friar were buried, she was surprised to see the rector sitting on an upturned pail in front of Friar Benedict's grave, his chin resting in his hands, and chatting away to him as if the friar were alive and well.

Maisey coughed.

Richard stumbled to his feet. 'You've caught me getting pastoral advice from my new friend!' he said, looking slightly embarrassed.

'He gave *me* advice from when I was a baby, so it must be very good by now,' she replied, smiling.

'It's the very best!'

'Have you met my daughter, Katherine?' Maisey asked, looking down at the tiny grave.

'I asked her if she might be my friend,' he answered. He continued, 'I'm so sorry. I didn't think to ask whose child she is. I didn't know Katherine is yours. I apologise for that.'

'How strange that you used the word *is* and not *was*,' Maisey questioned somewhat puzzled.

'I believe in God, and I don't believe death is the end of our lives. It might be the end for our earthly bodies, but our souls live on, as do your memories of Katherine and Friar Benedict,' he replied.

'The father believed that as well,' she said in a quiet voice, looking straight into his eyes as if seeking a reply to an unasked question.

'Most true men of God do,' the rector stated softly, returning her gaze.

Richard offered Maisey his pail to sit on whilst he sat on the ground. She told him about her daughter, about her short life that was so full of humour, happiness, and love. With bowed head, she then related the circumstances surrounding her death and the speed of the illness that took her from this life. The silent cleric gently reached up and squeezed her arm in sympathy and understanding.

Looking up again with her gentle smile, she started to tell her spellbound listener some of the stories surrounding Friar Benedict, magically transforming her tears of sadness into those of laughter.

It was late when the two walked back into the village, but the night was still and warm with a golden moon to light the way for the pony and trap that took them back to Mitcheldean.

After their departure, the glades of the Forest fell silent save only for the sounds of the bedtime chatter of the village children, and the calling of distant owls.

Grundwell and Gumshu were also warming to their new rector. Of late, he hadn't put a foot wrong in his sermons, with not a reference to wealth or power. What they didn't know at the time was that both the rector and Paul Milton, the Justice, had started working together in an effort to gather funds to build alms houses, an orphanage, and an ambitious project for a hospital, all to be within the town limits of Mitcheldean.

'There are many in this town who are of the opinion that I think I already own it!' Paul Milton said laughingly one day when they were looking at a possible site for their hospital. 'I don't think that at all. I just care for the people who live in it and want to see the best for them, rich or poor, but especially the poor.'

The two men, although having a twenty-year age difference, had become firm friends purely by chance when Paul had mentioned to the rector that he was interested in trying to build alms houses in the town. Richard told the Justice that he had been involved in a similar project in Bristol when he had been a curate in one of the city parishes.

The friendship, and the project, had grown from that one conversation.

Then had come the rector's finest hour!

He had been standing in his usual place after a Sunday morning matins service, wishing his departing congregation a happy day and that God be with them, when he heard a serious disturbance on the other side of the lych gate. Walking briskly from the church door, he saw four of the more undesirable residents of the town, who had obviously come looking for trouble, making a nuisance of themselves with some of the ladies of the congregation.

Giving the Bible and prayer book he was holding to Elizabeth, who happened to be standing next to him, he strode over to where the men were loitering and very politely asked them to stop annoying the ladies, and preferably go back whence they came.

Their replies were anything but polite, especially as they were addressing a man of the cloth. Gumshu, Grundwell, and John Dickens made to go forward in defence of the cleric, but they stopped short when they saw that there was definitely not a need.

Two of the men made a lunge at the rector, both coming at him from different directions. He caught the first to get within his range with a sweeping left-handed uppercut straight under the chin whilst the second got the benefit of a full force kick to the groin, and as he bent double, he felt the power of a clerical right jab to the back of the neck.

The result of the action was that both attackers fell inert upon the floor, unconscious.

The third member of the murderous group came at Richard with a wooden club in his right hand, which he produced from within his clothing; he raised it high above his head and started to bring it down towards the rector's neck. The young cleric stepped sharply to his left, taking hold of the man's arm as he did so; he swung it down and round so violently it went well beyond the arm's natural capability, dislocating the man's shoulder.

The reverend gentleman then spun him round so that they were square to each other and brought his knee up with all his force, and as the man bent double in pain, he dispatched him with what could only be described as a religious hammer blow to the back of the neck.

'Knife, Rector!' John called out, as he cocked the pistol that he had just drawn out from its usual place of concealment within his coat.

'Thank you, Captain!' Richard replied as he turned to face his fourth assailant, who was already heading towards him, brandishing an evil-looking blade. Richard stepped into the charge and grabbed the man's wrist, pushing it to one side, at the same time turning his back into him and bringing his other arm across so that the man's arm was caught as if in a gin trap. Then with a twist of his body, he sent the assailant over his hip, the man screaming in agony as his elbow snapped, ending up flat on his back with God's emissary kneeling on top of him.

The Mitcheldean incumbent then dispatched the man into oblivion with a sharp fist blow to the forehead. That last action resulted in the attacker losing his hold on the knife, sending it skittering across the grass and down the bank. Although evil looking, it had a fine long blade with a beautifully carved and decorated handle.

John disengaged his pistol and eased it back into its place of hiding.

'Just a precaution?' questioned a voice beside him.

'Just a precaution!' John replied, recognising the constable's voice.

Unnoticed, Grundwell walked down the slope and picked up the knife, sliding it inside his coat.

'Just in case it ever arises that I need such a thing,' he murmured to himself.

'Do you think he'd teach *me* to fight like that?' Maisey asked, innocently gazing up at Gumshu.

'Probably not. *No*, I'd say definitely not, my love!' he replied, laughing, remembering the penance he'd paid for not conferring with her about buying their home on Craven Street.

The rector walked back to where he had left Elizabeth holding his books, and smiling, he gently took them from her hands.

'Close your mouth, Daughter!' Sophie whispered in her ear.

'It's funny', Richard said some days later as he sat on his upturned pail talking to his friend, 'but since that little bit of a tumble outside the lych gate, I've had no trouble with the ladies who do the flower arranging, no trouble with the bell ringers, and no trouble with the choir master or his musicians. The choir boys have all been on time for choir practice, and Grundwell and Gumshu have stopped raising their coats with the comment "Honest, Rector, we ain't taken the poor box" each time they pass me coming out of church.'

The Reverend Rolland also took the advice of a laughing Justice of the Peace, who reckoned that now was the right time to approach the residents and businesses of Mitcheldean for donations to their building appeal, and he thought the rector would be more effective going around on his own.

'You're not suggesting that a man of God should use his brawling reputation to extract money from the people of the town, are you?' asked the horrified rector of his friend.

'Yes, I am!' came the instant response.

'In that case, I'll start today!' he replied, thinking how much Friar Benedict would have approved.

The rector of Mitcheldean only got one refusal in his first fund-raising trip around his town.

He had knocked on the front door of a cottage that was on the opposite side of the town from the church, and it was opened by a man with a heavily bound shoulder and arm, who let out a shriek and immediately slammed the door in his face.

'Well, how was I to know the cottage belonged to the man who had attacked me with a club?' he said defensively to a laughing Grundwell and Sophie as he sat in the large room in the house on Craven Street. 'But I *do* wonder where the others live!'

The Spinning Wheel ledger building was now completed and all the paperwork moved from the wooden warehouse, which still contained some three months of raw wool stock and so could not yet be demolished. Grundwell had also bought the two buildings that Edward had rented many years ago as the owner who had refused to sell them had now died. The first act of his will beneficiaries had been to approach the Spinning Wheel and offer them for sale.

'We won't store any more fleeces in them,' Grundwell instructed. 'I want the buildings taken down at the same time as the warehouse and *all* of them replaced with stone buildings under slated roofs, as we'd originally planned for our old facility. Alice, can you organise that, please?' he added, as he wanted to stop her from working so hard with the baby's imminent arrival. Tasking her with looking after the building work *might* just stop her prowling round the spinning and weaving buildings quite as much.

Alice looked at him with deep suspicion.

'You have been talking to John, haven't you? He's been trying to persuade me to slow down as well.'

'Well, if you don't, Alice, your offspring might be born with a loom in its hands,' Phillip said to her, laughing.

'Well, be it boy or girl, they'd better get the wool tension right. You know what the mother's like about loose tension!' Richard Beachwood added, ducking as Alice aimed a ledger at his head.

Emmy's life had also been transformed. Her love, and lust, had been returned by the man who was soon to become her husband with an enthusiasm that sometimes left her breathless.

They had actually decided to marry as soon as possible as Emmy wasn't quite sure which was going to come first, the wedding or the child.

Henry Milton, Paul's son, had been a lawyer in London working for his uncle but had now transferred to cover the local assizes in the counties around Mitcheldean. He had started to arrange the move the day of his near collision with the Hawk Mines carriage, hence his total lack of concentration on looking where he was going.

His father was obviously highly delighted with his son's return home and even more delighted when he told him that he intended to marry Emmy.

'The marital negotiations are going to be interesting. You're marrying into one of the wealthiest families in the south-west!' his father said with a concerned frown.

'Don't worry,' his son replied. 'I've already spoken to her parents, and they both assure me I've only got to match half their fortune, which will be cancelled out as soon as I actually marry Emmy, and then make sure that she lives with me, *not them!*'

'We still have to be seen to take our responsibility seriously, Henry,' his father cautioned. 'Remember that you're a lawyer and I'm a justice of the peace, so that puts us directly in the public eye.'

The meeting of the two families had been both humorous and productive, with an agreement reached that was acceptable to the two parties. No one ever knew what that agreement was, but Hawk Mines funded a large part of the cost of the community building project, as did the Spinning Wheel.

Paul Milton gave the young couple his house, as long as he had the right to live there until his death. He now lived alone as his wife had died some ten years previously, with Henry being their only child.

He only had one proviso. Much as he liked them sharing his home, he asked them if they could *please* move to a bedroom on the other side of the house, as their lovemaking sometimes shook the walls of his bedroom and kept him awake.

'And we haven't even used any of the love potions out of the large red bottle with the peculiar stopper yet!' Emmy explained to her blushing mother, when she told her what her prospective father-in-law had said.

The other children immediately demanded that what was left be shared between them, *'in case the need arose'* as Hannah put it.

'And what says that your mother and I still don't need it, young lady? Her father asked in a highly indignant voice.

'Old age!' came the joint reply from all of their children.

'What are you talking about?' Henry asked, as he sat listening to all the family banter.

'Don't anyone tell him!' Emmy said, going over to sit on his knee and covering his ears with her hands. 'He's bad enough without it. I'd *never* be out of bed if he ever got hold of that!'

The wedding was a Cumdean village affair on a fine summer's day, with the bride and her father arriving on a coal cart drawn by two grey horses, bedecked in ribbons and bells.

'I really do hope that's not been cleaned!' George said, as he was still removing coal dust from various parts of his anatomy after his sister had sent him to work on one of the coal-carrying collier boats for a month.

The Reverend Richard Rolland conducted the service and blessing, and then the newly-wed couple were taken around the village in another coal cart decorated with all the Forest leaves and flowers of summer.

'I'd hoped that one was dirty as well' commented a now somewhat disappointed George as he sloped off to join the other members of his family.

It was not until all the wedding party and guests had left the church and the wedding feast had begun, that Richard Rolland walked through the gate into the graveyard and sat down on his pail in peace and solitude to talk to his friend.

Maisey, too, had slipped away, and she stood by the wall of the churchyard, watching the young cleric for several minutes. She smiled, and after blowing her daughter and her friar a kiss, she turned away and returned to the celebrations.

A little later, Richard rejoined the festivities, and the first thing he did was to go quietly round the tables and sit down with every family, and every person, who had lost a loved one in the Cottrells' mine disaster. He left no one out, and after talking with them, he made the sign of the cross on the forehead of each person, just as Friar Benedict and William Benson had done in that cold grey dawn following the night of the collapse.

Gumshu watched him, totally fascinated, and then leant over to Maisey saying softly, 'How does he know? Neither I nor anyone else has ever told him. How does he know?'

Looking at her husband with her wonderful gentle and radiant smile, but with tears welling up in her eyes, she breathed, 'I can't tell you. I honestly can't tell you!'

'I think that you can,' he replied in all but a whisper. Then he kissed her tenderly on the cheek and continued, 'But I suspect that secret will remain between you, and your friar.'

Some time later, as the golden shafts of evening sunlight crept through the Forest, Maisey sat alone deep in thought, watching the dancing, listening to the music, hearing the laughter, and suddenly she knew that this was the time.

Unnoticed, she slipped away from the celebrations for a few minutes.

On her return, she called to her husband, she called to Grundwell, and then silently took them to the village churchyard.

She sat them down on the low wall by the gate and then knelt in front of them, at the same time drawing out a folded document and a small package from the pocket of her skirt.

The document was in the hand of Father Benedict.

Maisey opened it and very slowly read the contents to them.

It told the story of a dying woman; it told of the cause of her death; it told of her courage and determination; it told of her husband; it told of the families of both husband and wife; and finally, it told of the lives of both the brothers who were born as twins to the dying mother.

As the two men sat on the wall, dumbfounded by what they had just heard, Maisey slowly rose from where she knelt and carefully placed the package down on the wall between them, saying very softly, 'These were your mother's.'

Grundwell and Gumshu stared at it for a few moments before hesitantly opening it.

Within the soft hide wrapping nestled five exquisite rings, including a golden wedding band, two gem-encrusted brooches, and a cloak clasp bearing an heraldic coat of arms.

They both gazed down at the contents, and gently touched each item as if they felt that they contained their mother's spirit.

Then, without any further words, Maisey took their hands and led them through the churchyard gate down to a grave that was close to Father Benedict's and little Katherine's, with a headstone that was simply marked *Granuaile*.

And as the two brothers stood totally transfixed by the sight of their mother's last resting place, there came the beautiful and vibrant song of a nightingale, rising from the greenery of the overhanging oak tree.

Lightning Source UK Ltd.
Milton Keynes UK
UKOW052117230712

196452UK00002B/1/P